After a career in ~~...~~, Brenda Clarke began writing when her two children had left school. Since then she has written about twenty novels, many of which were published under her maiden name of Brenda Honeyman.

Also by Brenda Clarke

THREE WOMEN

and published by Corgi Books

WINTER LANDSCAPE

Brenda Clarke

CORGI BOOKS

WINTER LANDSCAPE

A CORGI BOOK   0 552 13261 6

Originally published in Great Britain by Century Hutchinson & Co. Ltd.

PRINTING HISTORY

Century Hutchinson edition published 1986
Corgi edition published 1988

This book is set in 10/11pt Plantin.

Corgi Books are published by Transworld Publishers Ltd.,
61-63 Uxbridge Road, Ealing, London W5 5SA, in Australia by
Transworld Publishers (Australia) Pty. Ltd., 15-23 Helles
Avenue, Moorebank, NSW 2170, and in New Zealand by Transworld
Publishers (N.Z.) Ltd., Cnr. Moselle and Waipareira Avenues,
Henderson, Auckland.

Printed and bound in Great Britain by
Cox & Wyman Ltd., Reading, Berks.

A sad tale's best for winter
William Shakespeare 1564 – 1616

PART ONE

Winter 1944–1945

Barren winter with his wrathful, nipping cold

CHAPTER ONE

It was warm under the bedclothes, the pillows tucked securely around her neck, her body curled beneath the blankets and eiderdown, generating its own pool of warmth. Only the tip of her nose was cold as it scented the early morning air, like the snout of some small animal emerging cautiously from its burrow.

Sally lay still, knowing that if she moved an arm or a leg by so much as an inch, she would encounter the icy touch of the surrounding sheets or the flabby chill of last night's hot-water bottle. Her first conscious thought was that it was Saturday; that this morning she would not have to face the seven-thirty darkness of the November streets in order to catch the 'bus into Bristol, nor wait this evening in frozen-toed misery in the city centre. She had finished the week-end's homework the previous night, and until Monday, could put all thought and worry of next summer's School Certificate examinations out of her mind.

Her second thought was that tomorrow was November the fifth, and for the sixth year running, there would be no celebrations. She had been nine years old the last time she had seen fireworks, and they had all been together then; her parents, her twin sisters and herself. She remembered how the rockets and sparklers and Catherine wheels had illuminated the gardens of the cottage, blossoming in the darkness like multi-coloured flowers. She recalled the twins, their faces nipped by cold, trying unsuccessfully to pretend that, at seventeen, they were too old to enjoy such juvenile pleasures. And she remembered wondering, as she had often wondered since, if she would grow up to resemble those two long-legged, elegant creatures whom she had admired almost as soon as she was out of the cradle.

'You'll be the prettiest of the lot,' her father had once told her. 'You look more like your mother than either Jennifer or Veronica, and one day you might even outshine her.'

It was the only time Bill Sherwood had uttered such a heresy in the twenty years of his marriage, and it had been said more to console Sally than from any real conviction. Bill Sherwood had adored his wife, thought her the most perfect woman in the world and was blind to her faults. On some level he had been aware of the veiled hostility between Dorothy and her three daughters, but the thought had made him uneasy and he had never searched for its causes.

The fact was that Dorothy Sherwood would have been happier with sons. She should have been the centre of an adoring, all-male family, because any woman was a rival to her, and she inevitably regarded daughters as future competition. She would have refuted the suggestion angrily, had it ever been put to her; but the twins and, later, Sally sensed her antipathy from their earliest years. Their mother's extrovert personality had swamped their more retiring dispositions, and, beside her, all three had paled into insignificance. It had been with a feeling of escape that, on their eighteenth birthday, two months after the outbreak of war, Jennifer and Veronica had volunteered for service in the WRNS.

The Women's Royal Naval Service was the most prestigious female branch of the three armed forces and the most difficult to get into. The twins' acceptance was due to the fact that Dorothy's father had been a Captain in the Royal Navy, and had won a posthumous VC at Jutland, in 1916. Dorothy was thirteen at the time, a year older than Sally had been in 1940 when Bill Sherwood failed to return from Dunkirk.

When the telegram announcing her husband's death arrived from the War Office, Dorothy had locked herself in her bedroom, refusing contact with anyone. She emerged

10

twenty-four hours later, red-eyed, white-faced, but perfectly calm and ready to meet life head-on. She, who had never worked, having married straight from the schoolroom at the age of seventeen, had taken a course in shorthand and typing, and was now secretary to one of the BBC producers based in Bristol. Sally had to admire her mother, even though she found it difficult to love her. After Bill's death, she had been deeply hurt by her exclusion from Dorothy's grief and the fact that she had been forced to turn for consolation to her Uncle Philip.

Philip Jackson was not really her uncle, but Dorothy's cousin; a tall, thin, weather-beaten man with very dark hair and eyes, inherited from an Italian grandmother. His face adorned the dustcovers of several reputable biographies and travel books, and his name was often bylined in the more serious newspapers, analysing, commenting or offering informed opinion on the issues of the day. He was three years older than Dorothy and had moved to Coldharbour village some years earlier, after the death of his wife. He gave as his reason the fact that Dorothy was his only surviving relative and that London was too big and impersonal a place for the lonely. Sally suspected that he was in love with her mother. If so, he was not alone. Practically every man with whom she came in contact succumbed to Dorothy's charm.

Sally eased on to her back, still keeping the bedclothes tucked around her chin and crooking her knees, so that her feet stayed on the same warm patch of sheet. But the bed was cooling rapidly and Sally resigned herself to the idea of getting up. She could hear her mother moving about in the next bedroom, getting ready for work. In a moment or two, she would cross the landing to the bathroom and run the five inches of water permitted for a daily bath.

Sally stared at the bedroom ceiling with its map of hairline cracks, charting, she imagined fancifully, some lost continent or unknown railway junction, and thought about her mother. Dorothy was not really beautiful; the nose was a shade too aquiline, the mouth a little too wide. But the

11

eyes, Sally had to admit, were lovely, dominating the face and even eclipsing the mane of jet black hair, worn in a classic chignon at the nape of her neck and providing a perfect foil for the creamy skin. The eyes, however, those huge, thickly-lashed, liquid brown eyes, inherited, like Philip's, from their Italian grandmother, were the feature which made the first and most lasting impact, and persuaded people, particularly men, that Dorothy Sherwood was beautiful.

Sally heaved an envious sigh. Her own eyes were brown, but lighter, more hazel, and the lashes would never be as thick as her mother's. Her hair, too, like the twins', was brown, not black, although all three girls had inherited their father's shorter, straighter, more aristocratic nose.

'But who ever heard of a man falling in love with a nose?' Jennifer had once grumbled to Veronica.

Sally heard her mother come out of the bathroom, and the next moment Dorothy was tapping impatiently on her door.

'Sally! Sally are you up? I have to be at work by half-past eight this morning and I've already overslept. That wretched alarm clock didn't go off again. It's really too bad!'

At once, Sally felt the knot of guilt begin to form in her stomach, as though, somehow, she were responsible for the alarm clock's failure. It was a familiar sensation and she resented it. It was also irrational, she told herself fiercely. Her mother's words had implied no blame.

But the tone of voice had . . . Sally suppressed the thought and got out of bed.

'I'll go down and make breakfast right away,' she called. 'I can bath and dress after you've gone.'

The bedroom was freezing. Sally pulled on her blue woollen dressing gown and snuggled her feet into her fur-lined slippers. While she combed her hair, she stared out of the window at the frost-bitten garden. It was still too dark to see it properly, but she knew the long, narrow strip of land so well that she could picture it even in the blackness.

Before the war it had been nearly all lawn, with one or two flower-beds and trees. But she and Dorothy had dug up most of the grass to grow vegetables. They had worked at it during the long summer evenings four years earlier, and found in the digging and planting a release for their pent-up emotions following Bill Sherwood's death. Sally could never look at the garden now without thinking of her father.

She ran downstairs to the stone-flagged kitchen, filled the kettle from one of the taps at the sink and lit a burner on the gas stove. While she waited for the water to boil, she cut two thick slices of bread and took a packet of dried-egg powder from a cupboard. By the time her mother appeared, she had made toast and scrambled eggs.

'Not that filthy powdered stuff, darling, surely!' Dorothy protested, wrinkling her nose in disgust. 'Couldn't Mr Greenhill find us a couple of under-the-counter eggs? Slip round this morning and ask him.'

Sally poured the tea. 'He gave us more than our ration last week,' she objected. 'It's only a small shop, Mummy. Mr Greenhill has other customers beside us. Anyway, it's not right. The Black Market, I mean.'

'You absurd child!' Dorothy didn't know whether to be annoyed or amused. 'Don't be so pi! You expect things like eggs to be more plentiful in the country. All right, if you don't want to ask Mr Greenhill again, go round to Barton Farm. Ellen and Bob Younger can probably spare us one or two.' Dorothy sipped her tea and chuckled. 'Bob will certainly let you have a couple if you say they're for me.'

Sally hated it when her mother talked like that. She said nothing, but her thin little face set in disapproving lines. Dorothy pretended not to notice.

There was a knock at the back door. The latch lifted and Philip came in. He looked paler than usual, having only just recovered from an attack of the chronic bronchitis which made him unfit for military service. He ruffled Sally's hair and smiled at his cousin.

'I have to go into Bristol this morning, Dorothy. Would you care for a lift? Fortunately, I have some of this month's petrol ration left.'

'Philip, you're an angel! An absolute angel!' Dorothy

waved him to a seat. 'Have a cup of tea. Sally, pour one for Uncle Philip.'

He winced. 'Do stop referring to me as "uncle",' he begged. 'It makes me feel so old.'

'You never used to mind,' Dorothy remarked, surprised.

'Sally was a child then. She's almost a woman now.' He smiled at her across the table. 'A very attractive young woman.'

'Nonsense!' Dorothy spoke sharply. 'She's only fifteen.'

'I shall be sixteen on New Year's Day,' Sally reminded her mother quietly. 'That's less than two months away.'

'You're still a schoolgirl! Good heavens!' Dorothy began gathering up her hat and gloves.

Philip, watching her shrewdly with eyes so like her own, thought that just so must the queen in Snow White have looked the first time her magic mirror suggested that Snow White might be a possible rival. Of all the men of her acquaintance, Philip Jackson was the only one who loved Dorothy without letting himself be blinded by her charm.

Dorothy adjusted her smart little black felt hat, studying her reflection critically in the mirror beside the kitchen door.

'I've decided to invite some of the American officers from Barton Court for Christmas this year,' she said, with a nonchalance which did not quite ring true. 'I thought perhaps a party the evening of Chrismas Day. It would be a friendly gesture, don't you think?'

'Very friendly,' Philip replied evenly. 'I assume Major Graham will be present.'

'Charles? Of course. You'd hardly expect me to exclude *him* from the invitation.'

Dorothy put on the new tweed coat which had cost her several months' supply of clothing coupons. It had been worth it, however, because it was so smart; a real pre-war style with a proper buckled belt and none of that excessive shoulder padding which made women nowadays look like all-in wrestlers. Her shoes, too, were real leather, slender and elegant, lovingly preserved from the past. Not for

Dorothy the clumsy horrors with hinged wooden soles, currently on sale in the shops.

Philip drank his tea and got up. 'Don't make it too big a party, Dorothy. Remember, these men are convalescent.'

'A select gathering of half-a-dozen of the fittest,' Dorothy agreed. 'That nice young Pete Kovaks is almost better. He must come.' She gave her cousin one of her most dazzling smiles.

Philip's heart missed a beat. He had been in love with Dorothy ever since they were children. His wife had never been more than second-best to him, although he had always been able to conceal that knowledge from her. It was knowledge which he had been able to conceal from almost everyone except, he guessed, Sally. That quiet, observant child, with her artist's eye, saw more than most people ever suspected. He had seen some of her sketches of their friends – sketches which Dorothy dismissively described as 'Sally's scribbles' – and had been amazed by her clarity of vision. It was a penetration all the more remarkable because she was unaware that she possessed it. She drew what she saw, without malice, without flattery. Philip wondered if any of her subjects realized how uncomfortably close to the truth about them she got.

Dorothy gave her daughter's cheek a hasty peck. 'Don't forget to go to the farm, darling. And Mrs Wakeman will be in presently to tidy up. Make her a cup of coffee, but don't use the good stuff. Essence will do. She won't appreciate the difference, anyway. Amuse yourself, angel. I'll be home about six. Philip, for heaven's sake let's get going or I shall be late.'

'I'm ready.' He leaned over and kissed Sally's forehead. 'So long, Snow White,' he said.

The existence of Coldharbour village, perched high on its range of hills, had first been officially recorded in the Domesday Book in 1086, but it was older than that. There had been a small Saxon community before the Conquest, but all traces of it had long since disappeared except in the

15

church, where the lowest course of stones at the east end of the chancel showed signs of Saxon workmanship. Some time after the Conquest, the church had been rebuilt and rededicated to Saint Andrew, being made a tributary of the Norman Abbey of Jumièges shortly before the death of William I.

Until 1538, most of the surrounding land, including what was today Barton Court and Barton Farm, had belonged to the ecclesiastical authorities. After the Reformation, however, Saint Andrew's had dwindled in importance to the status of a village church, and most of its property had passed to John Quintrell, a Bristol merchant who supported Henry VIII in his fight against Rome, and who wrote a loyal pamphlet to say so.

A Quintrell had remained in possession of Barton Court until the present day; but Sir Gilbert and his wife had been trapped and interned inside France at the outbreak of war, and Barton Court had been requisitioned by the Government. At first, it had been filled with evacuees from London and the eastern counties; but when it became obvious that the west country was as vulnerable to German bombers as anywhere else in the British Isles, many parents had taken their children home again. The few left were dispersed to private houses, and with the entry of America into the war, Barton Court was handed over to the United States Army as a convalescent home for officers.

Before June the sixth, 1944, it had remained relatively empty, but D-Day had changed all that. For the past five months, a steady stream of men, recovering from extensive and serious wounds, had occupied the house. Major Charles Graham was one of them.

He and Captain Kovaks were just coming out of the main entrance as Sally passed by on the opposite side of the road. In the old days, the grounds of Barton Court had been protected from public gaze by high iron railings, but these had been removed earlier in the war to be melted down for scrap. Sally saw the two men and waved shyly in greeting,

16

but she did not linger, hurrying along the unmade track which led to Barton Farm.

There was something about Major Graham she did not like, although he always went out of his way to be kind to her. Sally did not examine the reason for her antipathy too closely. If she had, she might have realized that it had something to do with his friendship with her mother.

It was half-past eleven by the time Sally, warmly wrapped up in her navy-blue school coat, over her green slacks and warmest jumper, squelched into the muddy farmyard. It was a time when she felt sure of finding Ellen Younger alone in the house, the farmhands and landgirls having been in much earlier for their mid-morning break. The company of too many people embarrassed Sally and she was uneasy in the presence of Bob Younger. She disliked the way he always wanted to talk about her mother. She much preferred his wife. She opened the back door of the farmhouse and let herself in.

Ellen Younger was in the kitchen, but she was not alone. A young man was seated at the table looking rather white, and Ellen was bandaging his hand.

'There,' she was saying, 'that should be all right now. It's not a deep cut, thank goodness, and I've put plenty of iodine on it. You should be as right as rain in a couple of days. All the same, get the doctor at the camp to take a look at it tonight.' She turned her head and saw Sally. 'Hullo, my dear. I shan't be a minute. Werner here has had a bit of an accident. Cut his hand on the edge of a spade. Now, you go and sit by the fire, lad, and I'll make us all a nice cup of tea.'

It was then Sally realized that the young man was one of the German prisoners-of-war who worked on the farms around Bristol. The Youngers had three, who were brought each morning and collected each night by a truck from the Portway camp. She often saw the trucks go past on her journey home from school in the evenings. It was easy to tell the Germans and Italians apart. The former were subdued and surly, whereas the latter hung out of the backs

17

of their trucks, whistling and calling to the girls. They would shriek and blow kisses and, occasionally, pantomime more primitive gestures. The girls would toss their heads, pretending not to notice, before collapsing in a paroxysm of giggles. The Italians were incorrigibly friendly; the Germans were hostile and rude.

The young man by the fire, whom Mrs Younger had referred to as Werner, looked like that now. His face beneath the straw coloured hair was closed and resentful. The blue eyes, which had briefly met Sally's as she entered the kitchen, were half-shut as he stared at the leaping flames of the fire. He was stocky and powerfully built, dressed in his ugly brown-dyed uniform, decorated with lighter, Dutch-boy patches for easy identification. Across his left cheek was the faint, white crease of an old scar.

'What can I do for you, love?' Mrs Younger inquired cheerfully, as she spooned tea into the black earthenware pot and tipped in boiling water from the kettle kept permanently singing and hissing on the hob.

'Does . . . Does he speak any English?' Sally whispered, nodding towards the German.

'Werner? Nearly as good as you or me. He told me once his mother was an English teacher, that's how he can speak it so well.' Ellen Younger lowered her voice and mouthed: 'That mark on his face is a duelling scar. It's still carried on over there, at the universities, he says.' She pulled a disapproving face. 'Just what you'd expect of the Jerries.' She poured the tea and carried a mug across to the young prisoner, who took it eagerly with his uninjured hand. 'Get that down you, lad, and you'll feel better. There's a spoonful of sugar in it, which is all I can spare.' She twitched her apron straight and turned back to Sally. 'Now then, my dear, what can I do for you?'

'Mummy wants some eggs, please, if you have any to spare.'

Ellen Younger passed Sally the second mug of tea and wiped her hand across her forehead. She was a stout woman with a florid complexion; a Somerset girl born and bred,

18

who had never known any other life but farming. Nothing ever discomposed her, not even the long tally of her husband's infidelities.

'I was just going to the hen coops when Werner was brought in, so I'll go now. You can keep him company while I'm gone.'

'I'd rather come with you,' Sally pleaded desperately. She did not want to be alone with this silent and hostile young man.

'There's no need,' Ellen Younger said firmly. 'You stay and talk to Werner. He won't bite.'

She went out, closing the door behind her. The fire crackled gently behind the black-leaded bars of the kitchen range.

Sally cleared her throat awkwardly. 'Have you . . . Have you been a prisoner long?'

The blue eyes looked at her without expression.

'A year and a half,' he answered. There was another silence.

'Where . . . Where were you captured?' Sally ventured again.

'Sfax. North Africa.' This time he did not even bother to look at her, but stared at the glowing red heart of the fire.

'You speak very good English.'

He shrugged, without answering, and Sally gave up. She sat down at the scrubbed kitchen table and sipped her tea.

It was a relief when Mrs Younger returned, carrying a paper bag containing two eggs.

'This is all I can let you have, I'm afraid, my dear. The hens haven't been laying at all well lately. Your mother can settle up when she sees me. Don't trouble yourself now. Werner been entertaining you, has he? How's the hand now, lad? I've told Mr Younger you'll be staying here until you feel better.'

Sally thanked her for the eggs and said goodbye. At the door, she turned and hesitated.

'Goodbye, Werner,' she added, but he did not look up. He was nursing his injured hand.

'Goodbye,' he grunted.

19

It was cold and damp outside, a chill which cut through to the bone after the warmth of the farmhouse kitchen. Sally began to run, dodging the holes in the rough, mud tracks before turning the corner into Manor Walk.

The Major and Captain Kovaks had disappeared, but as she crossed Church Lane, Sally heard Charles Graham call her name. She kept on going, pretending she had not heard him, but he caught her up as she reached the gate of Grace Cottage.

'Sally, are you running away from me again?' The deep, cultured voice with its faint trace of East Coast accent always surprised her. It was not how she expected Americans to talk. A hundred Hollywood films had conditioned her to a nasal Brooklyn twang.

'I'm sorry,' she lied, 'I didn't hear you. If you were shouting, that is.'

He smiled understandingly. He was very good-looking, she thought. The greying wings of hair visible beneath his cap were very distinguished. But she still didn't like him.

'Did you want something?' she asked, after a moment.

'Will you please tell your mother that I'll be round for lunch as usual tomorrow. The doctor doesn't want to see me, after all.'

Sally nodded curtly. 'Yes, all right.' She unlatched the gate and walked up the front garden path. Taking her key from her coat pocket, she unlocked the door and went inside.

CHAPTER TWO

'They look so skinny. The kids, I mean.'

Captain Pete Kovaks was blowing on his fingers as the Major rejoined him, before burying them deep in his overcoat pockets.

Charles Graham shrugged. 'Five years of war, more or less in the front line, what can you expect? The folks back home don't really know what this war is all about.'

'That's for sure.' Peter Kováks had been hit in the stomach by shrapnel during the D-Day landings on Omaha beach, and was only now getting back on his feet. Another two months' convalescence at least, the medics said. He didn't know if he could stand it: the quietness of this place was driving him crazy. 'Doesn't anything ever happen around here?' he demanded.

'I guess we're four years too late for the fireworks,' Charles Graham said. 'They say that during the blitz, you could see the whole of Bristol burning from this ridge. Are you really so anxious to get back to that hell on earth, in France?'

'Anything would be better than this silence,' his companion answered bitterly. 'Jesus! You can even hear the birds singing!'

The Major laughed. 'Take it a day at a time,' he advised. 'Thanksgiving at the end of the month. Christmas. New Year. Who knows? By that time the war might be over and we'll be going home?'

But Pete Kovaks, staring disconsolately along the village street, refused to be comforted. A thin wind had been whipping across the high ground all day, bringing with it flurries of chilling rain, and the trees threshed their almost leafless branches to its dismal, piping tune. Pete longed for girls, bright lights, London and dancing at Rainbow Corner, the US social club.

'It's all very well for you,' he grumbled, 'you've got something worth staying for.'

Under normal circumstances, he would never have referred to the Major's affair with Dorothy Sherwood, the Black Widow as she was irreverently called by the other inmates of Barton Court. But social and military barriers tended to get overlooked when people were bound together by mutual pain and suffering. All the same, he could see the Major didn't like it and hurriedly changed the subject.

'Who's going to win next Tuesday, then? Is FDR going to be returned for another term?'

His companion made no answer. The subject was no more welcome to him than the first.

Charles James Graham was forty years old, the only child of Ewan Ross Graham, a Democratic Senator who had backed Franklin Delano Roosevelt all the way from his first election to the United States' Presidency in 1932, through the New Deal, his second and third terms of office in the White House, his attempts to bring America into the war much earlier than Pearl Harbor, right up to the present and Roosevelt's almost certain re-election as President for the fourth time, the following Tuesday. Charles, himself, had been born in Washington DC and surrounded throughout his childhood by the cut and thrust of politics; by the backbiting, bitching and gossiping which made up so large a part of the capital's social life. He had reacted against it by announcing that nothing on earth would persuade him to become the fourth generation of the Graham family to sit in the House of Representatives. After Harvard, he had gone on to New York and entered the publishing firm of Lodge and Berryman. Two years later, he had married socialite Faith Lodge, his boss's daughter. They had two children, Kay, fourteen, and Teddy, twelve.

Charles and Faith Graham had begun their married life

in a fashionable brownstone, west of Washington Square. Now, they lived in a Park Avenue penthouse with a magnificent view of downtown Manhattan. Sometimes, in his blacker moods, Charles wondered if he had married his wife solely to spite his parents, who had never liked her. At others, he gave himself some credit for having felt a kind of tenderness for Faith, although it had evaporated within a very few years of the marriage; dried up by her coldness and constant preoccupation with her health. She had not wanted children and had been furious to find herself pregnant with Kay. After Teddy's birth, she had removed all her belongings to another bedroom, where she had slept ever since, the door implacably locked each night against her husband. It was the end of the marriage in any genuine sense of the word, but Charles had never asked for a divorce. Faith was a true neurotic, totally dependent on his continuing support. He had left her twice, and on both occasions she had tried to kill herself. His children needed him, too.

Pete Kovaks produced a packet of Lucky Strike from his pocket and offered it to the Major.

'Cigarette?'

Charles took one and lit it with a gold lighter which bore the inscription: To CG from FL. Always. June 1928. 'Always' had become a life sentence from which there was no escape.

The two men strolled slowly along Church Lane, past the row of cottages, whose front gardens, even at this time of year, were full of bright patches of colour; Michaelmas daisies, late flowering chrysanthemums, berberis spilling like blood over the grey stone walls. Charles was conscious that his legs were aching: he still found it painful to walk very far. He had sustained a compound fracture of the left tibia and a simple fracture of the right femur when his jeep had overturned as the American forces battled their way out of Normandy at the end of July.

Pete Kovaks glanced at his wrist watch.

'Say, d'you think the pub's open yet? I still can't get the hang of these dumb Limey licensing laws.'

'Lower your voice, Captain,' Charles ordered, abruptly pulling rank. He saw Pete's startled face and relented. 'Didn't you ever read your copy of the Guide?' he inquired more gently.

A Short Guide to Great Britain, which had been issued to every United States serviceman before he landed in the United Kingdom, warned about the vagaries of the British character. It also cautioned its readers against criticizing native customs and institutions, or boasting that their fathers came over to win the last war.

Pete Kovaks had lost his copy long ago, nor had he ever bothered to read it, but he did not say so. There was something forbidding about Charles Graham, and it was not merely his seniority in years and rank. There was something austere and withdrawn about the man. It had been all the more surprising, therefore, when he had made it so fast and so easily into the attractive Mrs Sherwood's bed.

'Three weeks. Three goddam weeks,' Pete would complain loudly to anyone who would listen, 'that's all it took before she invited him home for lunch. Three weeks out of hospital and still walking with a stick! Brother! I wouldn't have believed it if I hadn't seen it with my own eyes.' Pete had fancied his own chances with Dorothy – 'I adore older women who have legs like Betty Grable!' – and had been disconcerted by the Major's success.

The King's Head was just beyond the church, and at midday on a Saturday was full up with regulars as long as the supply of beer held out. Terry Ibbs, from Barton Farm, was describing in his high-pitched, penetrating whine the best way to drive a herd of young pigs.

'Bag o' beans, that's all you need. Keep droppin' one in front o' the leader an' all the other greedy little beggars'll come trottin' forrard t' see what 'e's got.'

A couple of the older men were recalling their youth and the New Year custom of Plough Monday.

'Blacked our 'ands and faces, we did, turned our coats inside out and dragged the old ploughshare round all the

24

'ouses in the district. Got a fair old whack of money. Those that couldn't give cash gave in kind.'

'All finished now,' the other man added gloomily. 'Can't do it no more, not since tractors and cultivators replaced the 'orse-drawn plough.' He consoled himself with a swig of ale.

As the two Americans approached the bar, there was a sudden hush. It happened every time, Charles reflected irritably. Surely the villagers must be used to the presence of their allies by now. One or two people smiled uncertainly, and a couple of the women giggled and batted eyelids in invitation, but most of the younger men looked hostile. After a few moments, heads turned away again and conversation was resumed. Pete and the Major were left to their own devices.

'Friendly lot of bastards,' Pete muttered under his breath, while the landlord, Ernest Jordan, inquired with false heartiness: 'Right, gents, what can I get you?'

'Two whiskies and sodas, please.' Charles had learned by this time not to ask for Scotch or Bourbon and certainly never to expect ice. He had also learned not to drink beer, partly because the tepid English variety was not what any self-respecting American was used to, and partly because the natives resented it if the Yanks failed to throw their money around.

'You're looking better, Major Graham.' Ernest Jordan pushed two glasses across the bar and indicated the siphon. 'Help yourselves to soda. And you, Captain Kovaks. Looking better, I mean.'

'Yeah.' Pete ignored the siphon and swallowed his whisky neat. 'I can't wait to get back to civilization. Can't even go to an evening movie in Bristol. The goddam 'buses stop running at nine.'

'Only the country 'buses.' Ernest Jordan was tetchily defensive. 'They took down all the signposts at the beginning of the war, in case of invasion, and with the blackout and everything, an inexperienced driver could get lost. End up in a field. Common sense, if you think about it.'

'Of course it is,' Charles agreed diplomatically. He steered Pete Kovaks to a corner seat. 'For pity's sake,' he told him, 'stop rubbing people up the wrong way.'

'They resent us!' Pete exclaimed hotly. 'We come over here to fight their lousy war for them, and they resent us!'

'That'll do, Captain. Of course they do, if they hear you talking like that. So shut up, unless you can say something friendly. Have another Scotch.'

Pete shook his head dourly, but was aware that the Major was not as angry as he sounded. Conscious of a dull ache in his guts, Pete vented his frustrated spleen on the Germans.

'Bastard Krauts,' he muttered.

Charles made no reply. The buzz of conversation continued all around them, the soft Somerset burr blending with the harsher Bristol accent. The King's Head was a very old pub; fifteenth century, some parts of it, Dorothy had told him. The saloon bar, where they were sitting, had low, smoke-blackened beams and a big, open fireplace, where logs and peat were burning, giving off an earthy, yet resinous smell. Horse brasses gleamed on the walls, and the wooden benches, ranged around the room, were dark with age. The shelves behind the bar counter were almost bare, the empty spaces testifying to five years of total war and the disappearance of so many luxury goods, hard liquor among them.

Charles had visited the pub on several occasions with Dorothy, but she always took him into the lounge, and this was his first time in the saloon bar. He leaned back against the settle and half-closed his eyes, wondering what he was going to do about Dorothy Sherwood. He had been a fool to discuss his marriage with her, but that particular day, he had needed a shoulder to cry on. It was the day he had first made love to her; the day he had received an especially abusive letter from Faith, in which his wife accused him of abandoning her and the children to 'go and play soldiers in Europe'.

26

'Daddy would have got you a safe desk job in Washington,' she had written petulantly, 'but you wanted to leave me. I've been extremely ill and unhappy. I hope you are satisfied, knowing what I've suffered on your account.'

It was the day his mending bones had been hurting him like crazy, and he had turned to Dorothy for comfort. She had given it in such generous measure that they had inevitably ended up in bed together. She had mentioned the word 'divorce' and had gone on mentioning it at regular intervals ever since. He couldn't seem to convince her that even if he survived the rest of the war, he wouldn't be coming back to England to marry her; that he had no intention of divorcing Faith. He found it even more difficult to convince himself that he wasn't a fool to pass up such a chance of marital happiness with a woman who so plainly adored him.

Or did she? Wasn't Dorothy really in love with the glamour of the Graham name? His family were very wealthy and very powerful, two well known aphrodisiacs where women were concerned.

Charles opened his eyes and finished his drink.

'Let's go,' he said to Pete Kovaks. 'It must be nearly lunchtime. We'd better get back to the house.'

They left almost unnoticed and walked along the road. It was raining harder now and Charles turned up the collar of his coat. As they passed the church, the vicar came through the lych-gate. He smiled and nodded at the two Americans.

'Terrible day.' The Reverend Nicholas Horobin was shortsighted and had to peer closely at Charles before recognizing him. 'Major Graham, isn't it? I thought I remembered your face.' He wagged an admonitory finger. 'You haven't been to church again, since that first time. We'd very much like to see you and any of your friends, you know.'

'Yes. Of course. I'm sorry, padre. I really will try.' Charles touched his cap in salute and hurriedly moved on. That morning visit to St Andrew's, some weeks ago now, had also been his first meeting with Dorothy.

It had been a day of pale sunshine, which had slanted through the stained glass windows to coagulate on the floor of the nave in pools of amethyst, emerald and palest rose. Charles had been sitting behind one of the Norman pillars, which almost obscured his view of the pulpit, wondering what had prompted him to come.

He had not been inside a church for at least twelve years, not since Teddy's christening. Marriages, funerals, baptisms; that seemed about his mark. His parents had never brought him up to be devout. Nominally Presbyterian, like their Scottish ancestors, politics were the Grahams' true religion. Charles did not even believe in that.

But this morning, quite suddenly, he had felt the urge to visit the village church. Perhaps it had been prompted by boredom; by the prospect of another seemingly endless Sunday spent reading, writing letters and listening to the American Forces' Network over the radio, in the company of a dozen or so semi-invalids like himself; men with whom he had nothing much in common. He had asked Pete Kovaks to accompany him before recalling that the younger man was a Catholic and would attend Mass at the Court with Father McBride.

> Oh come, oh come, Emmanuel,
> And ransom captive Israel . . .

The Advent hymn soared upwards, the sound echoing among the rafters and bosses of the roof. On the chancel steps, someone had arranged a brass jug of autumn leaves and berries, while the bronze cross and candlesticks on the altar caught the sunlight, glinting with fire.

Several people had stared at Charles as he entered the church, and now, as the elderly vicar droned through an uninspiring sermon, a few more nodded encouragement. A very smart woman, seated beside a young girl on the opposite side of the aisle, smiled at him in sympathetic amusement, and Charles found himself smiling in return.

After the final benediction had been pronounced, the woman had come up to him and held out her hand.

'I'm Dorothy Sherwood,' she said, and Charles noted that her voice was low and husky, every bit as attractive as her appearance.

'And I'm Charles Graham,' he answered. 'Chuck to my friends.'

The magnificent dark eyes beneath the brim of her chic blue hat twinkled up at him.

'I'm not quite sure where that leaves me. Perhaps on so slight an acquaintance, I'd better stick to – let me see – Major, isn't it? Major Graham.'

'No, no, please! You must call me Chuck.' All around them, people streamed slowly out of the building, but the two of them, as he later recalled, might as well have been on a desert island. The young girl, standing so quietly in her mother's shadow, was almost invisible.

Dorothy's well-defined eyebrows lifted provocatively. 'In that case, I feel I must do something to earn the privilege. Will you come to Sunday lunch with us, Chuck?' She laughed and shook her head. 'No, really, I can't call you that, when Charles is such a distinguished and dignified name.'

'Call me anything you wish. And I should be honoured to lunch with you, ma'am. I'll have to report back to the house first, though, to obtain official permission.'

'Of course. And I think you're very brave,' Dorothy added, 'forgoing all that lovely American food for British austerity fare.'

Charles cursed himself for a fool. He had been so anxious to accept the invitation that he had forgotten rationing.

'Is there anything I can bring?' he asked. 'I have friends in the stores.'

'Not a thing,' Dorothy assured him. 'Just don't expect too much, that's all. I live at Grace Cottage, by the way.' They were out of the church by this time, and she indicated the row of stone cottages opposite St Andrew's. 'The end one, next to the fields.'

*　　*　　*

An hour and a half later, Charles had leaned back in his chair and sighed with repletion.

'That was first-rate, Mrs Sherwood. The coffee was excellent.'

Dorothy smiled. 'High praise, indeed, coming from an American. I'm a rotten housekeeper, but a very good cook. And if I'm to call you Charles, you must stop addressing me as Mrs Sherwood. I'm Dorothy, but be warned! Unlike you, Major, I make no concessions to my friends. I never answer to Dot, Dotty, Doll or any of the other hideous diminutives of my name.'

'I'll remember,' Charles answered gravely. 'But tell me, how do you produce a meal like that on your rations?'

'Oh, Mummy doesn't manage on her rations.' Sally's voice chipped into the conversation, tinged with malice. 'She has so many admirers and friends, someone can always supply her with something under the counter.'

Charles turned and smiled politely, but he did not join in Dorothy's peal of laughter. Until that moment, he had considered Sally an odd, quiet little thing, rather gauche and badly dressed, not at all the sort of girl he would have expected to be Dorothy Sherwood's daughter; but harmless. Now, he thought her rude, as well.

'I'm afraid Sally's right,' Dorothy confessed ruefully. Her voice dropped to a confidential whisper. She smiled conspiratorially straight into the Major's eyes. 'I have a lot of friends and I must admit to taking a shocking advantage of them all.'

One of her hands was lying on the tablecloth, close to his, and he had to restrain the impulse to squeeze it. She was an extraordinarily charismatic woman. He had never felt attracted to anyone before as he felt attracted to her.

Sally's fresh young voice made itself heard again as she asked abruptly: 'Are you married, Major?'

Charles coloured angrily. 'Yes,' he answered shortly.

'Have you any children?'

'Two.'

'Boys or girls?'

'One of each.'

'How old are they?' The relentless catechism continued.

'Kay's fourteen, Teddy's twelve.' Charles glared balefully at his inquisitor. Sally glared right back.

'I expect they miss you, don't they?'

'Darling!' Dorothy had decided that it was time to intervene. 'I'm sure there's no need to guard my virtue quite so zealously. Major Graham has come for lunch. He's not intending to ravish me.' She gave her throaty chuckle and turned back to Charles. 'You must forgive Sally, but since my husband was killed, she feels she has to be the man of the family.'

Sally flushed scarlet and looked down at her hands in her lap. The Major's sympathy veered abruptly in her direction.

'I'm sorry about your father,' he said quietly. 'One of the men at the Court told me he was killed at Dunkirk. He must have been a very fine soldier.'

Sally made no reply and Dorothy pushed back her chair. 'He was . . . You must show me the snapshots of your family sometime, Charles. I'm sure you have some and I should love to see them. If Kay and Teddy are anything like their father, they must be a handsome pair.' She got to her feet. 'Shall we go into the lounge? You don't have to go right back? Sally, darling, I know you have homework to do. Leave the washing-up.' And she had led the way out of the room.

That had been the start of it, thought Charles, as he and Pete Kovaks turned into Manor Walk from Church Lane. The path leading to seduction had seemed so straightforward then. Now, all these weeks later, he was not so certain.

Sally saw the two Americans from her bedroom window, while she was taking off her coat. She was too innocent to realize the true state of affairs between her mother and Charles Graham, but she did suspect the Major of being Philip's rival for Dorothy's affection. Sally was very attached to Philip, and although, at present, she resented the thought of anyone usurping her father's place, she was sensible enough to know that it would probably happen one day. Her mother was still a comparatively young woman. She was almost certain to marry again, and Sally wanted the man to be Philip. He was one of the family already. His presence would make no material alteration to their lives, and he loved Dorothy as much as Bill Sherwood had done. If Major Graham ever got divorced and married her mother, it would disrupt their quiet existence.

All her life, since she was old enough to notice such things, Sally had seen the effect her mother had upon men. Even though Dorothy had adored her husband, she had never been able to resist exerting her power to charm and fascinate. It came as naturally to her as breathing. Bill had not seemed to mind, but Sally had resented Dorothy's behaviour on his behalf. Now, she resented it equally for Philip.

She went to the cupboard in one corner of her room and took out a sketching block and pencils. Within minutes, a wicked caricature of Charles Graham took shape on the sheet of paper, accurate enough to be immediately identifiable, but with every feature exaggerated. The strong nose looked hawk-like; the china blue eyes, beneath their thick lashes and brows, were smaller than in real life. The wide mouth was shut, trap-like, and the firm chin made to jut forward, its slight trace of a cleft deepened to an ugly double point. The military cut of the once dark, now greying hair was bristly and porcine. The whole effect was mean and predatory, and Sally sat looking at it for a moment or two before tearing the sheet of paper from the block and crumpling it up. She tossed it into the wastepaper basket. Her instinctive sense of fair play told her that Major Graham was not really like that: what she had drawn was a lie, however much she might want to believe it.

She began doodling idly on the pad in front of her. After a while, she saw that she had drawn another portrait, without even realizing what she was doing; a squarish face beneath a thatch of blond hair. The eyes staring up at her from the paper were hostile, and she remembered them as piercingly blue. A faint scar line shadowed the left cheek.

It was the young German prisoner-of-war whom she had seen that morning in Mrs Younger's kitchen.

32

CHAPTER THREE

Werner Neumann lay on the narrow bed and stared at the ceiling. A naked, low-powered bulb hung from its centre, giving the hut a depressing air of gloom. The windows were shuttered against the night and the threat of German bombers.

But German bombers were scarce over this part of England nowadays. The V1 and V2 rockets might be getting through to London and the south-east, but they weren't going to turn the tide of war in Germany's favour. They could have done so once, but not any more. It was too late. The war was lost, and had been lost as soon as the United States came in on the side of Britain. British bombers by night and American bombers by day were pounding Germany's cities into dust. Berlin, Düsseldorf, Dresden, Cologne and, above all, his home city of Hamburg were systematically being reduced to ruins.

The last letter Werner had received from his mother had been at the beginning of the year. Since then, there had been an ominous silence. The Camp Commandant, a decent enough fellow in his way, had instigated inquiries through the Red Cross; but apart from discovering that the street and house where Werner had lived with his mother and married sister, had been totally destroyed, the authorities could discover nothing concerning the fate of the two women. Had they been in the apartment when the bomb struck, or out shopping? Had they been killed or had they joined the thousands of homeless refugees now clogging Germany's roads, living rough, having lost everything?

The country was fast becoming one vast shambles as

Hitler's thousand-year Reich began to crumble and the allies pushed forward towards the Rhine. Werner no longer doubted the validity of the BBC news which he heard over the camp radio. He had realized many years ago that Nazi propaganda could not be relied on.

'The Führer has never visited Hamburg,' was its citizens' secret boast.

It was the one major German city which Hitler had seemed to avoid, made uneasy perhaps by the port's liberal traditions and spirit of tolerance. For centuries, the inhabitants had regarded themselves as having more in common with their Saxon cousins in England than with members of the other German states. In 1567, the city fathers had risked an open breach with the Hanseatic League by inviting the English Company of Merchant Venturers to establish themselves in Hamburg, and by granting them important trading concessions. The English had occupied one of the city's finest medieval buildings until the time of Napoleon's continental blockade.

But it was not only the English who had been welcomed in Hamburg. Its Assembly had offered asylum to anyone of any nation, Christian or Jew, who had fled his own country to escape political or religious persecution. From 1529 onwards, the citizens had had their own constitution, giving them the right to be consulted on all matters of administration.

The port at the mouth of the Elbe had always flourished, but its period of greatest prosperity had been from the late 1860s until the outbreak of war in 1914. By 1912, it was the world's third largest port, giving precedence only to London and New York.

If the Great War had meant economic depression for the city, the punitive Treaty of Versailles had spelled financial disaster. The Neumann family had been only four of its many victims. Before the German banknote became nothing but a useless piece of paper – terrible days when a billion marks would barely buy a loaf of bread – Werner and his sister, Sophia, had lived with their parents in a fine house near

34

Altona, bought by Bruno Neumann when he married his Elsa just before the start of the first world war. Neumann's had been a successful importing business for three generations, but in 1923, when Werner was four years old and Sophy eight, the firm went bankrupt. Bruno Neumann had taken his old service revolver to a quiet spot near the river and shot himself, leaving his wife and children to face the future alone.

Elsa had sold the house, moved to a seedy apartment near Hamburg docks and resumed her old profession of teaching English. The infusion of American dollars which had finally stabilized the German economy had been followed by the Wall Street crash and the Depression. Nothing seemed to change for the better.

And then, suddenly – at least, it seemed sudden to Werner, looking back on events which had happened when he was an adolescent boy – the Weimar Republic had fallen and the National Socialists had come to power. In fact, there was a four-year gap between the two events, but all Werner could remember was the feeling of euphoria and patriotism which had swept the country like a fever in 1933. Germany would be great again. The Fatherland would be revenged on the rest of Europe for a decade of humiliation and despair. Emotions had run high, even in Hamburg, and there had been very few protests when the Bürgeschaft, the four-hundred-years old Citizens' Assembly, had been dissolved and replaced by a Commissioner responsible directly to Berlin.

Elsa Neumann and her children had been part of the country's economic revival. They had moved to an airy, second-floor apartment with windows commanding a distant view of the smaller of the two Alster lakes. There was money for good clothes and food, and Sophy had married a young officer in the newly formed Schützstaffeln; the SS for short. In 1937, at the age of eighteen, Werner had obtained a place at Heidelberg University.

But for him, as for many people living in Hamburg, people who were unable to brush aside completely the freedom-loving traditions of the past, the Nazi dream had begun to turn sour. There were ugly whispers of neighbours disappearing in the night; of mysterious cattle trains with sides boarded up, bearing human cargo; of beatings, torture and killings. They were only whispers, however, and no one wanted to believe them. Life was too comfortable. Hitler was leading the Germans back to their true place in the world. They were once more a nation to be reckoned with.

It occurred to only a few that Hitler was also leading them into a war which they might not be able to win. And when, in 1938, the Führer persuaded the British and French governments to agree to his annexation of Czechoslovakia, the German man-in-the-street, as well as the British, had believed it was 'peace in our time'.

'Of course you'll come for Christmas Day. They'll let you do that, won't they? The twins have both got leave. It should be fun.'

Dorothy sat up in bed and lit a cigarette with Charles's gold lighter. She no longer found the inscription intriguing, and held the engraving away from her by dint of using her left hand.

Charles propped himself on one elbow and wondered, not for the first time, how Dorothy could bear to make love with that portrait of her husband looking down at them from the wall. No doubt it was hypocritical, but he was sure that in her place it would have made him uncomfortable.

'If I'm still at the Court and not pronounced fit by then,' he said, answering her question, 'naturally I'll come. And I've taken you at your word and invited Pete Kovaks and a few of the other guys round for Christmas evening . . . I keep meaning to ask you, who did that drawing? It's extraordinarily vivid and alive.'

Dorothy threw an indifferent glance at the portrait. 'That? Oh, that's one of Sally's scribbles. Bill was attached to it, so I've kept it for sentimental reasons. Why do you say "if I'm still at the Court"? The doctors aren't going to discharge you yet, are they? You're not properly fit.' Dorothy pulled the eiderdown around her shoulders for

36

extra warmth. Outside, the December night was bitterly cold, and it was little better in the bedroom, where the only source of heat was the hissing and spluttering of an old gas fire. 'You don't want to get sent back now. Not with Jerry making this push in the Ardennes.'

'If I'm passed fit, I'll have no choice,' Charles replied absently. He nodded again at the picture. 'Is it a good likeness of your husband? It really is a marvellous portrait. I didn't know Sally could draw.'

'You didn't know Bill, either,' Dorothy retorted acidly. 'How can you possibly judge whether it's a marvellous portrait or not? And Sally doesn't draw in the sense you mean. She dabbles a bit for her own amusement, but that's all. I've never thought it up to much, myself, though I believe her art mistress at school thinks she's not bad . . . Look! I didn't perjure myself to get an afternoon off work to talk about Sally!' Dorothy glanced at the bedside clock. 'She'll be home from school soon. If we're quick, we can make love one more time.' She snuggled down beside him.

Charles shook his head. 'Sorry, my dear, but I can't.' He kissed her lightly between the eyes. 'I apologize, but there it is.'

'Is it?' Dorothy's voice was edged, and she was conscious of the fact that, for once in her life, she was not in control of a situation. The intensity of her emotions for Charles Graham had taken her by surprise. She was not in love with him, but it was the strongest sexual attraction she had ever experienced. She wanted him and she wanted him for keeps. If he survived the rest of the war, she wanted to know that he would divorce his wife and come back to her. She intended to be the second Mrs Graham.

Most people, she knew, would find it hard to believe, but he was the only man she had ever been to bed with apart from her husband. Dorothy was well aware of the image she presented, and deliberately fostered, of a woman who had been 'around'. But although an incorrigible flirt, she was not promiscuous. Heaven knew that she had had her chances! Yet only a few weeks after her first meeting with Charles Graham, she had let him make love to her.

If she wanted to be sure of him, however, she must not appear possessive. She had recognized the shrewish note in her voice as she asked that last question.

'Of course you're tired,' she said easily, getting up and putting on the cream satin housecoat which she had bought at Selfridge's, just before the war. She crossed to the window and drew together the heavily lined curtains, but with less care than she would have used a year or even six months ago. Blackout regulations were not being enforced so strictly as victory in Europe was scented and confidence grew. Dorothy switched on the light and moved back to the fire. She began dressing.

Charles lay watching her, finishing his cigarette, conscious of a slight feeling of revulsion. The sensation was new to him and took him aback. He could offer no explanation for it. There was nothing unsatisfactory about the way she performed in bed, and after years of rejection by Faith, any woman who responded to him with more than a shudder of distaste should seem good. But there was something not quite right in his relationship with Dorothy which, until this moment, he had been unable to pinpoint. Now, he realized with a sense of shock that he did not really like her.

The revelation was so unexpected that he almost dropped his cigarette. As it was, a gobbet of ash feathered across the counterpane, burning a tiny hole in the pale pink silk. Hastily he stubbed out the butt in a convenient ashtray and swung his legs out of bed.

'Are you all right?' Dorothy asked, pausing in the act of pulling on a stocking. 'You look . . . odd.'

'I'm OK,' he answered, forcing a smile.

The silly thing was, he had no idea why he didn't like her. She was a most attractive woman. The sensation of dislike began to fade; a momentary paranoia, brought on perhaps by fatigue and the after-effects of some drug he was still being given. He went across and kissed her, letting himself respond to the urgency of her body as it pressed against his. They went back to bed and made love for a second time.

38

Later, returning to Barton Court, his coat collar turned up against a biting wind, he reflected yet again on his affair with Dorothy Sherwood. What had started as one of a million wartime flirtations was growing too serious for his peace of mind. He sensed her growing commitment to him; her ever increasing expectations of a future life together. It was easy to tell himself that it was not his fault; that he had never given her any reason to believe he would divorce his wife, but Dorothy was a woman used to getting her own way. She was imperious, demanding. He suspected that Bill Sherwood had always eased his wife's path, granted her every wish. Charles had known men like that, whose lives were ruled by gratitude. He had no intention of joining their ranks.

A thin moon peered through a broken rack of clouds above the trees, gleaming on roofs and leafless branches. 'It's goin' t' be a cold 'un,' Terry Ibbs had informed him that morning, referring to the winter months which still lay ahead. Whatever Terry's methods of foretelling the weather, Charles believed him. He had never known the sort of chill which he encountered in England; a dampness that seeped into the very marrow of his bones. He recalled with a shiver the seemingly never-ending rain which had lashed the Essex marshes and the south coast around Southampton, where the troops had gathered before D-Day.

Inside Barton Court it was reasonably warm, the United States Army having insisted on installing the rudiments of a central heating system before any of their sick and wounded officers were allowed within a mile of the place. Charles crossed the hall, with its black and white tiled floor. From the doorway on his left he could hear laughter and the radio blaring; the familiar, wise-cracking voice of Bob Hope. One of the doctors came through a door at the back, followed by a medical orderly. He raised his hand in greeting.

Charles mounted the central staircase. At the top, on the facing wall, was a copy of a Holbein line drawing of Sir Thomas More, which belonged to the house. Charles

39

paused, staring at it as, half an hour before, he had stared at the pen-and-ink portrait of Bill Sherwood. Was that the reason for his sudden dislike of Dorothy? he wondered; because she was lacking in kindness and consideration for the feelings of others, particularly those of her youngest daughter, Sally?

It was dark by the time Sally alighted from the green single-decker 'bus, outside the church. Her black school hat, with its band of red ribbon, was pushed inelegantly to the back of her head, her satchel, held by its strap, swinging and banging against her legs. Soon it would be the Christmas holidays. The crib had already been set up in the church-yard, but it was impossible to distinguish it properly in the gloom.

A truck rumbled down the track from Barton Farm, the German prisoners-of-war sitting in the back, under the cage of green tarpaulin. Most either stared straight in front of them, or turned their heads to glare resentfully at passers-by. The three men from Barton Farm, the last to be picked up, were right at the end, next to the tailboard. One of them, on the left-side row, suddenly waved to someone he recognized, but there was no accompanying smile. Sally knew him at once: she had drawn his face a dozen or more times since that Saturday morning seven weeks earlier, when she had seen him in Ellen Younger's kitchen.

On a sudden impulse, she called out: 'Happy Christmas, Werner!'

The German's eyes swivelled towards her in astonish-ment, but he made no response. The truck swung left, along Hill Road, making for the steep descent to the outskirts of Bristol. The tail lights glimmered for a moment, then disappeared over the brow of the hill. Sally stood on the pavement, feeling snubbed and foolish. Werner hadn't known who she was. Why should he? There was no reason to suppose he had remembered her face as she had done his; there was no reason why he should have remembered her at all.

She turned into Church Lane, passed the lych-gate of St Andrew's and stopped outside Philip's sprawling modern bungalow. There was no chink of light at the front of the building to indicate his presence, so she walked round to the back and knocked on the kitchen door. Philip opened it, a frying-pan held in his other hand.

'Hullo, Sally my child! Come in. I'm just going to cook myself bacon and egg. Have some with me?'

'I'd better not, thank you, Uncle Philip. I'll be having a meal with Mummy when she gets home.'

'That won't be for over an hour yet. Aren't you hungry? Sit down, then, and watch me eat. And stop calling me "uncle"!'

Sally grinned and chose a wooden chair by the kitchen table. 'I'll try, but it won't be easy. I've called you that for so many years . . . You haven't put any fat in that frying-pan.'

Philip swore and searched in the pantry for the bowl of dripping which he painstakingly accumulated, layer upon greasy layer, from the woefully inadequate pieces of meat which comprised his solitary ration. He flung two small rashers of streaky bacon into the pan and began to reconstitute some powdered egg.

'What can I do for you, my dear?' he asked.

Sally swung her foot, kicking the chair rung. 'I was hoping you might persuade Mummy to let me stay on at school. She wants me to leave at the end of the summer term and begin earning. She says we need the money.'

'Why? Education is never wasted.'

Sally grimaced. 'Try telling that to Mummy! She doesn't think that girls need a lot of education.'

Philip snorted. 'Typical!' he said. He poured the egg mixture into a saucepan and began beating it with a fork. 'Why do you want to stay on?'

'I want to go to art school and I can't do that until I'm eighteen. And anyway, I don't know how well I'll do in my School Certificate exams. If I flop, I could take them again next Christmas.'

'What sort of art do you want to specialize in? Commercial? Fabric design? Portraiture? What medium are you thinking of using?'

'I don't know yet. That's what I want to find out.'

'And Dorothy's against the whole idea?'

'She doesn't think anyone can make a living as an artist, in spite of Daddy. She says it would be different if he were alive to advise me, and if she weren't a poor widow, living on her pension.'

Philip smiled grimly. He could just hear Dorothy saying it; and believing it, too, that was the trouble. It was useless pointing out to her that apart from her war-widow's pension and the salary she earned at the BBC, Bill Sherwood, who had been a successful freelance illustrator, mainly of children's books, had left her reasonably well-off. 'Reasonable' was not an acceptable word in Dorothy's vocabulary.

Philip piled the bacon and scrambled egg on to a plate which he had forgotten to warm, cleared a place on the cluttered kitchen table and sat down opposite Sally.

'I'll have a word with your mother,' he promised, 'but I don't hold out much hope of its carrying any weight. It's costing her four guineas a term to keep you at school. A fair bit of money, but I'd be willing to help, if that's her only reason.'

Sally gave him the blinding, trusting smile which she bestowed only on the favoured few, but which transformed her from a rather plain adolescent into a young woman of incipient beauty.

'Oh, thank you, Uncle Philip!' She got up and came round the table, dropping a kiss on the top of his head. 'You're the one person she'll listen to, now that Daddy's . . . gone.' Philip noted that she still could not bring herself to use the word 'dead'. There was too much finality about it.

'You flatter me, my dear. I doubt if I have any influence with your mother whatsoever.' It was on the tip of his tongue to say: 'You should try Major Graham,' but he restrained himself, merely sprinkling salt and pepper liberally over his meal and cutting himself a slice of national wholemeal bread. Sally picked up her satchel from beside her chair, preparing to leave. Philip asked as casually as he could: 'Is Dorothy still seeing much of Charles Graham?'

'I suppose so. He's round at the cottage fairly often. They've been to the cinema and the theatre, in Bristol, a couple of times. Mummy's asked him and some of the other American officers for Christmas Day. The twins are both getting leave. Isn't that splendid?'

'Splendid,' Philip agreed. 'Am I invited?'

'Of course.' Sally crammed on her hat and slung her satchel across her shoulders. 'Mummy takes you for granted.'

The kitchen door closed behind her and Philip was left alone with his meal.

When he had finished eating, he lit a cigarette, one of a lavishly packaged carton of Chesterfields, which Pete Kovaks had given him. The two men had become friendly one evening in The King's Head, where they had both been lamenting the state of British beer. During that and subsequent conversations with the young American, Philip had learned from a word dropped casually here and there, of the state of Charles Graham's marriage. And when Dorothy had recently defended the institution of divorce, with surprising cogency for someone who had always had High Church leanings, Philip had grown uneasy. Whatever the Major's intentions might be, Dorothy's had become glaringly obvious.

Philip got up from the table and put the kettle on to boil, whistling tunelessly under his breath. When he had made himself a cup of tea, he carried it into the living room, where a small fire was burning. He knew he should be working on the final chapters of his latest book, but he was not in the mood. Tonight, the complications of the life of Rupert of the Rhine seemed unimportant when compared with those of his own.

Dorothy was hoping to marry Charles Graham. Perhaps he was misjudging her, but he did not think so. He knew her too well. He leaned back in the comfortable, chintz-covered armchair and stretched his feet towards the feeble blaze. He had not bothered to switch on the light, but sat in the glow of the fire, watching the shadows curtsey and flicker across the walls.

He loved his cousin and knew all her faults; her selfishness, her vanity, her pride. Charles Graham represented money and influence, two attributes Dorothy would find it very hard to resist. She had adored Bill Sherwood and he had kept her faithful, in spite of his lack of any real wealth. But now he was dead, Dorothy could give her ambition full rein.

Then there was Sally. Philip guessed that Dorothy's true reason for not wanting her to go to art school was purely selfish. She did not want a daughter who might be successful, perhaps even famous; a daughter in whom people might be more interested than in herself. It was a terrible suspicion to harbour about any mother, but deep down, Philip knew he was right. Sally would have to learn to fight for what she wanted. He would have to learn to fight, himself.

CHAPTER FOUR

The row of cottages in Church Lane had originally been artisans' dwellings, belonging to Barton Court, but the days had long gone when any estate could afford to be self-supporting. Sir Gilbert Quintrell's father had auctioned off the cottages soon after the end of the first world war, and Bill Sherwood, recently married, had bought the end one, next to the fields. In 1920, he had brought Dorothy there to live, and no amount of success in his chosen profession had persuaded him to leave it.

'It's near enough to a big city and remote enough for me not to be disturbed,' he had explained patiently whenever Dorothy grew restless. 'And you know how precarious my livelihood is. My income is never the same two years running. Besides, I like high places.

London-bred Dorothy had been just seventeen when she married her dashing ex-captain of the Somerset Light Infantry. She had found the village of Coldharbour aptly named, swept in winter by every wind that blew, and covered in snow for weeks after the city below them was enjoying a thaw. She had made the best of things, however, because she loved Bill Sherwood, and had done her utmost to make a niche for herself. She threw herself into village life, flirted with every man in sight, made some friends and even more enemies and, twice a week, went into Bristol by 'bus until, in the early 1930s, Bill had bought a second-hand Austin 7.

Dorothy had immediately learned to drive and motored around the village at a scandalous pace. She was the first woman in Coldharbour to smoke, using a long, amber cigarette-holder, the epitome of sophistication as typified in the pages of *Vogue*. It was she who had persuaded Bill, at one period of their lives when they were in funds, to have the front and back parlours of the cottage knocked into one, with French doors opening on to the back garden. The following year, she had had the paved area beyond the doors glassed in, stocked it with a variety of potted plants and two basket-weave chairs, and infuriated her neighbours by referring to it as 'my conservatory'.

'Conservatory, my foot!' Lady Quintrell had snorted in irritation, betrayed into one of the vulgarisms she so despised. 'Who does the upstart think she is?'

Dorothy had been unrepentant. Bill, cocooned in his work, had been oblivious to any undercurrents of feeling between his wife and their friends. He had not cared for the open-plan living room, finding his growing family of first two, and then three, daughters liable to be always underfoot. He had retired with increasing frequency to the 'studio', a wooden summerhouse at the bottom of the garden, which, since his death, had stood empty and musty-smelling, rapidly falling into decay.

The girls, too, had disliked the one big room, but Sally had to admit that for entertaining it was ideal. On this Christmas night it was possible for six American officers, the twins, her mother, Philip and herself to move around with ease.

The twins had arrived home the previous day, after travelling overnight on a packed train from Portsmouth.

'Delays all the way and an hour's wait at Salisbury,' Veronica had proclaimed cheerfully. 'Come and kiss me, Sallykins! You're looking extremely grown-up.'

'Too grown-up,' Jennifer had complained. 'She makes me feel positively hagged.'

The twins had laughed with all the assurance of women far too attractive to be fooled by such self-deprecation. They were full of vivacity and excitement, scattering their belongings untidily throughout the house, regaling Sally with outrageous stories of life in the Wrens until Dorothy came home, early because it was Christmas Eve. After that, it was their mother who moved naturally centre-stage, relegating them, as always, to their roles as supporting players.

'She doesn't change,' Jennifer moaned to Veronica, as they settled down to sleep in the bedroom they had shared since infancy. 'She still overwhelms you.'

'We mustn't let her,' Jennifer replied with unfounded optimism. 'At least it should be fun tomorrow, with half a dozen American officers invited to supper.'

In spite of a nation-wide fuel crisis, Dorothy had managed to obtain a hundredweight of coal more than her ration, Bob Younger had let her have some logs from his store at the farm, and with the red velvet curtains pulled against the winter night, the living room was pleasantly warm. Firelight shone on the glossy dark leaves of the holly. The pearled berries of mistletoe, which Dorothy and Sally had gathered a few days earlier, gleamed milky-white. A Christmas tree, with its jewel-bright trimmings, sparkled in one corner of the room. There were no other decorations, Dorothy having banished, with a shudder of distaste, the garlands of paper-chains and crêpe-paper twists which the girls had made when they were children.

The Americans had, as usual, been lavish with their gifts, bringing with them two bottles of malt whisky, an enormous box of what they called 'candy', and the inevitable present of nylon stockings for the women. Even Sally had received a pair, her first, and wondered how she would ever bring herself to put them on. The material was so fine and shiny, like spun glass, that it looked as though it would break in her hands.

'Fully-fashioned, too!' she had heard Jennifer exclaim in delight to her twin; and Sally could see, when she took the nylons out of their cellophane wrapping, that each was woven to the exact shape of the leg. She thought it might be awkward for anyone who had fat thighs or bulging calves, but she understood why women would queue for hours in the shops to get them. They were so much more sensuous than lisle or rayon stockings.

47

In another corner of the room was a small, upright piano, a relic of the days when Dorothy, in a short-lived burst of enthusiasm, had decided that the twins were going to be concert pianists. Pete Kovaks had been playing carols for the past half-hour, but now, with a sudden change of tempo, he began thumping out *Swinging on a Star* from the Bing Crosby film *Going My Way*. The twins, who, instead of wearing civvies, had elected to remain in uniform – the black stockings were sexier, Sally reflected with a cynicism too old for her years – started singing the words, standing one on either side of Pete Kovaks. The rest of the Americans and Dorothy joined in, crowding round the piano. Philip, one elbow propped against the mantelpiece, watched from a distance. Sally curled further into the depths of her armchair and took a date from the box on a nearby table.

'Aren't you going to sing?'

She jumped and turned to find that Major Graham had detached himself from the group and was standing by her side, smiling down at her.

'Oh . . . No. I haven't any voice. And I don't like this song very much.'

'Why not? Sounds a great tune to me.'

Sally shrugged, not knowing whether to explain or keep silent. Something in his face, some spark of interest, which she had not noticed before, made her continue.

'I saw the film last September, when Arnhem was on. The newsreels were full of it. The song reminds me, that's all. All that suffering and dying . . .' She paused, the colour staining her skin. 'You probably think I'm being very silly and childish. But I think war's wrong. I hate people who say the only good German's a dead one.'

'I don't think you're silly or childish.' Charles sat down on one of the high-backed chairs which had been brought in from the dining-room and placed along the wall. 'War is evil, and most have been unnecessary evils. But I don't happen to believe that's true of this one. I think that German National Socialism is a bigger menace even than war.'

Sally looked mulish and her colour deepened. Charles

48

realized that his attempt to speak to her as an equal had sounded censorious and patronizing. He was relieved when Philip strolled across to join them.

'Dorothy tells me you've finished your latest book,' he remarked, glad to change the subject. 'May I ask what it's about?'

Philip helped himself to a date and carefully took out the stone. 'A biography of Rupert of the Rhine. An attempt to flesh out the real man, as opposed to the romantic myth.' The words sounded pompous, even to himself, and he felt angry. He added rudely: 'I don't suppose you know anything about him.'

'He founded the Hudson's Bay Company, didn't he? And the Royal Society? And etching, wasn't he responsible for that?'

Philip smiled bleakly and swallowed the date. 'Congratulations, Major, you're very well informed.'

The blue eyes twinkled. 'For an American, you mean? Don't forget, I was in the publishing business.'

Sally said quickly: 'Prince Rupert and Colonel Henry Washington captured Bristol for the Royalists. Henry Washington was an ancestor of your first President.'

'You mean a Washington fought for the king?'

'Yes. There's a plaque somewhere, marking the place where the Colonel broke through the city defences.' She looked up at Charles, seeing him for the first time as an individual and not simply as an admirer of her mother's. She sat forward, clasping her hands round her knees. 'Do you like history, Major Graham?'

'I majored in it at college. The seventeenth and eighteenth centuries.'

'In that case, why don't I take you into Bristol during the Christmas holidays, and show you all the historic places? The city has sometimes been called the cradle of America.'

Charles looked down at her eager, smiling face and wondered how he could ever have thought her plain.

'I should like that very much,' he said warmly. 'How about Saturday? Is that a date?'

The singing finished and the party around the piano broke up. Pete Kovaks, flushed with too many whiskies, put his arm about Veronica's waist and attempted to nibble her ear. Jennifer subsided in a giggling heap on another officer's lap and began feeding him chocolates. Dorothy bore down on the little group in the corner.

'This is very cosy,' she drawled. 'Charles, you're being extremely anti-social, you know.' There was a strident note to her voice, and although she smiled at Philip, her eyes focused immediately afterwards on Charles and her youngest daughter. It was, Philip thought with wry amusement, a basilisk stare.

'We were talking about Prince Rupert,' he cut in quickly, instinctively protecting Sally from her mother's displeasure. 'Major Graham was asking about my new book.'

'Oh dear! My poor Charles! How boring for you.' Dorothy arched her eyebrows, her ill-humour evaporating. 'I've always thought Rupert's mother a much more interesting character. The Winter Queen, isn't that what she was called? Men found her absolutely fascinating, I believe. There you are, Philip.' She turned mockingly to her cousin. 'The subject for your next book. I read somewhere that Elizabeth's husband built an English garden for her at Heidelberg because she was homesick. He had a great stone arch raised overnight as a surprise for her, when she woke next morning. It bore the words *Elizabetae, Conjugi Cariss.*' Dorothy glanced provocatively at Charles Graham. 'That's what I call devotion.'

Charles laughed and got to his feet, suddenly too tired to join in her verbal games.

'Pete!' he called. 'Play something else, will you?' Pete groaned, but obligingly disentwined himself from Veronica's embrace. Charles added: 'Mrs Sherwood and I want to dance.' He glanced over his shoulder at Sally. 'Don't forget, now. That's a date for next Saturday.' He smiled lazily into Dorothy's eyes. 'Your daughter and I are going out on the town.'

* * *

'Aren't you going to sing carols?' Erich Rossman paused by Werner's bed, looking concerned. 'You hardly ate any dinner. Cheer up! The war will soon be over. This time next year, we'll all be home.'

Werner shook his head. 'I'm not coming. I'll stay here and read. I might come along later, if I feel like it.'

He watched his friend leave the hut, then dropped back on his pillow, hands linked behind his head.

Erich, in common with many men in the camp, still imagined that the Allies were going to make an honourable peace with the Germans before they crossed the Rhine. No one talked of the possibility of unconditional surrender: nobody wanted to believe that Germany could be beaten to her knees. They thought that Hitler would be forced to resign as Chancellor and that his successor would then treat with the Allies. Some even thought that this last push in the Ardennes might stave off defeat altogether. The most pessimistic of prisoners imagined that victory for the Allies would mean swift repatriation for themselves. They shut their ears to the warnings of the Camp Commandant that it could be years before they saw Germany again. The country had been so badly bombed, cities like Hamburg reduced to so many million tons of rubble, that the authorities would not dare add to the chaos by discharging thousands of ex-prisoners, many of them homeless.

Werner opened his eyes and stared hopelessly at the opposite wall. A row of pin-up pictures decorated the area just above the bed. And that was about as close as any of them would get to a woman, he reflected bitterly, for a very long time.

Then he remembered the young girl who had called out: 'Happy Christmas, Werner!' He had puzzled over her a lot these last few weeks. How had she known his name? Her face glimpsed briefly in the fading light, had been vaguely familiar. She must belong to the village. Had he seen her, perhaps, near the farm?

His eyelids drooped and he began drifting towards sleep. The fools in the common room would be singing *Still the*

51

Night, Holy the Night by now and crying sentimental tears into their ration of weak English beer. That was the trouble with the Germanic races, even the phlegmatic Anglo-Saxons, they were full of bottled-up emotion under that hard outer crust.

He jerked wide awake again. There was still no word from the International Red Cross about his mother and sister. Those in charge were apologetic, but Hamburg was in a mess, information difficult to come by. He wouldn't think about it, not tonight, at any rate. Not Christmas Day. His mind wandered again, weaving pictures of happy, carefree student days at Heidelberg.

He had been fortunate, getting into the country's oldest university. How proud his mother had been! When she visited him, she had been enchanted by the wooded hills and castle rising above the town and river, like a backcloth to some Viennese operetta. The castle had been partially destroyed during the Thirty Years' War. Werner remembered the English garden and the broken remains of an arch, raised by Frederick, the Elector Palatine, for his English bride . . .

The English had always spelled trouble for the rest of Europe. They had amassed their empire, but were continually trying to prevent other nations from amassing one, too. A smug, self-righteous, self-opinionated race! He could tolerate the Americans better!

A thin face glimmered between the veils of sleep; a young face, a girl's face; hardly more than that of a child.

'Happy Christmas, Werner!' She had known that he understood English. She had known his name.

'Are you tired? You look awfully pale.'

Charles Graham laughed. 'Never tell an American he looks pale. To a nation of sun-worshippers it's the final insult. But yes, I am feeling tired.'

'We'll sit down for a minute.' Sally took his arm and guided him to a seat with all the care and consideration she would have shown to an elderly uncle. 'In a moment, we'll go and have some tea.'

'Thank you,' Charles said, as gratefully as he could. She made him feel every one of his forty years.

He had had his guided tour of the city, and they were now seated among the waterfalls and lawns of Brandon Hill, a few feet from the Cabot Tower. Sally said, with the candour he was beginning to find so endearing: 'I didn't like you much when I first knew you. I expect you realized that. But now I've changed my mind.'

'I'm glad,' he replied simply, 'because I like you a lot.'

She giggled. 'You didn't to begin with. Come on, admit it! You thought I was a rude, ill-tempered brat.'

'I thought you . . . outspoken.' His eyes creased at the corners. 'All right. I didn't like you much at the start, I agree. So we're quits.'

She stared out over the surrounding city, her shoulders looking pathetically thin under her red woollen coat. With the sudden transition from childhood to maturity, so disconcerting in people of her age, she said abruptly: 'Mummy thinks you're going to marry her. Oh, she hasn't discussed you with me. It's just a hunch, but I think I'm right. She believes you'll get a divorce. Will you?'

He took a deep breath. 'No,' he answered steadily. 'I must stay with Faith – my wife – so long as she needs me. I'm sorry if Dorothy feels she's been misled.'

This time, it seemed, he had succeeded in talking to her as an equal without sounding any note of condescension. Sally turned and gave him one of her clear, direct looks. 'I expect she misled herself. Shall we go and get that tea?'

As they rose, a small boy sidled up to them. 'Any gum, chum?' he asked the Major.

It was such a familiar question, chanted by children all over the country to every American serviceman they met, that Charles had automatically reached into his pocket before the boy had finished speaking.

'Here! Have two packets.'

'Gosh! Thanks, mister.' The shrewd young eyes switched to Sally. 'You're a bit young fer this lark, ain't ya? 'E's a bit old fer you, an' all.'

53

'I shall be sixteen on New Year's Day,' she retorted indignantly, then stared in surprise as Charles boxed the boy's ears. 'Why did you do that?' she demanded.

He did not reply, and maintained his silence as they climbed Park Street to the Berkeley Café. She was such an intriguing mixture of maturity and innocence, he was not quite sure how much she knew. It had been immediately obvious to him that Brandon Hill, with its banks of trees and shrubs and sheltered arbours, was a night-time haunt for servicemen and their girls. He had noted the evidence among the general litter of sweet-papers and austerity chocolate-wrappers which lay scattered across grass and paths. He had recognized many of the condoms as those issued to American troops, but he had no idea if Sally understood their significance.

They went upstairs in the café, to a large room surrounded by gilt-framed mirrors, and ordered tea and hot-buttered toast. Sally had not repeated her question, but sat quietly regarding him, dawning comprehension at the back of her eyes. One or two people at neighbouring tables were looking at them, and one woman pointedly whispered behind her hand to her friend.

Charles cursed silently. He should have asked the twins to come with them, but he had always thought of Sally as a child; she was not very much older than his daughter. Now, it dawned on him that she was a young woman, and an attractive one, in her red coat and nylon stockings. Even those awful shoes with the hinged, wooden soles were acceptable on her small, slender feet.

She grinned at him. 'Those two women think I'm just another tart out with a Yank. A teenage delinquent. Let's give them reason.' And she laid a hand on his sleeve, staring into his eyes with what she fondly imagined was a seductive expression.

'Don't do that. You look constipated,' he informed her brusquely.

Instead of being offended, she dissolved in giggles, a child again. But that moment when their eyes met had disturbed him badly. Christ! he thought in disgust. What was the matter with him? He couldn't possibly feel like that about a fifteen-year-old girl. Yet he had been conscious of emotions he had never known before.

He forced down a second slice of toast. Soon he would be gone. The doctor had told him that morning that he would be fit in a few weeks' time. He had not told Dorothy yet: he wanted to postpone the inevitable scene for as long as possible . . . He looked up and saw Sally watching him curiously, her head tilted on one side, like a little bird. His heart missed a beat. He looked hurriedly away again. He didn't believe what was happening to him.

He pushed back his chair and signalled to the waitress for the bill. Sally gulped down her last mouthful of tea.

'Why the big rush?' she asked plaintively. 'I thought we were going to have some of those little iced cakes.'

'I'm not feeling too good,' Charles lied. 'This afternoon has been more exhausting than I expected.'

She was contrite. 'I should have thought. I'm sorry.' He had noticed before how quick she always was to shoulder blame, and had no hesitation in charging it to Dorothy's account. 'Bristol's so hilly,' Sally added.

He smiled at her, trying to feel avuncular and not succeeding.

'I'm sorry about the cakes. Would you like to go home in a taxi to make up?'

Her eyes glowed. 'You mean all the way to Coldharbour in a taxi? Yes, please!'

The woman at the next table hissed at her friend: 'D'you hear that? A taxi to Coldharbour! Disgraceful I call it! The Yanks have money to burn.'

But it turned out not to have been such a good idea. In the taxi, with Sally sitting beside him on the back seat, their arms touching, the Major was conscious of an overwhelming desire to kiss her; to feel those soft lips crushed against his. He started to sweat. He had read about men who fancied young girls, and had felt nothing for them but loathing and contempt. He was forty. It was ludicrous to suppose that

55

he could be falling in love with a girl less than half his age. A schoolgirl!

At Grace Cottage, he paid off the taxi, but refused to go in.

'Make my apologies to your mother. Tell her I'm tired.' He held out his hand. 'So long, Sally. It's been a great day.'

'You enjoyed it? Truly?'

'Wouldn't have missed it for the world.'

She raised anxious eyes to his as she took his hand.

'It's been a great day for me, too. I hope I haven't tired you out too much, though, dragging you around like that. Are you sure you won't come in? Mummy'll be expecting you.'

'I'll see her tomorrow. She's invited me and Pete for New Year's Eve.'

'Oh good! I thought she had, but I wasn't sure. Veronica will be pleased. She's rather keen on Pete.'

Charles laughed. It sounded strained. 'Pete's "rather keen" on her, as well,' he said, mimicking Sally's English vowels.

She was still holding his hand and he freed himself gently. Before he realized what she was about and could stop her, she reached up and kissed his mouth. There was nothing passionate in it; just the sort of kiss he had seen her give Philip, but he felt the blood surge in his veins.

'I must be going,' he said abruptly. 'Good night, Sally, my dear. Don't stand around. It's cold.'

She stared after him as he crossed the road and disappeared along Manor Walk. A truck was coming in the opposite direction. As it negotiated the corner into Church Lane, a voice from beneath the tarpaulin shouted: 'Happy New Year, Sarah!'

She swung round, startled, and saw Werner in his usual place at the back of the lorry. She was so surprised, she was unable to answer for a moment. Then, as the vehicle slowly gathered momentum, easing its way down the narrow road, she ran after it, waving.

'Happy New Year, Werner! How did you know my name?'

But it was too late. The truck swerved on to the main road almost without stopping and vanished into the evening gloom.

CHAPTER FIVE

When he finally recollected where it was he had seen her before, Werner asked Mrs Younger her name.

'Please. That young girl in the kitchen, the day I cut my hand. What is she called?'

Ellen Younger smiled. 'Goodness, Werner! You have a good memory. That was Sarah Sherwood. Everyone calls her Sally.'

He had not cared for Sally: Sarah was a much more dignified name.

When he saw her outside the cottage, he had shouted on impulse. The return of her friendly greeting was not something he had planned. It was not until later that he connected her with the United States Major, walking along the road where the big house stood. But she had been wearing a coat and staring after the American in a way that suggested they had just said goodbye. They must have been out together, that child and a man nearly old enough to be her father! For some reason, Werner felt depressed and angry.

He knew from things the camp guards said how much the Yanks were resented by British servicemen. GI Joe had better pay and a smarter uniform than the Tommies. He also attracted the women in their droves with his lavish gifts and courteous manners. Sometimes Werner got the impression that Englishmen disliked their allies more than their enemies. For his own part, he had always preferred the Americans to the British, but now, suddenly, he resented the US Major, sleek, handsome and well turned out. Werner rubbed his chilblained, dirt-stained hands against the rough cloth of his trousers. For the first time in almost two years, his appearance bothered him.

He had been one of Rommel's crack Afrika Korps. Today, he was just another shabby prisoner, doing the most menial tasks of a farmhand. Many of his fellow prisoners were glad to be out of the war; happy to be in the fresh air by day, instead of cooped up, a prey to depression and boredom. The hard, manual labour helped them sleep soundly at nights, instead of worrying about what was happening at home. They had grown apathetic about a war they were now convinced they could not win.

Eleven years. Werner reflected bitterly; that was how long the Führer's thousand-year Reich had actually lasted. He turned up the collar of his battle-dress and huddled beneath the canvas as it began to rain. The truck had accomplished the descent from the village and he could see the sluggish gleam of water as the ground evened out; a little stream bordering the road, caught by the glancing beam of the lorry's dimmed headlights. The wind-swept fields gave place to the city outskirts, where Christmas decorations still adorned the exterior of one or two shops.

Some of the prisoners were asleep, worn out by the day's exertions. A few were laughing and talking as though they hadn't a care in the world. Werner hunched himself still further inside his jacket, fighting off the desperation which so often gripped him. Looking into the future was like looking down a long, dark tunnel with no light at the end. Germany and the Germans would be made to pay again, just as they had after the first world war. The last-ditch stand in the Ardennes was over. The Allies had broken through on Boxing Day and were moving north towards the Rhine. The feared and hated Russians were closing in from the east.

Tomorrow was New Year's Eve. At that moment, Werner, wet, cold and tired, standing on the brink of a new year which held no hope or promise, was filled with hatred; hatred for the arrogant, well-fed Americans, for the even more arrogant, empire-building British, and for the men who had betrayed Germany with the promise of a golden

58

millennium, only to bring the country crashing down in ruins after less than a dozen years.

The truck swung through the camp gates and came to a halt in front of the main reception block. The men piled out into the chill twilight, their breath hanging on the air in clouds of steam. The icy rain stung Werner's face as he was checked in by the young soldier on duty, then raced for the shelter of his hut. After the cold outside, even its Spartan comforts seemed a haven of luxury and warmth. He sat down on the edge of his bed and started taking off his boots.

'Happy Christmas, Werner!'

'Happy New Year, Sarah!'

Through the turmoil of hate and killing, two enemies had reached out to one another. He and that girl had built a fragile bridge between two human beings . . .

He shrugged off his jacket, dropping it on the floor, and cursed himself for a sentimental fool.

'What do you mean, you're going? How dare you just walk in here and announce that you're off, the day after tomorrow!'

Dorothy had had a trying day. One of the speakers for an afternoon broadcast had failed to show up at the recording studio, and Dorothy had been blamed. She was furious. She was absolutely certain that she had sent the doddering old fool a letter of confirmation, but, unfortunately, no copy could be found. Some idiot of a junior clerk must have misfiled it! She had very nearly handed in her notice, but reason and self-interest had prevailed. She had no wish to be directed into a munitions factory.

Dorothy had reached home to find Sally only just in before her, no meal on the table or fire in the grate.

'It's one of my games evenings,' Sally reminded her mother. 'You know I'm always late Tuesdays and Thursdays. Netball and hockey practice.'

It irritated Dorothy that she had forgotten. It suggested that she might have been wrong about that letter.

While Sally warmed up a casserole in the oven, Dorothy

put a light to the dining-room fire, pouring herself a large whisky as she did so. She rarely drank that early in the evening, but tonight she felt in need of a stimulant. There was an air of desolation in the empty dining room, as the watery light of the January afternoon slowly seeped away. She drew the curtains and watched the flames take hold of the pile of newspaper and sticks in the grate, licking the soot-blackened chimney. Firelight sparked on the golden liquid in her glass. She took another sip, but felt no better.

The meal, eaten in the kitchen, was equally depressing; tasteless and tepid because they had not waited for it to heat through properly. Sally washed up before going to her bedroom to do her homework. Dorothy wandered into the dining room, to sit hunched over the fire.

The house was so quiet now that the Christmas and New Year festivities were over. The twins had gone back to Portsmouth at the beginning of the previous week, and even the Americans, as though fearful of wearing out their welcome, had not called for the past few days. Dorothy had not seen Charles Graham for almost a fortnight, and several times had been on the verge of telephoning him at the Court. It was not pride which had held her back, but the anticipation that when he did come, he would have something important to say. He must be putting his domestic affairs in order before he spoke to her again, and at this distance, it was bound to take time.

When the doorbell rang, just after eight o'clock, she hardly dared hope that it was Charles. She opened the door, steeling herself against disappointment, half-expecting to see Philip, and her welcome was all the more effusive when she saw the Major's tall figure on the step.

'Charles! How lovely! I was just thinking about you. Come in, come in. I'm in the dining room. There isn't enough coal left to heat the lounge, and I can't stand the kitchen all night.' She led the way through the door on her right. 'Whisky and soda? I'm afraid I can't run to ice.'

'No, thank you.' Charles's tone was constrained and he did not sit down. He said quietly: 'The doctor pronounced me fit this morning. I'm returning to my outfit the day after tomorrow, so I've come to say goodbye. It'll be a full day tomorrow. I'm having my final check-up and I have to pack.'

Dorothy, caught off guard and completely unprepared for the note of finality in his voice, exploded with rage. She could hear the shrill beginnings of hysteria as she flung her questions at him.

He answered steadily, not quite meeting her eyes: 'You've always known I'd have to go away sometime.'

'But not like this.' She turned, suddenly cold, to warm her hands at the fire.

Deliberately, he chose to misunderstand her. 'Whenever it came, it was bound to be sudden. Once the doc made up his mind I was fit for duty, there couldn't be any hanging about.'

'That's not what I mean,' she protested. She looked appealingly at him, a challenge in those magnificent dark eyes.

Charles hesitated, tempted to turn tail and run. If he stayed, he could not continue playing games. There would have to be some plain speaking and he hated scenes. But he owed her something. He sighed and pulled up a chair to the fire.

'Dorothy, I'm sorry if you feel . . . if you feel that I've misled you in any way. But I thought I'd made it clear from the beginning that I have no intention of divorcing Faith.'

'But you don't love her. You told me so, yourself. You also told me the way she's treated you all these years.'

'It doesn't make any difference. She needs me and she's my wife.'

'Some wife!' Dorothy put her empty whisky glass down on the table with a snap. 'But if she means so much to you, what were you doing, going to bed with me?'

'I've been to bed with a lot of women in the two years I've been in England.' He was purposely being brutal. It seemed the best way. 'It's one of the soldier's few perquisites of war.'

61

Dorothy rounded on him. 'Liar! You're not the sort. And you certainly knew that I wasn't just an easy lay.' Her lip curled. 'I believe that's the correct American expression. I'm not a camp follower; a cheap little tart, out for a few laughs and what she can get. We had something special going for us.' Abruptly, she changed tack, falling on her knees beside the chair, clasping his hands in hers. 'Charles! Darling! I don't mind waiting. I know a divorce will take time; that you can't really do anything until after the war. I'll be happy to wait, I promise. There's been no one else for me since Bill died. Only you. You must realize that you mean everything to me now.'

'Dorothy, please!' Charles released his hands and stood up. 'You have your family. You have Philip. All right. I admit you're special. You're one of the most fascinating women I've ever met. But I'm not in love with you. Even if I were, I have my children to consider. And I might not even survive the rest of the war.'

'I know that. Dear God, do you think I don't know that! I've prayed every night for months that the war would be over before you were sent back. But it can't be long now, and if you take care of yourself, don't do anything rash . . .' Her voice tailed off, silenced by the shuttered, almost inimical look on his face. Slowly, she, too, rose to her feet. 'Something's happened,' she accused him. 'Something or someone has made you change your mind.'

'You're talking nonsense.' His tone was unnecessarily sharp. She caught the defensive note in it and smiled triumphantly.

'I'm right, aren't I? Don't bother to deny it. There's someone else, though God knows who you can have met in this village.'

'Who could compete with you, you mean?' He regretted the sneer as soon as it was uttered. 'Dorothy,' he protested wearily, 'there's no one else. If you're fair, you'll admit that I've never mentioned the words "divorce" and "marriage".'

'You certainly gave me to understand that your marriage was finished, the first time I went to bed with you. Are you telling me I imagined that?'

62

'Yes,' he replied wearily. 'Dorothy, my dear, wartime affairs are like holiday romances. They're ephemeral. Evanescent. Transient.'

'They don't have to be.' She blinked back tears of rage and frustration, struggling to keep her voice under control. She hadn't cried since Bill died. 'Dozens of GIs are marrying British girls every day.'

'I am married,' he answered flatly, conscious of holding his family obligations between them like a shield.

'That isn't the reason,' she repeated stubbornly, refusing to admit that she could fail with any man she had set her heart on. 'Someone has spoilt things for us.'

Before he could contradict her yet again, the door opened and Sally came in.

'Hello, Charles,' she said. 'I thought I heard your voice. I've been doing my homework or I'd have been down sooner.' She sat at the table and took some knitting out of a cretonne bag, oblivious to the charged atmosphere of the room.

'I've come to say goodbye.' Charles held out his hand. 'I'm quite fit now. I shall be leaving here the day after tomorrow.'

'Oh . . . I'm sorry.' She took his proffered hand in hers. 'It's been nice knowing you. Is Pete Kovaks going as well?'

'Not just yet, but soon.' His heart was hammering in his chest so that he could barely speak distinctly.

'Tell him to keep writing to Veronica, won't you? She's still "rather keen".'

They both started laughing and Dorothy found herself excluded from the joke. It was a new experience for her to be the outsider in any company, but particularly in that of men. And to be pushed out by her own daughter was more than she could bear, coming as it did on top of Charles's rejection.

She looked from one to the other and made a startling discovery. However innocently Sally might regard the Major, he was certainly in love with her. Dorothy had seen that expression in men's eyes too often to be mistaken. She had seen it in Bill's, saw it almost daily in Philip's, and

63

noted it frequently, and with amusement, in Bob Younger's.

For a moment, she was genuinely shocked. The protective, maternal instinct flared briefly, to be extinguished immediately by a surge of jealous anger.

Charles was laughing at Sally's knitting, teasing her gently.

'What the hell is it? I've never seen a piece of work with so many knots.'

'It's a pair of gloves, made with skeins of darning wool. Darning wool,' Sally explained patiently, 'is not on coupons. Proper knitting yarn is. Lots of women use darning wool for knitting small items, like hats and mittens. I suppose I really ought to splice the strands together, but it's so boring and I haven't the time.'

It was an innocuous conversation, but to Dorothy, every word seemed charged with hidden meaning.

'And how long has this been going on?' she demanded with perilous calm.

Two pairs of eyes looked inquiringly at her, but only Charles, after a moment's blind incomprehension, understood. He went cold with fear and embarrassment. But surely Dorothy, who had somehow guessed his secret, could not intend saying anything in front of Sally!

'It's time I was going.' He offered Dorothy his hand, but she ignored it. He turned to her daughter. 'Goodbye, Sally. If you're ever in the States when this lot's over, be sure to look me up. My family would be delighted to see you. I've written them so much about you.'

'I bet you have!' Dorothy's tone was vicious. 'You're in love with her, aren't you? A child young enough to be your daughter, and you're in love with her! It's disgusting!'

Sally blinked in bewilderment, then gave an uncertain giggle. 'It's not true, Charles, is it? Tell her it's not true.'

'Don't play the innocent with me, miss!' Dorothy was too angry to consider her words. 'Don't tell me you don't know he'd like to sleep with you! It's written all over his face. Well, I'll tell you something, just in case you have any ideas. He's already been to bed with me.'

64

Before he knew what he was doing, Charles had slapped her face, a stinging blow which made her stumble back against the mantelpiece. Sally burst into tears and ran out of the room.

'You bitch!' he shouted. 'Jesus! I'd like to give you a thrashing. Did you have to destroy your daughter's illusions about you in that spiteful fashion? She thought you were faithful to her father's memory. Didn't you realize that? Or don't you care?'

'Don't you dare lecture me!' Dorothy put up a hand to her reddened cheek. 'Sniffing around young girls still in gymslips! God! What a mistake I made about you. Get out of my house. Go on! Go!' She shrieked the last word at him.

For a moment, he knew what it was to want to murder someone; then he swung on his heel and moved towards the door. His anger suddenly drained out of him. He felt sorry for Dorothy. She was a beautiful woman, used to, and needing, the admiration of men. Now she was past forty and lived in fear of losing out to a younger woman. It was doubly wounding to suspect that that woman was her daughter, who was just sixteen.

He turned back. 'Dorothy,' he urged, 'you're making a mistake. OK I'll admit to you what I've so far been afraid to admit even to myself. I am in love with Sally. The realization appals me just as much as it does you and, quite obviously, her. But that has nothing whatever to do with us. There never was any us. What I told you earlier was the truth.'

'I don't believe you.' Her voice was steadier, but she was still shaking with fright and temper. No man had ever lifted a finger to her in her life before, and she was discovering that physical violence was degrading, not the rather thrilling experience she had half-imagined it to be. 'I don't want to see you again, ever. If you don't leave at once, I'll call the police.'

'Don't worry,' he assured her, 'I'm going. I'm genuinely sorry that our friendship has ended this way.' He picked up his hat and gloves and went out of the room.

Sally was just descending the stairs. She had a coat on, as though going out, but when she saw Charles, she stopped, her eyes wide with alarm. She began to retreat upstairs.

'Sally!' He walked forward, reaching out a hand for the banister rail. 'I must speak to you. Please.'

She threw him a queer, scared glance and ran. A moment later, he heard her bedroom door slam shut.

The Major hesitated, one foot on the bottom stair, then realized that he dared not go after her. He swore softly, staring absently at a picture on the wall; a faded print of *Winter 1595*, by van Valkenborch. A fishmonger was chopping fish for two ladies in conical hats, who carried a basket and three large strings of onions. Beyond the stall, everything was covered in snow.

He let himself out into the freezing dark. The garden path was slippery, the top of the gate already rimed with frost. A stray shaft of light from a badly blacked out window in the neighbouring cottage showed a glittering world. It was going to be a bitter night.

Sally lay on her bed, shivering, still wrapped in her coat. She had been running to Philip, but now she had changed her mind. She couldn't face anyone. Her mother's revelation had shocked her; made her feel unclean.

In spite of doing biology at school, there was a lot about sex which remained a mystery to her. She was aware that many of her classmates were far more knowledgeable than she was, and that the war had been made an excuse for a flood of promiscuity which would never have been tolerated in peacetime. All sorts of taboos and shibboleths were being ignored. Throughout it all, however, Sally had retained the innocence of childhood. It had been like watching a film in the warmth and cosiness of a cinema: while she understood what was going on, it was merely a flickering shadow play on the screen.

Tonight had changed all that. The ugly little scene which had taken place downstairs had forced her to grow up in a hurry. Her mother had been Charles Graham's mistress,

66

and he wanted to go to bed with Sally herself. Without knowing how or why, Sally had accepted the truth of her mother's statements when she saw the Major standing at the bottom of the stairs. Her instinct and intuition, both working overtime, had recognized the look in his eyes.

Sally knew that most girls of her age would have been flattered and excited at the idea of having an older man in love with them, particularly one as handsome and distinguished as Charles Graham. She was frightened by the prospect. She had never had so much as a boyfriend, except one summer when, for a few short weeks, she had gone out with Terry Ibbs. Dorothy had soon put a stop to that, once she was aware of what was happening, and the twins had lectured their baby sister on the dangerous lack of morals in randy young farmhands.

Loosening her coat, Sally cautiously felt her breasts through the woollen material of her dress. Even bound in by one of Jennifer's old brassières, they seemed quite big. But the thought made her shy and she quickly buttoned up her coat again. She tried not to think of her mother and Charles Graham together in the bed which Dorothy had shared with Bill, but the image persisted. All her initial dislike of the Major came flooding back. She had been right to mistrust him.

There was a tap on the door and, without waiting for an invitation, Dorothy came in, switching on the bedroom light. Her eyes were swollen as if she had been crying, and she was huddled in an old shapeless cardigan of Bill's. Sally had never seen her like that before, her make-up smudged, her hair awry. It made her mother more human somehow, and Sally felt she would never be in awe of her again. They had reached a crisis in their relationship. The steps they had taken that night could not be retraced.

'Don't lie here in the cold and the dark,' Dorothy pleaded. 'Come downstairs where it's warm. Have some supper. I'll open a tin of Spam, and there's that homemade tomato pickle Ellen Younger gave me at Christmas.'

Sally nodded. She slid from the bed and took off her

67

coat, following her mother down to the kitchen.

'We'll eat here,' Dorothy said. 'The fire in the dining room's almost out.'

They ate in silence, each busy with her own thoughts and not yet ready to be friends. Later, however, when they were drinking hot milk before going to bed, conversation began drifting back to normal. Dorothy told Sally about the row in the office that day, making it sound much more amusing than it had actually been. Sally responded with small talk about school and the preparations for her School Certificate examination at the end of the summer term.

There was no reference, not even an oblique one, to the scene in the dining room. They were simply going to pretend that nothing had happened, always her mother's solution when anything unpleasant occurred. It papered over the cracks and maintained Dorothy's bright image of herself which introspection and discussion might tarnish. In the past, it had partially succeeded in preserving the illusion for Sally, but not this time. Tonight was different. Tonight, she had begun the process of growing up. She would never feel the same about anything ever again.

She said quietly: 'I'm tired. I'm going to bed. I'll see you in the morning.'

She did not give her mother the perfunctory, meaningless, goodnight kiss which had been mandatory since childhood; part of Dorothy's image-building as an adored and doted-upon mother. Instead, she left the kitchen without another word, leaving Dorothy alone, still sipping her milk.

PART TWO

Winter 1947 – 1948

Here shall he see
No enemy
But winter and rough weather

CHAPTER SIX

The Reverend Nicholas Horobin pronounced the final benediction; then, as the congregation rose from its knees, he held up his hand.

'One moment, please, before you go. There is a special announcement that I should like to make.'

'What now?' Dorothy whispered to Jennifer, who was sitting next to her. 'Not another appeal for the organ fund! It sounds perfectly all right to me.' She caught Bob Younger's eye, on the other side of the aisle, and made a moue of exasperation, which slid into a smile as he grinned admiringly.

On this grey November morning, there was no doubt that she brightened up the church. Clothes were still on coupons, just as food, coal and petrol continued to be rationed after two and a half years of uneasy peace. But in spite of that fact, the more fashion conscious British women had adopted Christian Dior's New Look with a hunger born of wartime austerity. They bought the almost ankle-length, full-skirted dresses, belling out from a nipped-in waist, with an astonishing enthusiasm. They sported hats, gloves and high-heeled shoes. They felt feminine for the first time in years.

Dorothy, this morning, was wearing a vivid scarlet coat in the New Look style, the collar and peplum trimmed with beaver lamb fur. A small scarlet hat, swathed in veiling, was perched at a rakish angle on her dark hair. Black shoes, gloves and handbag completed an outfit designed to catch the eye; and she knew by the number of male heads which kept turning in her direction that it had amply succeeded.

By contrast, the three girls, although smartly and neatly

dressed, looked dowdy, as did nearly every other woman in church. Philip had seen how Sir Gilbert and Lady Quintrell, home again after their internment in France and installed once more at Barton Court, had stared down their noses, and the flicker of resignation which had touched Ellen Younger's careworn face. All the same, there was no denying that Dorothy looked magnificent; a flame burning brightly and warming the drabness of the day.

One person who seemed unimpressed by Dorothy, Philip noted, was the young man Jennifer had in tow; Anthony Latham, one of the directors of the Bristol wine importing firm where she had worked ever since she was demobbed from the Wrens. Dorothy had high hopes that Anthony Latham and Jennifer would make a match of it, and was encouraging such an eligible suitor with all the zeal of a Victorian Mama. The young man would evidently be Philip's fellow guest at lunch. Veronica was still corresponding with Pete Kovaks, who had survived the war and was now helping to run his father's chain of drug stores in the States. There was some talk of his coming on a visit after Christmas.

And then there was Philip's favourite, Sally, whose wish to go to art school had been overborne by Dorothy, and who was at present a clerical officer with the Ministry of Labour and National Service. Sometimes, when he was angry with Dorothy, Philip felt he would never forgive her for that. It was a comfort to know that he, at least, had given Sally one brief moment of fame. No one regretted more than he did that nothing had come of it . . .

The Reverend Nicholas Horobin cleared his throat. 'As most of you will already be aware,' he said, 'an inter-denominational scheme was launched some months ago by the various churches to help the many hundreds of prisoners-of-war still in this country.' He cleared his throat a second time, conscious that the parents of Coldharbour's six war dead were among the congregation, and that he might be treading on delicate ground. Sir Gilbert and Lady Quintrell, too, had suffered at the hands of the Germans. 'As you know, it has not yet been possible to repatriate these men in any numbers, although the work is proceeding slowly. In the meantime, those that remain have been allowed outside the camps at weekends, but there is not very much for them to do. I am sure, whenever you have visited Bristol on a Saturday, you have seen them wandering aimlessly around the museum and art gallery or staring into shop windows.' The vicar's grip tightened on the pulpit rail as he encountered one or two hostile stares, but he continued bravely: 'During the week, they are kept busy. If you recall, we used to have three working in this village, at Barton Farm, before Alec and Ivor Ibbs returned home safely, for which we all thank God.'

'I don't think either of them ever went further than Aldershot,' Dorothy hissed in Jennifer's ear, and Jennifer suppressed a giggle. 'I wish he'd get to the point. My feet are freezing.'

The Reverend Horobin took a deep breath. 'So it was decided by the churches that it would be a humane and Christian act if we were to invite some of these unfortunate fellows into our homes at weekends. Now, I know that some of you will have strong feelings on the subject, but let us remember that we are all human beings and equally beloved of God. If you feel that you can help, please let me know as you leave the church, or telephone me later, at the vicarage. I will pass your name and address on to the appropriate authorities, and in due course you will be allocated your weekend guests. Thank you. One other thing.' Dorothy groaned audibly. 'Anyone who does not possess a radio and who wishes to hear the broadcast on Thursday of the wedding of Her Royal Highness, the Princess Elizabeth to Lieutenant Philip Mountbatten, RN, is welcome at the vicarage. Mrs Horobin and I will be delighted to see you. There will, of course, be refreshments.' And with a sigh of relief at having been able to finish on a decidedly more acceptable note, the vicar descended the pulpit stairs and made his way to the west door of the church.

'At last,' breathed Dorothy, getting to her feet. 'Philip, darling, I didn't see you behind me. Of course you're coming to lunch?'

'Well, what do you think, girls?' Dorothy asked suddenly, when they had all finished their meal and were drinking coffee. 'Shall we do it?'

'Do what?' Veronica's tone was curt. She hated the Sundays when Anthony Latham came to lunch. Seeing him and Jennifer smiling intimately at one another and holding hands made her miserable. Pete was so far away, and she wasn't even sure of his feelings for her any more. It was over two years since they had last been together; a brief, ten-day furlough, spent in Portsmouth, just before she had been demobbed. Pete had managed to cadge a lift on a US transport 'plane flying to England, since when she had been forced to make do with letters. She was quite sure that there was no one else as far as she was concerned. She wished she could be as sure of Pete. 'Do what?' she repeated irritably when her mother did not reply immediately.

Dorothy replaced her coffee cup in its saucer. 'Have a couple of Germans to tea on a Saturday. Or a Sunday. Or even both. What do you think?'

'Does it matter what our opinions are,' Sally asked quietly, 'when you have already made up your mind?'

'Who says I've made up my mind?' Dorothy leaned back in her chair, the wheel-backed carver which Bill had always used. She took a cigarette from the packet of Player's Navy Cut in her handbag and fitted it into her amber holder. 'Could I have a light please, Anthony? Thank you.' And she smiled into his eyes across the flame.

If Jennifer noticed, she was undisturbed. Anthony Latham, ex-Battle of Britain fighter pilot, was one of those rare men who were impervious to her mother's charms. He lit the cigarette politely and at once turned back to Jennifer.

A decidedly plain young man, Dorothy thought contemptuously, with that ginger hair and scrubby little moustache.

He might even run to fat when he was older. But the Lathams had plenty of money. Jennifer was showing her good sense there.

'Haven't you?' Sally challenged.

'Darling, don't sound so hostile all the time.' Dorothy drew on her cigarette and the tip winked and glowed. 'No, I haven't made up my mind, but I think it might be rather fun.' Her eyes flicked from Sally to her cousin. 'Of course, I can see why you and Uncle Philip might not agree.'

Philip had long since given up trying to persuade Dorothy to drop the word 'uncle'. It was a reminder to him that he was *her* admirer in a world of grown-up daughters, who were competing too successfully for attention.

Anthony Latham finished lighting cigarettes for himself and Jennifer, and turned to Philip.

'I've been meaning to tell you, sir, that I recently read your book on the Nuremberg trials. I thought it quite brilliant.'

Philip's pale, thin face showed a little colour. 'Thank you,' he said. 'I hope you found the line drawings equally brilliant.'

'The line drawings? I don't think I noticed them. The photographs were excellent, though.'

'Oh, really Tony!' Jennifer sounded unexpectedly cross. 'Didn't you read the credits, or whatever they're called, at the beginning of the book? Sally did the drawings. Philip took her with him to Germany when he covered the trials.'

'Oh God! No, I didn't notice. Sorry, Sally.' Anthony's ugly face creased into an apologetic grin.

'Don't worry about it,' she laughed. 'No one else noticed them, either. It didn't lead to fame and fortune.'

'I always said it was a stupid idea,' Dorothy remarked, expertly blowing a smoke ring. 'She'd only just left school, and I let Philip talk me into it, against my better judgement. He said it would be an experience for her and might lead to other commissions. Of course it didn't. I could have told him that, if only he'd listened. Drawing for your own amusement's one thing. Doing it professionally is quite another.'

'She should have gone to art school. It's a waste of talent,' Philip said coldly.

Dorothy stubbed out her cigarette. 'Oh, don't start that again! Doesn't anyone ever think of me? It was bad enough being on my own for all those weeks while she was in Germany with you. I couldn't possibly have been left alone for a couple of years.'

'It seems we don't count,' Veronica remarked, *sotto voce*, to her twin.

'I didn't know how long it would be before you two were home again,' Dorothy protested. 'Besides, I couldn't afford it, so there's no more to be said.'

'You know very well – ' her cousin began angrily, but Sally caught hold of his hand.

'Leave it, Uncle Philip, please! It doesn't matter now.'

'What did you make of Göring and Co.?' Anthony Latham asked her. He had a habit of treating social unpleasantness as though it didn't exist, concentrating single-mindedly on anything he wanted to know.

Sally shivered and glanced at Philip. 'I think the book said everything there was to say about them much better than I could express it.'

'Try,' Anthony persisted. 'Give me your opinion. That's what I want to find out.'

Sally shrugged helplessly. 'Horror at what had been done, I suppose. Especially . . .' She paused, considering her words. Philip propped his chin on his hand, listening attentively. Dorothy shifted restlessly in her chair. 'Especially,' Sally went on, 'because they looked such ordinary men. Sometimes . . . Sometimes, I actually felt sorry for them. And sometimes, I found myself laughing at something Göring had said. He could be very amusing. Really witty. I even found myself, on occasions, wanting to like him. And all the time I was listening to the awful details of what had been done to the Jews. Several times, I had to go to the cloakroom and be physically sick. It was frightening.'

'I haven't patience with all this fuss about a few Jews!' Dorothy exclaimed in annoyance. 'They weren't exactly popular here, at the beginning of the war. There were all sorts of stories about them racketeering and profiteering.

They probably were, too. No smoke without fire.'

'I don't remember that,' Sally objected.

Philip drained his cup. 'You were too young to take any notice. But your mother's right. In the end, the Chief Rabbi appealed to Churchill to scotch the rumours, which he did. After that, things simmered down and everyone pulled together. By the time of the blitz, no one cared if you were Christian, Jew or Hottentot.' He passed his cup to Dorothy for more coffee. 'But Sally's not talking about one or two slanderous remarks made by a few irresponsible journalists. She's talking about the systematic extermination of millions of men, women and children in the concentration camps.'

Dorothy handed back his refilled cup. 'I don't believe it. It's just propaganda.'

Anthony Latham lit a fresh cigarette. 'I'd believe it, if I were you, Mrs Sherwood. A friend of mine was one of the first people into Belsen. A big, strong chap without an ounce of imagination. He still suffers from nightmares.'

Dorothy gave a forced laugh. She hated being worsted in an argument.

'I don't think we can hold every German responsible for Hitler's atrocities, do you? Sally! You used to dislike people saying that the only good German was a dead one.'

'I suppose I still do.'

'Well then – !'

'I just feel a little more anti-German than I used to.'

Happy Christmas, Werner!

Happy New Year, Sarah!

She hadn't thought about the young German for years. After Nuremberg, she had resolutely put him out of her mind, a task made easier by the return to Barton Farm of the two elder Ibbs boys, who, with the land girls, made it unnecessary for the Youngers to use prisoner-of-war labour. Werner and his two companions had been redeployed elsewhere. Sally had torn up all the portraits she had drawn of him.

Dorothy pushed back her chair. 'Shall we go into the other room? Jennifer and Anthony have volunteered to wash

77

up.' She gave her throaty chuckle. 'Don't be too long about it, darlings.' She stood up, smoothing down the scarlet dress which matched her coat. 'You three carry on. Philip, switch on the wireless. There may be a repeat of *Twenty Questions*. I shan't be long. I'm just going to 'phone Nick Horobin at the vicarage.'

As soon as he saw the name Sherwood on the list, Werner knew that he would finally let Erich Rossman persuade him to change his mind.

Until now, he had steadfastly resisted all temptation to visit the British in their homes.

'I don't know what you've got against it,' Erich would complain bitterly, as they took shelter from the cold in shop doorways or the under-heated museum. The previous winter had been the worst the country had known for fifty-three years. Snowdrifts had blocked roads and pavements, then frozen solid in the icy winds. The terrible weather had persisted well into March and there had been a fuel crisis of epic proportions. At weekends, the Germans had voluntarily remained in their huts, but with the shortage of coal and coke, heating for prisoner-of-war camps had been low on the list of priorities. Erich saw no reason to suffer again this winter, now that the opportunity had been offered to avoid it. 'Think of it,' he would urge, 'a real house, a fire, home comforts, even if it's only for a few hours a week. Come on, Werner, what do you say? Let's put our names down.'

'You put yours down if you want to. I'm not going.'

'Why not? The British aren't so bad, when you get to know them.'

'Tell that to Heinz Drewer. He comes from Dresden. His entire family was wiped out. You haven't lost anyone. I have.'

'You don't know that.'

'All these years and not a word? Of course I do.'

But for some reason, when the Camp Commandant had announced that morning that he had a further list of families willing to entertain German prisoners, Werner had allowed Erich to drag him along to see the officer on duty. And when, reading the list upside down from the other side of the desk, he deciphered the name Sherwood and the address, Grace Cottage, Coldharbour, he knew that he was going to give in. He leaned over and indicated the appropriate line.

'I am acquainted with that lady and her daughter, Corporal. I was on the farm at Coldharbour since two years ago. I should like very much to be recommended for that place. If I can.'

'Don't see why not,' the Corporal answered good-naturedly. 'The lady'll take two.'

'Rossman will come with me.' He turned to Erich and rapidly translated what was going on. After four years, the extent of Erich's English vocabulary was: 'Hallo, darling!' and 'Fuck me!' Werner made a mental note to warn his friend against the use of either phrase in mixed company.

Erich was delighted, if somewhat bewildered, by Werner's sudden capitulation.

'I knew you'd see sense eventually. When do we go? This weekend?'

'They'll let us know. And you've got to behave yourself,' Werner added grimly. 'This is a family of women. A mother and three daughters. I think it must be the youngest one I knew.' Although 'knew' was hardly the word. A smile, a wave, a greeting, that was all it had amounted to in the end. 'No politics, no flirting.'

'I'm a happily married man,' Erich protested with an air of injured innocence. Werner remained unconvinced.

'It's years since either of us was near a woman. Just remember that it might be difficult at first.'

Erich nodded. 'Not to get a hard on, you mean.'

Werner gave up. Erich had a one-track mind. 'No, I didn't you randy bastard! I just meant it might be difficult to behave in a civilized fashion after all this time. Come on! There's the whistle for the midday meal. Let's go and eat.'

'So while I was in New York, I thought I'd call.' Pete Kovaks accepted the Scotch-on-the-rocks which Charles Graham handed him and sank into a chair. He glanced at the blue and white decor of the room. 'Nice place you've got here.'

'Faith's doing. She's just had the whole apartment redecorated.' Charles poured another whisky and sat down in the armchair facing Pete's. 'It's good to see you again. It's been too long.'

'Sure has. I wasn't certain, at first, if you'd gotten through the war in one piece. No more trouble with the legs?'

'No. And you?'

Pete swallowed some of his drink. 'Still get a pain in my guts now and then. I'm not supposed to have this stuff, but what the heck! Can't go through life like an invalid, not at my age. Specially not when I'm thinking of getting married.'

Charles raised his eyebrows. 'Congratulations. When is it to be?'

'I haven't asked her yet.' Pete downed the rest of his whisky, but reluctantly refused the offer of a second. 'Better not tempt Providence. As a matter of fact, you know the lady. Veronica Sherwood. I'm going over to England immediately after Christmas.'

Charles's hand tightened around his glass. 'You still keep in touch, then?'

'Yeah. Ronnie and I have written to each other ever since I left Barton Court. Any messages for . . . for anyone, when I go?'

'My regards. Remember me to Dorothy and . . . Sally.'

'Hey, she must be grown-up by now. Eighteen, nearly nineteen, I guess. I shall be taking some things with me. Stuff's still pretty tightly rationed over there.'

'Yes.' Charles put down his empty glass. 'I think that's the one thing I couldn't get over for a long time after I came home; the abundance of goods in the shops. It didn't seem right, somehow.'

'I know. I felt the same.' There was a pause in the conversation. To cover it, Pete asked: 'Not gone into politics yet, then?'

'Nope.' Charles got up and poured himself another drink. He looked inquiringly at Pete. 'Sure you won't have one?

No?' He returned to his seat. 'I think my father was hoping I'd have changed my mind, but publishing seemed safer.'

The door opened and a slight, fair-haired woman came into the room. She was dressed to go out for the evening in a full-skirted, strapless gown of rustling black taffeta, encrusted with bugle-bead embroidery. Pete Kovaks knew nothing about fashion, but even he could see that the frock was expensive. The woman hesitated in the doorway.

'You didn't tell me you had a visitor, Charles. I'm sorry. I'll come back later.'

'No, don't go.' The two men got to their feet. 'Pete, this is my wife, Faith. Darling, this is Pete Kovaks. We were together in the convalescent home in England. You may remember me telling you about him.'

'Oh, yes.' Faith Graham came forward and shook Pete's hand. Hers, he noticed, was sweating slightly, as though she were nervous or excited. A nice enough looking woman if you liked that fluffy kind of prettiness, but there was something unbalanced about her. Perhaps it was the expression of the pale-blue eyes which fluttered restlessly from one object to another, but never looked directly at the person she was addressing.

'Nice meeting you, Mrs Graham. Charles told me all about you, as well.'

She gave a sudden high-pitched neigh of laughter. 'And what exactly did he tell you, Mr Kovaks? That I'm neurotic? Don't bother to deny it. I'm sure he told you that I've tried to commit suicide twice. You ought to have changed by now, Charles. We're going to a Thanksgiving Day dinner, Mr Kovaks, with some friends.'

'Hey, Major, why didn't you say?' Pete began pulling on his overcoat. 'You should have told me it was inconvenient.'

'That's all right,' Charles said quietly. 'We've plenty of time. There's no need for you to rush away.'

'No, indeed. They're only friends of *mine*. It won't matter if we're late.' Faith Graham sat down and took a cigarette from a silver box on the table beside her. She lit it with a shaking hand.

81

Charles flushed angrily, but said nothing. He glanced apologetically at his guest.

'I have an engagement, myself, this evening, with a business client.' Pete smiled reassuringly. 'That's why I'm in New York instead of with my parents, in Washington, sharing their Thanksgiving dinner.' He wrote hurriedly on the back of an envelope which he found in his pocket. 'Here's my home address, Major. Next time you're in Washington, I'll expect you to look me up.'

'I shan't be with him. He never takes me to Washington,' Faith said. 'His parents don't like me. Nobody likes me.' And she began to cry.

Charles went over to her and gently patted her shoulder. 'Stop it, Faith,' he ordered quietly. 'You'll ruin your make-up. Your mascara's running. Go and repair your face, there's a good girl. I'll be along to change in a minute. Take one of your pills.'

'I've taken two already,' she answered, clinging to his hand. She stood up abruptly. 'I'll go and say goodnight to Kay and Teddy.' She moved to the door, then recollected Pete and glanced over her shoulder. 'Goodnight, Mr . . . Mr . . .'

'Kovaks. Goodnight, Mrs Graham.'

'I'm sorry about that,' Charles said stiffly, when the door had closed behind her.

'Hell! Think nothing of it,' Pete told him. 'My fault for calling unannounced. I should have given you warning. So long, Major. It's been real nice seeing you again.'

'Goodbye,' Charles replied. 'And I'm not "Major" any more, "Captain" Kovaks.'

Pete laughed, but once inside the elevator he let out his breath on a sigh of relief. It was small wonder that Charles Graham had decided that publishing was safer than politics with a wife like that. Poor devil! He should have done what Dorothy Sherwood wanted; divorced that embarrassing wife of his and married her instead.

CHAPTER SEVEN

'I can't see them yet,' Veronica said, peering through the living room window. 'Perhaps one of us ought to have met the 'bus.'

'The young man I spoke to at the camp assured me that there was absolutely no need,' Dorothy answered. 'He said one of them used to work at Barton Farm and knew his way about.'

Sally, who was busy reskeining the unpicked wool of an old jumper, glanced round sharply.

'One of the Germans used to work at Barton Farm? What's his name?'

It was Sunday, the thirtieth of November, and, in the morning, they had been to church to celebrate the patronal festival of St Andrew. For once, Philip had not been asked back to lunch at Grace Cottage.

'We want to get cleared away in a hurry today,' Dorothy had told him, 'and you know how you hate rushed meals.'

'Something happening?' he inquired, but not caring very much. His chest felt tight and he had begun to spit phlegm, both symptoms of an approaching bronchial attack. He would be better off tucked up warmly in bed.

'We're having our two Germans for the first time today. I hope to God they've picked me someone interesting.' And Dorothy had moved away, not even pausing to exchange a word with Bob Younger.

She said now, searching for a piece of paper in her handbag: 'One's called . . . let me see . . . what have I done with it? Ah, here it is! One's called Erich Rossman. He can't speak much English apparently. But the other one can. Quite well, I believe. His name is Werner Neumann.'

'You pronounce the "w" like a "v", Mother,' Jennifer corrected her, looking up from the jigsaw puzzle she was doing. 'Verner Neumann.'

Happy Christmas, Werner!

Sally lowered her arms, swathed in the wavy, unravelled, yellow wool and stared unseeingly in front of her. After all this time, she would be meeting him again. How would she feel about it?

It occurred to her that apart from their first encounter at the farm, they had never been in the same room together; never spoken except at a distance; never held any sort of conversation. And yet his face was as clear in her mind as when she had first drawn it, over three years ago. She had not known his second name until now. It hadn't seemed important. In some subtle way it changed him; gave him an identity. He had ceased simply to be Werner.

Other things had changed, too. She had been to Germany. She had seen those men in the dock, watched them, drawn them, been shocked and appalled by the revelations she had heard. The full horror of Nazi Germany had burst over her unsuspecting head. Then Philip had obtained passes for them to visit Dresden, and she had been horrified all over again; but this time by the ferocity of an Allied air attack which had razed a city to the ground. Three times as many people in Dresden alone had been killed as had died in the entire British blitz.

That had been 1945, the same year that the atomic bomb had been dropped on Hiroshima and Nagasaki, with the subsequent terrifying loss of life and injury. Sally had felt as emotionally muddled then as she did now, but it was something she had to resolve alone. She had never been able to discuss her innermost feelings. She found it difficult to talk about them even to Philip, the one person who really understood.

'They're coming,' Veronica called out. 'They're walking up the road now.'

'What are they like?' Dorothy asked, consulting her

handbag mirror to make sure that she looked her best.

'Mmm . . . Difficult to say. Wait a minute, I can see them better now. One's rather stocky, but quite nice looking. The other's tall and handsome in a Teutonic kind of way. Makes you think of Siegfried and Rhine Maidens and all that jazz.'

Veronica moved away from the window as she spoke, and, a few moments later, the front doorbell rang. Dorothy got up and went gracefully out of the room. The twins exchanged significant glances.

Then he was there, cap twisting nervously between work-roughened hands, the same inimical look on his face that Sally had seen so often in the past. By contrast, Werner's friend was grinning happily, introducing himself by the simple expedient of repeating over and over again: 'Erich Rossman. I am Erich Rossman. I am pleased to meet you.' He had evidently learned the words by rote, and gave equal emphasis to each one. Werner prompted him in German and Erich at once shook their hands, a proceeding which seemed to afford him great amusement.

'Eng-lish cus-tom,' he said, pumping Sally's arm up and down.

He was indeed tall and handsome, as Veronica had described him, but Sally only had eyes for Werner. Yet, perversely, as soon as he took her hand in his, she looked away, avoiding his gaze.

As soon as the women had resumed their seats, the two men also sat down. There was an awkward silence. Dorothy, as usual, had not looked beyond the initial stages of the project. It had not occurred to her to wonder how she was going to entertain the Germans.

'You found us all right, then,' she said, offering them each a cigarette, which they accepted with alacrity. 'Which one of you used to work at Barton Farm?'

'I did,' Werner answered, inhaling too deeply in his nervousness and coughing.

'Ah . . . You're the one who speaks English.'

'That is right.'

There was another pause, while Dorothy looked helplessly

at Sally and the twins for inspiration. They had rarely seen their mother at such a loss.

Sally turned to Werner and asked: 'Your hand . . . it healed up all right?' She added for the benefit of her bemused family: 'Werner and I met once, years ago, when I went to the farm for some eggs. Mrs Younger was bandaging his hand. He'd cut it on a spade.'

'Really?' Dorothy's interest was exaggerated. 'You never told me about it, darling. What a sly girl she is, Herr Neumann.'

'There was nothing to tell. Please call me Werner.'

Dorothy gave him a dazzling smile. 'I daresay I ought to call you by your military rank, but I'm afraid I don't know it. I probably couldn't pronounce it if I did.'

'There is no need,' Werner answered flatly. 'The war is over. We are all civilians now.' He turned to Sally and held out his left hand. The faintest pucker of a scar was visible across the palm. 'Yes, thank you. As you can see, it healed.'

For some absurd reason, she wanted to touch it, to trace its length with her finger. She went on skeining wool.

'You do speak English well,' Dorothy complimented him.

'My mother was a teacher of English,' he replied.

'Was?'

'I do not know what has happened to her. Or to my sister. Our house in Hamburg was bombed. I do not know if they were in it at the time.'

'Can't the Red Cross help?' Jennifer asked. It was the first time she had spoken since the Germans' arrival. She was not sure that she approved of the scheme. Anthony most certainly did not and had expressed his disapproval. The war was too fresh in his memory and he had lost too many friends. He felt it was too soon to try to heal the wounds.

'No,' Werner said, while Erich lay back in his chair, feet stretched towards the fire, wishing that someone would offer him another cigarette. 'Hamburg has been reduced to rubble. The city is in chaos. There are thousands of refugees now, in Germany, whose papers have been destroyed.'

Dorothy was annoyed by his hostile manner. How dare

he make her feel as though she, personally, were to blame?

'It wouldn't have happened,' she snapped, 'if you Germans hadn't started it. My husband, I should like you to know, was killed at Dunkirk. And Sally could tell you a thing or two, as well. She was at the Nuremberg trials.'

Erich had stopped smiling and was shuffling his feet. He sensed the charged atmosphere and had recognized the names Hamburg, Nuremberg and Dunkirk. He said sharply to Werner in German: 'Don't stir things up, or we shan't be asked again.'

Werner ignored him. 'You've been to Germany?' he asked Sally eagerly, and she nodded. 'What were the conditions there? Are they really so bad?'

Again she avoided his eyes. She could guess the terrible frustration prisoners-of-war must be feeling, not certain how much of what they heard was true, and desperate to get home. She could lie to him, she supposed, but that would be even more unkind.

'Conditions are . . . very bad,' she admitted. 'I didn't visit Hamburg, but I did see Dresden. It was . . . unbelievable. Devastated. All the same . . .' She broke off and raised her eyes to his.

'You think we deserve it.'

'Yes. You did elect Hitler to power.'

At the mention of Hitler, Erich shot upright in his chair, aware that the conversation must be moving on to very dangerous ground.

'Fuck me!' he exclaimed, repeating words which he had heard the camp guards use whenever they seemed to disapprove of something.

There was a moment's astounded silence, while Werner held his breath; then the four women burst into uncontrollable laughter.

'Oh dear, oh dear,' Dorothy said, dabbing her eyes with her handkerchief. 'We really shall have to do something about improving your friend's English, Werner. Now, how about a game of cards?'

* * *

By Christmas, the two Germans had learned how to play both rummy and whist, and had initiated Dorothy, Sally and Veronica into the simple pleasures of a card game called Müller. They had been introduced to mint sauce as an accompaniment to lamb, and Erich, whose English vocabulary was slowly expanding, had written down the recipe for his wife. He had also managed to squeeze Dorothy's hand on several occasions, and once, under the table, had contrived to smooth her thigh. He thought her a very beautiful woman, even though, in age, she could be his mother, and lusted after her in his heart. He had recognized at once that she automatically responded to men, but was not fool enough to believe that their little affair could proceed beyond the mildest of flirtations.

Werner and Erich were at the cottage most weekends. At first, they came Saturdays, to tea and supper; then it was Sundays as well. Philip discovered that if he wished to continue spending occasional Sunday afternoons with Dorothy, he must be prepared to tolerate the presence of 'my boys' as she called them, in her most proprietorial tone of voice. She was, like Mr Toad, in the grip of another enthusiasm.

Philip's feelings towards his fellow guests were mixed. He wanted to dislike them, to lay the blame for the horrors of Hitler's Third Reich at their doors, but he couldn't. They were two, nice, ordinary lads with whom it was impossible to associate the appalling cruelty of the concentration camps, the evil which had wiped out the villages of Lidice and Oradour-sur-Glâne, and the extermination of Russian peasants as if they were so much vermin.

Werner was no happier and no less confused. It had only been his sudden and inexplicable desire to see Sally again that had forced him into a situation which he had always been determined to avoid. When the churches had first proposed their scheme of reconciliation, Werner had sworn never to visit an English home. He kept remembering that awful May night, nearly three years earlier, when he and the other prisoners in the camp had listened in total silence to the ringing of church bells, the hooting of ships' sirens on the river Avon, the distant shouting and singing, and known that the fighting was finally over. Germany had surrendered. The war was lost.

He had gone to Grace Cottage that first Sunday fully expecting to have his prejudices about the English confirmed. With the exception of Sally, he had expected to meet the sort of arrogant, overbearing females who had helped their menfolk conquer a third of the earth's surface and build it into the greatest empire the world had ever seen. Instead, he had found four ordinary, pleasant women struggling to cope with life in the aftermath of a devastating war; preoccupied with the same feminine pursuits and problems as his mother and sister had been. Even the men – the cousin, Philip, who was so patently in love with Mrs Sherwood, and Jennifer's young man, Anthony – in both of whom Werner sensed a latent hostility, were polite. Werner often found himself sharing a joke with them, or discussing a subject of mutual interest, such as cars. Anthony Latham was an expert on the pre-war German Volkswagen, and one of its greatest fans. And one day, as he and Erich rattled back to camp in the green country 'bus, Werner had given up his seat to an elderly lady, who had smiled gratefully at him and murmured: 'You're very kind.' Werner wished he could be more like Erich who accepted without question that individuals were quite separate from their national image.

Their weekend presence was tolerated more readily in the village than in some other places, because Coldharbour had grown accustomed to Germans during the war. And Werner was remembered by people other than the Youngers, who greeted him, when they met, like a long-lost friend. There was occasional animosity, particularly from the friends and relatives of the six boys who had been killed, but nothing overt. By Christmas, two other families were playing host to German prisoners, and there were half a dozen of them catching the same 'bus from and to the Tramways Centre. Werner felt more confused than ever.

89

'How do you manage for money?' Dorothy had once inquired, and Werner got the impression she was prepared to fund them out of her own pocket if necessary.

'We are allowed a certain amount each week, most of which we save. There is nothing to spend it on, except the fares for the 'bus. Erich will buy clothes for his wife when at last he is sent home.'

'He'll need clothing coupons then,' Veronica said. 'Let us know when the time comes. We'll see what we can rustle up.'

Werner began to resent their kindness. He wanted his prejudices reinforced, not undermined. Philip felt the same way when the two Germans offered to dig his garden for him and plant his spring vegetables.

'I am used to it,' Werner laughed. 'I do harder work than that every day.'

Dorothy issued her invitations for Christmas, and he discovered that he was looking forward to it, instead of dreading the festival, as he had done for the past four years. So he found an excuse to refuse the invitation and stayed in camp. When Erich returned Christmas night to tell him what a fool he had been, Werner merely hunched his shoulders and went on reading his book.

Charles Graham knew from the beginning that he was making a mistake in accepting his parents' invitation to spend Christmas in Washington. Faith hated the house, the constant stream of friends and acquaintances who wandered in and out at will, the incessant political chat. She resented the way her parents-in-law spoilt Kay and Teddy, and, even more, their ill-disguised dislike of herself. Ewan and Margery Graham made very little attempt to hide the fact that they thought her a selfish wife and an incompetent mother. She had wanted to stay in New York where she felt safe among her own family and friends. For once, Charles had put his foot down.

'We're going,' he said, 'and that's that. I want to see my parents and I want to look up Pete Kovaks.'

Faith, unused to him in this mood, and afraid that if she

let him go alone he might not come back, had given in, albeit with a very bad grace.

On Christmas morning, she sat up in bed and sneezed. When Charles came in to see if she were ready for breakfast, he found her propped against her pillows in a lace-trimmed bed jacket, and the maid, Dorabelle, preparing a hot drink of honey and lemon.

'I knew I'd be ill if I came to Washington,' Faith accused him. 'I've caught one of my chills, and you know what that means. I always run a temperature. God! I hate this place! It's so cold. You'll have to make my excuses. I'm staying in bed.'

Charles was conscious of a surge of relief as he went downstairs. His mother looked down her aristocratic nose when he made Faith's excuses, and said it really didn't matter. He doubted if his father even heard.

'Where are the kids?' Charles asked, going to the side-board and helping himself to a liberal portion of kedgeree from the choice of dishes on their hot-plates.

'Gone out.' His mother sipped the cup of sugarless black coffee which was all she ever took for breakfast, an important factor in the preservation of her elegant figure. 'Sightseeing. Behaving like tourists, which they wouldn't feel inclined to do if you brought them to see us more often. I've told them luncheon at one-thirty sharp, and I won't tolerate lateness today of all days. Kay,' she added, 'is growing into a beauty. She'll have the heads turning here tomorrow night. Takes after me, of course.'

'Of course,' her son agreed ironically. 'And what about Teddy?'

'A nice, normal fifteen-year-old. I'm happy to say that your children don't favour their mother.'

'Now, Mama! Faith is my wife.'

'Hmph. You know what I think about that. You should have divorced her long ago.'

'What's that? Who's getting divorced?' Ewan Graham emerged from his reverie and became aware of his son. His long, thin face and lantern jaw, the typically Highland features bequeathed him by generations of Scottish ancestors, registered disapproval. 'Where's Faith? Time she was down.'

So Charles made his wife's excuses for a second time and was rewarded on this occasion by a grunt.

'She'd do better to go for a brisk walk, not molly-coddle herself in bed. Never mind. It gives me a chance to talk to you. Have you thought any more about what I said to you last night?'

'About going into politics? Father, you know it's impossible while I'm tied to Faith.'

'Get rid of her then.' Ewan Graham was noted for his bluntness. 'I'm nearly seventy and I can't go on for ever. America needs another Graham in public life.'

'Leave the boy alone,' his wife ordered, ignoring the fact of her son's grey hairs. 'Not that I don't agree with you, but Charles's life is his own affair. All the same,' she looked at him, 'I'd give a lot to see you happily married. Wasn't there some Englishwoman during the war?'

Charles raised his eyebrows. 'Now, how do you know that? But yes, there was. It didn't mean anything, however. Incidentally, Pete Kovaks, the guy I was telling you about, who was in the convalescent home with me, is going to marry one of the daughters. He's going over to propose after Christmas.'

Something in his tone made Margery Graham glance at him sharply. She said nothing, however, but went away to look up the Kovaks' telephone number and issue Pete with a pressing invitation for the following night. Christmas Day was to be reserved for the family, but on the twenty-sixth, there was to be a party in the evening.

It was unfortunate that Faith felt well enough – 'if she was ever really ill,' her mother-in-law snorted – to get up in time for the party. Why she insisted on doing so, Charles had no idea. She did not like the sort of gatherings laid on by his parents, but even so, all might have been well had she not taken exception to the presence of Pete Kovaks.

She had chosen to wear an elaborately fussy white dress, more suitable for an *ingénue* than the mother of two teenage children. She felt out of place the moment she came downstairs and saw the smart, svelte evening gowns of the other women. So she drank a little too much to give herself courage, and by the time Pete Kovaks arrived, around ten-thirty, she was growing sullen.

'Pete! Glad you could come. Nice to see you.' Charles held out his hand as he approached the doorway where Pete was standing, looking rather lost. 'Come and be introduced to my parents.'

Margery Graham, magnificent in a turquoise satin sheath by Balmain, smiled graciously.

'I'm delighted to make your acquaintance, Mr Kovaks. You're going to be married, I hear. An Englishwoman you met during the war.'

'If she'll have me, ma'am. I haven't asked her yet.' His eyes twinkled. 'Very remiss of me, I know, but I wanted to do it in person. To telephone or write a letter seems too impersonal somehow.'

'Very proper,' Margery Graham approved. 'I hope everything turns out well for you. I hope the lady accepts.'

'Ah, Mr Kovaks!' Faith was weaving her unsteady way between the knots of guests, a glass of champagne clutched in her hand. She spilled some of it down the bodice of her dress. 'We've met before, haven't we? A few weeks ago.' Her speech was only very slightly slurred, but there was a glassy look in her eyes. Charles took her gently by the elbow and tried to relieve her of her drink.

'That'll do, Faith. You've had enough for this evening.'

She freed herself angrily and turned back to Pete. 'Going to England to get married, I hear.' Her voice was raised and people were beginning to stare. 'Not the beau . . . beautiful Mrs Sherwood?'

'No.' Pete flushed. 'One of her daughters. Mrs Sherwood's a bit – well, a bit old for me.'

'More Charles's age, eh?' She laughed stupidly. 'You don't have to be discreet, Mr Kovaks. I'm quite sure that she and Charles were sleeping together. I can tell by the way he looks whenever he mentions her name. We haven't

93

been to bed together for years. My fault. I think what people do in bed is disgusting. But I don't suppose any man would agree.'

'Get her upstairs,' Margery hissed out of the corner of her mouth, 'before she says anything else.'

Faith rounded on her mother-in-law. ' "Get her upstairs",' she mimicked savagely. ' "Get her upstairs." That's all you've ever wanted to do with me, isn't it, ever since I married your precious son? Get me out of the way! Well, I don't care a damn about the Graham name, you stupid old woman! And I'll tell you this. If he ever divorces me, I'll go away and take Kay and Teddy with me. You'll never see either of your grandchildren again.'

She burst into tears, and Charles, ignoring the pitying or embarrassed stares of the people standing near, led her from the room. Upstairs, he handed her over to Dorabelle, feeling rather sick.

When he came down again, Pete Kovaks was in the hall, taking leave of his hosts.

'Mr Kovaks has decided not to stay,' Ewan Graham remarked. 'One understands how he feels. Presumably he will be followed by quite a number of my other guests. If you won't divorce that woman, Charles, the least you can do is keep her under control.'

'We're going back to New York tomorrow morning,' Charles said. He looked at Pete. 'When are you going to England?'

'A week's time. I'm sailing from New York on the *Queen Elizabeth*.'

'I'll come with you.' Charles closed his eyes for a moment, then opened them again. 'I must get away for a while. I've some time due to me, and my father-in-law isn't in any position to object. I'll book my passage tomorrow.'

CHAPTER EIGHT

'Charles is here?' Dorothy put down her knife and fork and looked at Pete Kovaks. 'In Bristol?'

'In Coldharbour. He's staying at The King's Head.'

There was something wrong somewhere, Pete thought. Charles had been very subdued on the voyage over and had refused to let Pete telegraph ahead to announce his arrival. And after docking at Southampton, he had been almost reluctant to accompany Pete any further.

'I think this visit's a mistake,' he had said. 'I'll book into a hotel and take a look round Hampshire while you go on to Bristol.'

'Nonsense! They'll want to see you,' Pete had reassured him stoutly. 'That's why you've come all this way, isn't it, to see Dorothy Sherwood?'

He had finally persuaded Charles to go with him to Bristol, but he and Veronica, who met them at Temple Meads station, had an even more difficult task to get him out to Coldharbour. Once there, Charles booked a room at The King's Head, resolutely refusing Veronica's pressing invitation to stay at Grace Cottage.

'We can make room, Charles, honestly. Sally can move in with Mother. They won't mind, not for just a few weeks.'

Charles, however, remained adamant. 'You tell Dorothy I'm here first and see what she says. Oh, and break the news to her gently.'

'What's all this about?' Veronica asked, as she and Pete got back into the taxi and were driven the few hundred yards round the corner to Grace Cottage.

Pete shrugged. 'Search me,' he said. 'Perhaps, after all,

he did come to a sort of understanding with your mother, which we know nothing about. And then, when he got home, he felt he had to stay with that wife of his. Poor devil!' Pete put his arms round Veronica and kissed her. 'Hey, never mind about Charles Graham. I haven't come thousands of miles to talk about him and his affairs. How's my girl?'

Veronica returned his kiss passionately, disregarding the interested stare of the taxi driver reflected in the mirror.

Pete's welcome at the cottage drove all other thoughts temporarily from his mind, and it was not until halfway through supper that he recollected Charles Graham and made his announcement. Dorothy's reception of the news reawakened his suspicions. Something had definitely gone wrong between them, but what intrigued him most was the sudden blush on young Sally's face and the way she abruptly lost interest in her food. Neither of the twins, however, seemed to notice anything amiss with their sister.

'What made Major Graham decide to come with you?' Dorothy's tone was as glacial as the north pole and her eyes flickered briefly in her youngest daughter's direction. There was a mystery somewhere connected with Sally, but what it might be Pete couldn't imagine. She had only been a child when Charles was here last.

Pete cleared his mouth of food and said: 'Family tensions. I guess he's had about as much as he can stand for the present. I was at a Christmas party given by his parents in Washington. Charles and his family were there, staying for the holiday. Faith Graham made an awful scene. She was drunk, that was part of the trouble. Not to put too fine a point on it, living with her must be hell.'

'The remedy is in his own hands, surely.' Dorothy's voice was no warmer.

'Maybe.' Pete laid his knife and fork together on his plate. 'But it's not quite as simple as that. The woman's neurotic. He couldn't leave the children with her.'

'I shouldn't have thought they could be classed as children any longer. However, if he wants to see us, tell him he can come.' Dorothy's invitation was grudging. 'Now, let's talk about you. How long are you going to stay?'

Pete grinned at Veronica. 'Well, truth to say, ma'am, I thought – if Ronnie's agreeable, that is – long enough to get married.'

There was a moment's silence, then Veronica was out of her chair and round the table, her arms entwined about Pete's neck.

'Darling! The answer's yes! You must know it is. I've been hoping you'd ask for ages.'

There was a chorus of congratulation from Jennifer, Dorothy and Sally, delivered with differing degrees of enthusiasm. Jennifer and Sally were genuinely pleased; Dorothy less so.

'But what about your parents?' Dorothy asked. 'Won't they want to be here?'

'I guess they'd like to be. But I couldn't make any definite plans until I had Veronica's answer. What's the earliest we can have a church wedding?'

'With a special licence almost at once. With the calling of banns, at least three weeks from next Sunday.'

Pete grinned. 'Banns it is, then. I'll cable my parents tomorrow. That'll give them time to get over.'

'And me time to plan the wedding,' Veronica added. 'I know Americans like to move fast, but this is ridiculous. I'll have to hand in my notice at work. Heavens!' She pressed her hands to her cheeks. 'I don't know if I'm on my head or my heels!'

'You're a Catholic, Pete,' Sally said quietly. 'Won't your parents object to you being married in a Protestant church?'

'Hell, no!' he answered cheerfully. 'My mother's not a Catholic and my father hasn't set foot in a church for years. I can't remember the last time he went to Confession.'

'That's all right, then,' Dorothy said. Her smile was brittle. 'I assume you'll be living in America?'

'Yes.' Pete looked apologetic. 'That's where my work is. Gee, I'm sorry, Mrs Sherwood. I should have thought. I'll be taking Ronnie away from you.'

'That's life, I'm afraid. One's children grow up and fly the coop.' Dorothy slid easily into her brave little woman act and smiled forgivingly. Jennifer grimaced at Sally as they began to stack the dirty dishes. 'Well, my dears, we have a lot to discuss. Plans to make. Let's take our coffee into the living room, shall we? We ought to get started. How fortuitous that Major Graham should be here to share this happy occasion with us.'

Sally had been dreading meeting Charles Graham again, and was thankful that Dorothy suggested he should come to tea on Saturday when Werner and Erich were present. Philip had been invited, as well. Dorothy was taking no chances of an awkward moment. There was safety in numbers.

They were all together in the living room when he at last arrived, twenty minutes late, after a long deliberation with himself about the advisability of the visit. In the end, his desire to see Sally again, to see what she was like now that she really was a woman, had overborne his better judgement.

She had grown was his first thought; so trite, so banal, that he had to suppress a grin. Otherwise, she was the slim, neat-framed girl that he remembered, with the same direct glance from her hazel eyes, the brown hair swept under in the style known as a page-boy bob, the wide, mobile mouth ready to tremble into a smile. There was a greater air of confidence about her than in the old days and she was less gauche; but she still dressed badly, as though clothes were of no interest to her, and she was still overshadowed by her mother. His heart contracted with a sense of love, of longing, so deep that it was almost a physical pain.

Dorothy was very little altered, as well. There were one or two more lines around the eyes, but the black hair was untouched by grey. She was as elegant as ever in a beige woollen dress with a very long, full skirt and a big cairngorm brooch pinned to the shoulder. Her manner towards Charles was brightly social, underscoring a studied indifference, and every spare moment was devoted to the handsome young German prisoner-of-war, whom she addressed as Erich.

'These are my two boys,' was the way she introduced them. 'Werner and Erich.'

Charles had known of the existence of the Germans, having been briefed by Pete.

'I shall never understand the Limeys,' Pete had said. 'One minute they hate your guts, the next they're falling over themselves to do you a favour.'

'You're marrying one,' Charles had pointed out, and Pete had shrugged fatalistically.

'God help me!' he exclaimed.

But he was so happy that his words did not ring true. He had cabled his parents in Washington and received their blessing. He and Veronica were counting the days until their arrival, and had booked them into the room next to Charles's at The King's Head.

Werner recognized Charles immediately as the American officer he had seen that night, three years ago, walking along Manor Walk; the one he was sure had been out with Sally. He also recalled Pete Kovaks, having noticed him at odd times around the village, and was struck by the thought that for these two men the war had long been over. They had been home, seen their loved ones, taken up the threads of civilian life again. For them, the war was receding into the past, already half-forgotten. But for himself and Erich and thousands of other prisoners-of-war, life was almost exactly where it had been in the winter of 1945, the last time he had seen the Americans. He still wore the same ugly uniform, was still under supervision, restricted in his movements. It was true that repatriation had started, but it was not yet the turn of either himself or Erich.

The old bitterness, never very far from the surface, welled up, making him resent these people who were all trying to be so kind to him. They meant well enough, but he could not forget that they were the conquerors, he the conquered. It was not quite so obvious with the British. They were still suffering with rationing and shortages: they still looked thin and underfed. But the Americans were different, in their expensive suits, offering round their packets of Lucky Strike and Camel, looking sleek and well nourished.

But there was another emotion mixed with Werner's resentment of Charles Graham. Jealousy. Jealousy of the way the ex-Major would occasionally look at Sally, when he thought no one else was watching. The man was in love with her; a man old enough to be her father. Werner found that his hands were trembling and clenched them into fists at his sides.

Dorothy and Veronica were discussing wedding plans with Pete, and Jennifer got up from her place beside Sally, on the couch, and joined them. After a moment's hesitation, Charles crossed the room and sat beside her.

'Sally,' he said in a low voice, hardly above a whisper, 'I was hoping to have an opportunity to speak to you.'

'I . . . I'm sorry, Major, but . . . but . . . Werner and I were going for a walk before tea, weren't we, Werner?' She got up as she spoke and turned to the young German, holding out her hand. 'We – ah – we're going as far as Culvert's End. Werner wants to see the view of Bristol from the ridge.'

'Yes, indeed.' Werner rose and bowed slightly to Charles, clicking his heels. A sense of triumph, out of all proportion to the event, surged through him. The look of chagrin on the American's face gave him an unholy feeling of joy.

'A walk?' Dorothy was saying. 'All right, but don't be long. Tea will be ready at half-past four. That gives you an hour.' She smiled vaguely in Werner's direction. He was not handsome enough, and not sufficiently attentive to herself, to be interesting. Not like Erich, who was playing gin rummy with Philip, and laughing. She was glad that Sally had so obviously snubbed Charles Graham. It served him right, coming to sniff around her after all these years, like a dog after a buried bone. She left the twins and Pete to continue the discussion, and went to sit beside Erich Rossman and help him with his hand. A few moments later, bored with cards, she murmured:

'Philip, be an angel, will you? Go and keep Charles Graham amused. Tell him all about your new book.'

'And over there,' Sally said, pointing, 'you can see the Suspension Bridge. On the other side of the Gorge are the grounds of Ashton Court.'

The city lay sprawled below them, where they stood on the very lip of the ridge; a collection of toy houses and roads, bridges and churches, carelessly flung down by some passing giant.

The day was still light, but a pall of cloud obscured the watery sun. It was very cold, and that morning there had been a flurry of snow. Now, it was beginning to freeze. The branches of the bare, charcoal coloured trees sparkled like tinsel and the houses were surrounded by silent white lawns. Sally tested a puddle with the toe of her shoe and found it already solid ice. Trapped in its depths was a cluster of bubbles, like a shower of tiny pale green stars. Her hands, in spite of her woollen gloves, were burning with cold and she tried to warm them inside the pockets of her coat. Werner, she noticed, had no gloves. His hands were raw red; work roughened and chapped by the winter cold. She wondered for the first time what he had intended to be in civilian life, once he left university.

'I never had time to decide,' he replied in answer to her tentative question. 'I went from Heidelberg into the army.'

Sally cried out in delight. 'Heidelberg! How lovely! I'd adore to go there. I remember Mummy and Daddy taking me to see *The Student Prince* before the war.'

That made him laugh, and she thought how nice he looked with amusement creasing the corners of his eyes. His face had momentarily lost its embittered expression.

'University life at Heidelberg is not truly like that. Romberg allowed himself . . . what do you say? . . . freedom.'

'Licence,' she corrected him. 'But Heidelberg is beautiful, isn't it? One of our princesses had an English garden there. She married the Elector Palatine, and Shakespeare was

101

called out of retirement to write a play for her wedding. It was his last play, *The Tempest*. The Germans had been almost drowned by terrible storms during their crossing to England, so I suppose that gave him the idea.' The striped woollen scarf wound twice around her neck was pearled with vapour, and she withdrew one of her hands from its pocket and tucked it into the crook of Werner's arm. 'Anyway,' she added, 'I'd love to visit Heidelberg.'

'One day, perhaps, I shall take you there.'

It was said so low that, at first, his words did not register in her mind. When they did, she raised her head and looked into his eyes, seeking confirmation that she had heard him aright.

'I'd like that,' she answered slowly. 'Oh, Werner, I'd like that very much indeed.'

Then she was in his arms and he was kissing her, their bodies strained so close together that they felt like one. The words: 'I love you, I love you, I love you,' kept going around and around in her head. It was as though he knew exactly what she was thinking, because suddenly he stopped kissing her and, holding her face between his hands, said passionately: 'And I love you, too. Until I die.' He turned abruptly and began to walk away.

Sally ran after him. 'Werner! Wait!' She didn't ask him what the matter was: she knew only too well. She caught him up outside the village school. 'Werner, we can't just go home like this. We have to talk.'

Beside them, the school playground lay empty and silent. Mrs Wakeham, trudging up from the village shop with her Saturday shopping, remarked acidly to her husband: 'Look at that! During the war it was nothing but Yanks. Now it's the bloomin' Jerries. I don't know what girls of today are coming to, I really don't.'

'There is nothing to talk about,' Werner said gently. 'There is nothing for us, Sarah. I have no home, no money. I do not know where is my family. When at last I reach Germany again, I must look for my mother and my sister. My sister's husband already is dead.' He took her by the

102

shoulders and gave her a little shake. 'But even if I have everything to offer you, it would not be good. Public opinion would not be for us. You know that well.' His English was losing its fluency as he became more distressed. The shape and feel of the language was beginning to elude him. 'I shall come not again. Erich, he can ask some other.'

'That's silly.' She clung desperately to his arm. 'Werner, I love you. You'll go home one day soon and sort things out. I can wait. I don't mind waiting for ever.'

He shook his head violently. He knew what he wanted to say; that she was too young, at nineteen, to waste her life in a hopeless cause; that he had no job, no prospects, no home; that he had no idea what chaos he would find when he returned to Germany. More than that, their respective countries had been on opposite sides in two murderous wars, both fought within the space of thirty years: it would take a long time for the breach to heal. And over and above that again, he sensed at times a certain antipathy deep inside her towards everything German, including, on occasions, himself. He understood that, because he had the same ambivalent attitude towards the English. But it was not a good basis for any kind of relationship, especially one involving marriage.

He could not find the English words to express all that he wanted to tell her. He could only stand there, shaking his head in that stupid fashion, like a clockwork doll with a broken spring.

Sally began to cry, the silent tears welling up and spilling down her cheeks.

'Werner,' she whispered, 'I love you. There won't ever be anyone else.'

'You do not know that. Now, please, let us go back.'

They walked, without speaking, the length of the village street and turned into Church Lane. Sally made no further appeal, common sense telling her that what Werner said was true. There could be no future together for a very long while, but she was young enough to feel that she had all the time in the world. She refused to believe that he would carry out his threat not to visit Grace Cottage again. It was so silly not to be together while they could. He was bound to reconsider his decision.

At the cottage gate, he paused, standing back to allow her to precede him. Her eyes and nose were red, but fortunately both facts could be attributed to the bitter cold.

She wanted to make him listen, but did not know how to do it. It had come as a complete surprise to discover that she was in love with Werner. Once the initial shock was over, however, it seemed so right, so natural, so inevitable that she could only marvel at her own obtuseness in not having realized it before. She could guess exactly what people would say if they knew; that it was a passing phase, a fancy, an extension of some schoolgirl crush. Or, more cruelly, they would remind her that women of the occupied European countries had had their heads shaved for the crime of consorting with German soldiers. It was probably what she would have said herself, had it been one of her friends. Only it wasn't. She didn't know how she could be so certain she loved Werner, a total stranger to her in many ways, but she was. She knew without doubt that it was a love which would last for the rest of her life.

The front door opened and Philip came out. 'I was just coming to look for you two,' he said. 'Tea's ready. For heaven's sake come in, both of you. You look frozen half to death.'

Charles Graham looked out of the window of his room at The King's Head. It was dark, but he could see a lighted window in Barton Court, and, further off, a glow from one of the outhouses at Barton Farm. It was strange to see lights at all in the village, and he recalled the blacked out streets of the war. A wind had risen and was blowing clouds across the face of a waning moon. The world had become a place of ghosts and shadows. He wondered why on earth he had come.

He pulled the faded curtains together with a sudden jerk, making the wooden rings clatter along the pole, then crossed to the door and switched on the light. The room was cold and bleak, the carpet threadbare, the bedspread mended and darned in several places. But the hotel where he and Pete had stayed for the night in Southampton had been like that. The evidence of deprivation and hardship caused by the war was still prevalent in Britain, in spite of the efforts of a Labour Government and the beginnings of the Welfare State.

Charles lit the inadequately small gas fire, which was the bedroom's only source of heat, and started to undress. Again, he asked himself what in the world he was doing in this chilly, miserable place instead of being in his own luxurious, centrally heated apartment in New York. But of course he knew the answer before the question was half-formed in his mind. In fact, there were two answers. One was Sally, the other was Faith.

After that dreadful scene at Christmas, he had to get away from his wife, if only for a few weeks, and his dislike of Faith had made him realize how much he needed to see Sally Sherwood again. He needed to see her if only to convince himself that what he had felt for her, and continued to feel ever since, was not just a momentary infatuation, a case of absence making the heart grow fonder, but something real. It had preyed on his mind to such an extent that shortly after arriving home from Europe, he had visited a psychiatrist. The doctor had been reassuring. Most men had fantasies about schoolgirls from time to time. It was nothing to worry about, particularly in the abnormal setting of a war.

Charles knew he should have been satisfied with that, but he wasn't. Neither was he certain that his feelings for Sally were the result of some sexual aberration; and when Pete had announced that he was going to England, it had seemed a heaven-sent opportunity to go with him.

Charles finished undressing and put on his pyjamas. There was no point going along to The King's Head's solitary bathroom. There would be no hot water at that time of night, so he cleaned his teeth at the wash-basin in the corner, turned out the fire and climbed into the icy bed. Too cold to sleep, in spite of putting his overcoat on top

105

of the bedclothes, he lay on his back and stared at the ceiling.

He had been prepared for his inimical reception at Grace Cottage, especially from Dorothy, but he had not been altogether prepared for the uprush of affection which he experienced as soon as he saw Sally again. He knew then, beyond any shadow of doubt, that he was in love with her, and had been for the past three years.

He still felt guilty about it because of the difference in their ages. Perhaps if he did not have a daughter of his own only two years younger than Sally, he could accept the disparity more easily. As it was, one half of him wanted to run away, to go back to the safety and comparative sanity of his everyday life by the first available boat. The other half needed to stay; to tell Sally how much he loved and wanted her; to get a divorce from Faith and make her his wife. At the same time, common sense whispered that Sally was completely indifferent to him. He could try to change that, couldn't he? God, what a mess! Eventually he fell asleep.

CHAPTER NINE

Sally normally finished work at one o'clock on Saturdays, but this particular day she was allowed to leave at half-past twelve. The supervisor of her section had granted her the extra time as a special concession, in order to choose her bridesmaid's dress. And then, at the last moment, Veronica had telephoned to say that she was unable, after all, to get into Bristol that afternoon. Sally had returned a noncommittal answer and said nothing to Miss Tate. She left as planned, promptly at twelve-thirty.

She ran down the steps of the old, grey house in Priory Road, where her department of the Ministry was lodged, and made her way round the corner to the Civil Service canteen. She would have lunch there, then wander down to Queen's Road and look at the shops. Everything was in such chaos at home, with the wedding only a week away, that she wouldn't be missed. Pete's mother and father had arrived in Coldharbour a few days earlier, and between Dorothy and Mrs Kovaks there had been instant hostility. Veronica and Pete spent most of their free time just trying to smooth things over. It had been a case, Sally reflected, of Greek meeting Greek.

Jennifer was staying out of it all, spending as much of her free time as she could with the Lathams. And Charles Graham, who had been persuaded to remain until after the wedding and act as Best Man, said very little. Sally wondered, but without much interest, what had brought him back to England. She still felt embarrassed in his company and avoided him when she could.

She pushed her tray along the counter and ordered what

looked like shepherd's pie, but which turned out to be cauliflower cheese. Like most of the canteen food, it was tasteless, shapeless and of a nondescript, uniform colour. She chose jam roly-poly with some of the ubiquitous custard to follow, a cup of what could have been either coffee or tea, found an empty place and sat down.

She had no idea what would happen now about the bridesmaid's dresses. They were very busy in the office and she hadn't the courage to ask for further time off. No doubt her mother and Veronica would manage something between them. Dorothy had taken a fortnight of her annual leave with the BBC.

Sally forked up a mouthful of the cauliflower cheese and swallowed, without tasting it. She had not seen Werner for over three weeks, and nothing nowadays seemed worthwhile. For the past two weekends, Erich had come by himself, saying that Werner was not feeling well.

'His company's no loss,' Dorothy had remarked at breakfast only that morning. 'He never says much. As long as Erich still comes! I shall be very sorry when he has to go back to Germany.'

'What she means, of course,' Jennifer had remarked to Sally, when they went upstairs to finish getting ready for work, 'is that Werner was very polite and gave us all an equal share of his attention.'

Sally finished her canteen lunch and left. She suddenly felt tired and listless, as though all the colour had drained out of the afternoon. She wandered aimlessly along Queen's Road, looking with lacklustre eyes at the goods displayed in the shop windows. Usually, she could see a dozen and one things she wanted to buy, but today there was nothing that she needed. She took one of her laddered nylons into Bright's to be mended, then decided to visit the Art Gallery. There might be an exhibition.

As always, the echoing halls and marble staircases of the various galleries exercised a peculiarly soothing effect. There was a greenish, sub-aqueous light which made it seem like walking through an underwater cave. There was no exhibition today, and Sally had to content herself with renewing acquaintance with old and familiar friends. Upstairs, in one of the side galleries, she found a collection of old Victorian paintings, their varnish dark and cracked; *Weston Sands* by William Hopkins and Edmund Havell, *Boulter's Lock* by Edward John Gregory, and Howard Geach's *Waiting for the Boat*. There were others, but those were the three she liked best. She sat down on a seat in the middle of the room, blinking back unbidden tears.

There was a footfall behind her and a hand pressed her shoulder. Werner's voice said: 'I saw you downstairs, so I followed.'

Sally sat perfectly still for a moment, almost afraid to breathe. She had been thinking about him, wanting him so badly, that for a fleeting second she was certain that it must be a trick of her imagination. Then she raised a hand and laid it over his.

She answered simply: 'I'm so glad you did.'

Werner came round and sat beside her, looking at the pictures lining the walls. He was wearing his overcoat with the collar turned up, and his cap pulled well down over his ears.

'It's cold and damp in here,' he said at last.

'Come down to the restaurant and have a cup of tea,' she suggested, but he shook his head.

'No. If you don't mind, I would rather stay here.' After another silence, he added: 'You were right that day. We have to talk.'

'I meant what I said, Werner. I love you. I always shall. Sometimes you just know these things.'

He smiled. Someone walked past the door of the gallery, paused for a moment, but decided not to come in. Werner's hand found Sally's and held it hard.

'Yes, I know,' he said. 'It is that way for me, also. But it is no good to think we have a future together, because we do not.'

'Why haven't we?' She turned her head and studied his profile, the strong line from the forehead to the jaw. She had drawn it so many times lately that it was like tracing a familiar map.

'Many reasons. Many which are simple, which I think you understand. But one, also . . .' He searched for the words in English. 'One not so simple. One which is deep inside yourself.'

She did not pretend to be ignorant of his meaning. 'I know,' she replied softly. 'But I can't help remembering all those men at the Nuremberg trials. All the terrible things that they did. The people of your country – you! – let that happen.'

Werner stared at a picture of a little girl sitting on a doorstep with an apronful of cherries.

'You do not believe,' he asked after a moment, 'that such things could happen here?'

'No, never!' Sally was horrified. 'We wouldn't let a man like Adolf Hitler come to power.'

'But then, you have been a nation for a very long time. We have been a nation for less than a hundred years.' He took off his cap and twisted it between his hands. 'You have not lost a war nor been punished for it, as we were. Now we shall be punished all over again.'

He wanted to explain to her what it had been like in Germany when he was a boy; the despair, the humiliation, the oppressive sense of guilt. They had almost been ashamed of being Germans. And then the National Socialists had arrived on the scene. They had brought the rallies and the banners, the renewed sense of identity and pride. No one had wanted to question too closely the regime which gave them these things.

'Don't you see,' he demanded, 'that we needed, we *had* to believe?'

She looked at him, wanting to understand because she loved him so much, but the war was still too close. He could see in her eyes that she loved him *in spite of* the fact that he was German. It was not an irrelevancy which she was able to ignore.

It was an attitude of mind which both hurt and angered

110

him, but which he knew he must accept, not simply because
he loved her, but also because, deep down, he had to admit
that part of it, at least, was justified. It was useless to tell
people that thousands of ordinary, decent Germans really
hadn't known what was going on in the concentration
camps, or among the Jewish and dissident sections of the
population. For the truth was that many of them had
guessed. But it wasn't easy to jeopardize everyone and
everything you held most dear. Principles looked less attractive when you were the one called upon to pay their price.

The silence stretched between them. At last, he broke it.
'What were you doing in Nuremberg with Mr Jackson? You
have never told me.'

He had not realized that she could draw. The revelation,
when she had finished explaining, was a surprise. The fact
had never been mentioned either by her or by any member
of her family. There were no examples of her work, that
he had seen, adorning the walls of Grace Cottage. Yet she
was good enough to have illustrated a book and for those
illustrations to have been accepted.

'But why, then, do you work in an office?' he asked,
frowning.

She leaned against his shoulder, closing her eyes. She felt
extraordinarily tired, and even talking was too much effort.

'Oh . . . reasons,' she murmured.

The gallery was freezing. Coal was in too short supply
for many of the public buildings to be heated. Sally's
toes were numb with cold and her fingers hurt. She shivered
and Werner wrapped part of his greatcoat around her,
holding her tightly against his side. She sighed with pleasure
and snuggled close.

He said sharply: 'Do not go to sleep, please, Sarah. I wish
to speak with you.'

'Mmmm. Let's get married, Werner. Let's get married
and to hell with everybody.'

'Do not be foolish! You know that is not possible. But
your drawing, that is possible. Why do you not go to . . . ?
Go to . . . ?'

111

'Art school?' She rubbed her cheek against the rough cloth of his tunic.

'Yes, to art school. Why do you not do that? I should like to be answered, Sarah, please.'

She lifted her head from his shoulder and grinned at him. 'I love it when you get proprietorial.'

'Do not use the long words just to confuse me. Is it your mother who has stopped you going?'

Sally gave another sigh, but this time of exasperation. She sat upright, pulling herself out of the circle of his arm.

'Yes, I suppose it is. Now you're going to lecture me, like Uncle Philip and the twins. You're going to tell me that I must stand up to her, not let her ride rough-shod over me. Well, I know all that, but old habits die hard. It's not quite as easy as it sounds. Mummy would have to pay for me. I haven't any savings of my own.'

Sally spoke quickly and the colloquialisms were not familiar to Werner. But he understood enough to say emphatically: 'If you have talent, you must use it. Mr Jackson, he would help you, would he not?'

'I suppose so.' She sounded impatient and cross. 'If I asked him.'

'Why then do you not ask him? He is akin to you, surely?'

'Related to me. Yes, he's my cousin. Oh, Werner, I don't know. I don't know if I'm really ready to leave home and branch out on my own. I'm not the adventurous type.' She regarded him, her head tilted to one side, and love surged through her. Why was it that one set of features, one face, put together in a certain way should make her stomach feel hollow and her knees feel weak? Werner wasn't handsome, not in the conventionally accepted Hollywood mould. She didn't even know him all that well. He was an alien and an enemy. Yet she had been aware, almost from the first moment of seeing him, that she liked him. It had taken so little to turn that liking into love. 'What do you want me to do?' she asked resignedly.

He leaned forward eagerly. 'I want you to promise that you will not waste your talent. That you will try to be yourself.'

112

'For your sake?'

'Yes, for my sake, if you like. But also for your own.'

She pulled on her gloves and picked up her handbag from the seat.

'All right,' she said gravely, 'if you'll promise to go on coming to see me as long as you're in England. If you'll stop playing the coward, so will I.'

He hesitated. He knew that Erich was planning to take one of the other men in their hut with him, next time he went to Grace Cottage, but nothing was definitely settled. Erich would be only too delighted if Werner changed his mind.

'Very well. I agree.'

Sally smiled. 'That's OK then. Not next Saturday, because that's the wedding. Veronica's getting married.'

'Yes. Erich told me. I shall see you on Sunday.'

'I think Mummy's having that day to recover. I shall see you in a fortnight's time.'

'A fortnight's time.' He repeated the phrase carefully, adding with his sudden grin: 'I need you, you see. To help me with my English!'

'Oh, Werner!'

Involuntarily, they moved towards each other, but just at that moment, someone turned into the gallery from the landing. It was a young man wearing RAF uniform, his service respirator slung over one shoulder, his greatcoat buttoned tightly to his chin. His eyes flicked from Sally to Werner and back again. A look of mingled disgust and disbelief crossed his face and he turned on his heel without a word. The silence settled oppressively behind him. Even the painted faces staring out from the canvases seemed to wear an air of disapproval.

Sally took a deep breath. To her surprise, her only emotion was that of anger on Werner's behalf. She moved towards the doorway.

'Where are you going?' Werner demanded.

'To find that airman and give him a piece of my mind. How dare he look at us in that way!'

113

'No, Sarah, no!' Werner caught her arm. 'It would do no good. It is something we Germans will have to accept for a long time to come.'

'Well, I'm English and I don't have to put up with it.' She wrenched her arm free and ran out of the gallery.

She clattered down the stairs, her shoes making a satisfactorily angry noise on the uncarpeted stone. The Aircraftsman was standing in the main hall, but she walked straight past him and down the short flight of steps to the swing doors. When it came to the point, she knew there was nothing she could say, because her sympathies were with the young airman.

Werner, leaning over the balcony, saw her leave. Then he went back into the gallery, sitting by himself on the seat which they had so recently shared together.

Sally, with Jennifer, followed Veronica out of the church, faintly surprised to find that the wedding had actually taken place.

The past week had been such total confusion that by Wednesday night, Veronica was in hysterics and threatening to call the whole thing off. This had been triggered by the discovery that they did not have sufficient clothing coupons between them to buy new outfits for the bride and bridesmaids, largely because Dorothy, who had promised to contribute, had used all hers on a new coat and dress.

'But darling,' she protested when Veronica reproached her, 'I am the mother of the bride. People will be looking at me. I must appear to advantage.'

In the end, Philip had, as always, come to the rescue, giving up all idea of a new summer suit. Only Sally was aware of this fact, and had been sworn to secrecy.

'You're a darling, Uncle Philip,' she had said, kissing his cheek.

'And so are you,' was his answer.

Mrs Kovaks was disappointed that it was not a white wedding, and said so. For once, her husband did his best to muzzle her.

'For Christ's sake, Mame, can't you see what conditions are like in this country? Everything's still rationed. As soon as the kids get back to the good old US of A you can have the biggest reception for them that your friends have ever seen. Until then, hold your tongue.'

Veronica had chosen a New Look style suit in brown velvet with a matching coolie hat and a ruffled blouse of pale beige silk. She carried a single orchid and her prayer book. Jennifer and Sally wore identical dresses and jackets of primrose yellow, a colour which suited neither of them. As ever, it was Dorothy who stole the show in a dramatic emerald green coat and carrying a huge, fur-trimmed muff. Her fur hat had bands of emerald green georgette swathed, wimple-like, around her neck and chin.

The reception was held at The King's Head, in the private room at the back; a buffet meal which allowed the guests to move around informally and chat. It was Jennifer who, as Chief Bridesmaid, should have partnered the Best Man, but Tony Latham claimed her early on, and it was Sally who found herself beside Charles Graham on one of the window seats.

They had not been alone together since that night, three years earlier, when Sally had realized that he loved her. They were not, she supposed, alone now, but it felt like it, islanded as they were in their stone embrasure, while the party flowed to and fro like some gentle tide, passing by, but never washing over them.

She thought he looked older. The intervening years had not treated him as kindly as they had treated her mother. At forty-three, his hair was very grey, with only here and there the original dark colour showing through. His face, with its cleft chin, was gaunter, the fine bone structure plainly visible beneath the skin. The china-blue eyes were veiled by the heavy lids as he leaned against one of the stone stanchions of the window, surveying the scene.

For his part, one of his earliest impressions, on seeing Sally again, had been that she was as much of a child as ever; but he had rapidly changed his mind. There was

115

something about her, these past few weeks, which he was finding it difficult to define. At times, she was the laughing, innocent schoolgirl of three years ago; at others, she was older than the Sphinx. Charles reminded himself that she had always been like that, a creature of mercurially changing moods; both Little Nell and ancient sibyl in the space of an afternoon. But it did not altogether explain the change he sensed in her nor the lurking sadness at the back of the eyes. He longed to be able to ask her to marry him. He wanted to protect her against the world.

The trestle tables bearing the remains of the food were being pushed back against the wall, and someone had put a Victor Sylvester record on the gramophone.

'Come on, everyone! Take your partners!' Veronica called, as she and her husband moved to the centre of the floor in a graceful waltz.

Bob Younger beat Philip and several other hopefuls to Dorothy's side to claim the honour of the first dance, while Jennifer and Tony Latham seized the opportunity to slip outside. Sally could see them through the window, her sister huddled within the encircling warmth of her fiancé's arm. Jennifer was laughing, her face turned to Tony's, his head bent to catch what she was saying. It was a moment of intimacy between two people deeply in love, and Sally was torn by a feeling of desolation. Would it ever be like that for her and Werner?'

'Sally!' She glanced round, startled, to see that Charles Graham had risen and was holding out his hands. 'Would you care to dance?'

'Oh . . . Yes, thank you.'

There was nothing she wanted less at that moment than to dance, especially with Charles, but it was impossible to refuse. He moved well, but the pressure of his body against hers, as he guided her round the floor, made her uncomfortable. She could never forget that he had once been her mother's lover.

A log crackled and fell in the grate, spangling the room with fire. Sally jumped and Charles's arm tightened around her waist. Other guests were laughing and exclaiming, leaping clear of the flying sparks. Ernest Jordan came in from the bar with another trayful of drinks, and flicked down the switches. The room became a cavern of light.

'You didn't go to art college, after all?' Charles asked suddenly.

'What? Oh, no. But I'm thinking of going. Someone's . . . Someone's persuaded me to change my mind.'

He felt a surge of jealousy for the unknown person, before deciding it must be Philip. After all, who else was there who could have so much influence with Sally? Even if Werner's name had occurred to him, he would have dismissed it as absurd. He had accepted the presence of the two prisoners-of-war with equanimity: he felt no great vindictiveness towards the Germans. But that any of the Sherwood women felt more for either one of them than that kindly, tolerant impulse of the British for the underdog, never so much as crossed his mind.

'When are you going back to the States?' Sally inquired politely as the waltz came to an end.

'I'm leaving for Southampton tomorrow. I sail on the *Queen Elizabeth* in three days' time.' He saw Pete coming to claim a dance with his new sister-in-law and asked hurriedly: 'Sally, will you write to me? I'd . . . I'd like to keep in touch.'

She was caught off guard. The request was unexpected and she did not know how to say 'no' without giving offence. To have refused would have sounded churlish.

'Yes. O – Of course,' she stammered, as Pete swung her exuberantly into a quickstep, shouting: 'Come on, Sal! I'm your brother now! You have to do as I say and accord me a little respect.'

She did not speak to Charles again. It was soon time for Pete and Veronica to leave for their brief, four-day honeymoon in Cornwall, after which they would return to Coldharbour for a week before departing, more irrevocably, for the United States.

Sally stood with the other guests in the biting cold outside The King's Head, waving goodbye as the taxi disappeared over the brow of the hill, taking the newly-weds into Bristol and Temple Meads station. As she turned to go back inside, she caught sight of her mother's disconsolate face and felt a sudden rush of sympathy and affection. It was not going to be as easy as she had hoped, telling Dorothy of her own decision.

CHAPTER TEN

Soon it would be spring. March had brought the milder, damper days and a promise of fair weather. The gardens in Church Lane were full of early flowering narcissi and crocuses, like purple and yellow flames. Then, suddenly, winter was back, trailing rain and sleet in its wake and bringing the bleak, ominous light that accompanies an easterly wind.

The second Sunday in March, the last Sunday that Werner was to spend in Bristol, he and Sally went for a walk across the fields. Clouds chased each other overhead, broken by momentary gleams of sunlight, cold as steel. In the distance, the spire of St Andrew's showed white against the sky, and the blown branches of trees rattled like angry skeletons. Sally shivered, and as soon as they were out of sight of the village, Werner put his arm around her. They leaned against a stile. The little stream which bordered the meadow was a dark, rough streak of broken water.

'When did you hear?' Sally asked. 'You didn't say anything yesterday.'

'This morning. Erich and I are of fifty from the camp to be sent home next Thursday. Not home at once, you understand. We go first to the transit camp at Salisbury.'

'But you are leaving Bristol on Thursday?'

'Yes.'

She took a deep breath, steadying her voice. 'I don't suppose I shall see you then, after today. At least . . . not for a while.' She had to persuade herself that one day they would be together again, or she would go mad.

He made no reply and she glanced up at him. The scar

on his left cheek stood out, livid in the cold. She lifted a hand and with one finger traced the pugnacious outline of his jaw.

'I love you,' she whispered. 'Oh, I do love you, Werner.' She rubbed her cheek against his coat.

'I know,' he answered huskily. 'I love you, too.' He tilted her head back and kissed her hungrily; forehead, cheek and mouth. She clung to him, trembling in every limb.

Looking back on the scene in later years, striving to recall each detail, she realized how innocent she had been, and how much he must have had to restrain his natural impulses in deference to that innocence. But at the time, it had seemed perfectly natural to her that their lovemaking should stop at kissing.

Werner pulled away from her, looking white and shaken, and gripped the top bar of the stile. His knuckles were blue and chilblained. After a few moments, he said harshly, in a voice totally unlike his own: 'I keep my promise to you, I have come with Erich these past two weeks. Now, you keep your promise to me. You have talent to become a famous artist.'

The naïvety of the assumption made her laugh. 'Oh, Werner! That's very sweet of you, but people don't just become famous artists. Painters' reputations grow, and it needs an awful lot of hard work, and even more luck, to get noticed.'

'You have talent,' he repeated doggedly.

The previous Saturday, he had arrived at Grace Cottage with Erich, and even Dorothy had been delighted at his reappearance. She was feeling deflated after the rush and bustle of the wedding; and two days earlier, she had said goodbye to Veronica and Pete at Southampton. She had not been so pleased, however, when, at Werner's request, Sally had brought down from upstairs a portfolio of her drawings to show him.

'Darling, Werner doesn't really want to be bothered with all that stuff. He was just being polite, can't you see that?'

But Werner had ignored her, preferring to spend the next

hour looking at Sally's pictures rather than join in the noisy game of Newmarket, which Dorothy was teaching to Erich. Dorothy had hunched an offended shoulder and decided that Werner was, after all, just as boorish and uninteresting as she had always thought him.

Werner had expected to be impressed by the drawings – no one was allowed to illustrate a book who was not competent to do so – but he had not anticipated being bowled over. It was the portraits, more than anything else, which caught his eye. The landscapes and various still lifes were good, but Sally's ability to catch people's expressions and put them on paper was outstanding. He saw, too, what Philip had seen long ago, that she was quite unconscious of this special talent.

Later, he had leafed through Dorothy's copy of Philip's book, entitled simply *Nuremberg*. It was the first time he had seen photographs of the trials and he was angered by what he saw, yet also shocked by the snippets of text which he managed to read. He sensed that there were elements of both hypocrisy and expediency in the trials which, at the same time, had been necessary, and this confused him. The dozen or so line drawings which Sally had done of the defendants told him that here were men capable of great self-delusion, that some were more wicked than others, but that all were ordinary human beings who had allowed themselves, to a greater or lesser extent, to be touched by evil. He found himself wishing that she had drawn likenesses of the lawyers and judges in the case. Those, too, he thought, might have been equally revealing.

Her talent was undoubted, but it needed refining and disciplining.

'You must be properly trained,' he said now, watching a flight of birds wheel and swoop silently above their heads, as the peculiar soundlessness of a winter afternoon lapped all about them. Spring had vanished, temporarily defeated. 'You promised me that you would do so if I came again to the cottage, and I have come. It is more important, now that I go away, that you should promise me. Now

121

perhaps that we do not see each other any more.'

'You're not to say that!' she answered passionately. 'We shall see one another again.'

She reached up to kiss him, but he held her off, repeating: 'Promise me.'

'If it's what you want, I promise,' she said. Then she was back in his arms, her lips on his.

'You put her up to this!' Dorothy exclaimed viciously, rounding on Philip. 'It was your idea!'

'No, it wasn't, Mummy. It was my own.' Sally stooped and put another log on the fire before turning to face her mother. 'Philip has just promised to finance me, if I can get a place at the Slade.'

'All the same,' Philip put in from his seat on the couch, in front of the dying fire, 'I can't pretend that I haven't tried to persuade you, over the years, to do exactly what you intend doing now. And I can't pretend that I'm not delighted to lend you whatever you need.'

Dorothy was tired. It was almost half-past eleven at night, and all she wanted to do was sleep. Instead, she was confronted by this scene. The fact that there would be no scene if she didn't make one, she conveniently ignored.

'And when was this little conspiracy hatched?'

Philip sighed. 'There is no conspiracy, Dorothy. Sally only broached the subject to me tonight, during the first interval.'

Philip had taken Sally to the theatre to see a revival of Pinero's *The Second Mrs Tanqueray*. Dorothy had been invited, too, but as she had already seen the play the preceding week, in company with Jennifer and Tony Latham, she had declined. She had spent a frustratingly solitary evening listening to the radio and reading a book. By the time she heard Philip's car draw to a halt outside the cottage, she was feeling thoroughly bad tempered. Even the absurdities of *Take It From Here* had failed to alleviate her boredom.

She had been surprised, and not altogether pleased, when

Philip had accompanied Sally indoors. Dorothy wanted to go to bed. Jennifer had her own key and could let herself in when she eventually decided to come home. Dorothy had forced herself to be polite, however, and offered Philip coffee, which, to her annoyance, he accepted. It was while she was in the kitchen, heating the water in the percolator, that Sally had come through to tell her about her plans, the decision to give up her job and apply for a place at art school. She had, she said, asked Uncle Philip to finance her, and he had willingly agreed.

Dorothy had left the coffee to boil all over the top of the stove and marched back into the living room to demand an explanation from her cousin.

'This nonsense,' she told Sally, who had followed her, 'has to stop.'

But Sally was proving adamant. It was a woman, cool and decisive, who faced her mother and said quietly that she had made up her mind.

There was something different about Sally lately, Philip thought. She seemed remote, withdrawn, unhappy. He wished he could help, but when he had tackled her this evening, she had declared that nothing was wrong. She needed to get away from her mother, and there, at least, he could assist her.

Dorothy looked at their two unyielding faces and lost her temper.

'And what about me?' she demanded angrily. 'What about me, left here all on my own? Selfishness, that's what it is, Sally! Sheer, unthinking ingratitude! Jennifer's being married in two months' time. Veronica's thousands of miles away, in America! And now you want to leave me. A great comfort and support my three daughters have turned out to be, I must say!'

She was pacing about the room, twitching at ornaments, rearranging them without having the least idea what she was doing. Philip thought how handsome she looked and how much he loved her, even while he was praying that Sally would not weaken and give in.

Sally had no intention of giving in. Since Werner's departure, all she had left was her promise to him. It had become her oriflamme.

'You have Uncle Philip,' she answered coldly, 'so how can you possibly say you're being left alone? And Jenny will be living in Bristol. If all goes well, I shall only be just over a hundred miles away, in London. You're being very childish, Mother.'

Dorothy stopped in her tracks, her mouth open. 'How dare you speak to me like that?' she gasped. 'You wouldn't have done so if your father had been alive. Philip!' Lost for words, she appealed helplessly to her cousin.

'She's right, you know, Dorothy,' he told her brusquely. 'You've always been a self-centred woman.'

'Oh!' He could see her calculating the possibility of getting her own way with a bout of hysterics, and then deciding against it. She opted for wounded dignity instead. 'I see. So that's what you think of me. It's nice to know the truth after all these years.' She turned to her daughter. 'If you wanted to go to art school that badly, you should have said so. As you didn't, naturally I assumed you were perfectly happy to be at home with me. Until you got married, that is. However, now that I know the truth, of course you must go. But please come to me for the money, not to your Uncle Philip.' She paused to see what effect this self-sacrificing speech was having on her audience, and was furious to note that Philip was still regarding her with amusement, unimpressed. Sally, at least, had the grace to look a little ashamed of herself. Dorothy added in her most martyred tones: 'We will discuss it tomorrow when we are alone. And now, if you'll both excuse me, I shall go to bed.'

The door shut behind her and Sally sank down on to the couch, beside her cousin.

'Phew!' she whistled. 'I'm glad that's over. Do you think she means what she says?'

Philip smiled. 'I should think so. Now she's realized you're serious, she'll keep to her word.' He patted Sally's

124

hand. 'I wish I knew what has happened to make you change your mind like this.'

He had not expected her to tell him, but neither was he prepared for the abrupt way she pulled her hand from under his, exclaimed petulantly: 'Nothing's happened! I wish you wouldn't keep cross-examining me! There's nothing to tell!'

It was so unlike Sally to be rude, it immediately warned Philip that something serious had occurred in her life, some kind of crisis, although what it could be he was unable to imagine. Normally, he would have made the obvious guess; a man. But Sally had no boyfriends that he knew of. She had always been rather a solitary child, depending on her family for company; one of the main reasons Philip wanted to see her free of Dorothy's influence.

'My dear child,' he apologized mildly, 'I'm sorry, I had no intention of prying.'

She burst into tears and groped blindly in her handbag for her handkerchief. The story of herself and Werner came pouring out.

'Nobody else knows,' she sobbed finally, blowing her nose. 'You're not to tell anyone.'

Philip was secretly horrified, though he tried hard not to show it. He was also upset that he should feel that way. He prided himself on his broadmindedness, and had bitterly despised the jingoistic fervour of the first world war, which he could vaguely remember as a child. He had always been thankful that there had been very few similar manifestations during the last war; but Nuremberg had left deeper scars than he knew. The evidence of Nazi atrocities had appalled him, more particularly because he recalled two very happy holidays he had spent in Germany during the nineteen-thirties. He had even, on one occasion, seen Hitler close to, in Berlin, and thought him an extremely charming man.

Another time, he had lectured a group of German students on the subject of Oliver Cromwell, drawing parallels between the English Lord Protector and the German Führer. He remembered his audience as pleasant, fresh-faced youths, sitting informally at small tables, drinking beer. Had the location been Heidelberg, Werner might have been amongst them . . .

Philip smoothed Sally's hair, murmuring: 'Hush, hush. Your mother will hear you. Of course I won't tell anyone.' But when she was calmer, he added: 'You must know yourself that it can't come to anything, Sally. There's no future in it for either of you.'

'Why not?' she asked defiantly, blowing her nose.

He made no reply, because there seemed no satisfactory answer; because in spite of the 'no fraternizing' rule, a few British soldiers had already married German girls. A quotation came into his mind, unbidden. *True love is drowned by no billows of mischance; true love fears no thunderbolts of fate; true love abides immortal, firm, unchangeable. To have loved once is to have loved for aye.* He thought of his own unshakable affection for Dorothy, however badly she behaved, however often he swore to himself that, this time, she had alienated him for good.

An idea occurred to him.

'This sudden determination to go to art school, is that something to do with Werner?' Sally nodded and Philip felt a momentary stab of anger that the German had been able to influence her, where all his own advice had failed. 'At least he's done some good.' Philip's tone was abrasive, but Sally did not even notice. He felt ashamed of himself and kissed her gently. 'Justify his trust in you then. Go to art school. You and he can keep in touch by letter. He knows your address. Later on, when things are more settled in Germany, when he's sorted out his affairs, you can see one another again. See how you both feel then.' Philip did not voice his opinion that the romance would die a quick and easy death. He felt that would have been unnecessarily cruel.

The front door slammed. There was a swift, firm tread in the hall and Jennifer came in.

'Hullo, Sal,' she said. 'What are you doing up? It's nearly midnight.'

'I'm just going to bed,' Sally mumbled. 'I've been talking to Uncle Philip. Mummy's gone on up.'

At any other time, Jennifer would have noticed her sister's tear-swollen face, but tonight she was full of her own concerns; in spirit still with Anthony, whom she had just left outside in his car.

'Right. Well, I'm going to get myself some hot milk. Want some? No? OK. Uncle Philip, I expect you can let yourself out.' She disappeared, and they could hear her moving around in the kitchen.

Philip grinned wryly. 'I sometimes think,' he confided to Sally, 'that of you three girls, Jennifer is the one most like your mother.'

Sally managed a watery smile, kissed him gratefully and went up to bed. A few moments later, she heard the front door close quietly behind him. She wandered over to the window, staring out at the darkened fields beyond the narrow belt of still leafless trees. It was cold in the bedroom, but she made no attempt to switch on the electric fire. Standing there, shivering in the gloom, she thought longingly of Werner and wondered where he was. Had he left the transit camp yet? She had no idea how long he had to stay there.

She tried not to think of the present, only of the future; of the day when she and Werner would be together again, but she could not picture it. The images eluded her. It was like trying to walk through an unknown landscape, and she gave up the attempt in despair. After a long time, during which Jennifer came upstairs and went into her room, Sally slowly began to undress and got into bed. She heard the church clock strike first one, then two. Finally, after what seemed an eternity, she fell asleep.

Werner looked out over the stern of the ship at the grey waters of the Channel and the creaming wake. He was going home. He repeated the words to himself. *He was going home.* After all this time, he ought to feel a sense of anticipation, at the very least. All around him, men were chatting, their voices charged with excitement. There were spurts of laughter. Within twenty-four hours, they would be on

127

German soil. Some of them had not seen Germany for more than eight years.

There were a few, like Werner, who did not share in the general rejoicing; men who had lost everything during the Allied aerial bombardment in the closing stages of the war; men whose homes and families were in the east, now under Russian domination. But the majority of men on board either did not fully understand, or did not care about, the conditions which lay ahead of them. It was enough simply to be going home.

Werner remembered the faces of the prisoners left at the camp, men whose date for release had not yet arrived; the looks of envy; the fond messages for mothers, wives and children, entrusted to any of the returning prisoners who could deliver them personally. And *he* had not wanted to leave! Had it not been for his uncertainty over the fate of his mother and sister, Werner believed he must have followed the example of a small minority of Germans who had opted to stay permanently in England. Six months ago, the thought would never have crossed his mind; the very idea would have seemed like treason. But six months ago he had not been in love with Sally.

Many of the prisoners – Werner still thought of them as that: it was difficult to appreciate that they were now free men – had carefully-wrapped parcels in their knapsacks or tucked under their arms, where no one could steal them. These contained luxuries like nylons and underwear for wives and sweethearts, tea and coffee, sugar and cigarettes. Many of their adopted British families had helped, where necessary, with clothing and food coupons. The Sherwoods had eagerly assisted Erich with whatever he had wanted to buy. It proved something about human nature, Werner supposed, if only that, in general, people left to themselves preferred to be friends rather than enemies. He himself was taking nothing back, except his own belongings. There had seemed no point. Common sense told him that his family were dead.

Someone slapped him exuberantly on the back. It was Erich, grinning from ear to ear.

'Cheer up!' he urged. He, too, leaned on the taffrail and stared at the receding expanse of water.

Werner said: 'You do realize we're not going back to the same country we left? We've been away a long time, first in the desert and then in England. Even if we hadn't lost the war, many things would have changed by now. As it is – ' He broke off, shrugging expressively.

'I tell you what it is, Werner,' Erich declared in disgust. 'You're getting like that Greek fellow, who was always prophesying doom.'

'Cassandra. And she was a woman.'

'That's him! Her! I don't know what's come over you lately. You're no fun any more.' And Erich went off to rejoin the new friends he had made in the transit camp, who had been prisoners somewhere in the north of England.

Werner watched him go, then turned back to his contemplation of the sea, wondering what Sally was doing. It was a weekday, so she would be at work, but he had no real idea of what it was that she did, except that she was a clerk in a government office. So he pictured her elsewhere, walking with him through the winter fields, showing him her drawings, sitting with him in the cold little room in the municipal art gallery.

The images crowded thick and fast on top of one another; Sally playing cards, teaching him how to play rummy, being taught herself how to play Müller; Sally knitting or sewing; Sally laughing or serious; Sally laying the table or clearing away; Sally, Sally, Sally . . .

Then, quite suddenly, she ceased to be real. With every kilometre the ship put between itself and the English coast, she appeared more and more to be part of a dream, insubstantial as air. There was only present reality; Germany and what he would find there. It was self-delusion if he let himself think otherwise.

Werner reached into the inside pocket of his tunic and brought out the piece of paper with Sally's name and address on it in block lettering. To destroy it would only be a symbolic gesture, because both his memory and his English

129

were good enough for him to send her a letter whenever he wished. Grace Cottage, Church Lane, Coldharbour, near Bristol, England; he could recite the direction in his sleep. But just at this moment, he was in need of a symbolic gesture. He tore the paper into a dozen pieces and tossed them over the side of the ship.

Sally saw the letter with the foreign stamp and her name on it as soon as she got home. It was lying on the mat, just inside the front door. She picked it up and ran upstairs to her room. Either her mother or Jennifer was already home. She could hear someone busy with cutlery and china, laying the evening meal in the kitchen. She took off her hat and coat and tossed them in a heap on the bed. When she picked up the letter again her hands were shaking.

Then she saw that the stamp was American and a great tidal wave of disappointment engulfed her. It took her a few seconds before she realized that the handwriting was not her sister's. Veronica must be ill. Pete was writing to her, rather than frighten Dorothy with the news. But it was not Pete's writing, either.

Sally slit open the envelope and drew out several sheets of notepaper, covered in a vaguely familiar hand. She turned to the last page, looking for the signature. There it was: Your Sincere Friend, Charles Graham. She threw the letter on the floor and flung herself, face downwards, on the bed.

PART THREE

Winter 1952 – 1953

For you there's rosemary and rue; these keep
Seeming and savour all the winter long

CHAPTER ELEVEN

Sally shifted the heavy carrier bag and brown paper parcel from one hand to the other, glanced up at the ornate iron gates and imposing facade of Rosetti's house and hurried along Cheyne Walk. It seemed to her that artists and men of letters who lived seventy or more years ago, could afford a greater degree of comfort than a rising young portrait painter of 1952. The studio and adjacent bed-sitting room which she now called home, with a shared bathroom on the landing below, was at the top of a house in a narrow cul-de-sac at the back of St Stephen's Hospital; not perhaps the most elegant part of Chelsea, but sufficient for her needs. And she was beginning to make a name for herself as a portrait painter in oils. The daughter of a distinguished politician and an Alderman of the City of London had been among her most recent sitters.

The late October sunshine was warm on her back as she crossed the King's Road, but there was a chill wind blowing off the river which heralded the onset of winter. Sally pulled her duffle coat more securely around her and fastened its leather toggles. The coat was a brilliant emerald green with a plaid taffeta lining. She giggled to herself, remembering two schoolboys, the previous day, waiting for a 'bus in Old Brompton Road. They had stared at her in frank astonishment before one had turned to the other and remarked in a hushed tone: 'Gawd! It's Robin bleedin' 'ood!' She had joined in their laughter, not at all offended, and earned herself the accolade of being 'a right good sport!'

Crosby House, named rather optimistically, Sally felt, because of its proximity to the fifteenth century Crosby Hall, was the corner building on the left hand side of the cul-de-sac. She let herself into the dark, linoleumed hall and glanced through the small pile of mail on top of the meter boxes to see if any of the letters were for her. There were two; one from her mother and one with an American stamp, from Veronica. As she went up the three flights of stairs to the top of the house, Sally reflected, almost with satisfaction, that after four and a half years, she no longer expected a letter from Werner.

He did not, of course, know her present address, but in the days when she had first come to London as a student, she had waited daily for a letter to be forwarded from Grace Cottage. She had become quite a joke in the boarding house where she had lodged, because of the way she rushed into the hall each morning to collect the mail, and searched the afternoon post when she returned at night. Nothing had arrived, however, although Dorothy heard regularly from Erich. But Erich had lost all contact with Werner after their return to Hamburg. Sally's cautious inquiries had at least elicited that information from her mother.

She unlocked the door to her attic flat and let herself into the studio. It was by far the larger room of the two, covering almost the entire loft space of the house and featuring a big skylight. Sally dropped the brown paper parcel, containing two new tubes of paint, on to the table beside the easel and crossed to the bed-sitting room. The carrier bag, with its groceries, she dumped unceremoniously behind the door, threw her coat untidily over the back of a chair and lay down on the bed to read her letters.

She opened her mother's first. It was shorter than usual, there being, so Dorothy said, a dearth of news. There were snippets of village gossip; Philip had taken her to see *Measure for Measure* at the Bristol Old Vic; her immediate boss at the BBC was leaving and being replaced by a man she did not like; Jennifer was expecting a baby.

'Not before time,' Dorothy wrote waspishly. 'I had very nearly resigned myself to not being a grandmother, especially since you show no signs of getting married, and Veronica and Pete have decided against becoming parents. Such a selfish attitude, I always think! Not that grandchildren in America would be much comfort to me, but there you are! I don't complain.'

And it was in fact true that Dorothy complained far less than she had once done, either overtly or by those self-sacrificial little remarks which stuck like barbs in the conscience of her youngest daughter. Or perhaps, Sally reflected, it was just that she was more impervious these days to her mother's reproaches.

There was a postscript at the bottom of the final page.

'PS. Philip has asked me to marry him. I don't know yet what my answer will be. I can't make up my mind.'

Sally nearly dropped the letter in astonishment. She was quite sure that this was not the first occasion on which Philip had proposed, but it was certainly the first time that Dorothy had ever mentioned it, let alone intimated that she might be considering the offer. Sally found herself wondering cynically if the unexpected and extremely lucrative success of Philip's latest book, a biography of Charles I, had anything to do with her mother's changing attitude towards her cousin.

'Don't be mean!' Sally admonished herself severely, and turned to Veronica's letter, ripping it open with her thumb.

In contrast to Dorothy's letter, it was exceedingly long, the neat, precise writing covering sheet after sheet of the thin airmail paper. A great deal of space was, as usual, devoted to Veronica's social life; cocktail parties, bridge afternoons, shopping trips to New York and the recent Pharmaceutical Convention she had attended with Pete in Denver. Then there was a page devoted to the forthcoming Presidential Election, and the hopes of Republicans, like Pete and his family, that Eisenhower would win.

'The Grahams, naturally, are for Stevenson, but I don't believe he'll get elected. Everyone is sporting campaign buttons. The Democrats are "Madly for Adlai". I wear my "I like Ike" button everywhere, except in bed, and I don't think Pete would really mind if I wore it there.

'I saw Charles Graham the other day at a party in the home of a mutual friend. I thought he looked ill. He's certainly looking older. Of course, he is forty-eight. He and his children had come to Washington to stay with his parents for a week or two. I imagine that dreadful wife of his is playing up again. It must be a terrible life for all of them, though the kids seem sane enough. When I say "kids" they're grown up now. The boy is twenty, he told me, and his sister is nearly your age. Charles asked after you. He always does.

'Now, what about this visit you say you're going to pay us, but never do? You're as bad as Jenny and that husband of hers. Next summer, Pete has promised me a trip to England. We shall have to stay with Mother, but I'm determined to be in London for the Coronation. Coronation fever is even getting a grip over here. The Americans are wild about Lizzie. I bet it's funny singing *God Save the Queen*.

'Sally dear, you're becoming quite famous, did you know? You painted the portrait of a friend of a friend of my mother-in-law, while she was staying in London last year. She was absolutely delighted with it, and I was terribly proud to be able to say that you're my sister. My standing has risen by several notches in everyone's estimation. Since then, one or two people have approached me to find out more about you. So you see, you could make it a working holiday over here if you wished . . .'

The letter continued for another page to finish with the sprawling signature. Sally grinned and lay back against the pillows, hands linked behind her neck. She tried to remain unimpressed by her sister's information, but the words 'you're becoming quite famous' and 'terribly proud' kept circling around in her head. She felt a tingle of excitement, which she forced herself to ignore. It would be all too easy to get an inflated idea of her importance as an artist. Nevertheless, she was good. She knew it, and it would be hypocritical to pretend otherwise. She owed a lot to Uncle Philip – and to Werner.

It was the first occasion she had allowed herself to think

more than fleetingly of Werner for a very long time. When he had failed to write, the mental agony had been unbearable: the memory of him had lain like a bruise at the back of her mind, at first too tender even to touch. But gradually, like all bruises, it had begun to fade, and there had been so much to do, so much to learn during those years at college, that her life had been fully occupied.

Lately, however, his name had once more started to intrude upon her thoughts, but she had managed until this moment to suppress it. But now, as daylight faded and the roar of the city traffic was muted to a gentle hum by closed windows and the surrounding network of small side streets, memories of him flooded back, as strong and clear as on the day he went away. The old unanswered questions pushed themselves once more to the forefront of her mind. Why had he never written? What had made him break his promise?

Sally unlinked her hands from behind her neck and beat with clenched fists on the bedspread, suddenly overwhelmed by frustration. She could feel the hysterical sobs rising in her throat . . .

She must stop this! Angrily, she swung her legs over the side of the bed, her feet groping for her shoes, then went back into the studio, switching on the lights. She twitched the cloth from the canvas she was working on and stared at the painted likeness of a well-known minister of the cloth. The florid face stared back at her from beneath the greying hair. The heavy grooves which ran from either nostril to the corners of the mouth gave an impression of power and strength, and also conveyed a strong sense of animalism. Sally shook her head. It wasn't quite right. She had overdone it. It looked more like a portrait of the actor Donald Wolfit, in full flight as Marlowe's Tamburlaine. And yet some memory of that towering performance, which she had seen the previous year at the Old Vic in the Waterloo Road, must have found an echo in the face and personality of her subject. All the same . . .

With a sigh, Sally unhitched her old smock from the back of the studio door, unpacked the tubes of paint which she had bought that afternoon, and turned once again to the portrait. If she concentrated fiercely enough, she could block out that other face and those memories which were insistently clamouring for her attention.

The apartment was very quiet when Charles unlocked the front door and let himself in. He stood for a moment or two, just listening, but there was no sound. Kay, he knew, was at an eve-of-election party in the home of one of her friends. Teddy was away at college. Probably Faith had gone out, too, in order to teach him a lesson for leaving her so callously that morning in the middle of one of her tantrums. Her voice, rising to screaming pitch, had pursued him down the hallway as he had left for work.

'I hate you! I hate you! You don't care what happens to me! You don't love me! You never have! I know all about your other women. You fucking bastard, you!'

She had stood there in her nightdress, her hair a tangled mass about her shoulders, and as the front door shut behind him, he had heard the thud and crash of something thrown. Whatever it had been, the pieces had been tidied away.

Charles went into the living room, but there was no one there. He switched on the television, flicking from channel to channel, but it was nearly all election news. Excitement was rising as the pundits foretold a victory for Eisenhower. Charles switched the set off again, comforting himself with the recollection of Truman's victory in 1948 against all the predictions of the polls.

The kitchen, too, was empty and silent, unnaturally so. Usually, either Dorabelle or McMasters, the English butler whom Faith had insisted on hiring, were somewhere around. Then Charles remembered that Monday was McMaster's night off, and if Faith had gone out, Dorabelle had probably been given permission to do so, as well. There was no sign of anything being kept hot for him. Faith had evidently assumed that he would eat out. He glanced at the clock on the wall, and was surprised to see that it had turned half-past-nine. Tonight's meeting must have gone on longer than he had realized.

138

There was a cold chicken in the refrigerator and some pasta salad. He would make himself a meal from those later on, when he had showered and changed. He went along the corridor, with its pastel blue walls and huge vase of flowers standing on a Sheraton table, to his bedroom. The door to Dorabelle's room was ajar, giving on to total darkness. He had been correct, then, in his assumption that she had been given the evening off. The door to Faith's room was also open, and there was again no sign of life.

He went through to his bathroom, shedding his city clothes as he went. He had received invitations to several pre-election parties, but had no desire to go to any of them. All he wanted was a stiff drink, some food and a long, dreamless sleep. Since his return to Washington, things between himself and Faith had gone from bad to worse. The rows had become even more frequent, and twice he had had to call Doctor Foy to her in the middle of the night, to administer an injection, because the oral sedatives she took had ceased to work. On the second occasion, the old man, who had known Faith from her birth, had taken Charles aside and advised him to think seriously of having her committed to a sanatorium.

'She might get worse during the menopause. It takes some women that way. If not for your own sake, then for the sake of the children.'

Charles suspected, however, that Teddy would never return home to live, and Kay would not remain for much longer. There had been talk lately of her getting her own apartment. He wished she would find herself a job. Times were changing, and very few girls, however rich their parents, were content nowadays to lead a purely social existence.

His head began to ache, and Charles decided to take a bath rather than shower, to relax his work-weary muscles. Later, with a towelling robe flung over his pyjamas, he returned to the kitchen. By the time he had percolated coffee and made himself a plate of chicken salad, his headache was worse; a dull throb, like the steady, rhythmic beating of a drum. He pushed aside his food untasted and lit a cigarette, which he smoked down to the butt before accepting that he would have to do something to relieve the pain. The drugs' cupboard was in Faith's room, where she kept a supply of preparations which would put a pharmacist's storeroom to shame. He left the kitchen and went along the passage to her room.

Outside, he paused to stub out his cigarette end in a big glass ashtray, set on a cabriole-legged table against the wall. Above the table hung the only item he had ever bought for the apartment: everything else had been chosen by Faith. It was a copy of *Winter 1595* by Lucus van Valkenborch, which he had found in a little antique shop, somewhere between Forty-fifth Street and Third Avenue. It was the frame he had paid for – late eighteenth century gilded walnut, originally made to hold a mirror – but it was the picture he had wanted. It reminded him of Grace Cottage and Sally.

She seemed to be gaining quite a reputation for herself as a portrait painter. That Mrs Voorhees, whom he had met at one of his mother's parties in Washington, was delighted with the likeness Sally had done of her. Veronica kept promising a visit from her younger sister, but so far, Sally had not come.

Charles shivered suddenly, in spite of the central heating. He mustn't think of Sally: it did no good. The pain in his head increased, pounding afresh behind each temple. He pushed wide the door to Faith's room and switched on the light.

Sally had given herself the day off. Resolutely, she had shut the studio door behind her at half-past nine and set off for Westminster. Today, she was going to behave like a tourist.

It was Tuesday, November the fourth and the first State Opening of Parliament by the new, young Queen. Throughout the capital, there was an undercurrent of excitement; the anticipation of a new and golden Elizabethan Age. It seemed to Sally that every time she had switched on the wireless during the past few months, someone was either singing or playing the song *Let's All be Good Elizabethans*. This sense of expectation, of a fresh beginning after years of austerity and suffering, in no way diminished the country's enormous feeling of loss at the death of King George VI. He had died at Sandringham in February, and had been genuinely mourned by subjects who had come to love him for his steadfastness and courage during the dark days of war. But a twenty-six year old Queen, with a handsome husband and two young children, gave everyone a lift, and the name Elizabeth evoked an older and more glorious age.

On her way to the Houses of Parliament, Sally stopped to post Jennifer's birthday present, a little silver locket and chain, which was all she could afford. Veronica's had been despatched to Washington weeks before. She also paused to look longingly at fireworks in stationers and toy shops; Catherine wheels, sparklers, rockets, from a penny each to big boxes priced at half-a-crown, five or ten shillings. They brought back memories of those pre-war Bonfire Nights, when life and relationships had seemed so simple and straightforward.

The crowds of people jostling one another on the pavements were tremendous, and Sally, wedged between a fat woman with a fractious, whining child, and the woman's husband, was afraid that she would be unable to see anything when the moment arrived. But in the event, she had a clear view of the young Queen, resplendent in evening gown and flashing jewels, a white fur stole around her shoulders. Later, Sally pushed her way along the Mall to see the Royal family come out on to the balcony of Buckingham Palace, the Queen and Prince Philip joined by the nearly four-year-old Prince Charles and the two-year-old Princess Anne, both children in sensible, buttoned-up coats.

It was almost five o'clock before Sally finally returned home, exhausted but happier than she had been for a long time. The cheerful, good-natured crowds, the glittering occasion, the transmitted belief that they all stood on the threshold of a brilliant future, had banished her sense of gloom and foreboding, which had troubled her now for weeks; ever since she had once more begun to think of Werner.

She crossed the studio without glancing at the easel, a reminder that she should have spent her day working. She was beginning to get more commissions: perhaps she would start charging a higher fee. She unwrapped the newspaper parcel of fish and chips, which she had bought on her way home, and spread the contents on a plate. Then she lit the gas in her tiny oven. As she slid the fish and chips inside to reheat, the telephone rang. She went over to the bedside table and lifted the receiver.

'I have a long distance call for you. Trans-Atlantic from Washington,' said the operator. 'Please hold the line. I'm putting the call through now.'

'Sally?' It was Veronica's voice, rather faint. 'Sally, darling, I was going to 'phone tomorrow to say thank you for my lovely present, but Pete's mother has just told me a piece of news I can't possibly keep until then.'

Sally wondered what item of information the redoubtable Mrs Kovaks senior could have imparted that could possibly be of interest to her, but all she said was: 'Can you speak up, Ronnie? There seems to be an awful lot of background noise.'

'Oh, that's our election day party. I'm giving a buffet lunch to some of Pete's Republican friends. It's the Presidential Election today, in case you didn't know in that little backwater of yours, over there.' Veronica's laugh sounded above the crackling of the wires. 'Anyway, it appears that Margery Graham − Charles's mother − called Pete's mother about half an hour ago. They're not really that friendly, being on opposite sides of the political fence, but they keep in touch for the sake of the boys.' It took Sally a moment or two to realize that her sister was speaking of Pete and Charles Graham. 'Well, my dear, what do you think? Charles's wife has committed suicide.' Veronica's voice sank to an awed whisper and Sally had to strain to hear her. 'Last night, while Charles was working late. She took an overdose of sleeping tablets. Charles found her. It must have been awful for him. A terrible thing to have happened, but no one's really surprised. She was totally unbalanced. It was bound to happen one day. As Pete's mother says, it's probably a blessing in disguise. Sally? Sally, are you still there?'

'Yes. I'm still here.'

'You don't sound very shocked.' Veronica was plainly disappointed. She had expected her news to make a bigger impact.

'Well. I never met Charles's wife. It's not easy to get upset about someone I didn't know.'

'You know Charles!'

'Yes . . . I'm very sorry for him, of course.'

'Does he still write to you? I know he did for a while after our wedding.'

'He writes now and then, and I always answer. But it's difficult to find something to say. We haven't seen one another for over four years. It's months now since I last had a letter from him.' Sally did not add that she had never encouraged the correspondence.

'A pity,' Veronica said. 'I think he was trying to keep in touch with Mother through you. Things had obviously gone wrong between them.' Sally heard a swell of whooping and cheering in the background, audible even at that distance. 'It sounds as though Ike's carried another state,' Veronica shouted. 'I must get back to my guests. Sal, try to keep in touch with Charles Graham. He's a free man now. 'Bye, darling! 'Bye! Pete sends his love.'

The line went dead. Sally replaced the receiver on its cradle and stood staring at it for a moment. The room suddenly seemed very quiet.

She was sorry about Charles Graham's wife, but it didn't really concern her. Charles belonged to the past. He had no place in the present, nor in the future she had once planned to spend with Werner. Abruptly, with a little shake of her head, as though to clear it of unwanted thoughts, she turned away from the telephone and got her meal out of the oven.

143

CHAPTER TWELVE

'I can't really believe you've had the good sense to say "yes"!' Sally put her arms around her mother. 'But congratulations to you both. I'm absolutely delighted.'

Sally had returned to Coldharbour for Christmas, to the depleted family circle of the past four years; for most of the time, just herself, her mother and Philip. Jennifer and Tony came to dinner on one of the two main festival days, but spent the greater part of the holiday with the Lathams. Jennifer and her mother-in-law were the best of friends, a relationship Jennifer had never succeeded in achieving with Dorothy. This year, it was Boxing Day before she and Tony put in an appearance, so the news had been saved until Boxing evening, when they were all gathered around the fire in the living room.

Sally lounged in an armchair on one side of the hearth, helping herself every now and then from the box of chocolates at her elbow. Jennifer, as yet showing no signs of pregnancy, but already suffering from backache, sat on an upright chair drawn close to Tony, who sprawled in the other armchair, replete with too much food. Dorothy and Philip were side by side on the couch.

There was a small Christmas tree in one corner of the room, its tinsel decorations reflecting the light from the fire. Branches of holly and mistletoe had been stuck behind the frames of pictures, and, in general, a greater effort seemed to have been made this year than for the previous four. Sally had arrived late on Christmas Eve, and so far, she and her mother had had little time for an exchange of confidences. But then, Dorothy had never encouraged intimate, mother-

and-daughter chats. If she had something to say, she preferred an audience.

And Dorothy did have something to say. She and Philip were going to be married.

Sally was genuinely pleased, less for her mother than for Philip, whose years of dogged devotion were at last to be rewarded. Whatever her mother's reasons for accepting him, there could be no doubt that Philip's proposal was founded in love. Sally got up from her chair and hugged them both, a demonstration of affection she had not made, towards Dorothy, at least, since childhood. Jennifer, too, expressed unqualified approval.

Dorothy smiled wanly. 'It's nice,' she said, 'to be in everyone's good books for a change.'

Jennifer raised expressive eyes to heaven. Later, she asked Sally: 'What do you think her reasons are for accepting Uncle Philip?'

The two women had complained of the heat from the fire and had gone into the little conservatory to get cool; but both knew that it was really a ploy to have a few minutes' private conversation.

Sally sank into one of the basket-weave armchairs, now so old that they creaked ominously under the slightest pressure, and looked back into the room where their mother was watching Philip and Tony play at cribbage.

'I should guess loneliness. The fear of old age.'

Jennifer lowered herself into the other chair, having first dusted it carefully with her handkerchief. She was, Sally reflected, becoming rather tiresomely finicky in her ways, probably due to the influence of the elder Mrs Latham.

'Mother looks remarkable, considering she's forty-eight,' Jennifer objected.

'But that's the point. She is forty-eight.' Sally moved in her chair, which groaned in protest. 'You think back twelve years, nineteen-forty, the beginning of the war. It doesn't seem very long ago, does it? That length of time again, and Mummy will be sixty.'

'Mmm. I always thought there might be something

145

between her and that Major Graham. You don't think, now that his wife's dead . . . ?' Jennifer's voice trailed off inquiringly.

Sally shook her head. 'No. I'm sure of it. There was never . . . as much between them as was thought. You know how people gossip.' She could feel the colour creeping up under her skin and changed the subject. 'How are you feeling? What are you hoping for, a boy or a girl?'

The conversation flowed effortlessly into other channels, and by the time the two women returned to the living room, the topic of Charles Graham had been forgotten. Jennifer joined her mother to watch the men's game, while Sally drifted aimlessly about the room, examining the signatures on the Christmas cards. One, with an unseasonable display of pink roses on the cover, inside disclosed the name Erich in flowing German script.

'You still hear from Erich Rossman, then,' she said, turning to her mother.

'What? Oh, Erich! Yes. We exchange cards at Christmas and Easter, and he writes once or twice a year. I write back.'

Conscious of Philip's eyes upon her, Sally continued, 'He . . . He never mentions that friend of his . . . the other one . . . Werner?'

Dorothy laughed. 'Darling, you remember the extent of Erich's English! It was a little better by the time he went home, but it hadn't improved that much. His letters, if you can call them that, are confined to essentials. 'I am well. Are you well? My wife has had a baby.' His poor wife always seems to be having babies. The first one, born nine months after his return to Germany, was named after me. I was rather flattered.' She shifted her position on the arm of the couch so that she could look directly at her daughter. 'I seem to recall having had this conversation with you several times before. Why are you so interested in Werner?'

Sally busied herself replacing Erich's card on top of the bookcase. When she answered, she made her tone as casual as she could.

'No particular reason. I just wondered if you knew what

146

had happened to him. If he ever found his mother and sister.'

Satisfied, Dorothy shrugged and resumed her watch on the cribbage game.

'I should imagine they're both dead,' she said dismissively, 'or surely, in all those years, he would have heard something!'

Werner lay on his back, staring up at the ceiling and cursing himself for a fool. It had been sheer carelessness on his part that he had neither seen nor heard the truck approaching as he crossed Ost-West-Strasse the previous Tuesday; and, as a result, he was condemned to spend Christmas in hospital with a broken leg. Then he reminded himself that the alternative would have been to spend Christmas alone in his apartment. Even his father's old friends, Elsa and Ludwig Fischer, had family commitments at this time of year. They would be in to see him when they could, but they would be involved for the next few days with children and grandchildren.

It had been purely by chance that, six months earlier, Werner had literally bumped into Ludwig Fischer in the Kaiser-Wilhelm Strasse, when he had stepped aside to allow a woman with a pram and two small children to pass him. In doing so, he had trodden on someone's foot, and, turning to apologize, had found himself face to face with his father's old friend. The reunion had been tearful, and when they parted, the older man had extracted Werner's promise to take his evening meal with him and Frau Fischer that night.

'But the food,' Werner had protested. 'Everything's so hard to come by and so expensive. I can't take your rations.'

'You will come to please us!' Ludwig Fischer had told him sternly. 'Otherwise, we shall be deeply offended.'

It had been a long evening, lasting well into the small hours of the following morning, there was so much to be said by the three of them. The Fischers were able to confirm what Werner had already discovered for himself, that his mother and sister were dead. Both women had been indoors when the bomb struck. Elsa Fischer had been visiting her

147

sister-in-law that afternoon, in the same street, and had spoken to both Frau Neumann and Sophie by telephone only minutes before they were killed. Elsa Fischer had been in hospital for many months afterwards, having been buried for over four hours in the rubble of her sister-in-law's house, which had been partially wrecked by the blast.

'What was it like in England?' Ludwig Fischer had wanted to know. 'Pretty bad, eh? We gave them as good as we got?'

Werner had nodded, not having the heart to disillusion him. How could he tell people who had suffered so much that in spite of the Luftwaffe and the Blitz, in spite of London, Plymouth and Coventry, in spite of the V1 and V2 rockets, the deaths from air raids in Hamburg alone had equalled those in the whole of Britain? And the casualties from one raid only on the city of Dresden had been more than three times as great. How could he explain that, mentally prepared as he had been for what he would find on his return to Germany, he had nevertheless been stunned by his first sight of Hamburg?

More than half of all buildings and eighty per cent of the harbour installations had been destroyed. There had even been talk of rebuilding the city on another site, but this had finally been rejected. And Werner was painfully aware that he had not seen the worst of the devastation. By 1948, the fallen masonry had been cleared away, leaving gaping, but tidy spaces. He remembered the long walk from the railway station into the centre of Hamburg that first afternoon, often only knowing where he was by the names of the streets, some of them simply chalked up on the sides of the ruined buildings. He had almost cried for joy when he saw the green-topped spire of St Michael's church, which had miraculously survived the destruction.

Things were better than they had been. Germany's economic recovery had already begun. No German was frightened by the prospect of hard work, and there had been no repetition of the Treaty of Versailles. American dollars were bolstering the German economy, and the Reichsmark

148

had been replaced by the Deutschmark. Businesses, old and new, were struggling back into the competitive market. At first, Werner had done any job that he could get – labouring, trying to sell obsolete, pre-war machine tools, gardening – but recently he had been offered the position of salesman with a toy manufacturing company, and he was determined to make a go of it. Germany had once been the greatest nation of toy makers in the world. He also moved from a sleazy basement room to a small apartment in one of the new blocks which were gradually being built. Life was slowly but surely returning to normal.

He thought of Sally often, and on more than one occasion had written her a letter, only to tear it up before it was finished. He had expected her memory to fade after the first few months, and had been dismayed to discover that her image was as fresh in his mind as it had been on the day he left England. But he still had so little to offer her, nor did he know if she still felt the same way about him. Common sense suggested he write and find out, but something deterred him, and it was not just the uncertainty of his own and Germany's future. Seeing the havoc wreaked on German towns by the Allies had rekindled old hatreds and resentments. These were not helped by the unhappy realization that some of the blame had to be laid at the door of the Germans themselves. With the revelations about the concentration camps had come a terrible, almost unbearable sense of guilt, which the condemnation of the rest of the world did nothing to ease. The German people drew together, closing in upon one another and presenting a united front to outsiders . . .

There was a diversion from the evening's boredom as some of the nurses and orderlies came into the ward to sing carols, but the choir was small. Hospital conditions remained chaotic, with too few buildings and staff and too many patients. The nurses and office workers were run off their feet. The result, all too frequently, was confusion. Only yesterday, Werner had been given the medicine which belonged to the man in the next bed but one; although this was a forgivable error as his fellow patient was also called Neumann. Gunther Neumann. He looked to Werner a very sick man, and one of the other men in the ward had whispered knowingly: 'Cancer. They say he'll be lucky to last out the week.'

Werner glanced sideways at him now, but the man appeared to be asleep. The skin had a waxy sheen to it, and the nose stood out sharply from the surrounding face. Werner turned his eyes quickly, suddenly uneasy, conscious of being in the presence of death, and concentrated on the carol singing, trying to ignore the pain in his broken leg.

'You must stop blaming yourself, Charles.' Margery Graham laid down her pen and glanced across from her desk to her son, who was standing by the study window. He had been there, unmoving, for the past fifteen minutes, and his silence was beginning to get on her nerves. 'It's Christmas, for goodness' sake! Try to snap out of this depression! Think of Kay and Teddy.' When he didn't answer, she lost her temper. 'It isn't even as if you were fond of Faith!'

The words seemed to find their mark. Charles turned slowly and came back to the fire, stooping to warm his hands.

'That's probably the reason I'm feeling so guilty.'

'Nonsense! Why should you feel guilty? You did everything for that woman that you possible could. Most men would have ditched her years ago. Or had her shut up.' Margery Graham put aside the letter she was writing and rose awkwardly from her desk. She had been conscious lately of the stiffening of her joints, and her doctor had mentioned the dreaded word 'arthritis'. She went across to her son, putting a hand on his shoulder.

'There's something more, isn't there? You're in love with someone. I've sensed it since quite a while back. I first noticed it after you returned from that trip to England, when Pete and Veronica Kovaks were married. Is it that widow? Veronica's mother. What's her name? Dorothy something. My memory's failing along with my body.'

Charles took a deep breath and straightened up, smiling

at his mother. 'You're a very shrewd woman,' he told her. 'There isn't much that's failing about you. You're right, of course, I am in love, but not with Dorothy Sherwood.' He hesitated for a second before adding defiantly: 'It's her daughter, Sally, who's two years older than Kay.'

'I see . . . It couldn't be just an infatuation, could it?'

He shook his head. 'I've been in love with her for the past eight years, ever since she was fifteen. I assumed at the time that I'd get over it, but I haven't. Distance, absence don't seem to make any difference to my feelings for her. Nor the difference in our ages.'

'And is she in love with you?'

'I should think it highly unlikely. Incidentally, Veronica tells me that her mother is getting married again soon. To her cousin, Philip Jackson. Veronica had a call on Christmas Day, giving her the news.'

The house was very quiet with a Sabbath calm. Obeying his wife's instructions, Ewan Graham had insisted on his grandchildren accompanying him to church, overriding their protests.

'I want to speak to Charles alone,' Margery had said. 'There's something troubling him and I want to find out what it is.'

The Senator thought her fanciful, and said so. He considered that Faith's death and Charles's discovery of the body were enough to depress any normal man. He had been as anxious as Margery to get the family to Washington for Christmas, but he thought any further interference unwarranted. Time should be left to do its work. He had even desisted from telling Charles to his face that he was damn lucky to be shot of that neurotic woman.

It was a beautiful day, the December sun hanging redly in the milk-white sky, frost crackling and winking on eaves and posts, frozen grasses crunching underfoot. It reminded Charles of mornings in Coldharbour, and he realized with surprise that an English winter was not entirely the way he remembered it, all dampness and gloom.

'What are you smiling at?' his mother demanded. 'You

151

haven't . . . You haven't seduced that young girl, have you, Charles?'

'No.' His tone was sharp. 'And I must remind you that she is no longer a child. She must be almost twenty-four. Her birthday is New Year's Day.'

Margery Graham frowned, fiddling absently with the belt of her elegant wool dress, an elusive champagne colour. She asked: 'Are you going to remain with Lodge and Berryman?'

At first, Charles was thrown by the abrupt change of subject, then he saw how his mother's thoughts were moving, in an arc, ready to come round full circle.

'There's no good reason why I shouldn't. Faith's parents don't blame me for her death.' His mouth twisted in a sudden grimace. 'And they are Kay's and Teddy's grandparents.' He felt it necessary to give his mother a timely reminder: she was all too apt to think of the children solely as Grahams. 'But I have been considering a move. I've been offered a job on the board of de Courcy's.'

'Another publishing house? Your father and I thought that now, you might think seriously of giving up publishing for politics.'

'By "now" I presume you mean now that I'm free of Faith, who was undoubtedly a drawback to a political career.'

'There's no need to use that ironic tone of voice. I never made any secret of my opinion of your wife, and neither has your father. He, as you are aware, has always dreamed of your following him into public life. He's getting on. We both are. We should like to know that you would step into his shoes. I had thought, these past few days, that you were giving it serious consideration.'

'I have done.' Charles was brusque.

'Well? And what conclusion have you reached?'

'None yet.'

'Then before you do, rid yourself of the notion you are so obviously harbouring, of marrying a girl young enough to be your daughter. It wouldn't look good.'

'For me or for you?'

'Don't be stupid, Charles. Apart from all else, it wouldn't

be fair to Kay and Teddy. Particularly Kay. To saddle her with a step-mother who is young enough to be her sister, could be embarrassing for her.'

'I wish you'd let Kay speak for herself,' Charles retorted angrily. 'She's a woman, not a child. I hope she'll be getting married herself someday.'

'And supposing you and this . . . this Sally have a child? After all, why not? She's young. She'd want children of her own. She won't be content with a ready made family. Good heavens, Charles! If that happened, you could have a son or daughter the same age as your grandchildren.'

Charles sighed and dropped down wearily on the couch beside his mother, taking one of her hands in his. In spite of the carefully tended finger nails, lacquered a pale rose pink, and the expensive creams and lotions rubbed in nightly, it was an old woman's hand, with ridged and brittle nails and swollen joints. He felt a sudden rush of pity for her; a desire not to hurt.

'Mama.' He squeezed her hand affectionately and saw her smile. 'Mama, you're jumping the gun. I haven't asked Sally to marry me yet. Maybe I never shall. And I don't know that she'd have me if I did. I haven't seen her for over four years.'

'Do you write to her?' Margery's tone was accusatory; and when he didn't answer immediately, she added triumphantly: 'You do!'

'And if I do, there's nothing to hide! Sally and I have simply kept in touch since her sister's wedding. But it hasn't been lovers' correspondence. I think she regards me in the light of an elderly uncle.'

'I'm glad to hear it. Of course, you'll marry again some day. You're not old enough to remain celibate. But there are plenty of eligible women your own age around, without making a fool of yourself over a young girl!' Margery leaned forward and kissed him. 'I'm giving a dinner and dance on New Year's Eve. Celeste Adams will be coming.'

Charles laughed and got up. 'Mama, I'm not interested in Celeste Adams or any other female on your list of eligibles. It's much too soon after Faith's death.'

'There's no harm in looking around,' his mother advised him dryly.

He smiled, but without warmth. 'I'm going for a walk,' he said. 'I promise I'll be back in good time for lunch.'

She nodded, sensing his need to be alone, and returned to her desk to finish her letter.

Georgetown, on a winter Sunday morning, was quieter than usual, the gardens lying silent and hidden behind their high brick walls. No children's voices broke the silence; the old Chesapeake and Ohio Canal glittered in the sunshine. Charles walked along the towpath, deep in thought.

He understood his mother's concern, but resented her interference. His life was his own affair. He thought again of the night he had found Faith lying on her bed, the bottle of sleeping tablets on the table beside her and the smell of whisky permeating the room . . . His mind shied quickly away from the picture. He did not want to remember it now. He thought instead of Sally; of the way she tilted her head, when speaking; of the smile in her voice and eyes; of her total lack of feminine wiles. Honesty and unaffectedness were not virtues he naturally associated with women.

After ten minutes, he turned and walked back towards the lock. The beautiful weather made him suddenly optimistic. Why shouldn't he be able to persuade Sally to love him now that he was free? The difference in their ages seemed of little importance in the brilliance of the morning sun. The cares and worries of his life with Faith, the haunting memories of her death, melted away. He felt young again. Nothing at that moment seemed impossible.

He left the towpath and walked rapidly along the brick sidewalks, under the overhanging, leafless trees. Mr and Mrs Kovaks senior lived not far from the university, and Pete and Veronica visited them every Sunday. He would call in and wish them a happy New Year and work again on Veronica to invite Sally to Washington for a visit.

'So why don't you come over for a week or two? Pete and

I would love to have you. We've told you that so often, you can't possibly be in any doubt. If money's the problem, don't be too proud to say, and we'll arrange the fare. Don't forget that I'm married to a disgustingly wealthy man.'

Sally turned the first page of Veronica's letter and switched on another bar of the fire. Rain and sleet drummed against the windows of her room. With her other hand, she hopefully extended a slice of bread, impaled on the prongs of a toasting fork, to the insufficient heat.

Her sister's letter had been waiting for her when she returned to London at the beginning of the year. Dorothy and Philip had both tried to persuade her to stay on at Coldharbour, but she had pleaded pressure of work. In fact, she was without a sitter for the moment, but she had felt the need to get away. Her mother's personality was still too dominant. Even after years of independence, Sally could not wholly overcome a feeling of inadequacy in Dorothy's presence.

Veronica's letter continued: 'We saw Charles Graham this morning. He called at Pete's parents' house while we were there. He was down from New York for Christmas, and said he might remain here for a while. The publishing house he works for – his in-laws', I think – has given him compassionate leave. As a matter of fact, he asked if you would be coming over any time. He said he'd very much like to see you again.'

CHAPTER THIRTEEN

'How are you feeling? More rested?' Veronica looked up from her morning paper and regarded her sister's wan appearance with some concern. 'Flying knocks you up, doesn't it? It's the change of time zone. When you travel by sea, it's a gradual transition.'

Sally took a seat at the breakfast table, opposite her sister. Pete's place was empty. The litter of eggshells and broken crusts of toast testified to the fact that his day had already started. Sally glanced guiltily at her wrist watch. It was gone half-past nine.

'I ought to be feeling thoroughly wide awake, I suppose,' she apologized. 'If I were at home, it would be the middle of the day. But for some reason, I'm exhausted. Am I dreadfully late for breakfast?'

Veronica crowed with laughter. 'Goodness no! Not for my breakfast. Pete's off early, of course, but I'm a lady of leisure. I'm very often finishing my meal at half-ten.'

Sally accepted a cup of coffee, but refused anything to eat. She swallowed her glass of orange juice gratefully. The breakfast room, with its white-painted walls and light coloured chintzes was bright and sparkling, but outside, the sky was a melancholy grey; rain spattered against the windows. Sally wondered, not for the first time in the last thirty-six hours, what had prompted her to accept her sister's invitation, which she had resisted for so long. She had had plenty of opportunity to come up with the answer during the long flight, with its refuelling stops at Reykjavik and Goose Bay. But when, the previous evening, she had at last stepped out of the 'plane into the gathering Washington dusk, she had been no wiser.

Perhaps it was the sense of aimlessness which had gripped her since Christmas; the sudden hiatus in a hitherto steady flow of work; the realization, painful as an open wound, that Werner had never intended writing. It was a part of her life which she must put behind her; she must stop harbouring immature and sentimental dreams. Maybe the decision to grow up had helped her to make up her mind to pay this visit.

Or had it been that sentence in Veronica's letter which said that Charles Graham had been inquiring after her? His interest and concern had never flagged, and all at once, it had seemed desirable to be of importance to someone. The gap between their ages, which had looked so vast when she was barely sixteen and he forty, no longer appeared to be unbridgeable. He was now exactly twice her age instead of more than double, and the distance would seem to lessen with every passing year . . . She pulled herself up short. She was being ridiculous. It was almost as if she were thinking of marrying Charles Graham. She took another sip of the hot, sweet coffee.

'What do you do with yourself all day?' she asked Veronica.

'Lunch with friends, visit the hairdresser and the beauty parlour, bridge parties, dress fittings.' She caught sight of her sister's face and laughed. 'Sally, my child, you should see your expression! All starchy disapproval at my hedonistic existence.'

'It does seem a bit pointless, you must admit,' Sally observed bluntly.

'Not altogether. I'm on a number of charity committees. We do very good work. But I suppose you're set on improving your mind. A tour of the art galleries and museums.'

'Well, yes . . . I had hoped . . . I mean, it seems silly to come all this way and go home again, without even seeing the Lincoln Memorial or the Smithsonian.'

Veronica gurgled. She was looking particularly fetching in a cream lace housecoat with fluttering, baby-blue ribbons.

'You're a glutton for punishment, Sal, but don't worry, I've got it all arranged. Of course, you've missed the great social occasion of this Season, Eisenhower's Inauguration. We gave a dinner and dance here on Inauguration Night. Remind me to show you the dress Pete bought me.'

'What did you mean just now; you've got it all arranged?'

Veronica finished her coffee, placed her elbows on the table and clasped her hands together. Over her linked fingers, she grinned at her sister.

'As soon as you cabled to say that you were coming, I rang up Charles. He and his daughter are still staying with Senator and Mrs Graham. I think the boy, Teddy, must have returned to Harvard by now.'

She paused for a moment, lost in thought, and Sally prompted: 'You telephoned Charles Graham? Why?'

Veronica emerged from her reverie. 'To take you around, naturally. He knows far more about Washington than I do, and he's interested, as well. You know how I hate history! As a matter of fact, he volunteered for the job as soon as I told him you were coming. Remember how you once took him around Bristol?'

'Yes.' Sally flushed. 'You shouldn't have accepted his offer, Ronnie. It's an awful imposition. I should be perfectly all right on my own.'

'Rubbish!' her sister exclaimed scornfully. 'I've told you, he wanted to do it.' Her eyes narrowed. 'Sal . . . I always used to think it was Mother he was after, but it wasn't, was it? It was you.'

The colour in Sally's cheeks deepened. 'I don't know what gives you that idea,' she hedged.

'Because I'm not a fool and I use my eyes and ears. You might as well tell me the truth. I intend finding out one way or another, while you're here.'

So the story which had been a secret between herself, her mother and Charles Graham for all those years, came stumbling out.

'There you are,' Sally said finally, avoiding her sister's eyes. 'Not much of a story, after all. I'm sorry to disappoint you.'

Veronica laughed. 'You haven't disappointed me, darling.

158

And I suppose you, you little Puritan, were horrified to find that this handsome, older man was in love with you, when most girls your age would have been jumping for joy.'

'I was only just sixteen!'

'Good God, Sally, I despair of you! I really do! When I was sixteen, I had a more adult approach to life than you do now. Jennifer, too.' Veronica poured herself another cup of coffee with cream and sugar. Sally had already noted that her sister was putting on weight.

'Mummy was shocked.'

'Of course she was!' Veronica was derisive. 'She was shocked to discover that while she was around, a man she'd set her heart on could even look at anyone else, let alone her baby daughter.' Veronica looked curiously at her sister. 'Haven't you ever been in love, Sally? Not even once?'

Sally busied herself rolling up her napkin and restoring it to its silver ring.

'There was Terry Ibbs,' she offered brightly. 'But I recall you and Jenny being just as stuffy as Mummy over that affair.'

'What affair? A spotty little farmhand! Don't give me that! You never cared tuppence for Terry Ibbs.'

'I did have a crush on one of his older brothers when I was younger, but I can't remember now if it was Alec or Ivor.'

'You're begging the question,' Veronica accused. 'There has been someone, hasn't there?' Sally made no reply and Veronica set down her cup and saucer. 'OK. I won't pry.' The black maid, Lily, came in with a tray to clear the breakfast things, and Veronica pushed back her chair. 'I'd better warn you, I'm having a party in your honour, next Tuesday. It's no good groaning. All my friends want to meet my talented sister. That portrait you did of Mrs Voorhees has been greatly admired. So, if you want to buy a new dress, we'll go shopping this morning. You can see *my* Washington first.'

The first week of Sally's projected two week stay was over almost before she realized it. She went shopping and visiting

159

with Veronica, whose friends lionized her in a way calculated to go straight to her head. She had to remind herself sharply on several occasions that the name Sarah Sherwood as yet meant very little in the art world.

Charles Graham called at the Kovaks' home the second day of her visit, and bore her off in the most avuncular fashion possible to see the sights. Not once during that or their many subsequent excursions did he so much as hint at any warmer feelings than those of a very old friend. And Sally realized with a certain cynical amusement that she was disappointed.

Her feet ached from so much walking. She saw Lafayette Square, with its statues of the foreign, Revolutionary heroes – Lafayette himself, Rochambeau, Baron von Steuben and Thaddeus Kosciusko – and its fine equestrian statue of Andrew Jackson. She toured the ground floor rooms of the White House, which were open to public display, rode the elevator to the top of the Washington Monument and admired the breathtaking view, and walked across Potomac Park, although it was too early in the year to see the Japanese cherry trees in flower. She lunched with Charles and Senator Graham in one of the Capitol restaurants and tasted the famous bean soup, visited the Smithsonian Institution and went to the Freer Gallery. At the end of the week, she was exhausted, but happy; and on Saturday evening, she, Veronica and Pete dined with the Grahams at the Georgetown house.

Veronica noted that Sally had taken more trouble than usual with her appearance. She was wearing the dress which Veronica had insisted on buying for her as a belated birthday present; a sophisticated, straight-skirted, pale brown taffeta with a cowl neck. With it, she wore a simple string of amber beads and matching stud earrings, and Veronica's hairdresser had done away with her anachronistic pageboy bob, cutting it to one of the shorter lengths which had become popular during the last few years.

At the dinner table, Sally found herself seated between Pete and Kay Graham, an arrangement artfully supervised by Margery, with the object of reminding her son how close the two young women were in age. Margery had viewed the events of the last week with growing concern, as Charles spent some part of every day in Sally's company, leaving the house with a light step and returning at night, tired out, but obviously happy.

In the beginning, Margery Graham had had no intention of inviting the Kovaks and their guest to visit her; but in the end, her curiosity had got the better of her, particularly after Sally had lunched at the Capitol, and Ewan had spoken of her warmly as a pretty and intelligent girl. Watching her now, talking animatedly to Kay, Margery could see her attraction. Part of it, and not the least part for a man who, until recently, had been tied to a self-centred hysteric, was her quiet assumption that she was of insufficient importance to intrude either herself or her affairs on the general notice. Margery would have preferred her to be a little more pushy. It would at least have given her something to cavil at.

She tried to draw the girl out, to get her to say something about her work, but Sally remained infuriatingly modest.

'I'm truly not that well known yet, Mrs Graham. One of the reasons I'm visiting Veronica now is a lack of sitters.'

'But you're good.'

'I think I'm good, but not everyone might agree with me.'

Sally smiled her cool little smile, and Margery Graham reflected how much she disliked the English habit of self-deprecation.

The conversation became general, with politics inevitably to the fore. The new President and Vice-President were mentioned, Senator Graham nobly subduing his prejudices against Eisenhower and Nixon in deference to Pete's Republican sympathies. Kay, bored, asked Sally if she had seen *High Noon*, and didn't she just adore Gary Cooper?

Sally found Charles's daughter a bright and lively young woman, yet possessing something of her grandmother's forbidding quality. Margery, with her patrician features and Boston accent, frightened Sally to death, although she was determined not to show it. She preferred the Senator, in spite of his tendency to blunt speaking. She wondered what

161

the absent Teddy was like, then frowned to herself. She was
beginning to think about them like a prospective family,
and she was not even in love with Charles Graham. It was,
she realized suddenly, Veronica's fault. For the past few
days, her sister had been talking almost as though, at some
future date, Sally might be settling in Washington. It was
absurd. And anyway, Charles lived in New York.

After dinner, Kay excused herself: she had a prior commitment to some friends, made before her grandmother's
invitation to the Kovaks was issued. Veronica and Margery
Graham, seated side by side on the drawing room couch,
were discussing mutual acquaintances. Pete and the
Senator were arguing about politics, following a taunt of
Ewan Graham's about the split in the Republican Party;
the so-called 'Old Guard' Republicans, led by Bob Taft.

Charles got up from his chair and went to sit beside Sally,
who was seated on the other end of the long velvet couch.

'I expected you to be worn out,' he said, 'but you look
ready and raring to go for another week's sightseeing, as
from Monday.'

Sally laughed. 'I've enjoyed myself,' she admitted. 'And
you owed me something for that day I dragged you all over
Bristol.'

He said thoughtfully: 'That was a long time ago, now.
Eight years.' He had been staring into the flames of the fire.
Now, he lifted his eyes to hers and asked abruptly: 'Have
you forgiven me?'

Despising herself for doing it, she hedged: 'Forgiven you?
For what?'

'For falling in love with you.' His tone was so low that
only she could hear what he said. Nevertheless, she felt
Margery Graham's suspicious eyes on the two of them.

She answered in a voice as quiet as his own: 'Yes. Yes,
of course I have,' and discovered that she meant it.

'I've been wanting to ask you all this past week, but I
hadn't the courage, in case you said "no". I still am in love
with you, you know.'

Sally made no reply. She no longer knew what she felt

162

about him. Seeing him like this, in his proper setting, his own country, had made a difference. And the sort of devotion he was offering her suddenly seemed very attractive. The disparity in their ages could be a plus, not a minus. He would never let her down.

Then, unexpectedly, the longing for Werner overwhelmed her again; a physical ache so strong that she wanted to scream with the pain. Instead, with infinite care, she placed her coffee cup and saucer on the little table in front of her and smiled at Charles.

'We'll talk on Monday,' she promised.

'Aren't you going back to New York?' she asked.

They had done very little sightseeing that morning. They had just walked, on and on, through the raw, bitter cold of the February day, and had stopped now in the little triangular park off 18th Street. Sally stared absently at the imposing statue of Bolivar.

'I don't know yet,' Charles answered. 'There's too much there to remind me of Faith, and I need to forget. My father's urging me to give up publishing and go into politics.'

'Yes, he told me the other day, when we had lunch with him. Do you want that?'

Charles shrugged. 'I don't know what I want.' The cold was making his legs ache. 'That's not true, of course. I want you to marry me. Will you?'

Sally was startled. She had not expected him to get to the point so quickly. Since Saturday evening, she had been prepared for the fact that, sooner or later, he would propose, but she needed time to think.

'Charles . . . I . . .'

He cut in swiftly: 'There's no need to give me an answer yet. Go home, back to England. Think about it. There's plenty of time. I shouldn't have asked you so soon after Faith's death. What is it? Three, four months? But I didn't feel anything for her except dislike and pity. It would be hypocritical to pretend that I did. And I've loved you ever since you were "sweet sixteen". Let's walk again, shall we?'

163

They had gone some way, oblivious to the buildings and traffic around them, before she spoke once more.

'You're right. I have to think about it. I couldn't give you an answer now, even if you wanted one. I'm not in love with you, but I have grown very fond of you these past days.' She was surprised to realize that this was true. Until this visit to Washington, she would have said that, at best, she was indifferent to Charles Graham, at worst, she disliked him. Then she recalled that for a brief while, eight years ago, she had felt drawn to him, until her mother had deliberately shattered her illusions.

'I don't mind if you don't love me,' he told her, quite aware that he was deluding himself, but convinced that once they were married, he could make her love him. He shut his thoughts against the warning voice which whispered that he, of all men, should know that people do not easily change.

'There are your children,' Sally went on, as though he had not spoken. 'They might object to your marrying someone so near Kay's age. And your mother doesn't like me.'

'Nonsense! It's just that she thinks I'm far too old for you. Leave her to me. As for Kay and Teddy, they're grown up. They must be free to lead their own lives, and so must I. The important thing is that you haven't said "no". And you're not in love with anyone else.'

She was silent again. She thought of Werner, but the anguish she had experienced on Saturday night did not return. His image seemed more shadowy than she had ever known it. Perhaps, at last, she had exorcized his memory.

She felt tired and unexpectedly listless. 'Let's get some lunch,' she said. 'I'm starving.' She tucked her hand into the crook of Charles's arm, giving it a friendly squeeze.

Veronica said miserably: 'Do you have to go home tomorrow? Couldn't you cancel your flight and stay another week? It isn't as though you have anyone but yourself to please.'

Sally grinned and stretched her feet to a blazing fire. Outside, it was cold and raining.

'All the more reason why I should get back and drum up some work. When you're self-employed, you don't get paid for idling. Sometimes I wish I was back with the good old Ministry of Labour.'

'No, you don't. You hated it. If money's the only problem, you know very well that . . .'

'No,' Sally answered firmly. 'And I'm quite sure Pete's had enough of his sister-in-law's company. I notice he keeps sneaking off in the evenings.'

'He goes back to the office, that's why,' Veronica retorted acidly. 'Sometimes I wonder which is more important to him, his father's business or me.'

There was an acerbity in her voice which made Sally wonder, for the first time, if everything was all right with her sister's marriage. Veronica was certainly still in love with Pete, as, so far as Sally could tell, he was with her. But she sometimes got the impression that Veronica was lonely, in spite of all her social engagements. She had plenty of acquaintances, but no real friends. She was, moreover, homesick. She had never admitted it in so many words, but Sally guessed from the nostalgic way in which her sister spoke of England. She was looking forward with desperate eagerness to her visit home in the summer, for the Coronation.

It explained, too, why she was so unsubtly trying to prod Sally into accepting Charles Graham, and Sally wondered if she had been wise to tell her sister of Charles's proposal. On Tuesday, at the party she had given in Sally's honour, Veronica had practically thrown her sister at Charles Graham's head. Margery Graham had been visibly annoyed and Kay had looked uncomfortable. Furthermore, Sally had overheard one of the formidable Washington matrons remark to another that Charles seemed hell-bent on cradle-snatching. 'So soon after his wife's death, too.'

After that, Sally had tried to avoid Charles, but when supper was over, he had followed her into the room Pete used as a study, where she had retreated for a moment's peace and quiet. The crescendo of laughter and conversation and the blaring radiogram were making her head ache. Even

Sinatra records could pall when played too loud and too long. Charles had come up to her and taken her hands in his. For a moment, she thought he was going to kiss her, and wondered how she would react if he did. He did indeed kiss her hands, first one and then the other, but that was all. He said gently: 'I shall miss you. Come back as soon as you can.'

She had made no promises, but she had felt a sudden rush of affection for him, which, if she had never known Werner, she might well have mistaken for love.

'Will you come to see me off on Friday?' she had asked.

He shook his head. 'I don't think so. Veronica and Pete will be with you, and I should resent them, wanting you all to myself. Besides, I must go home. There are things I must decide, and I shall decide them better uninfluenced by my parents. Sally,' he had looked earnestly at her, 'promise me that you won't let yourself be swayed by anyone's inclinations but your own. Not mine, not Dorothy's, not your sister's or my mother's. The decision must be yours alone.'

She stared now at the fire, listening with only half an ear to Veronica's voice, wondering what that decision would be. Or would she, once home, simply shelve the responsibility of making up her mind? Would she continue to drift, a prisoner of the ever-fading hope that one day a letter would come from Werner, or that he would turn up in person to claim her? And what would she say if he did? Was her affection for him no longer the real thing, but simply a romantic dream? It was, she decided, time to lay his ghost to rest once and for all. She would go to Germany to find him.

CHAPTER FOURTEEN

Sally's plans, however, had to be delayed. She arrived home to find a letter from Dorothy, announcing that she and Philip had decided to get married at once, instead of in the autumn as they had originally planned.

'It seems ridiculous to wait longer than necessary,' her mother wrote, 'so we asked Nick Horobin to put up the banns. Philip is going to sell that ugly monstrosity of a bungalow and move into Grace Cottage, for the time being, at least. The wedding is planned for Saturday the fourteenth. Saint Valentine's Day. So romantic, don't you think?' Below Dorothy's signature was a postscript. 'PS. Hope you enjoyed your trip to the States. Tell me all about it when you come.'

Sally returned the letter to its envelope with a grim little smile: no formal invitation to the wedding as such, just a calm assumption that of course she would be there. No inquiry after Veronica or Pete. Self-absorbed as always, Dorothy had issued her summons and expected it to be obeyed without question. In a few days' time, Sally, having just returned from America, was expected to be in Cold-harbour. She grimaced to herself, knowing full well that she would be there. She felt a secret gratification in having an ulterior motive: she wanted to consult Philip as to how she should begin her search for Werner.

There were two other communications; prospective clients wishing to make appointments for a sitting and to know her terms. The work was beginning to flow again. She was home.

Still feeling disorientated after the long flight, and more than a little tired, Sally made herself some tea and, leaving her unpacking until morning, fell into bed. Once there, however, she found herself unable to sleep. Too many images kept floating around in her brain; too many questions were demanding an answer.

Instinctively, she pushed the more personal problems to the back of her mind, concentrating on her mother's change of plan. Sally would have expected her mother to postpone her wedding, rather than bring it forward, and wondered what had happened. A superficial answer was that Dorothy had had a row at the office, or was tired of working and had handed in her notice in a fit of pique. But second thoughts convinced Sally that her mother had realized that if she did not marry her cousin at once, she probably would never do so. Sally had never supposed that her mother was in love with Philip, or that the projected marriage was anything to her but an insurance against the loneliness of age.

So Dorothy's heart was at war with self-interest, and self-interest had inevitably won, but she could not allow herself time to think about what she was doing. She would marry Philip and have her regrets afterwards, when it was too late to do anything about them.

The next four days were busy ones for Sally. She arranged first sittings for both her new clients, bought a new suit for the wedding with some of the cash advance, treated her studio and bed-sitting room to a spring clean they did not need, went to the cinema to see a revival of *Limelight*, which she had missed when it was released the previous year, and altogether made certain that she had no time to think or change her mind about going to Germany.

She arrived at Temple Meads station late on Thursday evening and took a taxi to Coldharbour village. It reminded her of the occasion when Charles had taken her home in a taxi during the war, and how scandalized the two women in the Berkeley Café had been... The lights of Bristol dwindled and vanished behind her, as the taxi began its ascent to the village between the crowding hedges and the blown, bare branches of the trees. Then they were approaching the ridge, where the hedges gave place to gently sloping earth banks, scarred with the dark patches of scrub. Sally could just make them out in the blackness, recalling how she and Terry Ibbs used to play hide-and-seek there, when they were children and there was practically no traffic on country roads. Dorothy, scandalized, had put a stop to it when she found out, scolding Sally for behaving like 'a common little girl'.

It had started to rain, and the car tyres hissed softly on the wet surface of the road. The lights of the first cottages appeared above the horizon, golden buds, slowly beginning to flower at their approach. As the taxi lurched round the bend and on to the flat, the whole village was strung out before her, like a daisy chain, under the lamps.

She leaned forward and addressed the taxi driver.

'Drop me at the bungalow next to the church, will you please? Here's the turning, Church Lane.'

The taxi headlights picked out the white name board with its black lettering as the driver swung round the corner and drew up outside Philip's bungalow. Sally paid him and got out, clutching her handbag and overnight case.

There was a glow behind the drawn curtains, indicating that Philip was at home. She opened the front gate and entered the garden, pausing to glance at the For Sale notice board, planted in the earth. It looked so alien that she felt a pang of regret at Philip's leaving the place where he had lived for so many years; as many years as she could remember. Then she told herself to stop being foolish. Philip was getting what he had wanted for most of his life, and she didn't have to worry that he was going into the marriage with his eyes closed. No one understood her mother better than Uncle Philip.

She rang the front doorbell, and after a few moments, Philip answered it. A sudden squall of rain caught him in the face.

'Sally! How lovely! Come in.' He saw her case and raised his eyebrows. 'Haven't you been home yet?'

'No. I got the taxi driver to drop me off here. There's something I want to talk to you about, and I knew I shouldn't easily escape Mother's clutches, once I'd set foot inside Grace Cottage.'

He laughed, kissed her affectionately and led the way through to the kitchen, pausing to switch off the drawing room light.

'Everywhere's a shambles, I'm afraid. The furniture in the front room is under covers until I decide what to do with it. I was just packing up my books when you arrived. But anything that isn't done tonight or tomorrow will have to wait until after the honeymoon. Dorothy's sudden decision to bring the wedding date forward hasn't left me much time to plan things properly. Were you surprised?'

He flicked on the kitchen light. Even there, there were empty spaces on the shelves, packing cases containing cutlery, china and saucepans ranged against one wall. The piece of worn blue carpet, which had made a pathway from sink to back door, had vanished – into the ashbin, Sally hoped.

Philip turned on the electric fire and pulled out a chair from under the table.

'Sit down,' he invited, 'and I'll make us both a cup of tea.' He busied himself fishing cups and a teapot out of one of the cases, and getting his last pint of milk from the larder. 'Well, were you surprised?' he asked again.

'Ye-es. That is, no, not altogether. What I mean is . . .' Sally broke off and cursed herself under her breath. Why did she always have to be so honest? Philip splashed milk from the bottle into the cups, glancing shrewdly at her across the table.

'I know what you mean,' he answered dryly. 'You don't have to explain. However – ' he filled the electric kettle with water from the tap and plugged it in – 'I shouldn't complain. It's what I want. On any terms. Now,' he spoke more briskly, 'you said you needed to talk to me about something. By the way, did you have a good time in Washington? I know I should have asked you that first, not waffled on about my own affairs.'

'I enjoyed myself very much. It's partly because of something that happened while I was there, that I want to talk to you.' She put up a hand and pulled off her soft felt hat. Raindrops fell from it in a sparkling shower.

'Fire away,' Philip said. 'You know that if there's anything I can do . . .' He had no need to finish the sentence.

By the time the kettle boiled, he was in possession of most of the facts; mainly those she had told him, but also a few of those that she hadn't.

While they waited for the tea to brew, he said quietly: 'Sally, dear, if you find Werner and he's married, or engaged to be married, what then? It won't make you more in love with Charles Graham, you know. I can't see what you hope to gain.'

'Peace of mind, I suppose,' she answered slowly. 'It suddenly seems essential to find out why he broke his promise to write. Maybe he found out that he wasn't in love with me, after all. I don't know. The important thing is, how do I start looking for him? He came from Hamburg, but that's a big place, and he may have moved from there. Oh, I realize it's probably a wild goose chase, but I have to try.'

Philip poured the tea and spooned sugar into the cups from a bag. The liquid was brown and very strong, the way he liked it.

'I don't know that I can help you much, my dear. You could make inquiries of the War Office. They must have lists of prisoners-of-war. Or perhaps the Home Office: you should try both, but even then, there may be no records of the men's home addresses. It would have been up to the German authorities to notify the prisoners' families of their capture.' He stirred vigorously to dissolve the sugar in his tea, which he sipped thoughtfully. 'It's really the German records that you want, and so many of them were lost . . . The truth is, Sally, I know no more than you do. But when we get back from Paris at the end of February, I'll make some inquiries.'

'But that'll take months,' she objected bleakly. 'I thought you'd be sure to know what I ought to do.'

171

'I'm sorry to shake your faith in me, but what on earth's the rush? Why this urgent desire all at once to settle your future? Have it all cut and dried? You're young. You're on the threshold of a brilliant career.' But he thought to himself: 'She's lonely. She's never found it easy to make friends.' He reached across the table and held her hand. 'Sally, listen to me. Marrying one man because another doesn't love you, or has fallen out of love with you, or whatever the reason is that Werner didn't write, simply isn't the answer. Anyway, Charles Graham is old enough to be your father.'

And suddenly, Philip could see that that was probably Charles's chief attraction. Without consciously being aware of it, Sally still missed Bill Sherwood; more, perhaps, than either her mother or her sisters. The twins had always had each other, and now they had their husbands. Dorothy was marrying him.

Philip added pressingly: 'Darling, you know you can always make your home with us, if you want to.'

Sally smiled and said absently: 'Yes, I know. Thank you, Uncle Philip.'

She changed the subject, telling him about Washington, about her flights there and back, about her new clients. But Philip could see that her mind was elsewhere. Eventually, she rose and picked up her case.

'I'd better let you get on with your packing, and Mummy will be wondering where I am.' She kissed him. 'Goodbye, Uncle Philip. I'll see you tomorrow, or Saturday, in church. I'm delighted you're going to be my step-father. I shouldn't have liked Mummy to marry anyone else.'

Trudi Rossman cleared the table and carried the dirty plates into the kitchen, stacking them carefully in the sink. This was the time of day she liked best, when the children were safely in bed and Erich was home from work. They were very lucky to have this apartment in one of the new blocks which had gone up in the last couple of years; lucky, too, that Erich had got his old job back, working in the dockyard. Eight years after the war had ended, there were still plenty of people with no proper homes or employment; rootless, drifting people, living in temporary camps.

Of course, things were already much better than they had been in 1945, although Trudi accepted that even then, she had been extremely fortunate. She had been living with her parents, and their house had not been bombed. Nevertheless, she could vividly remember the hunger, the lack of electricity and water supplies, the grey, dusty rubble stretching endlessly, street after street.

Erich had known nothing of that. By 1948, conditions had improved. Reconstruction had started and the tensions between victors and vanquished had eased a little. It was ironic that in many ways he had been better off as a prisoner in England than if he had been at home in Germany. He had once complained bitterly of the newspaper shortage; a single sheet of newsprint appearing just twice a week. In Bristol, he had subscribed to three newspapers a day and four monthly periodicals. Somewhere at the back of Trudi's mind was a suppressed resentment that Erich had not had to suffer as she had done. More overtly, she resented the fact that he still kept in touch with the English woman who had befriended him. Only last week, just because Frau Sherwood had written to say that she was getting married again, Trudi had been obliged to tramp around the shops looking for a card to send her.

Erich wandered into the kitchen and began to wipe the plates which Trudi had put to drain. Her spurt of bad humour died. Her brother and brother-in-law laughed at Erich for what they called 'this mad English habit'.

'All British and American husbands are henpecked,' they mocked. 'You're not a prisoner forced to do the polite thing now, you know, Erich.'

Erich took no notice of them, however, and continued to help with the washing-up whenever the fancy took him. It was true that before his visits to Grace Cottage, like any other self-respecting German male he would never have dreamed of being seen with a tea-towel in his hands. But

173

on those long-gone Saturdays and Sundays, when he had assisted Dorothy or one of her daughters in the kitchen, he had found the act of drying cutlery and china very soothing. So he turned a deaf ear to his brother's and brother-in-law's taunts and continued to lend Trudi a helping hand whenever he felt so inclined.

He and Trudi worked in silence for a while before she suddenly remarked. 'Oh! I forgot to tell you! I saw old Frau Dietrich yesterday. The woman who used to run the delicatessen on the corner of our street.'

Erich tried to look interested and failed. He recalled the shop which had stood at the end of the street where Trudi's parents lived, but the site was now nothing but weeds, with bits of bomb-blasted masonry thrusting through them like broken bones. Frau Dietrich, the owner, he could not remember with any clarity.

'Yes?' he said, seeing how many cups he could balance, one on top of the other, without the column toppling over. 'How is she?'

'She's all right. But she was telling me her son's been in hospital. Appendicitis or something. I forget what she said exactly.' Trudi transferred the last saucepan from the sink to the draining-board and said sharply: 'Don't be foolish, Erich! I don't want any of this china broken. It was my mother's and it's irreplaceable nowadays.' She dried her hands and began putting things away in a cupboard. 'Anyway, it appears there was someone you know in the same ward with Egon Dietrich. Your name cropped up one day in conversation and this man overheard. He told Frau Dietrich he knew you. You were prisoners together. Said his name was – wait for it! – Werner Neumann.'

'Good God!' Erich nearly dropped the plate that he was holding. '*Werner*! Fancy hearing of him after all these years! What was he doing in hospital? Did Frau Dietrich say?'

'I asked her that, but she was a bit vague. Couldn't even tell me if it was serious or not. I did discover that Egon was in the men's general ward. It's that temporary hospital they've put up somewhere near the broadcasting station.'

174

There were so many temporary buildings at present that Erich had to think hard for a few seconds.

'I know the one,' he said slowly. 'I think it's known as the Stockmeyer.' He put down the tea-towel he was holding and moved back into the sitting room. 'I'm going to telephone and inquire about Werner.'

'He may not be there now,' Trudi called. 'This was some weeks ago. Christmas.'

'They might at least be able to give me his present address. Werner! Well, I'm damned! I was certain he must have left Hamburg.'

Trudie heard Erich lift the receiver and went on with the rest of the drying. She could hear the low rumble of his voice through the half-open door. He seemed to be having trouble getting the necessary information, and it was quite a while before he reappeared in the kitchen.

'That took you long enough.' Trudi had her back to him, reaching up to the top shelf of the cupboard, where she kept her plates. 'What was wrong with him, did they say?'

Erich made no answer, and when she turned with an inquiring lift of her eyebrows, Trudi could see that he was white and shaken. He was leaning against the door jamb for support.

'Erich! What's the matter? Is it bad news?' She went to his side, putting an arm about his shoulders.

'He's dead. Werner's dead,' Erich mumbled at last. 'Just after Christmas. It was cancer.'

'Dear God!' Trudi whispered. 'So young.' She had never known Werner, but the dread word 'cancer' was sufficient to enlist her sympathy; and Erich had written a lot about Werner in the old days. They had been as close friends as men of such different temperaments and education could be. Initially, they had been drawn together simply because they were from the same city, but liking and a certain affection had grown between them. It had hurt Erich when Werner had lost contact with him after their repatriation.

Trudi asked: 'Did they give you any details?'

Erich shook his head. 'No. It took them ages to find the

175

records. There'd been some mix up in the filing system, due to illness. I must have spoken to four different people.'

'Come and sit down,' Trudi urged. 'I think there's some whisky somewhere.'

Erich followed her into the sitting room and sank into a chair. Werner! Cancer! He couldn't believe it. Something seemed wrong to him somewhere. But the last nurse he had spoken to had been very emphatic. The patient, Neumann, had died of lung cancer at the beginning of January.

Dorothy's wedding to Philip was a very quiet affair. Even the village evinced very little curiosity. Some people did not realize that the marriage had been brought forward, but many of those who did considered it not worth their while to turn out of doors in the miserable winter weather for an event which they had long decided was a foregone conclusion. Yet others had better things to do with their Saturday than crowd into a badly heated church. The result was a small congregation, and the reception at The King's Head consisted of Sally, Jennifer and Tony, the Reverend and Mrs Horobin, the Youngers and the newlyweds themselves. Sally couldn't help reflecting that it was all very untypical of her mother, and wondered what Philip was thinking.

If his expression was anything to judge by, he was perfectly happy, accepting congratulations as though he truly appreciated his luck, and making a short speech stressing his contentment. Tony, who, as Best Man, was far less at ease, faltered over his words and told a couple of jokes at which nobody laughed. It was obvious that, like his wife and sister-in-law, he was dubious of Dorothy's motives in marrying her cousin.

Jennifer, whose pregnancy was beginning to show, asked Sally: 'What are you doing after Mummy and Philip have left? You don't have to stay at Grace Cottage on your own, you know. You can come back with us.'

Sally shook her head. 'No thanks, Jenny. I'm going straight home to London. But I'd be grateful for a lift to the station.'

'Of course.' Jennifer was so patently relieved at having her invitation refused that Sally almost laughed aloud. Each meeting between the sisters underlined how little they had in common these days; how far they had drifted apart. Jennifer and Tony were absorbed in each other, his parents and the Latham wine importing business. When the child was born, they would be an even more complete family unit. There would be very little room for outsiders.

Sally thought how different her relationship was with Veronica and Pete. During her visit to Washington, they had become great friends. They were welcoming with the open-handed hospitality of most Americans.

The speeches and toasts over, Dorothy and Philip left for Paris, and there seemed no point in the guests hanging around. When Sally returned to the warmth of the pub's private room, after waving her mother and step-father goodbye, the Horobins and the Youngers were on the point of departure. Their farewells, she thought, were rather restrained. Sally's overnight case was still at the cottage.

'Tony's gone to fetch it,' Jennifer said. 'He'll pick us up on his way back and we can go straight into Bristol.' She started to pick at the debris of the buffet meal, spread out on the table. Pregnancy was giving her violent indigestion, which, in it's turn, made her ravenously hungry.

Sally wandered restlessly about the room, pausing at last beside the pile of telegrams and cards which had been brought from the cottage. She leafed through them without much interest. Most of them were from people she did not know. There was a cable from Veronica and Pete, and one from Charles Graham. The rest were mainly from acquaintances of Philip; his publishers, his agent and one or two friends. But right at the bottom was a card made of very cheap paper, displaying an assortment of bluebirds and wedding bells. The wording was in German, and when Sally opened it, she saw that it was signed: 'From Trudi and Erich Rossman.'

Erich! Of course! If she went to Hamburg, she could contact him. He did not know where Werner was, Dorothy

177

had told her so often, but he might at least have some idea how she should set about looking for him. He would know who to contact. Her mother must have Erich's address somewhere. Probably in the red leather address book beside her bed!

'I'm sorry,' she told an astonished and displeased Tony, when he walked in a few moments later, carrying her case, 'but I've changed my mind. I'm going to stop at the cottage tonight, after all. There's some unfinished business I want to take care of.'

CHAPTER FIFTEEN

She could hardly take it in. It was like a bad dream. Werner was dead.

Sally stared down into the street below, at people hurrying home from work, at women laden with shopping. A crowded 'bus passed the end of the road, its interior lights blazing momentarily in the evening gloom, but nothing seemed real any more.

A gong sounded, summoning the inmates of the little guest house to dinner, but Sally did not move. She wasn't hungry. She lay down on the bed, pulling the quilt around her to comfort the sudden shivering in her limbs. Her restless mind went over and over the events of the last few hours.

She had arrived in Hamburg earlier in the day, having caught a morning flight from London airport. As she had expected, Sally had found Erich's address in the book beside her mother's bed, and from that moment, nothing would satisfy her but to get to Germany as quickly as possible. The desire to discover Werner's whereabouts had suddenly become of paramount importance. She had not even stopped to consider the difficulties which lay ahead of her, in a country where she knew nothing of the language. A moment of sanity had prompted her, half an hour before her 'plane was due to leave, to buy an English-German phrase book, but she had not opened it once during the journey.

She had been fortunate, at Hamburg, to find a taxi driver who spoke good English, and who informed her that he, too, had been a prisoner-of-war, in Scotland. He was able to recommend a small, clean boarding-house where English was spoken, the Gasthaus Dreier. During the drive, he entertained her with the story of how, shortly before he was sent home in April 1948, he had hitch-hiked from the Scottish border to London, where he had seen a matinée performance of *Oklahoma* at the Aldwych Theatre.

Sally had protested, laughing: 'But, surely, you weren't supposed to go outside a five mile radius of the camp!'

The driver shrugged. 'In those days, everything so . . . so . . .'

'Lax,' she suggested.

'*Ja*. Lax. You can do anything. Men in my camp marry British girls. Stay on. Nothing here in Germany for them.'

Sally peered from the taxi window. 'It's a lot better than I expected. Last time I was in Germany was just at the end of the war, 1945.'

'Bad then. My family tell me. New money makes things better. Reichsmark out, Deutschmark in.'

She laughed again and overtipped him. At least, she presumed she had overtipped him from the beaming smile he gave her as he pulled away from the kerb.

The Gasthaus Dreier had proved to be everything the driver had claimed for it, and the owner, Frau Dreier, spoke enough English to make herself understood. When Sally had unpacked her case and eaten a belated lunch in the over-furnished dining room, with its heavy Victorian furniture and potted palms, she had set out in another taxi for the Rossmans' apartment, Frau Dreier having obligingly directed the driver how to get there.

The apartment was in one of the new blocks springing up on the city outskirts. As the taxi drew up outside the main entrance, it occurred to Sally for the first time to wonder if there would be anyone at home. Erich would undoubtedly be at work, and she had no idea if his wife worked or not. She did not even know Frau Rossman's first name. She had an idea that it had been on the wedding card, but at the time she had not taken much notice, and now could not remember.

She had, Sally told herself bitterly, acted completely irrationally. She had long ago decided that if Werner did

180

not write, it was because he wished to be free; because the romance, for him, had not outlasted his return to Germany, and she must be willing to let it go at that. Now, here she was, five years later, pursuing him like an avenging fury, determined to track him down. Moreover, she had made no plans; given no thought to anything except finding Werner.

As luck would have it — more luck, Sally acknowledged, than she deserved — Trudi Rossman was at home, having just returned from visiting her parents. She had left the three children in her mother's care for the rest of the afternoon, and was looking forward to putting her feet up and reading a magazine before it was time to prepare the evening meal. The face she presented when she answered the apartment door was not encouraging.

'*Ja?*'

Sally stumbled over: '*Guten Tag. Wie geht es Ihnen?*' before relapsing hopefully into English. 'My — My name is Sally Sherwood. I knew your husband Erich, when he was a prisoner in Bristol.'

Trudi knew very little English, but she recognized the words 'Sherwood' and 'Bristol'. She motioned Sally into the apartment and offered her coffee, a word almost universally comprehensible. Sally accepted gratefully with a heartfelt: '*Danke schön.*'

It was when she mentioned Werner's name and saw the horrified look on Trudi Rossman's face that Sally realized something was amiss. Gradually, with the help of her phrase book and an old German-English school dictionary of Trudi's, the story had been pieced together.

At first, Sally refused to believe it: Werner had always been so strong and full of life. It was impossible to think of him dying of cancer. But slowly, Trudi convinced her. The hospital had confirmed it. How could the authorities be wrong? Eventually, she had thanked Trudi and left, refusing what she recognized more by intonation than understanding, as an invitation to share the Rossmans' evening meal. She would not wait even to see Erich. The overwhelming need was to be alone.

She had walked a long way, through a maze of streets, before arriving, more by accident than design, at the main road and a cruising taxi. She gave the address of the Gasthaus Dreier, amazed at her outward display of self-control, when inwardly she was numbed by grief and shock. Once back in the seclusion of the boarding-house, she went straight to her room and stayed there. No one had seen her come in, so no one would question her absence at dinner.

A flickering pink neon light probed the darkness of the room from time to time, from a café just across the street. Sally found herself counting the seconds between each searching beam; a way of preventing herself from thinking. After a while, she got up and drew the curtains, then curled up once more under the quilt, forcing herself to consider what the news of Werner's death really meant to her.

She had lived with the idea of being in love with him for so long that she was not quite sure where reality began and fantasy ended. Five years without contact of any kind had made him a shadowy figure; someone without substance except in her mind. Their romance had been so brief, so abortive, that she was not even sure any more that she had truly known him, or that the man she was mourning had in fact existed outside of her imagination. If she had met him again after all this time, she might not even have liked him. He might not have liked her.

But he hadn't married. She had specifically asked Trudi that question, making certain she understood by indicating the third finger of her left hand. The other woman had shaken her head: the hospital had told Erich that Werner was single. How long had he known he was seriously ill? she wondered. However long it was, he had made no attempt to contact her.

The news had been the more unexpected because, as far as Sally knew, Erich had known nothing of Werner; had lost all trace of him since their return. Sally had approached the Rossmans merely with the idea of finding out the best way to set about finding Werner.

It was very cold. Sally slid out of bed and switched on

the electric fire. She also put on her coat. All at once, she began to cry; terrible sobs that racked her from head to foot. She felt incredibly lonely; completely isolated from the rest of the world. All these years when she should have been going out with other boys, she had drifted, dreaming of Werner. Now the dream was over and she was alone.

She sat on the floor in front of the fire and the trembling in her limbs gradually stopped. She poured some water into a glass from the carafe on the bedside table, and sipped it slowly. Werner hadn't wanted her, anyway.

She told herself severely that this mood of desolation would pass; that it was partly the result of being alone in a strange hotel, in a foreign city on an icy February night. She had her work and, somewhere in the background, was the comforting presence of Charles Graham. She was conscious of the deliberate avoidance of the phrase 'paternal presence'; but it made her feel comfortable to know that he was there.

She got up from the floor and switched on the light over the dressing-table mirror. From her handbag, she took the vanity bag containing her make-up, and, with a still slightly shaky hand, started to repair the ravages to her face.

'He's never even kissed me,' she thought; then paused, staring at her reflection in the glass, her lipstick poised halfway to her lips. Who had never kissed her? She must have been thinking of Charles Graham, because Werner had kissed her many times. Yet she had had the image of Werner in her mind. How odd that she should have got the two of them mixed up.

She was suddenly aware of an awful lassitude. She needed food and plenty of hot, strong coffee. It was only twenty minutes or so since the dinner gong had sounded. If she went downstairs right away, she would probably not be too late. She could also ask for her bill. She would leave first thing in the morning. There was no point in staying on in Hamburg now.

By the middle of March, Sally found herself something of a celebrity. Her most recent commission, the portrait of a well-known actress, had caused a stir. The lady herself had refused to pay for the picture when it was finished, declaring it was nothing like her, and had been furious when a Bond Street gallery had put it on display. One of her arch rivals had bought it, saying that the mean expression of the eyes and mouth were exactly typical of 'darling Ju-Ju'. The press got hold of the story, and the resultant publicity, plus the fact that the portrait was an extremely good likeness, did Sally no harm at all, and overnight she became mildly famous. For the first time in her career she had more clients than she could cope with. Towards the end of the month, she went home to Coldharbour for a long weekend.

She had not seen her mother and Philip since the wedding, although she had received letters from them both. She had written to tell Philip of her visit to Hamburg and its tragic outcome; a private letter, addressed to the bungalow, which had not yet been sold. She did not want her mother to see it. Sally had never told anyone but Philip about herself and Werner.

It seemed strange to have a man living at Grace Cottage again. It evoked memories of Bill which Sally would rather have forgotten. But if someone had to take her father's place, she preferred that it should be Philip.

Her mother was suspiciously bright. 'Darling! How lovely to see you! Quite a celebrity, nowadays! Bob Younger was speaking to me only the other day about my famous daughter. "So pretty, too," he said.' Dorothy's smile was strained. 'Dear Bob. He always had an eye for the women.'

Sally ignored this. 'Where's Uncle Philip?' she asked.

Dorothy shrugged. 'My dear, how do I know? He ought to be down at the bungalow, finishing the sorting and packing of his things, because until that's completed, we can't sell it. And God knows, we could do with the money. But I expect he's in the garden studio, which he seems to have appropriated as his own. I hardly see him. Being married to a writer is even worse than being married to an artist. Something or other is always gestating, and they have to rush away and write it down before it withers and dies.'

She ran her hands over her hips, which were as slim as ever. 'Do you like my dress? Philip bought it for me, in Paris.'

'You look very well and it's a beautiful dress,' Sally answered levelly. 'It's good to know that you're happy.'

'Who says that I'm happy?' Dorothy opened her brown eyes in a wide, reproachful stare. 'What is happiness, anyway?' she demanded with a dramatic sweep of her arm.

Sally beat a hasty retreat to her bedroom. She was in no mood for one of her mother's philosophical discussions.

Ten minutes later, there was a tap at the door, and Philip's voice called: 'Can I come in?'

'Yes, of course,' she said. As he appeared, she grinned. 'I'm sure it's perfectly right and proper, now that you're my stepfather.' She indicated the chair by the window and perched herself on the end of the bed, swinging one slender, nylon-clad leg.

'Your mother said you were asking for me,' Philip observed, sitting down. 'You look tired. You've had a bad time.'

She did not deny it.

'Stupid, isn't it, after all these years to mind so much? It was like clinging on to the dead. Wasn't there a Spanish queen who wouldn't let her husband's corpse be buried?'

'Yes; she carried it around in a coffin with her, wherever she went.'

'I feel a bit like that.'

'Nonsense! Juana was mad. You, on the other hand, are one of the sanest people I know. If you clung on to the memory of Werner, it was because you loved him.'

'I thought he loved me . . . So you see, people can be mistaken.' She looked at him, in a typical pose, her head tilted a little to one side. 'Mother didn't see my letter?'

'No. Fortunately, she wasn't with me when I visited the bungalow that day. In any case, I should have concealed it. As you can imagine, it came as a great surprise to me to learn that you'd already visited Hamburg.' He smiled. 'Talk about cutting the Gordian knot! I hadn't thought about Erich.'

185

'I didn't, either, until I saw the card he sent you and Mother for your wedding. Even then, I only expected him to be able to give me some advice . . . But I told you about that in my letter.'

'You didn't see Erich, himself? You didn't go back in the evening?'

Sally pushed her hair away from her forehead with a weary gesture.

'There didn't seem much point. Frau Rossman was quite definite. I just wanted to get away from Germany as fast as I could.'

'You couldn't possibly have been mistaken in what Frau Rossman told you? You said she didn't speak much English.' Sally shook her head. 'In that case,' Philip continued, 'I'm very, very sorry. What are your plans now?'

'I shall work.' Sally got to her feet and went to stand beside him, looking down into the garden and the studio-summerhouse at the end. 'And there's still Charles Graham's proposal.'

'You're not seriously considering marrying him?'

'Why not?'

'Because you're obviously not in love with him, for a start. If you were, you wouldn't have been searching for Werner.'

'Werner's dead,' she answered flatly.

Philip took no notice. 'And then there are the practical considerations.' He rose and stood beside her, one hand resting lightly on her shoulder. 'In twenty years' time, you could be a youngish woman nursing an old and sick man.'

Philip's repugnance sounded in his voice, and Sally moved a pace or two away from him, shaking off his hand.

'And I might not be. Charles is very fit. I'm fond of him, and he's in love with me. He can offer me affection and security; two things very much worth having.'

'Can't your mother and I offer you affection and security in equal measure?'

Philip looked so hurt that Sally's antagonism evaporated. She put her arms around his neck, her head resting on his shoulder.

'Of course you can,' she answered, a little too quickly to be convincing. 'But in a different way.' She kissed his cheek and moved back to sit once more on the end of the bed. Philip sat beside her and held her hand.

'Sally, love, just because you've discovered that Werner's dead, you don't have to rush into marriage with someone else. You're only twenty-four. You've all the time in the world.'

'The years go by so fast,' she answered quietly, 'and I'm lonely. Don't look so worried. I have no intention of accepting Charles this minute. But I am considering his offer very carefully, and I must warn you, I shall' probably, at some time or another, accept. I can paint portraits as well in America as I can over here, and earn more money.' She turned to Philip, suddenly appealing, her eyes bright with tears. 'Can't you understand that I've had enough of uncertainty? Of waiting and hoping and being let down? And for what, in the end? Nothing! Emptiness! Death. A great, gaping void in my life where warmth and sharing ought to be.' She attempted a smile. 'And you know that nature abhors a vacuum. You keep telling me I'm young, but at the moment, I feel old and tired and jaded.'

'That will pass, I promise you. No one grieves for ever.'

'Maybe not. I certainly don't intend to.' Sally stood up again. 'Now let's go downstairs, or Mother will be wondering what we're up to.'

It had been a typical March day of sunshine and showers, which had given place, towards evening, to a biting wind blowing in across the docks from the Elbe and, beyond that again, from the wild North Sea. Werner was glad to be home, the door of his small apartment shut and the electric fire glowing on the kitchen wall. He had eaten out, and all he now had to do was to make himself coffee. He set the pot on the gas ring while he reviewed the day's events with satisfaction.

He had been grateful that his job was still open for him after two weeks in hospital with the broken leg, and he was determined to show his gratitude. With persistence and hard work, he had managed to clinch a contract with a string of Danish toy shops which ensured his firm's solvency for some time to come. The Managing Director had been delighted, and Werner had been promoted to Chief Sales Representative on the spot. He could soon think of moving to an even bigger apartment.

The doorbell rang. Werner consulted his watch in some surprise: he was expecting Ludwig Fischer for a game of chess, but not at half-past six. The Fischers ate late, and in this bitter wind, the old man might well not come at all.

The bell was pushed again, urgently, and the note sustained. Werner turned down the flame beneath the coffee pot and went through the living room to the front door.

He had no idea who to expect when he opened it, and was completely taken aback at the sight of Erich Rossman. He had not deliberately avoided Erich since their return to Hamburg, but it was a big city and their paths had never crossed. And he had been content to have it that way.

His greeting was brushed aside as Erich pushed past him into the apartment, where he swung round and said accusingly: 'I thought you were dead!'

Werner gave an uncertain laugh, astounded by the other man's aggressive attitude.

'Well, I'm not, as you can see. Look, Erich, I'm sorry if you think I should have kept in touch, but, somehow . . .' He broke off, at a loss.

'I mean,' and Erich's chin jutted dangerously, 'I really thought you were dead. I was told so by the hospital. And then tonight, they telephoned to say they'd made a terrible mistake. The man who died of cancer was a *Gunther* Neumann. You just had a broken leg.'

'I know I had a broken leg.' Werner was bewildered. 'For God's sake, sit down and explain everything slowly. First, how did you know I'd been in hospital? Why were you inquiring about me? Hang on a minute. I'll get some coffee. I don't know about you, but I could do with a cup.'

Fifteen minutes later, Werner was in possession of the

relevant facts. He said, draining his cup and replacing it on its saucer: 'What a mess. Can't say I'm surprised, though, really. The nurses and staff in general were so hard pressed. But I still can't see – though I'm flattered, of course – why you're so upset.'

'I'm upset,' Erich retorted, 'because Sally Sherwood has been in Hamburg looking for you. She came to see me a few weeks ago, but I was out. Trudi, my wife, told her that you were dead.'

'Sally!' Werner was shaking. 'In Hamburg? Looking for me?'

'Yes.' Erich accepted more coffee. He looked curiously at Werner. 'You know, I half suspected that there was something between you two, but I was never absolutely sure. Trudi said Sally was in a terrible state when she told her the news. She wouldn't stay to see me or anything. Just blundered out. So when I heard tonight that you weren't dead, after all, I badgered the hospital into giving me your address and got over here as fast as I could. Can you get in touch with Fräulein Sherwood? You must know her address.'

'Ye-es,' Werner answered slowly. 'I can remember it.'

Erich echoed sharply: 'Remember it? You mean you've never written to her? Not once since you got home? Nor to Frau Sherwood, who was so kind to us?' His anger spilled over and he shouted: 'What the hell's the matter with you, Werner? Why have you got this chip on your shoulder? The war's been over for years!'

'My mother and sister were both killed,' Werner answered.

Erich calmed down a little and finished his drink. 'I'm sorry. I didn't know. I've wondered, naturally. You're bitter about it.'

'If it had been Trudi, wouldn't you be?'

'Yes, of course. But there were English casualties, as well. Frau Sherwood's husband was killed at Dunkirk.'

'I realize that. But it's different for us Germans. For us, there's the additional burden of guilt. The Jews. The concentration camps. We'll never be allowed to forget them. We'll be the pariahs of Europe for a long time to come. *Our*

189

dead will be forgotten unless *we* keep their memories alive.'

Erich got up and buttoned his overcoat to the chin. 'You think too much, Werner. You always did. And it doesn't get you anywhere. My motto is "Take life as it comes." ' He moved towards the door. 'Well, I've done my bit to put matters right. What course of action you take now is your affair.' Erich drew an old envelope from a pocket and handed it to Werner. 'Here's my address. Now we've made contact again, don't let us lose touch. Come and see us sometimes.' He grinned suddenly and held out his hand, English fashion. 'So long.'

Then he was gone and Werner was left alone with his thoughts.

PART FOUR

Winter 1957 – 1958

How like a winter hath my absence been

CHAPTER SIXTEEN

Sally called: 'Kay, bring Claudine over to this window. She can see better and there's not so much danger of her falling out.' She smiled at her step-daughter's husband, who, with Charles, was pouring champagne, which accompanied the cold buffet lunch. 'It's very good of you, Mitch, to let us all use your office like this.'

Mitchell Everard laughed. 'Hell! It's a pleasure. There won't be any work done today, anyway. Leastways, not until your Queen and Prince Philip have gone by. Excuse me a minute. I'm just going next door to see that the girls have the ticker-tape ready.' He went into the adjoining room and closed the door.

Kay had moved to sit beside Sally at the open window, her daughter, Claudine, perched on her knee. The sill here was one of sufficient height to prevent an active two-year-old from scaling it if she was put to stand on the floor, but not high enough to obstruct the two women's view down the canyon of Broadway. Sally could see the fluttering red white and blue of the Stars and Stripes and the Union Jack, as the flags waved in the October breeze. Crowds of people lined both sides of New York's most famous thoroughfare, waiting patiently and good-humouredly for the Queen of England's motorcade.

Sally had long given up trying to persuade the Americans that Elizabeth II was Queen of Great Britain or the United Kingdom. It was a losing battle, and the Scots, Welsh and Northern Irish would have to wage that particular battle for themselves. Indeed, living in the United States was not as easy as, in her ignorance, Sally had assumed it would be in the months before her marriage to Charles.

It had taken her a year of increasing loneliness to answer Charles's proposal, and it had not been until the autumn of 1954 that she finally said: 'Yes.' During that year, Sally had immersed herself in work, cashing in on her growing reputation, and leaving little time for any kind of social life. If she left London at all, it was only for brief visits home; and even these became fewer as the tensions in Grace Cottage mounted. There were no rows – it might, Sally thought, have improved matters if there had been – only an increasingly unhappy atmosphere. It was obvious that neither her mother nor Philip was wholly to blame, and Sally refused to take sides, much to Dorothy's annoyance. When she tried to unburden her troubles, her youngest daughter simply went back to Chelsea and stayed there.

In spite of her increased affluence, Sally remained at Crosby House, partly because the studio accommodation would be difficult to better, but also because she had no interest in moving; until one sunny autumn morning when she stood in front of her easel, staring at the half-finished canvas under her hand, and wondered what on earth she was doing with her life. And, on an almost spur of the moment decision, she had telephoned Charles in New York.

'Do you still want to marry me?' she had asked him.

Charles, groping through the veils of sleep to a stunned recognition of her voice at six-thirty in the morning, had sat up in bed, his hand excitedly clutching the receiver.

'You must know I do,' he told her. 'Haven't I repeated the question often enough? Every letter, every telephone call for over three years.'

'You've been very patient,' she replied, keeping her tone resolute. 'And now you shall have an answer. I shall be happy to become your wife, Charles, as soon as you like.'

They had been married in St Andrew's church three weeks before Christmas, 1954, and left at once for America. Sally had vacated the Chelsea flat some weeks earlier, and moved back to Coldharbour; and those weeks had largely been spent reassuring Philip that the marriage was what she wanted.

'Everything will be fine,' she said, kissing her stepfather's worn cheek. 'Charles is a very nice man.'

If Philip considered it a less than enthusiastic description of her future husband, he had resisted the temptation to say as much to Sally. Besides, he had problems of his own . . .

There was an increase of noise from the street as people began shouting and cheering. Charles moved across his son-in-law's office to stand by his wife, one arm encircling her shoulders as, together with Kay, they craned over the window sill. Below them crawled the long line of shiny limousines, surrounded by policemen on foot, on horses and on motor cycles. The air was full of whirling pieces of paper; a ticker-tape snowstorm, which Sally had seen so often on the cinema screen but never before experienced first-hand. It was impossible, at that height, to see either the Queen or the Duke of Edinburgh; it was enough just to know that they were down there. It reminded Sally of the day she had gone to see the State Opening of Parliament and of the Coronation procession the following summer, which she had witnessed in the company of Veronica and Pete. She suddenly felt desperately homesick. She suppressed the feeling for Charles's sake, and tried hard not to let her unhappiness show.

'Let me have Claudine,' she said to Kay. 'It will give you a rest.' She took the child in her arms.

The small, pliant body snuggled against hers, and a soft little hand patted her cheek.

'Pitty Sally,' Claudine murmured confidingly. 'Pitty Sally.'

'You're pretty, too, darling.' Sally kissed the smooth, pale skin.

Kay's marriage to New York businessman, Mitchell Everard, had taken place shortly after her father's, and Claudine had been born ten months later, only weeks before Sally's first miscarriage. There had been a second miscarriage at the beginning of this year, and Doctor Foy had advised Sally and Charles to wait a while before they tried again. Sally had been unable to escape the conviction that

195

Charles was relieved. However staunchly he denied it, a child of his own younger than his grandchild was bound to be an embarrassment.

Mitch had come back and was standing behind his wife, watching the motorcade as it slowly disappeared from view.

'Well, that's that,' he said at last. 'Shall we go and eat?'

The front door of the apartment closed behind them and Sally dragged off her hat.

'Thank God for that!' she exclaimed. 'I've never known New York so crowded. I thought we should never get home.'

The coloured maid, Louanne, who had replaced Dorabelle, appeared to relieve her of outdoor things.

'Mr McMasters says tea is ready in the drawing room, Mrs Graham.'

Sally smiled her thanks and preceded Charles into the big room, where tea was already laid out, English fashion, on the oval table. Nothing so alien as tea-bags lurked inside the delicate china pot, and there were freshly baked scones and tomato sandwiches.

Sally grimaced as she and Charles took their places. 'I do wish McMasters would rid himself of the notion that this is what I'm used to,' she protested. 'I can't persuade him that tea at Grace Cottage was a no-cloth, jam-jar on the table affair. Mother and I rarely had time for anything else.'

'If I know Dorothy,' Charles smiled, 'that's a wild exaggeration. Tea was always beautifully laid out whenever I was there.'

'Oh, I suppose . . . For visitors. Mother always liked to impress.' Sally poured two cups of tea and handed one to her husband. 'You know that she and Uncle Philip are coming over to stay with Veronica and Pete for Christmas?'

Charles bit into a scone, having first spread it liberally with butter.

'You told me yesterday. And Mama's expecting us all in Washington, too. You, me, Teddy, Kay, Mitch and Claudine. So it will be a houseful. At least since my father's death there's some extra room.'

Sally said nothing. Senator Ewan Graham had died eighteen months earlier from a massive heart attack, and Sally missed him. He had always been kind to her – was fond of her, she flattered herself – and had never blamed her marriage for Charles's decision not to embrace a political career. Margery Graham, on the other hand, had made little attempt to like her daughter-in-law, making it as obvious as she dared that she held Sally responsible for Charles's decision to remain in publishing. Nor had she attempted to conceal her relief at Sally's seeming inability to bear children.

Charles asked suddenly: 'Would you like your own house in Washington? Then we wouldn't have to stay with Mama every time we're there.'

'Oh Charles! What extravagance!' Sally managed to smile. These perpetual bids to buy more than her affection, that love which Charles was beginning to suspect would never be his, made her feel guilty.

'We can afford it,' he said. 'Besides, an apartment isn't really a home, not in the way that a proper house and garden is. And you've never once complained about living in what was another woman's home, although I'm sure you haven't enjoyed it. You haven't even taken up my offer to redecorate.'

'It would be a shame to alter something that's perfect, just for the sake of it.' Sally sipped her tea. 'And then, I'm at the studio so much.'

Charles pushed a half-eaten sandwich around his plate. 'I think we should do it,' he said. 'You can find a new studio in Washington. I'll keep this place on and use it during the week. I can fly down at weekends.'

'Hey, wait a minute.' Sally put down her cup and stretched out her hand. 'You're moving too fast for me. One minute, out of the blue, you propose we should have a weekend house in the capital; and before I've had time to assimilate that idea, you're talking about us *living* in Washington, and you staying here alone during the week. Are you getting tired of me, Charles?'

'No. It just hit me that after three years of marriage you

ought to have a house of your own. I had no right to bring you here in the first place. I thought your presence would exorcize Faith's ghost.'

'And it hasn't?'

'Not altogether. Perhaps that's not quite the truth.' He looked at her, a little frown creasing his brows. 'I get the impression sometimes that it's not the memory of Faith that comes between us. There are times, especially when we make love, I feel you are not seeing me at all, but someone else.'

'Nonsense!' she retorted stoutly, getting up from the table and moving to stand beside his chair. She leaned forward, slipping her arms around his neck. 'All the same . . . Yes, I'd like to live in Washington. I'd be close to Veronica and Pete. And perhaps proximity would help your mother to like me better. I could specialize in portraits of Senators and their wives.'

She despised herself for clutching so gratefully at this chance, so unexpectedly and generously offered, of leading partially separate lives. She wondered what had prompted Charles to make the suggestion. Uneasily, she suspected another bribe.

She had thought, naïvely, before she married, that she could give Charles everything he needed, even if she did not love him. She was fond of him; admired and respected him. Surely he would be content with that. But she had quickly discovered that her husband was a passionate man, and passion – her passion – was the one thing lacking in their relationship. Sally had tried, when they made love, to simulate, at least, some of the emotion she had experienced with Werner, but it was impossible. What she felt for Charles was a deep-rooted, filial affection, so akin to what she had felt for her father, that the act of sex seemed, at times, almost incestuous. Within a month of her wedding, Sally knew that she had made a disastrous mistake.

Her whole life, since then, apart from her work, which she loved and which was flourishing, was geared to keeping Charles as much in ignorance of her true state of mind as possible. He had been through one terrible experience with Faith: if Sally could help it, he should not suffer the second time because of her ignorance and error.

But in spite of all her good resolutions, she was not strong enough to refuse the offer he had just made her. The thought of having to maintain the pretence only at weekends was too great a temptation to resist.

He reached up and patted her cheek. 'Good,' he said. 'That's settled then. We'll fly down this Saturday and start house-hunting. Would you object to Georgetown, if we could find a property there? I know it would be near my mother, but it's the loveliest part of the city.'

'I shouldn't mind a bit,' she assured him. 'Now, if we're going out to dinner, I must go and get dressed.'

He watched her vanish through the door with a sense of elation. This time, he really believed that he had found the answer to making her happy. He should never have stayed in New York, let alone in this apartment, once they were married. It had been not only foolish, but wrong not to make a fresh start. A home of her own in Washington, near to her sister, was the obvious solution, and he cursed himself for not seeing it before. It would mean separation for five nights of most weeks, but even that could work to his advantage. It might help Sally to sort out whatever inhibition it was that prevented her from loving him as he desired.

Charles poured himself more tea from the nearly cold pot, then grimaced distastefully as he sipped the tepid liquid. He pushed the cup away. He, too, must go to get dressed. He and Sally were dining tonight with Mr and Mrs de Courcy; and the publishing house of de Courcy was far more thrusting and publicity conscious than Lodge and Berryman. Moreover, Charles, at fifty-three, was finding it less easy to compete in a world of increasingly younger men. But there was the chance of a partnership and he wanted it badly, for his own self-esteem, but most of all to impress Sally.

Sally . . . She had rarely been out of his thoughts for so many years, he had wanted her so desperately since she was

199

little more than a child, he could not bring himself to admit that his marriage to her was a disappointment. He could sense that under the gentle, loving creature who submitted to his embraces, there was a passionate and exciting woman, but he could not reach her. He shut his mind against the thought that perhaps he never would. There had to be an answer; something he had, or had not done; something he was able to do. Today, watching her face instead of the motorcade below, he had come up with what he thought was the solution, one he should have considered long ago. He was so convinced that it was the answer to his problems, that he whistled to himself as he made his way to the bathroom for a shower.

Philip walked through Broadway into Victoria Street and made for the Albert pub. He had been visiting his agent in Tothill Street, delivering his new typescript in person because there were one or two points he had needed to discuss, and now he was hungry. He was planning a new biography of Mary, Queen of Scots, and after he had eaten, he walked back across Dean's Yard to Westminster Abbey, in order to take a look at her tomb.

It was years sinse he had set foot inside the Abbey; not, he thought, since he was at school and had visited it with a second form party. The soaring French Gothic of Henry the III's eleventh century building left him literally and figuratively cold; a musty, echoing barn of a place, filled with sightseers and overseas tourists, each one with a guide book clutched in his hand. Even the beautiful Henry VII chapel, with its Torrigiani black and white touchstone tomb, failed to move him. He spared a glance for the tombs of Mary and Elizabeth Tudor, although only Elizabeth's had an effigy, and walked around to look at Mary Stewart's, with its painted and gilded wood and stone. He shivered. The place depressed him and he wished he had not come. For Philip, there was some spiritual lack in the great English cathedrals and abbeys; something which the Reformation had destroyed.

He suddenly wanted to get home, back to Dorothy. He

missed her when they were apart. He had asked her to come with him, but she had refused.

'I know your idea of a day in London,' she had jeered. 'Poking about among a lot of musty old buildings and museums. No, thank you. When I go, I'll go to do some shopping and see a show. I might get Jenny to go with me.'

She knew as well as he did that her daughter would decline any such invitation. With three children to look after and a large house to run, Jennifer was totally absorbed by home and family. She had become, as Dorothy once commented acidly to Philip, 'the complete *Hausfrau*. Dowdy and just a little bit boring.'

Philip moved towards the west entrance and the Jerusalem Chamber. *But bear me to that chamber; there I'll lie; in that Jerusalem shall Harry die*. The quotation went through Philip's head almost in the same instant as he noted the man staring down at the tomb of the Unknown Warrior. Something about the stance, the way the fair hair grew on the nape of the neck, was familiar to him, stirring a chord of half-forgotten memory. Then the man turned and Philip saw the faint tracing of old scar tissue on the left cheek, the bright blue eyes. He licked his lips and formed the word: 'Werner!' But he made no sound. The German moved swiftly towards him, taking his arm.

'Mr Jackson. Please. Sit down. You look as though you have seen a ghost.'

'I have,' Philip croaked. 'I thought . . . I was told you were dead.'

Werner said nothing, but with a supporting hand under the older man's elbow, guided Philip into one of the rows of seats placed in the nave. He kicked two of the hassocks out of the way and pushed Philip's head between his knees.

'Is your friend OK?' An American lady hung solicitously over them, the inevitable camera swinging from a strap around her neck.

'Yes. Yes, thank you. He will be all right now.' Werner smiled confidently up at her, and, with an anxious, backward glance, she moved away.

201

With an effort, Philip pulled himself together and sat upright. He said slowly: 'Sally believes that you are dead.'

Werner stared down at his hands, now clenched together in his lap. 'Yes, I know,' he answered.

'You *know*?'

'Yes. Erich came to see me a week or two after Sally had been in Hamburg. I had been in hospital. A broken leg.' Briefly he outlined what had happened, concluding: 'So, when he was told a mistake had been made, Erich got my address from the hospital and came to see me at once.'

'And you did nothing? Werner, I don't understand. Why did you never write to Sally? You seem to have cut yourself off from Erich, as well. What was the point of it all?'

'We cannot talk here,' Werner said. 'I am staying at a hotel near Eaton Square.' He glanced at his watch. 'I have a business meeting at three o'clock, but that gives us an hour and a half. I will buy you a drink at my hotel. I owe you an explanation.'

'Not me,' Philip replied grimly, getting a little unsteadily to his feet: he was not as young as he was, and shocks were bad for him. 'Sally.'

'How . . . How is she?'

'She's married and living in New York. Do you remember Charles Graham? The American. You met him once or twice at Mrs Sherwood's. By the way, she is now Mrs Jackson. We're married.'

Werner muttered something that could have been congratulations, but his mind was still on Philip's previous disclosure.

'That old man!' he exclaimed contemptuously.

'He's four years younger than I am,' Philip responded, nettled.

'But old for Sally. She is . . . what? . . . twenty . . .?'

'She's almost twenty-nine.' Philip's tone was dry. 'You haven't seen her for a very long time.'

Werner's eyes dropped again. 'No. Please, let us go.'

They were silent for most of the walk along Victoria

202

Street. Only once did they speak, when Philip asked Werner what he was doing in London.

'I am here on business. I work for a toy manufacturer. I am having talks with representatives of one of your toy shops. I fly back to Hamburg tomorrow.'

No more was said until they were settled in a couple of armchairs in the lounge of a small commercial hotel, just off the King's Road. Werner went to the bar and came back with two double whiskies and a jug of water, which he placed on the glass-topped table between them.

'So? Why did you never write to Sally?' Philip asked again. 'Even if you found you weren't in love with her, it would have been kinder to tell her so.'

'I was in love with her. I still am. There has never been any other woman for me.' Werner's voice was so low that, for a moment, Philip thought he could not have heard him correctly.

Then he spluttered: 'But for God's sake, why then? Why didn't you get in touch with her? Can't you imagine what the uncertainty, the waiting, was like?'

Werner twisted his glass between his hands, watching the refracted golden light.

'I know. It was just . . . I could not marry her, but I could not make myself, either, to give her up.' His English was so good that the odd grammatical slip was like an unexpected bump in a smooth, straight road. 'My mother and sister were killed.'

'Ah! I'm sorry. Naturally you were – are – bitter. And at what you found in Germany.'

'You begin to understand. I am grateful. Not all Germans understand. Not those like Erich, who were lucky. Erich lost nothing; not his wife, not her parents, not his parents, not one member of his family. I could not bear to be with those persons. I had lost everything.'

'Couldn't you try to explain that to Sally?'

Werner sipped his whisky. The lounge was very quiet. Most residents were in the dining room, finishing their lunch.

'Perhaps. But it was not only that. There were other

203

things. Belsen. Auschwitz. Dachau. Six million murdered Jews.'

'And you feel responsible?'

'Guilty, I think. Also . . . cut off from the rest of human-kind. How long before people stop pointing the accusing finger at us?'

'You're exaggerating, surely. People are already beginning to forget.'

'They may trade with us – Europe needs a strong West Germany as a bulwark against the Eastern bloc – they may also forgive us in time. But they won't forget. Also, my country is now two countries. That might have been avoided, I think.'

Philip rested his elbow on the table and cupped his chin in his hand. 'You, also,' he said, 'find it hard to forgive and forget.'

'In thirty years, there have been two wars fought between our peoples. Such a legacy of bitterness and hate.'

'Then isn't it time for reconciliation? Isn't it worth trying to forget?'

Werner drained his glass. 'You were at Nuremberg. Do you find it easy to do so?'

Philip sighed and finished his drink. 'No,' he admitted.

'And Sally was with you. I don't suppose she has forgotten.'

Philip had a train to catch and he could not prolong the conversation, much as he would have liked to have done so. He made his excuses and rose, holding out his hand.

Werner took it, asking: 'Will you tell Sally that you have seen me? That, after all, I am still alive?'

Philip hesitated. 'No, I don't think so,' he said, after a moment or two. 'I told you; she's married. It wouldn't be fair to her husband.' He smiled sadly. 'Because she's still in love with you.'

CHAPTER SEVENTEEN

'With my love.' Charles handed Sally the oblong package wrapped in shiny Christmas paper, tied with silver ribbon and an elaborate bow. 'I decided not to wait until tomorrow to give it to you. I thought you could wear it tonight.'

Sally, seated at her dressing-table, combing through her short, fashionably cut and styled hair, opened the package with reluctant fingers. As soon as she saw the flat, blue leather case and the famous name picked out in gold, she knew that her worst fears were realized. It was yet another expensive piece of jewellery; yet another attempt, like this lovely Georgetown house, to force from her what she could not voluntarily give him.

Inside the case, on a bed of paler blue satin, was a narrow rivulet of diamonds, fastened by a clasp set with tiny sapphires. It was beautiful and, as always, in the most perfect taste. Charles took it out of the box and clasped it round her neck.

'Oh, Charles, you shouldn't spoil me so. It's gorgeous.'

She got up from the stool and put her hands on his shoulders, kissing him gently on the mouth. His arms slid round her waist, holding her tightly against him. He returned her kiss savagely, bruising her lips. She tried to respond with equal fervour, but couldn't. He felt her flinch and released her with an angry little laugh.

'Charles,' she said desperately, 'I'm sorry. I do try.'

His expression softened. 'I know. It'll come in time.' He was reassuring himself rather than her. 'And you'll be the prettiest woman at your sister's tonight. That dress suits you.'

'Thank you. It's the new "A" line. It hides all the imperfections of my figure. The blue matches the sapphires in your necklace. I wanted black, but it doesn't suit me. Black is so much more sophisticated. However . . .' She realized that she was babbling and made more of an effort to control her tongue. She turned back to the bed to pick up her fur stole and evening gloves. 'See if the others are ready, darling, will you, while I find my purse?'

He nodded and left the room. Sally sat down once more on the dressing-table stool and hid her face in her hands.

Charles had been delighted when they found this lovely house with a room at the back which could be converted into a studio. He had been so sure that this move to Washington would do the trick; that the civilized atmosphere of the capital, her proximity to her sister and the excitement of furnishing and redecorating her own home would make gratitude burgeon into love. Sally had hoped so, too, but, instead, it had only made matters worse. The freedom of her days, but particularly of her nights, Monday to Thursday, made it harder to welcome him with any pleasure when he returned from New York on Friday evenings. She wondered if Charles had guessed that her pressing invitation to Kay and her family, to Teddy and his girl-friend, to join them for Christmas, rather than impose themselves on her mother-in-law as originally planned, was really a safeguard against being alone with him for the holiday period. Charles was no fool: it was not easy to deceive him.

Sally took her brocaded evening purse from the drawer where she had left it, slipped the mink stole around her shoulders, made sure she had both long gloves and went downstairs. She must not let any mood of self-criticism or depression mar this Christmas Eve when, for the first time in years, she and most of the family would be together. Her mother and Philip had arrived in Washington the previous day, and Sally had not yet seen them.

Kay looked up and smiled as Sally entered the dining room, where the others were already assembled.

'Claudine is nearly asleep. Louanne is singing to her. You

look great, Sally. I love the dress.' Her eyes took in the necklace. 'Hey! Pop's been splashing out again, by the look of it!'

Teddy slouched over to kiss his step-mother. Since graduating from Harvard Law School, he had entered a Chicago-based law firm as, in his own words, 'general factotum and dogsbody'. Charles and Sally saw very little of him, even though, like his sister, he seemed never to have resented his father's second wife. Whenever he did put in an appearance, it was usually with some extremely beautiful, but dumb blonde in tow. The latest in a long line of 'Teddy's broads', as Kay insisted on calling them, was named La Verne.

'Like in the Andrews Sisters,' she had explained with a high-pitched giggle.

Mitch Everard also kissed Sally's cheek and said with a sly grin, because he knew how much she disliked it: 'Hello, step-mother-in-law.'

Sally could never accustom herself to the way in which the Graham family constantly touched and kissed one another. They had only been out of one another's sight for just over an hour, while they dressed for Veronica's party, and here they all were, greeting her as if they had been separated for weeks. Looking back, Sally could see that Dorothy had always discouraged too much physical contact between herself and her daughters. Perhaps that was what was wrong with her, Sally thought. But she hadn't felt that way with Werner . . .

She mustn't think that about Werner. He was dead and gone; a fragment of the past. She buried his memory again, as deeply as she could.

'Right,' Charles said. 'If everyone is finally ready, shall we go?'

The car journey across Washington was pleasant, under a bright, clear sky, peppered with stars. The house itself was crowded, bulging at the seams, and the noise was deafening. A famous band had been engaged for the evening and was belting out *Love and Marriage* as the Grahams entered through the front door, which was standing open. In spite of the cold outside, the house was like a furnace, the heating going full blast.

Veronica, who had put on more weight, and was wearing a most unsuitably revealing Jacques Griffe sheath, pushed through the crowd to greet them.

'Sally, darling! Kay! Go on up and leave your outdoor things. One of the maids'll show you which bedroom.' The wave of her hand, clutching an Old Fashioned in a pink-tinted glass, also embraced La Verne. 'But hurry down. Mother's dying to see you.'

Sally thought Veronica's remark a probable exaggeration, and she was proved correct after fighting her way downstairs into the cream-panelled drawing room, where Dorothy was sitting on a couch, discussing the present state of the British theatre with a charming, white-haired Senator from one of the Southern States.

'It's all this kitchen-sink rubbish, nowadays,' she was lamenting as Sally approached. 'Ever since the success of that awful Osborne thing, *Look Back in Anger*. Every playwright in Britain wants to jump on the bandwaggon and be an Angry Young Man.' She half-turned, in order to give the Senator the benefit of her left profile and saw her daughter out of the corner of her eye. 'Darling,' she said coolly, 'how lovely to see you.'

With obvious reluctance, she introduced Sally to her companion, and was plainly annoyed when the Senator gallantly insisted on leaving them alone together.

'Such a courteous man,' Dorothy murmured, as Sally squeezed into the vacated seat beside her. 'So interesting and intelligent.'

Sally pecked her mother's cheek. 'Where's Philip?' she asked.

Dorothy shrugged. 'My dear, I don't know. Pete took him off somewhere, just now, probably to the bar.' Her eyes focused sharply on the diamond necklace. 'My, my!' she remarked caustically. 'You must have been a good girl.'

Sally felt herself blushing, and hurriedly sipped the cocktail she had obtained from a passing waiter. Her mother seemed to be growing increasingly bitter. Her looks were fading, too. The eyes were as brilliant as ever, and for a woman of fifty-three, there was surprisingly little grey in the still abundant dark hair. But the face had thinned. The cheeks sank in below the bones, which now stood out with a skeletal prominence. The careful make-up was not quite careful enough, the heavy rouge and eye-shadow only accentuating the increasing gauntness of the features.

But Dorothy was as elegant as ever in a dark green velvet cocktail dress and matching shoes. Diamonds gleamed in her ears. Sally remembered the earrings as a pair which her father had once bought for Dorothy's birthday. She could not recall which one, and decided it would be tactless to ask.

Having glanced around the room to see what, if any, attention she was attracting, Dorothy switched her eyes back to her daughter. Sally became uncomfortably aware that she was being scrutinized intently by her mother.

'Is something wrong?' she inquired at last.

'No . . . I was just thinking what a dark horse you've turned out to be, that's all.'

'I don't understand you. What do you mean?'

'Oh . . . nothing. All this. Marrying money. Becoming a successful painter. I suppose that's what I meant.'

Sally peered at her mother, but Dorothy's face was bland. Yet there was some expression of the eyes which suggested a secret with difficulty suppressed. But what she could know, Sally found it impossible to imagine. She decided she was being fanciful.

'Let's look for Charles,' she suggested. 'I think he went into the breakfast room. Oh, and there's Kay with Teddy.'

Dorothy dutifully rose and followed her daughter through the crush. It had taken all her willpower not to reveal that she knew about Sally and Werner. On his return from London to Coldharbour, Philip had still been so shocked that, without thinking, he had blurted out to Dorothy the fact that Werner Neumann was still alive, forgetting for the moment that she had not known that he was supposed to be dead. And he had compounded this error by adding: 'Don't tell Sally.'

After that, Dorothy had prised the whole story out of him, bit by bit, until she was in full possession of the facts. She had been by turns indignant, at having been kept in the dark, angry, for not having realized what was going on under her own nose, and deeply jealous that the youngest and, in her estimation, plainest of her daughters should once again have proved to be more irresistible than herself. It had always annoyed her that Werner, unlike Erich, had never fallen victim to her charms, but she had explained away the phenomenon with a number of perfectly satisfactory reasons. It had never occurred to her, not even after the lesson of Charles Graham, that he might have been attracted to Sally.

Philip had forbidden her, on pain of his greatest displeasure, to indicate to Sally, either by word or look, that she knew anything at all of the matter. Dorothy had agreed with reservations. If, at any time, she could use the knowledge, or turn it to her advantage, she would not hesitate to do so. She knew that Philip had a temper when roused, but she was not afraid of him. Indeed, on reflection, she thought it might be quite exciting to make him angry. It would make her marriage less boring if, occasionally, she and Philip could have a row. It would add a little spice to her existence.

'Do you intend telling Sally that Werner is alive?' she had asked during the trans-Atlantic flight, as they were nearing their journey's end.

'No,' Philip had answered shortly.

'Does Charles know about Werner?'

'I have no idea. That's Sally's business. There isn't that much to know. Not the way you make it sound. You brought her up too well for that.'

'Just be thankful that I did,' Dorothy replied virtuously, at the same time wondering uneasily if Philip had any idea that she and Charles Graham had once been lovers.

The same thought occurred to her again as she kissed her son-in-law's cheek. Her son-in-law! How absurd that a man the same age as herself should bear that title.

'You're looking very well, Charles.' She smiled at him from beneath her lashes. 'Veronica tells me that we're dining with you tomorrow.'

'Yes. I thought it would be nice for Sally to have a real family Christmas, to celebrate our new home. Did you have a good trip? How long are you staying?'

'A month, at least. Longer if Veronica gets her way. Our previous visits have been much too short.' Dorothy smiled and patted his hand. 'And now, if you'll excuse me, I must speak to Pete's parents. I can see them on the other side of the room.'

She turned and jostled her way to the far door. Sally and Charles were left standing, side by side. He put an arm about her to protect her from the crush, and she smiled up at him, gratefully.

'I should prefer not to be sent to America,' Werner repeated obstinately. 'Isn't there anyone else who can go?'

'This is an important contract, Werner. Probably the most important we shall land this year.' Kurt Gabler stared across his desk at the man sitting opposite him, nonplussed by this untypical behaviour. Normally, Werner was not only willing but eager to go anywhere, do anything, in the interests of the firm. Now suddenly, he was acting as though being asked to make a journey to the United States was synonymous with being asked to visit the moon. Kurt could not understand it. If he could go himself, he would. America! The land flowing with milk and honey! 'We need the best man we've got out there,' he urged. 'This new line's good, excellent in its way, but it might take a bit of pushing. You're the only one whose English is up to it.'

Werner looked out of the window, at the snow feathering across neighbouring rooftops, at the winter sunlight glancing off frost-encrusted eaves. Through the badly fitted windows, he could hear the harsh, grieving cry of a seagull and smell

211

the crisp tang of the sea, wafted inland by a vagrant breeze.

'I don't know New York,' he protested feebly. 'I've never been there. I don't know America at all.'

It was no excuse, and he knew it. It didn't surprise him at all that Kurt's initial amusement was rapidly giving way to anger.

'You'll go and like it,' the Managing Director snapped. 'Anyway, our contact's not in New York. He's in Washington. And the war has been over now for nearly fourteen years.'

'I wasn't thinking about the war,' Werner answered slowly. 'Why didn't you say before that it was Washington? Of course I'll go.'

Kurt Gabler blinked, confused by this abrupt change of attitude, but nevertheless relieved. An odd chap, Werner, in many ways. Secretive; not a man you could easily get to know. Kurt wondered – or, to be accurate, Frau Gabler wondered and passed her thoughts on to her husband – why Werner had never married. It must be an isolated and lonely existence living in that apartment, all by himself. Of course, he had been a prisoner-of-war in England for many years. Perhaps that captivity had left its mark. Not like being a prisoner of the Russians: very few of those men had ever returned to Germany; but a traumatic experience, none the less. Kurt silently thanked God that he had been too young to fight in the first war and too old for the second. He returned to the matter in hand.

'That's settled, then. Splendid. Everything's arranged. You should be in Washington by the second week in January. And I repeat, this toy is good. If the Americans do decide they want to manufacture it under licence, we want a decent price. But I know I can rely on you for that.'

Werner nodded and went back to his office, closing the door. There were some letters to be dictated to his secretary, but they could wait. He had seen this American visit looming and had hoped that he would be able to wriggle out of it. He did not want to run the risk of running into Sally, which was possible, even in a city the size of New

York. But now that he had discovered the destination to be Washington, it didn't seem to matter any more.

And yet the feeling of disappointment, of wretchedness, was so strong that he needed to be by himself for a while. The last thing he needed was his elderly and devoted secretary fussing over him, asking him what was wrong. He went across to his office door and locked it. Then he returned to his desk and sat down.

Since that meeting with Philip Jackson in London at the beginning of November, there was hardly a waking hour of the day or night when Sally was out of his thoughts. The ache, the longing for her had grown into an obsession with the knowledge that she was married to another man. And to Charles Graham, of all people! The US Army Major, whom he had first seen around Coldharbour village during that last winter of the war!

It was useless to tell himself that he had had his chance to marry Sally and deliberately thrown it away. It was equally pointless to remind himself that a marriage between them might not have worked out, haunted as it would have been by forty years of prejudice and suspicion. And they were too alike: they both, as Erich had accused him of doing, thought too much. Neither had that carefree attitude towards life which would have smoothed their path. Yet he knew now that it would at least have been worth the effort to try; that he had let something infinitely precious slip through his fingers.

As the ormolu clock on the mantelpiece struck midnight, glasses were raised. Philip hugged Sally and kissed her cheek.

'Happy New Year, my dear! And a happy birthday.'

'Yes, happy birthday, love.' It was Veronica's turn to embrace her sister and Pete followed suit. There was a general chorus of congratulations and the rustle of paper as gifts were produced. Charles moved amongst his guests, refilling their glasses.

Sally had insisted that, like Christmas, this New Year's Eve party should be a family affair.

213

'There will be quite enough of us without inviting out-siders. Although we'd better ask Pete's parents, I suppose.'

Charles had felt that the combination of Mrs Kovaks, his own mother and Dorothy would be potentially explosive and easier to control in a larger crowd, but in the end he gave in.

'Whatever you want,' he had said, ruffling her hair.

So far, the three older women had behaved themselves, only occasionally unsheathing their claws.

Mrs Kovaks said now to Sally: 'It must be very convenient, having your birthday on New Year's Day. No one can forget it.'

Sally, who was still unwrapping presents, laughed. 'Mummy obviously had a fixation with festivals. Veronica and Jennifer were born on November the fifth.' Pete's mother looked blank, and she added in explanation: 'Bonfire Night.'

'When Guy Fawkes and the Catholics tried to blow up Parliament,' Dorothy murmured dulcetly. She was perched on the arm of a chair, slender legs crossed to give a provocative display of fine, dark nylons. 'You Catholics have always been a thorn in our side. Look at the Irish.'

'I should have thought,' Mamie Kovaks retorted hotly, 'that whatever happens in Ireland is the fault of the British!'

And they were all away, in a noisy babel of argument just as Dorothy had intended, with Margery Graham, of old Convenanting Presbyterian stock, condemning the Pope, the Vatican and the whole College of Cardinals; Veronica noisily challenging her husband, who came to the defence of his mother; Teddy and Kay putting forward the theory that all religion was hokum; while Sally, Philip and Mitch Everard tried, without much success, to cool things down and sound the voice of reason. Teddy's girlfriend, La Verne, sat with her lovely mouth open.

Dorothy slid off the arm of the chair and touched Charles on the shoulder.

'Let's leave them to it, shall we?' she asked. 'I'd love to see the rest of the house. I didn't get much of a chance when we were here on Christmas Day.'

214

Charles, who hated arguments, a legacy from his first marriage to Faith, was thankful to escape, and led the way out of the drawing room, just as Veronica changed tack to bring in the race riots at Little Rock, Arkansas, the previous summer.

'How you Americans can be so self-righteous . . .' she was saying accusingly to her mother-in-law as Charles closed the drawing room door. The rest of the sentence was mercifully lost.

'Did you start that on purpose?' Charles demanded, and Dorothy laughed.

'Now would I do a thing like that? Don't bother with the kitchen. I've seen it. And most of the ground floor. The first floor, I think you call it over here. Let's go upstairs.'

'Sally would make a much better guide,' Charles protested, as he mounted the elegantly curving flight of stairs behind his mother-in-law.

Dorothy glanced down and over her shoulder. 'I doubt it. Not for what I have in mind.' Her tone was suggestive. She led the way into the nearest bedroom, switching on the light, and turned to face him.

His eyes were wary. 'Look, Dorothy, I don't know what you're up to . . .'

'Oh yes, you do.' She advanced and put her arms around his neck. 'You and Sally aren't happy, Charles. That's quite apparent to me, even if other people pretend not to notice.' She rubbed one leg against his. 'You made a mistake, you know, choosing the daughter and not the mother. We had something very special going for us once. Why not again?'

'Because we're both of us married to people we happen to be fond of. I am at least.' He made an attempt to push her away.

'Fond!' Dorothy repeated scornfully. 'What a pale, unimaginative word! Like "nice"! I like a man who excites me, and you always did that.' She released him suddenly, moving fretfully to the other side of the bed. 'Why didn't that wife of yours kill herself sooner, when you were still in love with me?'

'I was never in love with you,' he answered roughly. 'I've never felt for anyone what I feel for Sally.' His palms were damp and the sweat was pricking at his body, inside his shirt.

'Sally! Sally! Why is it always her men fall for? In spite of what Bill used to say, I never thought she was as pretty as her sisters.'

Charles frowned. 'What do you mean, "men"? Sally told me . . . I always understood that there wasn't anyone else. She never seemed to have any men friends.'

Dorothy bit her lip, struggling with the temptation to tell him all about Werner. But the prospect of Philip's anger deterred her, although she was not quite sure for how long. She was not used to accepting orders, even in the interest of self-preservation. And it might be exciting to provoke Philip's rage. For the moment, however, she was prepared to be good. She moved back to stand by Charles once more.

'Forget Sally,' she urged. 'She isn't making you happy. I can tell that. Remember the afternoons at Grace Cottage? It would be pleasant, just one more time, before I go home, to renew old acquaintance. What do you say?'

Charles said nothing, he simply laughed. Then he swung on his heel and left the room.

CHAPTER EIGHTEEN

Sally threw down her paint brush, wiped her hand on an oily rag and swore. The half-finished portrait on the easel in front of her was not going well. Her subject, a Senator's wife, was due for another sitting that afternoon. She did not like the woman, and had only undertaken the commission as a favour to her mother-in-law. Margery Graham rarely asked her for anything, and Sally had hoped that it was a chance to make friends. Now, she wished she had refused, as instinct had promoted her to do. The painting was proving difficult.

At least the house was quiet, and she was free from constant interruption now that the Christmas holiday was over. Teddy and La Verne had departed for Chicago, Kay and her family had returned to New York. Charles, too, was absent once again from Monday morning until Friday evening. The only possible callers were Veronica, her mother and Philip; and even those visits would cease in a few weeks' time, when Dorothy and Philip went home.

Sally stood back and surveyed the canvas, but could not concentrate. She kept thinking about Charles; how patient, how tender, how kind he was; and how increasingly distressing she was finding it to let him anywhere near her. She should never have agreed to marry him without being in love. She had thought it would be all so easy, once she knew that Werner was dead.

Faintly, at the front of the house, she heard the doorbell ring, and waited for Louanne to answer it. McMasters had gone back to New York to look after Charles. A few minutes later, Louanne knocked at the studio door.

'Mrs Kovaks and Mrs Jackson to see you, Mrs Graham. I've shown them into the drawing room. I'll go make some coffee.'

'Thank you, Louanne.' Resignedly, Sally took off her paint-stained smock and hung it on a nail. In her navy slacks and white, polo-necked jumper, she looked much younger than her twenty-nine years.

Dorothy and Veronica had obviously been shopping, judging by the mound of parcels dumped at one end of the couch on which her mother was sitting. Dorothy was smoking, the filter-tip stuck in her amber cigarette holder, and she was looking, Sally thought, like the cat who had just had a saucerful of cream. She was watching Veronica with an air of anticipation, and Veronica did not let her down.

Once the necessary greetings were out of the way, she said to Sally: 'You'll never guess who we've just seen!'

'Father Christmas?' Sally, irritated by her sister's air of mystery, was flippant. 'Although I suppose it's a bit late for him now.'

Veronica was too full of her news to take exception to the sarcasm. She continued blithely: 'Mother and I have been shopping, as you can see, and we were in 16th Street when we saw him coming out of the Jefferson Hotel. He's evidently staying there, because the doorman spoke to him and got him a cab. We both yelled – at least, I did; Mother just stood there like a stuffed owl – but he didn't hear, and the cab drove away before we could reach it. It was really strange seeing him again after all these years, but I knew him at once. So did Mother, even though he's a bit thinner than I remember him.'

Sally looked appealingly at Dorothy. 'Who on earth is she talking about?' she demanded.

Dorothy made no answer. Charles Graham had insulted her and she saw the perfect way to be revenged. She could easily have prevented Veronica from making her disclosure by taking her into her confidence before they arrived at Sally's, but she had remained silent. Nor was she breaking her promise to Philip.

218

Veronica clapped a hand to her forehead. 'Heavens! Didn't I say? It was Werner Neumann. You remember! One of those two German prisoners-of-war who used to come to Grace Cottage. Surely you can't have forgotten! He was the fair, stocky one, who spoke English.'

The room spun and Sally put a hand on the back of the couch for support. 'You must have been mistaken,' she said faintly.

'Of course we weren't mistaken!' Veronica was indignant. 'I must admit I was surprised to see him in Washington, but Mother says he's with some toy manufacturers and gets around quite a bit. Philip met him in London last November.' She glanced at her sister's white face. 'Sally? Are you all right? You look ghastly. What on earth's the matter? What have I said to make you look like that?'

At that moment, Louanne came in with the coffee, giving Sally a respite. But it wasn't long enough to stop herself shaking, although she managed to get her voice under control.

She turned to her mother. 'Is that true? Did Uncle Philip see Werner in London last November?'

Dorothy spoke for the first time, gesturing airily with her cigarette. The tip made a glowing red arc.

'Yes. In Westminster Abbey, of all impossible places! It seems they had quite a chat.'

Sally made no attempt to pour the coffee. She knew that if she did, she'd spill it.

'Was . . . Was Uncle Philip surprised to see him?'

Dorothy regarded her daughter with large, limpid eyes. 'As a matter of fact, he was. He had some peculiar notion that Werner had died. But apparently, it turned out that it was another man called Neumann. The hospital had got the records muddled. All Werner had was a broken leg.'

If her mother knew that much, then she knew the whole story, Sally concluded, with that part of her brain which still seemed to be functioning normally. There was no way in which Philip could have told Dorothy those facts without disclosing the truth. Sally did not blame him for that: the

219

unexpected meeting with Werner must have shocked him. But she felt bitterly hurt and resentful that he had not also told her.

'I wish someone would explain what's going on,' Veronica said plaintively. 'What's all this about Werner being dead? And aren't we going to have coffee? I'm dying of thirst.'

'I'll pour it,' Dorothy offered, stubbing out her cigarette in a heavy glass ashtray and putting the holder away in her handbag. Looking at Sally's face, she was torn by a momentary guilt. In her eagerness to disrupt Charles's marriage to Sally, she had given very little thought to her daughter's feelings. Now, suddenly, the mother took over from the rival and she was trapped by a brief moment of compassion. 'Your sister's had a shock, so don't ask questions, Veronica. I'll explain later. Just drink your coffee and we'll go. I think Sally would like to be alone for a while.'

For the remainder of their curtailed visit, Dorothy took over the reins of conversation, sparing Sally as much as she could from the necessity of participating. As she and Veronica were leaving, weighed down by bags and parcels, which they piled into the back of a hastily summoned cab, she even went so far as to kiss Sally's cheek. But as the taxi moved away from the house her expression began to change.

'You're looking very pleased with yourself, Mother,' Veronica accused her. 'So now, suppose you tell me what it's all about.'

Werner was tired. He had had a long and difficult day with his American contact, not only having to think almost constantly in English, but in a racier, less precise English than was spoken in its country of origin. The effort had left him physically as well as mentally exhausted. Nevertheless, it had been a rewarding day, with a contract for the new Gabler walking, talking robots to be made under licence in the States, safely signed and witnessed. The price, too, had been above the minimum limit set by Kurt, who was delighted when Werner telephoned him with the news. He

220

did not even object to being woken from sleep, although Frau Gabler was less accommodating.

'Stay over there for a few days,' he urged. 'See the sights. My dear Werner, you've earned a holiday.'

Werner demurred. He felt lonely and a long way from home. 'I'll think about it and let you know,' he had finally promised.

But he did not really think he would stay. He had a few drinks at the hotel bar, watched some television, then went upstairs to his room.

It was dark, the curtains pulled against the cold January night, his bed turned down. Some people passed along the corridor laughing and talking. Outside, in the streets, the busy life of a capital city proceeded, taking no account of the strangers in its midst. There was no place on earth so lonely as a big city, Werner told himself, when you were on your own; then grinned at the unoriginality of the thought.

The telephone buzzed beside his bed. He lifted the receiver and gave his room number. The voice of the hotel switchboard operator sounded nasally in his ear.

'Herr Neumann? There's a lady down here, in Reception, asking to see you. A Mrs Charles Graham. Do you wish her to come up? Herr Neumann! Are you still there?'

'I . . . Yes . . . I am here. Please . . . Yes, ask Mrs Graham to . . . come up, if she will.'

He dropped the receiver with a clatter, no longer having the strength to hold it. He was shaking so much that he had to sit on the edge of the bed, gripping the blankets with both his hands. He was unable to think straight. Everything was blurred as though seen through a veil, and the only thought in his head was to wonder what Sally looked like now.

When he at last opened the door in answer to her knock, she seemed to him just the same. It was not until much later that he began to notice the differences wrought by the ten years since they had said goodbye. To his eyes, in that first moment of reunion, she looked exactly the same as when he had left her; the wide, mobile mouth, the straight little

221

nose, the direct hazel eyes, all adding up to that expression of courageous, rather childlike innocent, which was the thing about her that he best remembered.

She stood in the open doorway, her gaze unwavering as though she could hardly take it in that he was actually there, in front of her.

'W-Werner?' she stuttered hesitantly. She put out a hand and touched him gingerly, as though frightened that he would melt, ghostlike, into the air. 'It . . . It is you, isn't it? You're not dead, after all.' And she burst noisily and convulsively into tears.

Making love with Charles had never been like this; the passion, the frenzy, the explosion of happiness that burst inside her as she responded to the urgency of Werner's body.

She couldn't recall taking off her clothes and getting into bed, only the feeling, like an electrical charge, which had affected them both the moment they touched one another. The years rolled back and vanished. The two of them might have been standing in the meadows outside Coldharbour, or in the little room of Victorian pictures in Bristol Art Gallery. Only this time, their love was too strong to hold them apart: the restrictions of their former relationship had disappeared. He was no longer a prisoner-of-war, nor she his hostess's daughter. They were simply a man and a woman . . .

Sally struggled free of Werner's embrace and got out of bed.

'*Leibchen*,' he murmured sleepily, 'where are you going?'

She stood in the middle of the floor, looking around her in a daze, her body firm and arrow-straight, the light from the bedside lamp dappling her pale skin with gold.

'Sally!' Werner's voice grew more urgent. 'Come back to bed.'

'No.' She picked up his dressing gown, which had been laid ready, with his pyjamas, on top of the bed, and put it on. 'What on earth's the matter with me?' she demanded, more of herself than of him. 'Haven't I any pride? Any self-

222

respect? You ignore my existence for almost a decade; you don't even bother to let me know whether you're dead or alive; and the moment I see you again, I fall into your arms and let you seduce me, in spite of the fact that I'm married to another man. And a good man, at that. For God's sake, what's wrong with me? I should have slapped your face. Told you to go to hell! Ignored your presence in this city as you obviously intended to ignore mine! Really, I disgust myself!' She turned away and began gathering up her clothes from where she had dropped them, her eyes blinded by tears.

Werner also got out of bed, but made no attempt, for the moment, to touch her.

'I know,' he said. 'I know. But if it's any consolation to you, I never stopped loving you. No one ever replaced you in my heart.'

'Then *why?* Why didn't you write?' The words were torn from her on a wrenching sob, her face contorted with bewilderment and despair.

'I don't know,' he answered. 'I thought I knew. I thought all my reasons were good ones.' He held out his hand, which she ignored. He shivered. 'I can only say to you what I said to Mr Jackson, when I saw him last year, in London.'

'Ah yes! Philip! I shall have something to say to him, the next time I see him. He and my mother are here in Washington, visiting my sister, Veronica. That's how I knew you were here and where to find you. My mother and sister saw you this morning, coming out of this hotel.' Sally breathed deeply to calm herself, and sat down on the edge of the bed, dropping her clothes back on the carpet in an untidy heap. 'Well? What did you say to Philip when you saw him in London?'

So Werner repeated, as well as he could, the reasons which had held him silent for so long. Sally, curled up at the foot of the bed, Werner's dressing gown hanging loosely on her slender frame and making her appear like a little girl in adult clothes, playing at being grown-up, listened without interrupting. Her expression, hostile and angry to begin

223

with, gradually softened, although there were still things she found hard to forgive.

When he had finished speaking, she said quietly, 'You admit you knew I thought you were dead, yet even then, you did nothing to get in touch with me. And you say you thought I was living in New York, or you would never have agreed to come to Washington.' She regarded him with that clear, direct gaze he recalled so well. 'Yet you ask me to believe that you love me. Have continued to love me all these years. I don't find that easy, Werner.'

'Haven't I just proved it?' he pleaded.

She made no answer, lowering her eyes and plaiting and unplaiting the fringe of his dressing gown sash. She understood the reasons for his silence better than she would admit; two wars, the memory of her father, of Werner's mother and sister, of six million Jews and the dead of Dresden stood between them like uneasy wraiths, who refused to be appeased.

But she couldn't lose him again, not now that she had found him. Ghosts had to be laid: there came a point when they could no longer be allowed to overshadow the lives of the living. Sally slid off the bed, letting the dressing gown drop to the floor, and crossed the room to Werner, her arms wide open. She could feel the hard taut muscles of his body as he gathered her against him and lifted her back into bed.

Sally refused to think about Charles until she had to, when he returned from New York on Friday evening. Meantime, she had three whole days to spend with Werner. She locked her studio, cancelled her sittings and told Louanne that she had been called out of town. She packed a small case, picked up Werner from the hotel, in the drop-head tourer which Charles had given her for her twenty-eighth birthday, and drove into the country to a secluded wayside motel. There, they registered as Mr and Mrs Neumann, newlyweds, and spent most of the time in their chalet, in bed.

Kurt had been genuinely delighted when Werner called him to say that he had changed his mind and would not be flying home until Friday.

224

'Enjoy yourself! You deserve it! Going out of town? A good idea! See something of the country while you're there.'

Werner grinned and lit a cigarette. He and Sally were lying in bed, watching the short winter day fade and darken beyond the closed curtains.

'I wonder what Kurt would say if he could see me now,' he murmured. 'I do not think this qualifies – is that correct? *Gut*! – as seeing "something of the countryside".'

'Oh, I don't know.' Sally smiled and lay back against the pillows. 'John Donne referred to his mistress as "Oh, my America! My new found land!" I think I'm as interesting a sight as you'll find in the States, don't you?'

Werner put down his cigarette and rolled on to his side, propping himself on one elbow. With his free hand, he gently cupped one of her breasts, leaning forward to kiss the other.

'I think you are the most beautiful sight I could see any time, anywhere,' he answered simply.

After that, it seemed the most natural thing in the world to make love again. When they had finished, she lay quietly in his arms, curled into his body, her hands caressing him. The room was now almost completely dark, a thin spiral of smoke from Werner's forgotten cigarette threading the blackness.

Sally said: 'I'm starving. I could murder a nice juicy hamburger with all the trimmings. Let's get dressed and eat. There's a place a few yards down the road. I remember passing it, just before we arrived here.'

Half an hour later, they were seated on a white wooden bench at a red-topped table, a jukebox blaring away in one corner of the cabin. In front of them, on paper plates, were two of the largest hamburgers Sally had ever seen. The look of horror on Werner's face, as he contemplated the best way to tackle his, started her giggling.

'If a Hamburger doesn't know how to eat a hamburger,' she asked, 'who does?'

The feeble, childish joke set them both laughing. They were like a couple of schoolchildren released from school.

Sally told Werner about the taxi driver she had met in

225

Hamburg, who had also been a prisoner-of-war.

'He hitchhiked all the way from Scotland to London and went to the theatre. When he got back to camp, no one had missed him.'

Werner removed some tomato ketchup from his chin with a paper napkin.

'A fellow from our camp did the same thing, and went to a concert at the Royal Albert Hall. He brought us back the programme to prove it. During the concert, a very charming gentleman spoke to him and asked if Dieter would like to go with him to his home for a meal. Dieter said he would be delighted; but when they were in the back of the taxi, this so charming gentleman began to stroke Dieter's thigh, and tried to unbutton his trousers.'

Sally choked on a mouthful of hamburger. 'Whatever happened?'

Werner shrugged. 'As soon as the taxi stopped at some traffic lights, Dieter jumped from the taxi and ran like hell.'

Sally was convulsed by laughter. When she could finally speak, she said: 'I have this vision of Britain in nineteen-forty-eight; all these German POWs running amok over the countryside. Discipline must have gone by the board.'

'It had. It got even worse, I understand, later in the year, after my draught had gone home, just before the very last prisoners were repatriated.'

They finished their hamburgers and wandered out, hand in hand, into the night. The girl behind the counter looked after them with a puzzled expression.

'Couple of looney people,' she remarked to one of the other waitresses. 'Life ain't that funny. English, maybe.'

The next two days passed all too quickly. On Thursday evening, Sally glanced up from packing her overnight bag to find Werner watching her from a chair on the other side of the bed.

'I've settled our bill,' she said, 'so we can make an early start. I'll get you back to the Jefferson in time to pick up the rest of your things before I drive you to the airport. You'll be in plenty of time for your flight.'

'I know. I am not worried. I don't care if I never go home. Now that I've found you again, I can't let you go.'

Sally left her packing and walked round the bed to kneel beside him, covering both his hands with hers.

'I don't want you to go, but you can't stay in America indefinitely. You know that.'

He leaned forward, releasing his hands and cupping her face between them.

'Come with me,' he pleaded.

Sally shook her head. 'No. I can't just walk out on Charles without a word of explanation. He's been very good to me. I'm fond of him. I couldn't serve him such a backhanded turn. He was there when I needed him.'

'And I wasn't!' Werner threw himself back into his chair and covered his face with his hands. '*Gott in Himmel!* What a fool I've been!'

'No. You haven't. I understand.' Sally tugged at his hands, forcing them away from his face. She went on quietly: 'Truly, I do understand. Last night, I went to sleep so happy and contented just to be with you, and then I had this dream. I was back at Nuremberg, only I was in the dock with all the Nazi leaders, and the prosecuting counsel was my father.' She laid her cheek against his knee. 'Then the whole scene dissolved, the way dreams do, and I was somewhere else. But it was so vivid that when I woke up this morning, I could recall every detail. Am I feeling guilty, deep down, because I love you?'

They stayed silent for a moment or two, Werner stroking her hair. At last, he said: 'What a waste war is. What a waste of . . . of *people*!'

She raised her head at that and smiled at him through her tears.

'I shall tell Charles,' she promised. 'I'll tell him I want a divorce and explain the reason. But I must do it in my own way, in my own time. You mustn't hurry me. As soon as I can, I'll cable you to let you know when I'm coming.'

He kissed her again and again. 'I don't deserve that you should love me so much,' he whispered. 'I swear that I'll

227

make you happy for the rest of your life.' He stood up and drew her up with him, unbuttoning her dress with shaking hands. 'I love you, and in spite of what you must think, I have never stopped loving you, not since the first moment I saw you, all those years ago, in Mrs Younger's kitchen.'

CHAPTER NINETEEN

Veronica came back into the white painted breakfast parlour and resumed her seat at the table.

'Any luck?' Pete inquired through a sticky mouthful of pancakes and syrup. 'Is she home yet?'

Veronica shook her head. 'But Louanne is quite sure she'll be home before Charles returns from New York tonight.'

Dorothy stirred her coffee and pouted. 'I think it's too bad of Sally, rushing off like this, without a word to anyone, right in the middle of my visit. She knows I shan't be here for much longer. After all, when do I get to see my family these days, with two daughters living in America?'

Philip studiously ignored this plaintive cry and asked: 'Can't you think of any reason. Veronica, why Sally might have gone off in this way?'

Pete rose from the table, wiping his lips on a napkin. He kissed his wife's cheek. 'See you tonight, honey. 'Bye, mother-in-law. So long, Phil.' The parlour door closed behind him.

'He works too hard,' Veronica sighed, but her concern for her husband was less than it was for her sister. She turned to her mother. 'You know, I've been thinking. Sally behaved very oddly Monday morning, after we'd told her about Werner Neumann.'

Philip drew in his breath, sharply. 'Werner Neumann?'

'Yes.' Veronica looked surprised. 'Didn't Mother tell you about it? I was sure she would, because she said you'd met him, last November, in London.'

'Dorothy?' Philip's tone was full of barely suppressed anger.

His wife lit a cigarette and inhaled the smoke deeply. 'I forgot,' she said airily. 'The incident slipped my mind. We've been so busy these past few days. Theatres, the cinema, Mr and Mrs Kovaks' party. The holiday's going so fast, I haven't had time to think.'

Philip looked at her disbelievingly, then at Veronica. 'Tell me what happened,' he commanded.

'It was nothing to do with me, darling,' she protested. 'Ronnie was the one who told Sally we'd seen him.' She added: 'Of course she didn't know the story then. I had to tell her.'

Veronica said, horrified: 'You don't think Sally's gone off with Werner Neumann, do you? She couldn't! She's married to Charles.'

'That's not always a deterrent,' Dorothy replied sweetly, and Philip glanced at her with sudden suspicion. She was up to something, but he couldn't quite figure out what. There didn't seem to be a motive.

'Sally wouldn't just desert Charles without a word,' he said. 'And if Louanne says she's coming back today, then she probably is.' He rose from the table and headed for the door. 'Excuse me, Veronica.'

'Where are you going?'

'I'm going to see Sally. If she isn't home yet, I'll wait until she arrives. All day if necessary. May I borrow your car?'

Sally, returning home mid-afternoon, found Philip still waiting for her. She dumped her case in a corner of the room and dragged off her fur-lined jacket.

Without greeting or preamble, she demanded angrily: 'Why didn't you tell me that Werner was alive?'

Philip, who had been smoking heavily, added yet another butt to the growing pile in the ashtray.

'What good would it have done you to know the truth? You're married now, to Charles.'

She stared at him for a second or two, as if having difficulty in understanding him. She sat down, rubbing her arms, cold in spite of the central heating.

'You told Mother,' she accused him.

'Of course, I told her.' Philip was suddenly as angry as she was. 'I blurted out the news that Werner wasn't dead without thinking. After that, I had to tell her the truth. Perhaps it would have been better if you had done so from the beginning!' Philip's eyes met Sally's. 'Have you been with Werner these past three days?' he asked her.

'Yes.' She was defiant; and at the thought of Werner, her face softened, her eyes grew tender. He was on the first leg of his long journey home. She ached to be with him.

Philip had no need to inquire what had happened between her and the German. Her expression told him everything he needed to know.

'What about Charles?' he asked.

Sally breathed as though in pain.

'I shall ask him for a divorce,' she said, after a moment's silence. 'There's no need to look like that. I'm not proud of myself, believe me. I'm perfectly well aware that I shall hurt him.' She jumped up and began wandering aimlessly about the room. 'I know I shouldn't have married him without loving him, but I honestly thought I could make it work. I was very fond of him, in a way. I still am. And with Werner dead, as I believed, Charles seemed to represent security and affection and all the other things I appeared to lack.' Philip made no comment, but she answered as though he had. 'All right! I admit I used him, and it's wrong to use people. I suppose I've always known that, but I couldn't bring myself to admit it. Charles loved me. I couldn't see any reason why, given time, I shouldn't grow to love him.'

'But you didn't.'

'No.' Her anger had evaporated, leaving in its place an intense feeling of exhaustion. 'I've been thinking about asking him to set me free for a long time. Finding out that Werner is alive, meeting him again, has just precipitated matters, not altered them.'

'And you really believe that Charles will agree to a divorce?'

'I don't know. If he doesn't, I shall still go to Werner.'

231

'And "live in sin" as the novelists say? My dear,' Philip's voice, too, had softened. 'I know moral standards are a great deal laxer than before the war, but even today, nineteen-fifty-eight, it's still frowned upon, especially in Europe.'

She sighed wearily and sat down again, this time beside him. 'I don't care,' she said. 'I don't care what people will say.' She smiled, a little shamefacedly. 'I'm sorry for the way I bit your head off when I first came in. You've always been my greatest friend and I know you wouldn't do anything deliberately to hurt me. I've come straight from the airport after saying goodbye to Werner. I'm feeling like death.'

Philip put his arm about her shoulders. 'Sally, all I want is your happiness. Yours and your mother's. And, of course,' he added with a cynical smile, 'my own. But that's another story. I just don't think you'll find happiness by deserting Charles. That, however, is your affair. When are you going to tell him?'

'I don't know. I want to do it as gently as possible. I need to pick my time. Maybe tonight, maybe not for a week or two. Please don't say anything to the others.'

Philip grimaced. 'I'm afraid Veronica already knows the story and she's bound to tell Pete. There's going to be speculation, whatever I do or don't say. Moreover, I refuse to keep your mother in the dark again. Having secrets from her is neither fair nor kind; and I think she has a right to know.'

'Very well,' Sally conceded grudgingly. 'But I don't want it to go beyond those three. I don't want any hint reaching Charles's ears before I'm ready to tell him myself.'

'What do you think?' Dorothy hissed in her husband's ear. 'My guess is she hasn't told him yet.'

Philip sipped his cocktail.

'I think you're probably right, although neither of them looks very happy.'

He reflected with pleasure that, in a fortnight's time, he and Dorothy would be on their way home to Coldharbour village and the peace and quiet of Grace Cottage. He could start planning his new book; and, for once, instead of being a necessary chore, the prospect afforded him infinite pleasure. He was tired of Washington and the endless round of parties. The kind of frenetic social life led by Veronica and Pete profoundly depressed him, the more so because Dorothy so patently enjoyed it. The longer she stayed, the less she wanted to go home.

This party, given by Margery Graham, was like every other party Philip had attended during the past weeks; a crush of people, too much to drink and the incessant flow of political gossip and scandal. He could understand why Charles Graham had wanted to escape from it, and considered it a pity that he had ever brought Sally back here to live. Had he not done so, she would never have renewed her acquaintance with Werner. It was one of those dirty tricks which Fate played on all human beings from time to time.

Margery Graham, resplendent in a beaded Dior cocktail gown, but moving with increasing difficulty as the arthritis spread throughout her body, made her way to Philip's side.

'Mr Jackson, there's someone here I'd like you to meet. Her name's Celeste Adams and she's a great admirer of your books.'

Philip glanced at Dorothy, made an impatient grimace which his hostess fortunately did not see, and followed obediently in Margery Graham's wake.

Dorothy waited until he was lost to view in the crowd, then pushed her way to where Charles was standing. A few moments earlier, he had been talking to an elderly couple, but they had now been claimed by other friends. He was temporarily disengaged.

'What a lot of people.' Dorothy gave Charles her most seductive smile. She had taken especial care this evening with her perfume and make-up, and had chosen an emerald green chiffon dress with a high collar and long sleeves to conceal those most age-vulnerable parts of a woman's body, her neck and arms. Her legs, as good as ever, were sheathed in her favourite sheer, dark stockings. She perched on the arm of a chair, allowing her skirt to ride up slightly, revealing her knees.

Charles smiled faintly in return. 'My mother has always had the deplorable habit of inviting as many guests as possible to her parties.'

Dorothy sipped her Old-Fashioned, looking at Charles in wide-eyed concern.

'You're looking tired,' she told him. 'You're working too hard. And then there's all the travelling. I know it's none of my business, Charles, but do you think this move to Washington was really a good idea?'

'Sally needed to be near her sister. She knew no one in New York.'

'She'd lived there long enough without finding it too much of a strain. She never complained; at least, not in her letters to me.'

'Sally doesn't complain,' Charles answered shortly. 'She endures.'

Dorothy gave a delighted crow of laughter. 'She does, doesn't she? What a beautifully apt description of her.'

Charles felt uncomfortable. What had been intended as a compliment to his wife, had somehow been twisted. Dorothy made him feel as though he had been disloyal to Sally.

Dorothy went on: 'I shouldn't think the separation could be good for your marriage. After all, Sally is that much younger. Like can't help being attracted by like.'

Charles swallowed the dregs of his whisky. 'Is that supposed to mean something?' he inquired with icy politeness.

'Oh, don't be so stuffy and stand-offish, Charles,' Dorothy protested. 'Anyone would think our only relationship was mother and son-in-law, instead of having been to bed together.' She held out her empty glass. 'I'll have another, if you'd be so kind as to get one for me.'

'You're drinking too much,' he retorted. 'And for God's sake, keep your voice down.'

'My, my! Your temper's on a very short rein. Just one more Old-Fashioned and then I'll get my wrap. You can

234

take me for a stroll in the garden. What could be more romantic than a moonlit winter's night?'

He had been a fool to come; to let Dorothy inveigle him into this walk along the terrace. He felt instinctively that she was up to mischief. Wrapped in her heavy fur coat, she was smiling a little, cat-like smile of triumph.

After a moment's silence, and ignoring the impression that he was playing straight into her hands, Charles demanded abruptly: 'Why did you imply just now that Sally has met someone else?'

Dorothy's eyes were guileless in the moonlight. 'I'm sure I said nothing of the kind. Or even implied it. But marrying a girl young enough to be your daughter, Charles, was always a chancy business. One big pitfall, in fact.'

They had moved from the terrace down into the garden itself, and were standing close together beneath the shelter of a willow. The branches glittering with the night's new frost; overhead, a broad stream of stars flowed across the heavens. The faint, crackling silence of a winter's night lay all about them.

Dorothy moved closer to Charles, and the pressure of her body was surprisingly familiar after thirteen years. Without meaning to, he put an arm around her.

'Now that,' she said, 'is what I call a friendly gesture.'

He released her at once. 'It wasn't meant to be,' he said harshly. 'I don't want to go to bed with you, Dorothy, if that's what you think. It was only a passing amusement at the time.'

She drew away from him on a gasp of anger. 'How dare you!' she breathed. 'How dare you speak to me like that! My God, what a fool you are, Charles. You always have been. I should have made you a much better wife than either Faith or my daughter. But you couldn't see it, could you? You hankered after the unobtainable; a child the same age as Kay! And in the end, with patience and perseverance, you got her. But what a bad bargain you struck, dear boy! Your precious wife is cuckolding you, Charles!'

The old-fashioned word fell between them like a stone. The sudden silence was filled with the long, ululating cry of an owl.

'I don't believe you,' Charles said in a voice he scarcely recognized. 'You're making it up.'

But he knew she wasn't. For the last two weekends, he had been unable to get near Sally. She had pleaded headaches, tiredness, nausea; all the classic ailments with which, for centuries, women had fended off the unwelcome attentions of their men. His marriage was failing in spite of all his proffered inducements. It was not going to work. His mind started to spin as everything began to fall into place.

'Who is this other man?' he asked at last.

Dorothy's anger was cooling and panic was beginning to set in. She had given Philip her solemn promise to say nothing to anyone except Veronica and Pete. If he found out what she'd done, and why, he might leave her. She was startled to discover that the idea frightened her. She hitched her coat more firmly about her shoulders.

'It's cold out here,' she said. 'I'm going in.'

Charles gripped her arm, and she could feel the pressure of his fingers, even through the thickness of her sleeve. His look of dark and brooding anger terrified her. This was a Charles Graham she had never seen.

'No you're not. Not yet. Not until you've answered my question. Who is this other man?'

'Ask her yourself,' she gasped, trying to twist free of him. 'She's intending to tell you, anyway.' He let her go suddenly and she almost tripped and fell. She rubbed her bruised arm. 'If that's an example of the way you treat Sally, I'm not surprised she wants to leave you.'

'I would never treat Sally in that way. She does nothing to deserve it.'

'Oh, what a little Goody-Two-Shoes she is!' Dorothy flung at him. Recovering her nerve. 'Goody-Two-Faced would be nearer the mark.'

The look he gave her was full of contempt and disgust.

'You always had a vicious tongue, Dorothy. Age hasn't taught you to control it.'

'Age!' Her voice rose in fury. 'You're a fine one to talk about age, you . . . you cradle-snatcher!' She spun on her heel. 'I'm going in. Getting a divorce from you, will be the best day's work my daughter has ever done.'

She ran across the grass, losing one of her high-heeled satin slippers on the way. She picked it up almost without stopping, and arrived in the hall out of breath and shoeless, just as Philip emerged from the brightly lit, overcrowded drawing room. He paused in astonishment when he saw her.

'I was just coming to look for you,' he said. He took in her coat and raised his eyebrows. 'You haven't been outside? Whatever possessed you? You've caught a cold by the look of you. You're as white as a sheet. I'll get you a drink. A good, stiff whisky.'

'I don't want a drink!' Dorothy exclaimed. She glanced at his concerned face and was overcome by a rush of affection. She went up to him and put her arms around his neck, not caring who might be watching. She felt suddenly warm and safe and protected. 'You married a fool, did you know that? Well, I don't suppose I'll change overnight, but at least now *I* know it. Philip, darling, I'm tired and fed up with this noisy place. Take me back to Veronica's.'

Sally and Charles drove home through the quiet Georgetown streets. It had always seemed to Sally that Americans had a built-in aversion to walking, however short the distance; and she and Charles lived only a block or two away from the house occupied by his mother. Nevertheless, he had insisted on taking the Buick.

But now, she was glad of the car; she felt completely drained of energy. The party, so far as she was concerned, had not been a success. It had been noisy and overcrowded, and the strain of keeping up the pretence that all was well between herself and Charles had been the hardest part of all. But she wanted to give him no unnecessary pain until she had to; until she thought he was ready to bear it. She told herself that she was a coward postponing the evil day; but it was more than that. She had known for a long time that Charles had good and bad days; periods when he was more depressed than at others. Occasionally, he had nightmares. She recalled one time, in New York, when she had found him sleepwalking. The expression on his face had haunted her ever since: he had looked so anguished.

While Charles put the car away, Sally let herself into the silent house. Louanne had gone to bed, but she had left a tray of sandwiches and a flask of hot milk on the dining room table. The heating had switched to the night-time temperature, but the rooms were still pleasantly warm.

Charles came in, and she smiled wearily at him.

'Do you want anything? There are sandwiches – smoked salmon, I think – and hot milk, if you'd like your usual nightcap of hot milk and whisky. I'll pour it for you before I go up.' She kicked off her shoes and began to unscrew the cap of the thermos flask. 'I can't remember when I've felt so tired. Margery's parties are always exhausting, although I was surprised Mother and Philip left early. Mother enjoys those affairs so much.' Sally paused in the act of pouring hot milk into a glass, suddenly conscious of her husband's silence. 'Charles? Are you all right? You're very quiet.'

He sat down in a leather armchair by the empty grate. A large blue vase, containing sprigs of winter jasmine, stood on the deserted hearth. Sally thought irrelevantly that central heating had a lot to answer for: it had destroyed the pleasures of an open fire.

Charles said sombrely: 'Dorothy tells me you want a divorce. Is that true? If so, I'd rather have heard it from you, than at second-hand from your mother.'

Sally was adding whisky to the hot milk, and the decanter almost slipped from her hand.

'Damn Mother!' she exclaimed with uncharacteristic vehemence. 'Damn her! Damn her! Damn her!' She drew a deep breath and closed her eyes. 'I saw her go into the garden with you, but I never dreamed what she was up to. Philip promised me that she wouldn't say anything.'

238

Charles raised his eyebrows. 'So Philip knows, too? The old adage seems to be true: the partner is always the last one to know.'

Sally opened her eyes. 'Charles . . . I'm sorry. But there were reasons why — '

He interrupted her. 'It's true, then. You do want a divorce. Is there any particular reason?'

She made no attempt to go to him, although the sadness shadowing his face made her want to put her arms about him and cradle his head against her breast. But the comfort that she longed to offer him would not be the sort he either wanted or needed. Instinct warned her to keep away.

'Yes.' She strove to keep her voice level. 'I'm in love with somebody else. Someone I thought had gone out of my life for ever, long before I married you.'

'But he has come back.'

It was a statement, not a question, and Sally made no attempt to answer it. She just stood there, on the opposite side of the oak dining table, a skin forming on the rapidly cooling milk. She noted with detachment that she had spilled whisky on the polished wood, but made no move to mop it up. The fact that the spirit would leave a stain seemed unimportant.

She asked: 'Do you want me to tell you about it?'

Charles raised his eyes to hers, meeting them squarely for the first time since he came into the room.

'I think it would be as well, don't you?' He indicated the second armchair, on the other side of the grate.

He listened without interruption, his eyes half closed, until she had finished. When, finally, she ceased speaking, he leaned forward, his hands clasped together between his knees. He looked, suddenly, like a very old man.

But it was a trick of the shadows. When he got up and moved into the circle of light around the table, he appeared as he always did; a handsome, greying man in his early fifties. He had his features well under control, and hoped Sally would not recognize the effort it was costing him. He even managed to bite into a sandwich,

239

though it turned to dust and ashes in his mouth.

Charles remembered the German. They had met several times during the period of Veronica's wedding. It had never crossed Charles's mind that there was anything else but friendliness between Werner and Sally, so well had they concealed their feelings for one another. He put down his half-eaten sandwich and turned to face her.

'Thank you for being honest with me,' he said at last. 'You obviously love this Werner Neumann very much. If you want a divorce, then of course you must have it. I'll go to see my lawyer, Sam Brownlow, as soon as I get back to New York.'

CHAPTER TWENTY

'I never thought I should say it, but I'm glad to be home.'
Dorothy glanced around the living room of Grace Cottage
and sighed with contentment. Philip, who had just paid off
the taxi and was carrying the cases indoors, wondered how
long this state of euphoria would last.

'I'll just put the kettle on,' Dorothy said and headed for
the kitchen. 'Switch the gas and electricity on at the mains,
darling, will you? Oh good! Mrs Wakeman received my
letter. She's left the groceries I asked her to get, and here's
the spare front door key.'

Later, when they were finishing a makeshift midday meal,
Dorothy remarked: 'I can't see why Sally wouldn't come
back with us. I should think staying with Veronica and Pete
is most uncomfortable for her. They are both so blatantly
disapproving of the divorce.'

Philip poured himself a cup of strong tea. He had refused
coffee, saying that he was awash with the stuff.

'You have to remember that Pete and Charles were wartime buddies. And Veronica doesn't want to lose the only
family she has in the States. Moreover, they both think that
Sally is treating Charles badly. Which she is.' He added
another lump of sugar to the two already in his cup. 'As
for the reason she didn't return with us, she told me there
was still a great deal to see to. She didn't feel that she could
just walk out and leave everything to Charles. It wouldn't
be fair.'

'Oh, who cares about fairness?' Dorothy asked irritably.
She was feeling grateful towards Sally, who had plainly not
told the tales out of school. All the same, she could not resist

adding: 'Whoever would have thought, when they were children, that Sally would turn out to be my problem child? She was always so much quieter than Jennifer and Veronica. But first she marries a man old enough to be her father, and now it's an ex-POW. It isn't all that many years since the Germans were our mortal enemies.'

'You invited them here,' Philip pointed out. 'You were very fond of Erich. Besides, times change. Life would never progress if we went on cherishing old hatreds. Look at us and the French. We fought each other for centuries, but for a hundred years or more we've been allies.' He changed the subject abruptly. 'Are you really glad to be home?' He had thought her strangely subdued these past two weeks, and was uneasy as to the reason.

Dorothy laughed, drawing on her cigarette, and answered his question obliquely.

'I think this American trip has made me realize that I'm getting, not old, but older. It's such a young and energetic country.'

'You look exactly the same to me as you've always done,' Philip told her.

'Yes. That was something else I realized. If I have a fault,' Dorothy conceded magnanimously, and saw her husband's mouth twitch, 'it's a tendency to underrate my blessings. You and Bill . . . you've been the best of them.' She noted his look of astonishment and blew him a kiss. 'Make the most of this mood while it's on me,' she advised. 'Knowing me, who can say how long it will last?'

Sally found her sister at breakfast. She had deliberately waited until she heard her brother-in-law leave the house before coming downstairs. Pete's disapproval was harder to cope with than her sister's. She had suggested that she move to an hotel, but that idea had upset them even more, so she had decided to stay and make the best of it. It would not be for long.

'I'm going to the house to pack the rest of my things,' she said in answer to her sister's lift of the eyebrows as she took in Sally's outdoor clothes. She also wanted to telephone Werner, and preferred to do so where she could not be overheard. A tearful Louanne had been paid off and the house shut up. Charles had returned to New York and stayed there. He no longer came to Washington at weekends.

'Have you set a date for leaving?' Veronica asked.

'I'm booked on a flight in a week's time. February the twelfth. I shall go home for a short visit, then I'll fly on to Hamburg. Werner's looking for a bigger apartment. Once I've settled in with him, Charles will be able to instigate divorce proceedings.'

Veronica lowered her eyes again to the morning paper. 'I hope to God,' she said devoutly, 'you know what you're doing.'

'I was never more sure of anything in my life; not even of wanting to paint.'

'You know, I suppose, that you're ruining the life of a very nice man?' Veronica spoke without raising her voice. 'A man who has already had his life spoiled by another woman.'

Sally gripped her handbag tightly with both hands. 'Charles is quite willing to let me go. He's put no rub of any kind in my way. He knew I didn't love him when I married him. He also accepts that I would not have married him had I known then that Werner was alive.' Veronica said nothing, so Sally added: 'I'd like to take this opportunity of thanking you and Pete for letting me stay here these past few weeks. It would have been hellish being entirely alone.'

'You're my baby sister,' Veronica said roughly. 'Do you really think I would have let you go to some beastly, impersonal hotel?'

On impulse, Sally went over and kissed her. Her voice was too choked with tears to say more and she hurried out of the room.

On the way to Georgetown, she stopped at a delicatessen and bought sandwiches and a carton of apple juice. She would make the rest of her packing last all day. In spite of what she had said to her sister, it would be a relief to be on her own for a while.

The house was like ice, the heating having been turned off weeks ago, and there was only a handful of burnt-out ashes in the boiler. Sally went from room to room, just to make sure that everything was in order, and that no one had broken in. There was an uncanny silence because all the clocks had stopped, and she was seized with a sense of foreboding. Everything had been made too easy; not just by Charles's lack of opposition, but also by an even greater lack, her own feelings of guilt. She was so happy at the prospect of being with Werner for the rest of her life, that she found it difficult to accept what she must be doing to her husband.

She had received no word from either of her step-children, although she felt sure that Charles would have been in touch with both Kay and Teddy. Nor had she heard from Margery Graham. But then, her mother-in-law was probably delighted by the news of the divorce. She had never concealed her disapproval of the marriage.

Sally telephoned Werner earlier than she had intended, in an effort to dispel her growing sense of desolation, and the sound of his voice sent the shadows slinking back into their corners. It was mid-afternoon in Hamburg, he told her, and a beautiful day. The street beyond his window was bathed in sunlight.

'I was afraid you might be out,' she said, 'or away on another trip.'

'I should have let you know somehow. Darling, I have found an apartment. No one will know us there. We can be Herr and Frau Neumann without anyone being the wiser.'

'Have you told . . . what's his name? . . . Kurt.'

'I thought it best. He was bound to find out.'

'What did he say?'

'That my private life is my own busines. He will not be bringing his Magda to see us, however, until we are properly married.'

They both laughed. 'Oh, Werner, it is good to hear your voice,' Sally said gratefully. 'I was feeling so – oh, I don't know – so down! Only another three weeks, darling, and then we'll be together, for always.'

'I know. I am counting the days.'

They talked a little longer, each reluctant to let the other go, but eventually Werner said Kurt was asking for him and he must ring off.

Sally replaced the receiver with an unutterable sense of loss, as though she had just said goodbye to him for ever. The silence flooded back. It no longer seemed such a good idea to spend the rest of the day alone in the empty house. She would pack the rest of her things, eat her lunch and return to Veronica. And she would not wait until next week before she left Washington. Whatever was not settled now, would have to be done by correspondence. She would telephone the airport to find out if they could get her on an earlier flight.

She went first to the studio. The unfinished portrait of the Senator's wife was still on the easel. It would never be completed now. Sally lifted it down and stacked it against the wall. Whoever did the final clearance of the house, could decide what to do with it. She took her palette and tubes of paint, threw away the dirty rags and a half-empty bottle of thinner and ditched her old smock in the trash can. A yellowing pile of newspaper cuttings, favourable reviews of her work, followed it. The unused canvases could also be disposed of when the house was sold. She carried the heavy canvas bag containing those items she wished to keep through the house to the waiting car. Then she returned indoors and went upstairs.

There were very few of her clothes left hanging in the wardrobe. All the furs and jewellery which Charles had given her during the course of their marriage were carefully laid to one side. She neither wanted, nor would she need, them in her new life with Werner. It did not occur to her that, by rejecting his gifts, she would hurt Charles more than if she had taken them with her.

When she had stowed her case in the boot of the car, alongside the canvas bag, she went into the house for a third time. She ate the chicken sandwiches and drank the apple juice standing up, the one thought in her mind being that

245

she must get away. She swept up the crumbs, pushed the empty box and carton down the waste disposal unit and prepared, with an enormous feeling of relief, to leave.

She had her hand on the front door latch, ready to open it, when the telephone rang. The sound, cutting into the unnatural silence, made her jump, and she could feel her heart thumping against her ribs. She hesitated, unwilling to answer the imperious summons.

'Go now,' whispered a voice inside her head. 'Go straight to the airport and get on the first available 'plane. Veronica can send on the rest of your things. Just take what's in the car and go!'

But it was impossible to shake the habit of a lifetime. A telephone bell was for answering, whenever it rang. It was not easy to ignore its insistent demands.

It was probably Veronica. No one else knew she would be at the house. She went into the dining room and picked up the receiver.

'Hello,' she said into the mouthpiece.

There was a series of clicks; then, McMasters's impeccable English tones sounded at the other end of the line.

'Mrs Graham? This is Henry McMasters. Mrs Kovaks told me I should find you at the Georgetown house. Mrs Graham, Mr Graham is seriously ill. He has pneumonia. Dr Foy wanted him to be removed to hospital, but the master refused to go. I'm looking after him, together with a resident nurse. The reason for my call is that he has been delirious all night and he keeps asking for you. Madam, do you think you could come up to New York right away?'

During his lunch break, Werner took himself for a walk to clear his head. He had been at a conference all morning, and the cold February air was like wine after the stuffy, overheated atmosphere in Kurt's badly ventilated office. He moved briskly through the maze of old warehouses and bridges near the Rödings Markt, watching the ripples of sunlight on the canals which linked the Elbe and Alster rivers.

He was thinking of Sally, and a frown creased his

246

forehead. He had not heard from her for over a week, but she should have left Washington by now and returned to England. She should be telephoning him any day to say when she planned to arrive in Hamburg.

He told himself that he was being foolish to worry, but the silence was unlike her. Then he remembered his own silence, spanning almost ten years, and felt ashamed. If she had not sought him out in Washington, he would still be condemned to a loneliness of his own creating. She had made it plain that she loved him as much as he loved her. Why, then, should he feel afraid?

Yet he did. He had woken in the night, sweating and uneasy, as though from a nightmare, but he could not recollect any dream. He would make some excuse this evening to leave the office early. Surely there would be a letter waiting for him when he got home. Or tonight, Sally would telephone.

The new apartment was ready, and next week he was moving in. Kurt had given him three days' leave of absence and offered to lend him one of the firm's two delivery lorries, to save the expense of a removal van. Kurt was being generous and understanding; and none of his friends had so far condemned him for what, at first, would be an irregular household. Both the Rossmans and Elsa and Ludwig Fisher had promised to call.

Everything, in short, was going smoothly, running on well-oiled wheels. All the more foolish, therefore, for him to feel this way, as though something were about to go wrong. He retraced his steps to the factory, realizing he had eaten nothing. No matter; he wasn't hungry. He would make up for it tonight, when he got home and had read Sally's letter, which surely must be there. Then he would have a celebratory meal.

He went through the factory gates and round to the two-storey office block, which backed on to the road. He had a long, very busy afternoon ahead of him. he was glad: he would have no time to brood.

*   *   *

Sally sat by Charles's bed, holding his hand. He was asleep, breathing quietly and normally for the first time in days. The fever had abated and the crisis was past.

'He'll be fine now,' Dr Foy had said before quitting the apartment, half an hour earlier. 'Careful nursing, that's all he needs, and he'll make a full recovery. But it was touch and go there, for a while.'

The nurse had nodded her head in agreement, and Sally had sent her off to the dining room to eat a belated dinner.

'I'll stay with my husband. If he wakes, I'll call you.'

The nurse had looked at her significantly. 'It's you he'll want to see, Mrs Graham.'

And Sally, however much she wished to avoid the knowledge, knew that this was true. In his delirium, Charles had spoken her name over and over again, begging her not to leave him.

Sally had been in New York for over a week. After receiving Henry McMasters's call, she had telephoned her sister and taken the first flight out of Washington. Veronica and Pete had driven up at the weekend with her clothes. They had been as shocked as Sally to see how ill and wasted Charles had become, as he fought for breath, assisted by a tube in his throat. Veronica had wanted to stay, but Sally had refused the offer of company. She wanted to be by herself, to think, free from anyone who would try to influence her future actions.

She had written to Werner yesterday, explaining what had happened. She had refrained from speaking to him by telephone, nor had she given him the New York number. She knew if once she had heard his voice, she would be lost.

'So you see,' she had written, 'I must stay with Charles until he is well again. I owe him that, at least. But it won't make any difference to us, darling. I am still coming to Germany. It just means that we have to wait a little longer than we thought, before we can be together. I love you.'

Yet she had not told Werner of her suspicion that she was pregnant. The reason she gave herself was that after two miscarriages, it would be cruel to raise his hopes until she was certain that she would carry the child full-term. She refused to admit that there was a deeper, underlying uneasiness, which whispered that she had made a mistake in coming to New York; that she should have closed her ears and heart to McMasters's pleas; that, somehow or other, she had walked into a trap.

'Mr Graham hasn't been eating or sleeping properly, madam, since he returned to New York,' McMasters had said. 'He's been overworking and not taking proper care of himself, in my opinion.'

Sally had not wanted his opinion. That was the moment when she should have turned tail and run for her life. But how could she have done so and, afterwards, lived with her conscience?

'Make up the bed for me in Miss Kay's old room,' she had said. 'I shall be staying until Mr Graham has fully recovered.'

She had desperately tried to believe that, these past few days, and she told herself fiercely, as she sat beside the bed holding Charles's hand, that as soon as he was better, she would go. She must! She had to be with Werner.

The room was very quiet, only the rhythmic ticking of the bedside clock breaking the silence. The heavy red brocade curtains were pulled across the windows, rimmed by the dim light of a February evening. The temperature was a steady seventy degrees, controlled by the air conditioning and the central heating. The Americans were so much more advanced in these matters than Europeans, Sally thought resentfully. The war had hardly touched the civilian population. She looked at the man in the bed. It had touched Charles Graham. She remembered the American officer with the shattered legs.

As though aware that she was watching him, Charles opened his eyes and smiled at her.

'Sally,' he murmured weakly. His eyelids drooped again, before he suddenly came wide awake. 'Sally?' he repeated, on a note of interrogation. 'I . . . I thought you'd be in Germany by now.'

'Hush,' she answered, 'don't talk. You must save your strength. You've been very ill, you know.'

'Yes,' he assented. 'Bad dreams.' There was a long pause, during which the ticking of the clock sounded even louder. Then he muttered: 'Demons.'

'What?' Sally was startled. She leaned closer to him. 'I'm sorry, Charles. I didn't catch that last word.'

He shook his head with an effort. 'Nothing. Doesn't matter.'

'I thought you said "demons". You mean you had nightmares? Everyone does when they're delirious.'

He made no answer, and she saw he had once more drifted into sleep.

The nurse put her head around the bedroom door and raised her eyebrows.

'Its OK,' Sally told her. 'You get some rest. I'll send for you if I need you.'

The nurse checked her patient's pulse and, apparently satisfied, went away to lie down on her bed.

Sally settled herself more comfortably in her chair and picked up a book, a copy of *Room at the Top,* which her mother had sent her. She had only read a few paragraphs, however, when Charles moved, and she saw that he was again awake. She put aside the novel and smiled at him.

'How are you feeling?'

'Fine. Better for knowing that you're here.' His fingers convulsively gripped hers, like a drowning man clinging to a lifeline. Once more, she had the sense of being trapped. The clawed teeth of the gin were inexorably closing.

She tried to speak confidently. 'I'm going to stay as long as you need me. Werner won't mind waiting a few more weeks, until you're up and about.'

She had deliberately introduced Werner's name, and the sound of it lingered in the room, echoing faintly among the solid, old-fashioned mahogany furniture. Then Sally saw with horror that Charles was crying, the tears running silently down his thin cheeks.

He said abruptly: 'I killed her you know. I killed Faith.'

Sally was alarmed. He was wandering in his mind again. The fever had returned. She half rose to call the nurse, but Charles's hand detained her.

'Sit still and listen,' he begged. 'Please. I must tell someone. I can't keep it to myself any longer.' His voice was weak and it was costing him an effort to speak.

Sally sank back into her chair, realizing that he was perfectly lucid. She said sharply, panic setting in, the jaws of the trap beginning to bite: 'I don't want to hear!'

Charles paid no attention, concentrating all his mind on what he had to say.

'When I went into her room that night, she was lying on the bed. She'd been drinking heavily . . . smell of whisky everywhere. She'd been sick, too. Vomit was on the floor and bedclothes.' His voice faded for a moment, then rallied. He went on: 'I felt no pity for her; nothing except disgust. The sight of her made me − ' he searched for the word he wanted ' − angry.' He considered this, then nodded. 'Yes, angry. All those wasted years of my life. It was worse because . . . I'd just been thinking about you.' His eyes flicked to the van Valkenborch picture, which now hung in his bedroom. 'We'd had a fight that morning. When Faith saw me, she started right in again, pouring out abuse. Then she began to cry. I still didn't feel anything. I was just sickened. She asked me to give her some of her sleeping tablets in water. She was too drunk to dissolve them herself . . . Of course, I knew she shouldn't take them on top of all that alcohol. Told her so, but she just began screaming more filth.'

'Don't say any more, Charles, please!' Sally urged. 'Leave it at that.'

He continued as though she had not spoken. 'Something snapped. Silly expression, but that's exactly how it felt. I thought, "Why not? No one will even suspect that I was in her room." So I dissolved the tablets in water and gave them to her to drink. Then I went into the living room and switched on the TV. I listened to all the election news and tried to pretend I didn't know what was happening in that

251

bedroom . . . Later, when I couldn't stand it any longer, I went to look at her. I could see that she was dying . . . I telephoned Dr Foy . . . and that was that.'

'You didn't really kill her,' Sally argued desperately, clutching at straws. 'Faith asked you to give her the sleeping tablets. And you did, that's all. If you hadn't given them to her, she would probably have managed to get them for herself.'

'But I could have prevented her.' Charles sounded exhausted, his face so white it almost merged with the pillow. 'I should have 'phoned the doctor then, and stayed with her until he came. It's no good, my darling. I've used every possible argument, over the years, to justify what I did, but . . . they won't hold water. I killed Faith, and I have to live with that knowledge.'

'And it's killing you by degrees,' Sally thought, filled with desolation. 'If I leave you, you'll have to go on bearing the burden alone, and I can't stand the prospect of what it will do to you.' She stroked his damp hair back from his forehead, and remembered his kindness and strength when she had needed him most. Now, he needed her, and he was too proud and too concerned for her happiness to say so.

In that seemingly endless moment, Sally said her goodbye to Werner, even though every fibre of her being screamed out against the sacrifice. For a few precious seconds, she tried to persuade herself that Charles would feel differently once he had fully recovered. It was only weakness and what he called the demons of his delirium that made him so frightened. But the self-delusion could not last. Her hand tightened over his slackening fingers.

'Don't worry,' she said bleakly, 'I won't leave you again, I promise.'

Seconds later, he was soundly and dreamlessly asleep.

PART FIVE

Winter 1963 – 1964

Fear no more the . . . winter's rages

CHAPTER TWENTY-ONE

'So Pete and I wondered if you'd like to come with us.' Her sister's voice sounded persuasively at the other end of the telephone. 'I remember you saying you've never been to Texas, and I should be glad of the company. Pete'll be tied up with his conference most of the week.'

Sally hesitated, rubbing her free, paint-stained hand against the leg of her jeans.

'The end of next month? I don't really see why not. I don't think Charles would be able to get away, but I'm sure he wouldn't mind my going with you.' She leaned forward thumbing through the pages of her appointments' book. 'November sixteenth to twenty-third . . . I haven't any sittings that week.'

'There you are, then!' Veronica exclaimed triumphantly. 'A break will do you good. Louanne will love to take care of William. You know how she dotes on that boy. She'll see he drinks his milk and eats his spinach.'

Sally laughed. 'You're out of date, Ronnie. Milk and spinach aren't rated very highly in the dietary charts these days. You're still living in the era of Popeye and Sunny Jim.'

'Well, I am nearly forty-two,' Veronica said in extenuation. 'Don't forget you have an eight year advantage over Jenny and me.'

Sally shifted her position at the window seat, balancing the studio extension precariously on her knees.

'How is Jenny? I haven't heard from her for ages.'

'Fat, prosperous and very, very smug,' Veronica responded tartly. 'I had a letter yesterday, full of nothing but the latest addition to the Latham family. Six children now, would you believe it?'

There was an edge to her sister's voice, and Sally wondered, not for the first time, if the Kovaks' decision to have no family of their own had been a truly mutual agreement. She often watched Veronica with young William, and thought that there was a deep vein of maternal affection just waiting to be tapped.

She said: 'Of course you'll be coming next Monday for William's birthday? I'm counting on you for moral support. The prospect of a dozen or more hyperactive five-year-olds running riot all over the house fills me with horror. Charles, the craven, is going back to New York. He categorically refuses to ask for leave of absence.'

'I don't blame him,' Veronica chuckled. 'But I'll be there. I've always been a glutton for punishment. That's why I married Pete.' On which cryptic note she said her goodbyes and hung up.

Thoughtfully, Sally put the telephone receiver on its rest and replaced the instrument on the seat behind her. She wandered over to her easel and took up her brush, staring absently at an almost finished portrait. A well-known face from the Kennedy administration stared smilingly back at her, but suddenly she was no longer in the mood to continue the work which Veronica's call had interrupted. Sally covered the canvas, stripped off her smock and went through to the main part of the house.

It was very quiet, the late October sun pouring in at the windows and staining everything gold with a Midas-like touch. Yesterday, it had been cold and wet, with a biting wind blowing off the Potomac. Winter, it seemed, had arrived. Now, today, the capital was being given a last, tantalizing glimpse of autumn. Louanne was out shopping and William was at school. In three days' time he would be five years old.

Five years, Sally thought grimly, as she paused in the hallway, since Werner's son had been born; the son he had never seen; the son he did not even know existed. And it was more than five years since she had stood on this very spot, listening to the ring of the telephone, and had disobeyed her instinct to ignore it.

Slowly, she walked into the dining room, just as she had done on that long-gone afternoon. The telephone crouched, malevolent and black, on the selfsame corner table. She sat down on one of the dining-chairs and stared across at it, casting her mind back over the last five and a half years, searching for a lost self and trying to make some sense from the broken pieces of her life.

She and Charles had never again discussed the manner of Faith's death. It was a secret never referred to, but which bound them irrevocably together. As long as he needed her, she would stay. In return, he had accepted William as his son, given him the Graham name, and was genuinely fond of the stocky, fair-haired boy, who looked so much like Werner.

Charles's attitude had stilled any overt speculation that the child was not his; and even Margery Graham dared not treat William as anything but a grandchild. On the one occasion she had tried to prise the truth from her son, she had experienced the full blast of Charles's anger. Kay and Teddy had accepted William as their half-brother without question: they must have had doubts, but they never expressed them. They were only too happy that the divorce between Charles and Sally had been averted, and that their father seemed so happy. Kay and her husband did have some reservations, however, about Charles's decision to withdraw the Georgetown house from the property market and resume the pattern of living which he and Sally had established before his illness.

'Surely, it would make sense if Sally came back to live in New York,' Kay had protested.

Sally herself had made the same suggestion, but Charles had proved adamant.

'You and William need time to be alone together,' he had said, and no argument that either she or Kay could advance persuaded him to change his mind. The only concession he made to his daughter's concern for him was to sell the New

York apartment and move in with her and Mitch from Monday to Thursday.

It was an arrangement that worked to everyone's advantage, enabling Charles to spend time with his grandchildren – Claudine now had a two-year-old baby brother – and providing his daughter and son-in-law with a convenient child minder during the week. Again, if Kay and Mitch thought it odd that Charles preferred the company of their children to young William's, they kept their opinion to themselves.

Nor had they ever queried the decision to call the boy William Philip, thus ignoring the Graham side of the family completely. Even Margery had accepted Sally's choice of names without demur, and raised no objection to the selection of her sister and step-father as god-parents.

'Of course, they must know that William isn't Charles's son,' Sally thought wearily.

It was odd that she had never been able to carry either of her husband's children, but had borne Werner's son through the full nine months and given birth to him with comparative ease. The fact seemed full of significance to her on this morning of chilly sunlight, as she watched the dust motes whirl and gyrate along its beams. There had been many times during the past five years when she had longed to write to tell Werner of his son's existence. But it would only have added to the anger and perplexity he had felt at her decision to abandon all thought of divorce, and remain in America with her husband.

For Sally, that had been the most agonizing part of the whole affair; not being able to tell Werner the reason for her decision. But Charles's secret could not be shared with anyone else. She dared not risk confiding it even to Werner, in case, by some roundabout way, the knowledge might lead to her husband's arrest.

She had written to Werner, the day following her promise to Charles, a long, impassionate letter, willing him to understand. He had answered it with a few, stiff, formal lines, his deep unhappiness and bitter disappointment reflected in every word. They had ended: 'I feel that I have no right to reproach you, when so much of what has happened to us has been my fault, but you made me a promise, too. It seems, however, that the one you have made to your husband is more important to you. I suppose that is as it should be. I cannot complain. I think it best if we do not correspond again. From now on, we must live our own lives.'

He was right, of course. To continue writing could only prolong the agony. Charles was not an old man. He had fully recovered from his illness, had apparently regained his strength and could live for many years.

Sally still received sporadic news of Werner from her mother, who maintained her fitful correspondence with Erich Rossman. Sally knew that Werner was still unmarried, although there had been several women in his life during recent years. She lived in dread of the day when Dorothy would write to say that there was a Frau Neumann sharing the flat which Werner now rented in the same apartment block as the Rossmans.

Sally got up abruptly from her seat and ran upstairs. She could not bear to be in the house by herself a moment longer. She would change and go shopping, or to a matinée: anything to stop herself thinking.

She was used to these moods of restlessness and had learned not to resist them. In the early days, when William was a baby, she had tried to ignore them; to concentrate on her painting, with the child asleep in his carry-cot in the studio. But she had driven herself perilously close to a nervous breakdown, and had realized just in time, how foolish she was being. Louanne, who had been re-engaged immediately after Charles's decision to retain the Washington house, adored the baby, and liked nothing better than to be left in charge. So, whenever the mood was on her, Sally handed William over and took herself off for a couple of days.

In the bedroom, she stripped off her paint-stained jeans and old polo-necked jumper, then went through to her bathroom and took a shower. The flow of warm water over her naked body gave her a kind of sensuous pleasure, and she ran her soapy hands down across her breasts and thighs. A longing for Werner siezed her. Her life suddenly seemed so empty that she wanted to scream aloud.

She and Charles no longer lived as man and wife. Although, at weekends, they shared a bedroom, they had separate beds. When Charles suffered from his recurring nightmares, or was unable to sleep, Sally was there to comfort him. When she was restless, he would talk gently and soothingly to her until she fell into a doze. She had once said to him: 'We don't have to live like this, if you don't wish it,' but had realized, almost as soon as the words were out of her mouth, that it was impossible for them to resume any sexual relationship. The thought of William, the knowledge that she was still in love with Werner, would always come between them. Charles needed her desperately. Her affection, support and understanding kept the demons of guilt and remorse at bay. He was content with that. He no longer asked for – and perhaps did not want – the kind of love she had never been able to give him.

Sally stepped quickly out of the shower and dried herself. It was a sort of betrayal, she felt, to want Werner so badly. She dressed, selecting from her wardrobe an oatmeal coloured, Chanel-type suit, a dark red blouse and one of the round, pillbox hats that the President's wife was making so popular. The United States capital had never been so fashion conscious as it had been these past three years, since John and Jacqueline Kennedy had inhabited the White House. Skirts were getting shorter; they had risen almost above the knee. Sally, giving herself a final glance in the mirror, thanked God that she had good legs. Then she picked up her handbag and gloves, and ran downstairs.

It was strange, Werner thought, to be back in Bristol. He had not seen the place for fifteen years. Then, he had been one of an army of German prisoners waiting to be sent home, tolerated by the majority of Britishers as a necessary evil in their midst. Now, he was Herr Neumann, junior partner of Gabler and Neumann, toy manufacturers, a welcome visitor, who was inspecting the city with a view to making it the British headquarters of Gabler and Neumann (UK). He had been wined and dined and given the VIP treatment by the local Chamber of Commerce, and had finally returned to his hotel, having promised his hosts to let them have his company's decision as soon as possible. He had refused, politely but firmly, the arrangements made for his evening's entertainment, on the score that he had had a long day and wanted to make an early start for Birmingham in the morning. Bristol, he pointed out, enjoying his sense of power, was not the only city on his list.

The truth was that he was in no mood for a drinking session in some stuffy club, where strippers were bound to prove inferior to their counterparts in Hamburg's notorious Reeperbahn night spots. When he had realized that Bristol was high on the list of English cities being considered by the company for its United Kingdom base, he had believed that visiting it would cause him no problems. Its association with Sally was something he was perfectly able to handle. He told himself firmly that she meant nothing to him any more.

But he had been wrong. Ever since he got off the train that morning, she had walked at his side like an unquiet ghost. It had needed all his willpower to concentrate on the matter in hand, and attend to what his hosts were saying. Alone, at last, in his hotel bedroom, he could no longer delude himself that his love for her was a thing of the past.

There was a telephone on the table beside his bed and, beneath it, a local directory. With a finger which was not quite steady, he traced down the long list of Jacksons until he came to Philip R. He and Dorothy were still there: Grace Cottage, Coldharbour, near Bristol. He lifted the receiver and asked the hotel switchboard operator to get him the number . . .

Shortly after eight o'clock, he was standing in the cottage's narrow hallway and Philip was relieving him of his coat. Dorothy emerged from the living room, smoking the inevitable cigarette.

With her appearance, the sense of *déja vu* was overpowering. Werner half glanced over his shoulder, expecting to see Erich just behind him, and ran surreptitious fingers along the seams of his trousers to make sure they were not the rough, brown-dyed uniform of the POWs. And as he followed Dorothy into the well-remembered living room, he had to remind himself that he was Werner Neumann of Gabler and Neumann, courted and fêted visitor of eager British businessman, all anxious to bring some of the thriving West German industry to their city.

'You didn't mind my telephoning you?' he asked, when they were seated. 'I know from Erich that Mrs Jackson is kind enough to inquire about me whenever she writes.'

'We were delighted to hear from you,' Philip assured him. He appreciated the quiet Teutonic thoroughness which assigned Dorothy her proper title, although this was the first occasion on which she and Werner had met since her remarriage. Half the people in the village still referred to her as Mrs Sherwood. 'Are you in Bristol on business?'

Werner explained, and was gratified to note that they both looked suitably impressed.

'Well, well! Dorothy exclaimed, stretching her legs to the fire. 'Werner, the tycoon. How's Erich?'

'Very prosperous. Running to fat. He and Trudi now have four children.' He accepted a glass of whisky which Philip had poured for him. 'Your very good health. Mrs Jackson.'

An awkward pause ensued, while they all racked their brains for something to say without involving Sally's name. Dorothy, with relief, followed Werner's eyes to the display of photographs on top of her china cabinet.

'My grandchildren,' she explained. 'My daughter Jennifer's children.'

'Ah! May I please take a closer look?' Werner got up and crossed the room, peering with feigned interest at the various permutations of six plump, smiling faces. There was a collection of studio portraits and a scattering of snapshots, wedged into the frames. It occurred to Werner that the display was rather oddly arranged, bunched to one side of the cabinet roof, almost as though other photographs had stood there and been removed. He turned to his seat and sat down.

Philip sipped his whisky and asked: 'Is this your first visit to Bristol since your POW days?'

'Yes. And it is very strange. Before lunch today, I was driven past the place where the camp used to be. It was an eerie sensation. It was as though it had never been. As though none of it had ever existed outside of my imagination . . .'

His voice tailed off, and he sat looking into the heart of the blazing fire, such a lost expression on his face that Dorothy's animosity towards him vanished. She leaned forward in her seat and touched his shoulder.

'I think we all experience that feeling from time to time,' she said gently. 'Especially as we get older.'

He smiled faintly. 'You will never be old, Mrs Jackson.'

Dorothy was taken aback by a compliment from such an unexpected quarter, particularly as it was spoken with such genuine feeling. In the old days, Werner had seemed totally unaffected by her charms. She glanced triumphantly at her huband, and Philip knew that from now on, she would be firmly on Werner's side and against Charles Graham. It was so simple to win Dorothy's approval. He guessed that she was now itching to tell Werner about young William, and stepped in hurriedly to divert her attention.

'Your English is almost perfect now, Werner. Almost colloquial. Do you find you can think in the language?'

'Sometimes. It is necessary to be able to speak it. It has become the international tongue.'

'The result of empire,' Philip answered, and the conversation became general rather than personal. There was one dangerous moment, when President Kennedy's June visit to West Germany, and to West Berlin in particular, was mentioned, with reference to his *Ich bin ein Berliner* speech. Philip was afraid that it would lead them, via the United States and Washington, to Sally; but the reference passed without being followed up, and shortly afterwards Werner rose to go.

'It has been very nice seeing you both once more,' he said,

263

shaking hands. 'May I call again, if I find myself back in Bristol?'

'Of course!' Dorothy was almost gushing. 'You must promise to come and stay with us, mustn't he, darling?'

'If he wants to. But we are off the beaten track,' Philip reminded her. He was at present not only in the middle of writing a book, but was also committed to two regular political columns, one in a national daily and the other in a well-known monthly magazine. His time was precious. Moreover, he could not trust Dorothy to keep her mouth shut now that Werner had so unexpectedly instated himself in her good graces.

The front door closed behind the German, and the sound of his hire-car's engine dwindled away into the night.

'Winter's coming,' Philip said. 'You can smell the cold. It reminds me of childhood, and those couple of weeks between Trafalgar Day and Bonfire Night, when you realized that autumn was over and that Christmas was on the way.'

Dorothy was busy with her own thoughts.

'You know, I've misjudged that young man,' she purred, settling herself once again in her armchair and consulting the *Radio Times*, to see what was on television.

'Hardly young,' Philip demurred. 'He fought in the war. He must be getting on for forty.'

'And we're both over sixty,' Dorothy retorted sharply. The recollection made her smile. 'But I must say,' she added smugly, 'after Werner's compliment, I don't think that I have any need to worry.'

When he reached the end of Church Lane, his left indicator flashing, Werner suddenly changed his mind. There was no other car in sight, so he abruptly switched indicators and swung right along Hill Road, then right again at The King's Head, into the lower end of Manor Walk. A few hundred yards past the pub, he turned into the still unmade track leading to Barton Farm.

The Youngers were delighted to see him, and if they were less impressed by Werner's affluent appearance and business sucess than Dorothy and Philip had been, that was only because they knew very little of the commercial world outside of farming.

'Well, it is nice to see you again,' Ellen Younger said, when her husband had excused himself and gone out to see that the cows were safely shut up for the night.

'You've got to keep your eyes on that Terry Ibbs,' Bob had grumbled, 'every minute of the bloody day.'

Werner could not remember ever having been in the farm parlour before, and would have preferred the familiar homeliness of the kitchen. But Ellen evidently regarded his visit as a social occasion and insisted on lighting the fire in what she called 'the best room'; and they sat awkwardly, and in considerable discomfort, one on either side of the uneasily smoking fire.

'Now,' Ellen invited, 'tell me about yourself, my dear. What you've been up to all these years.'

Werner complied to the best of his ability. It was soon obvious that Ellen knew nothing of his affair with Sally. Philip and Dorothy had kept it to themselves.

'And you've not married?' Ellen queried in surprise. 'That is a shame, a nice looking man like you. Haven't you ever met anyone you fancied? Not one of those pretty blonde *Fräuleins* that we see on the TV news?' Werner shook his head, not trusting himself to speak. 'Well, I never!' Ellen Younger looked for a moment as if she were going to pursue the unwelcome subject, then changed her mind. 'Of course,' she said, suddenly remembering, 'you used to visit Dorothy Sherwood, didn't you, after the war? She'd like to see you again, I expect.'

'I have already been there,' Werner smiled. 'Then I thought I should like to see you and Mr Younger again, so . . . here I am.'

'I'm very glad you've come, my dear. And I expect Mrs Sherwood was pleased to see you, as well. It's a bit lonely for her with two of the girls living in the States. I suppose she told you about Sally and Veronica. They both married Americans. Met them here, in the village, during the war.

There's the other twin, Jennifer. She still lives in Bristol.'
Mrs Younger became confidential, delighted by the unlooked-
for chance to gossip to someone who did not already know
her news. 'But she doesn't visit her mother that often. Six
kiddies, so what can you expect? A shame, though, that
Dorothy doesn't see more of her grandchildren. And the
other one lives in America. I'm referring to Sally's little
boy, young William. Did you notice the big photograph Mrs
Sherwood keeps in her living room, at Grace Cottage?' Ellen
Younger's eyes suddenly narrowed, focusing intently on
Werner's face. 'Now, there's an extraordinary thing! It's
never struck me until this moment, but that boy looks
exactly like you!'

CHAPTER TWENTY-TWO

At the end of October, Charles suffered a mild heart attack. Kay telephoned with the news just as Sally had finished a rather trying session with the four-year-old twins of a prominent Washington socialite. It had proved almost impossible to keep the boys still for any length of time, and both their mother and Sally were exhausted.

The door had hardly closed on the lady and her sons, when the telephone rang. Louanne appeared from her sitting room to answer it.

'Whoever it is, I'm not in,' Sally mouthed, making once more for her studio. 'I'll fetch William from school today.'

But she had barely time to cast a dissatisfied glance at the painting on the easel, before Louanne reappeared, white-faced at the studio door.

'It's Mrs Everard, Mrs Graham. Mr Graham's been taken ill.'

Kay, however, was reassuring. 'A very mild heart attack, Dr Foy says. But Papa must have a few weeks' rest.'

Dr Foy himself confirmed that there was no immediate cause for concern, when Sally arrived that night in New York. By chance, he had dropped in at the Everards' apartment on his way home from the theatre, just to check on his old friend and patient. He and Sally had ridden up in the elevator together.

Charles was asleep in the room which had been put permanently at his disposal by his daughter and son-in-law.

'How bad is he?' Sally asked.

'He collapsed at the office, first thing this morning.' It was Mitch who answered, Kay having disappeared into the

267

kitchen to prepare sandwiches and coffee. 'Bob de Courcy insisted that they send for an ambulance, but by the time it arrived, Chuck was conscious and demanding that he be brought home. Kay contacted Dr Foy at once.'

Mitch turned towards the older man, as though renouncing any further responsibility for the story, and Dr Foy continued: 'Indications were that it was a very mild heart attack, as I've already said. But I took the precaution of calling in a second opinion. Charles needs nothing now but rest.'

'Will he have another attack?' Sally asked, frowning. 'The Senator died of a heart attack.'

'If Charles takes life more easily, avoids shocks and stress as much as possible, there's no reason why he shouldn't live to a ripe old age.' Dr Foy patted her hand comfortingly. 'I've given him some pills, just in case, but if he heeds the warning he's been given, he may never have to take them. He's lucky. I've told him so. Not many people get such a gentle advance notice that something could be wrong.'

'Can he travel? Can I take him back to Washington?'

'In a day or two. No problem. Just make sure he doesn't exert himself more than he has to.' Dr Foy got to his feet as Kay appeared with the tray of coffee and food. 'Nothing for me, my dear, thank you. I must be going. I've left my wife sitting in the car. She'll be growing impatient.'

When Kay had seen him out she returned to pour coffee. She glanced at Sally, but made no comment. Sally gave her back look for look.

'You think I should insist on moving to New York, don't you? I suppose I should. I'll talk to Charles about it, when he's fully recovered.'

Kay seated herself beside her husband on the couch and passed Sally the plate of sandwiches.

'I don't know that Papa would agree to that. He likes it here with the kids and all. No, I was just thinking how glad I am that you decided to stay with him. He needs you, Sally.'

'Yes.' The monosyllable fell flatly between them. Mitch raised his eyebrows.

'Regrets?' he asked.

Sally shook her head. 'No, of course not.' She caught his eye and grimaced ruefully. 'All right, sometimes. But not as often as I used to have them. I'm very fond of Charles, in case either of you has any doubts.' She paused, stirring her coffee. 'This heart attack, did Dr Foy offer any explanation?'

'Just age, overwork.' Kay sent her husband a reproving glance as he wolfed down the sandwiches. 'And what he suffered during the war. The operation on Papa's legs probably put a strain on his heart . . . For heaven's sake, Mitch! Those are for Sally!'

'It's all right,' Sally said, laughing. 'I'm not hungry. I ate on the 'plane. I feel too tired to eat.'

Kay jumped up at once. 'Of course you do! Come on, I'll show you to your room, so you can unpack and get some sleep.'

In the bedroom, with its soft, variegated shades of pastel green, Sally asked awkwardly: 'Kay, is Charles unhappy? Is that what put him under a strain?'

'Because you don't live together as man and wife, you mean?' Kay's frank gaze met Sally's and she laughed. 'Don't look so horrified. Papa hasn't discussed it with me. I just guessed. No, he's certainly not unhappy, as far as I know. Not so long as he can count on you being there whenever he needs you. I think he'll do as he's told. He has a lot to live for. He's devoted to Claudine and young Chuck. And now Teddy's getting married, finally, after all these years! Oh no! Papa will behave himself, don't worry.' She said goodnight and closed the door behind her.

It was only later that Sally realized her step-daughter had made no mention of William. Did she and Mitch guess? Probably. It wouldn't take much imagination to arrive at the truth. Besides, the boy didn't look like either her or Charles.

He was the image of Werner.

Werner couldn't sleep. In spite of being dog-tired – he had flown in from Holland only three hours earlier, and was off to France at the crack of dawn tomorrow – he was unable

269

to settle. As on so many other nights, the thought of the son he had never seen made him restless, his busy mind going round and round in circles.

He had no doubt that Sally's child was his. He had pressed Mrs Younger for such details of the boy's birth as she could remember, without arousing her suspicions. Fortunately, she had no idea that Werner had ever been to America, and so had been able to laugh with him over the odd quirk of fate which had given young William Graham his features. She knew the child had been born in the autumn of nineteen-fifty-eight, but had been unsure of the actual date.

'October, some time, it was, my dear. Late October, I think.'

To add weight to what already amounted to certainty in Werner's mind, was the recollection of the odd arrangement of grandchildren's photographs on the top of Dorothy's china cabinet; the impression he had obtained that there were at least a couple missing. They would, of course, have been of William. If the likeness between himself and the boy was so marked, Dorothy would have taken the precaution of removing them.

Werner had been tempted to return to Grace Cottage and demand the truth, but in the end, had decided against it. He liked Philip, and owed Dorothy a debt of gratitude for her hospitality, all those years ago. They were not to blame for the fact that he had not been informed about his son. The secrecy was Sally's.

It was this which he found so difficult to forgive. It was hard enough to accept that she had changed her mind so quickly and easily after his departure; that she had apparently made very little effort to resist the persuasions of her husband and family. But also to conceal the fact that she had borne his son, to deny him all knowledge of his child, made him not just hurt, but angry. The old animosities, which he had thought dead and buried for ever, floated to the surface once more. 'Perfidious Albion' seemed suddenly personified in Sally.

He switched on the bedside lamp and lit a cigarette, watching the smoke curl and feather away towards the ceiling. To his bitterness was added the frustration of knowing that there was nothing he could do to ease the situation. If Charles Graham had accepted the child as his, as apparently he had, then it would need a long and costly court battle to prove otherwise. It would mean spending a lot of time and money in the States, neither of which Werner could possibly afford. He had considered writing to Sally, but abandoned the idea after tearing up the drafts of half a dozen letters. Mere written words were not adequate to express his sense of betrayal.

There were other underlying causes, however, to fuel his unhappiness. With the visit of President Kennedy to West Germany and West Berlin in June, a feeling of euphoria had gripped him, in common with that of the rest of the country. To be German was respectable again. Foreigners no longer clung to the idea of collective guilt, and seemed suddenly willing to judge each German on his or her own merits. Then, yesterday, he had gone into a restaurant in Amsterdam, and immediately three people at the next table to his had got up and walked out. They had heard him address the waiter who had shown him to his place, and recognized his accent.

He had caught, as he was meant to catch, the words 'Boche' and 'Hun', spoken with a spitting contempt. Heads had turned, and he could feel dozens of eyes boring into the back of his neck, but he had stuck it out, ordering his meal in a steady voice and forcing himself to sit through all three courses. No one else had left the restaurant or treated him with anything but civility, but the incident had been unsettling, indicating as it did the residue of ill-feeling still remaining, eighteen years after the end of the war.

Werner propped himself on one elbow and lit a second cigarette from the stub of the first. Who was he kidding? More than a residue of hatred and resentment existed against the Germans. Was that why Sally had decided, after all, to remain with her husband? Had she been unable to face life with him, here in Hamburg? If only she had offered some

271

sort of reasonable explanation, instead of the excuse that Charles Graham needed her. She must have known that, when she promised to leave him, but it had not influenced her then . . .

His mind was trapped like a squirrel in a cage, and would not let him sleep. He got up and padded into the kitchen, his bare feet noiseless on the fitted carpet of the new apartment. The one he should have shared with Sally had been sold to another couple; but he had been unable to remain in his old apartment with its memories, however brief, of excitement and anticipation. It had been Erich who had informed him of the flat to let in the block where he and Trudi now lived; luxury apartments, but as a single man with a good job, Werner could easily afford one.

He made himself a hot toddy, took a bath, then crawled back between the sheets, willing himself to sleep. But even when he did so, it was only to dream that Sally was standing with him outside Grace Cottage, telling him that they had never had a son.

'It's all nonsense!' she was saying, laughing at him, displaying empty hands. 'You didn't really believe it, surely!'

He woke to the shrilling of his alarm, heavy-eyed and unrefreshed. He packed his case for the fourth time in three days, and made himself some breakfast.

'How are you feeling?' Sally perched on the end of Charles's bed as he sat up, eating his breakfast. The pale November sun gleamed fitfully, lightening the gloom of the winter morning. Yesterday in Washington had been a day of mud and rain and gusting winds. Today, the weather had relented.

'I'm feeling like a fraud,' Charles said, starting on his second boiled egg. 'I'm perfectly fit, and you and Louanne are waiting on me hand, foot and finger.'

'And that's how it's going to stay,' Sally answered. 'You know what Dr Foy said. Rest for several weeks.'

She did not tell him that in the middle of the night, she had wakened to find him standing at the foot of her bed, his eyes wide open, but his senses shut. When she spoke to him, there had been no response, and she had guessed at once that he was sleepwalking. After a moment or two, he had moved to the bedside table, lifted the glass which stood beside the water jug and offered it, not to her, but to the person his sleep-drugged mind believed her to be. Faith.

The hair had risen on her scalp and beads of perspiration had pricked across her body, but she had known better than to touch, or try to rouse him. Presently, Charles had put the empty glass back on the table, returned to bed and, within a very few minutes, was breathing peacefully. But Sally had remained awake for almost an hour, ready, if he should need her, to keep away the 'demons'. It came to her suddenly that it was the stress of guilt which was making him ill. He could not forgive himself for what he had done.

She blew him a kiss. 'I've just remembered,' she said, 'that I promised to go to Dallas with Veronica and Pete at the end of the month. Pete's going to attend some pharmaceutical conference, and Ronnie wanted company during the day. She isn't very keen on the company wives; and, as the wife of the boss's son, her presence tends to inhibit them. However, she'll have to make out on her own. I must 'phone and tell her I shan't, after all, be going.'

'Why not?' Charles paused in the act of spreading his toast with marmalade. 'I shall certainly be up and about by the end of the month. When exactly is it Veronica and Pete are going?'

'Well, I suppose it's not really the end of the month. November sixteenth to the twenty-third. But of course I shan't go now! Don't be absurd. I shouldn't dream of leaving you.'

'You might not have to. If I feel up to it, and I'm sure I shall, I'd like to come with you. It could be interesting. That's the week the President's campaigning in Texas. And he can't very well go to Texas without visiting Dallas, however much his aides might wish he could avoid it.'

'Why should they wish that?' Sally, even after nine years in the States, still found the political affiliations of her adopted country more than a little perplexing.

'Texans are mostly dyed-in-the-wool Republicans, the radical right, and they don't like the President. That's putting it mildly. There's been a recent demonstration against his administration in Dallas.'

Charles had had the story from his mother. A week or so earlier, Adlai Stevenson had visited the city to give an address on United Nations Day. Throughout his speech, he had been harassed, heckled and spat at. Members of the audience had waved handbills and placards bearing photographs, full-face and profile, of John F. Kennedy, beneath which was the legend: 'Wanted for Treason. This man is wanted for treasonous activities against the United States.'

'And that's not just an isolated incident,' Margery had said. 'I recall that during the nineteen-sixty campaign, even Lyndon and Ladybird Johnson received some very rough treatment in the lobby of the Adolphus Hotel.' And she had stared down her aristocratic nose as she contemplated the antics of the newly-rich citizens of Dallas, whose wealth was founded on the discovery, in the nineteen-forties, of the East Texas oil pool. The population of the city had doubled in just over twenty years.

Sally leaned forward and removed the tray from her husband's knees.

'If there's going to be any excitement of that nature,' she said, 'we're certainly not going. You're supposed to be taking it easy from now until after Christmas.'

'You'd like to go,' Charles said. 'I can see it in your face. And I won't have you disappointed.'

She tilted her head to one side and looked at him with eyes sparkling with tears.

'You're much to good for me. You always have been.'

He stretched out a hand and clasped her fingers. 'Dear Sally. I couldn't do without you, you know. You're the best thing that ever happened to me.'

'In spite of everything?' Her voice broke in the middle.

'Because of everything. You're the sheet anchor of my life. I couldn't go on without you.'

'You won't have to,' she answered, kissing him.

The bedroom door opened and William came in, a tough, sturdy five-year-old, with a mat of fair hair and the piercingly blue eyes of his father. Sally, standing beside the bed, holding Charles's hand, felt the shockwave of resistance go through him, as he braced himself for William's greeting. A moment later, however, he was returning the boy's bear-like hug with enthusiasm. What it cost him in effort, Sally thought, God alone knew!

'Why aren't you at school, young man?'

'I'm just going. Louanne's waiting for me in the hall, but I wanted to say goodbye to Pops.' The soft, nasal American twang never failed to sound alien to Sally in her and Werner's son. 'You feeling better today, Pops?'

'I'm feeling just fine.' Charles kissed the smooth cheek. The fresh young skin smelled faintly of apples.

'Good.' William scrambled off the bed and raised his face for his mother's kiss. ''Bye, Mom. See you later, alligator.'

She knew her response. 'In a while, crocodile.'

Her son shunted through the door, puffing loudly and hooting like a train whistle. She could hear him on the stairs.

'Hi, Louanne! Get ready with the signals. The freight's come into the siding.'

Sally turned back to her husband. 'He'll be sure to want to tell you about his day at school, this evening. Don't let him tire you.'

'He won't.' Charles looked up at her and squeezed her hand. 'I am very fond of him.'

She smiled reassuringly and kissed his forehead. 'I know you are. Now, get some rest.'

He nodded, yawning. 'I do feel tired this morning. I don't know why. I slept extremely well.'

She made no response, but waited until Charles had settled himself, then quietly left the room. She closed the door and went downstairs. Louanne and William had gone: she consulted her watch. Ten past nine: she had a sitting in twenty minutes. She made her way to the studio and put on her smock, uncovering the canvas which stood on the easel.

275

The day was uneventful. Her sitters arrived punctually and did as they were asked, without argument. She looked in on Charles four or five times, and on all but one occasion, he was sleeping. Sally did not even trouble to wake him for lunch, and she and Louanne ate cheese and salad in the kitchen. Veronica telephoned to know if Sally's trip to Texas was on or off, and was informed of Charles's proposal.

'What a splendid idea! It'll do him good. The presidential visit will add an extra interest. It's always a pleasure to see what Jacqueline's wearing. That woman has style. Incidentally, I have heard . . .' And Veronica plunged into the latest piece of Washington scandal.

Altogether, Sally reflected, as she cleaned her brushes and prepared to close the studio for the night, it had been one of those quiet, run-of-the-mill days, which made no physical or emotional demands, but still left one feeling pleasantly tired. Charles would get up for dinner – he was already running his bath the last time she had peeped in to see him – and afterwards, they would read or watch television. They might even stay up for the late night movie.

As she entered the hall from the back of the house, Louanne and William came through the front door and the telephone started to ring.

'I'll get it!' William yelled, dropping Louanne's hand and rushing headlong into the dining room to pick up the receiver. He loved talking to people on the telephone and would fight tooth and nail to be allowed to answer it whenever he was around.

'Hullo!' His young voice was urgent with excitement. After a pause, Sally heard him say: 'Yeah. I'm William. How d'you know my name?' There was another, longer pause before he went on: 'OK. I'll tell her. Hold on, please.' He appeared in the doorway. 'It's for you, Mom.'

'Who is it?' Sally whispered as she passed him, but he shrugged.

'I dunno. Just a man, I guess.'

A client, Sally thought. She picked up the receiver. 'Hullo. This is Sally Graham.'

There was a moment's silence, then Werner's voice said: 'Sarah . . . How are you?'

Her heart began to slam with long, slow strokes against her ribs. Her legs felt so weak, she was forced to sit down. She had not expected to hear from him ever again.

'Sarah,' he repeated, 'are you still there?'

'Yes, I'm here,' she croaked. 'I . . . Werner . . . What do you want?' She had not intended to sound so abrupt, but shock had robbed her of the power of polite conversation.

'I want to see my son,' he answered tersely. 'I'd like to come to Washington, later this month.'

'No!' Panic left no room for soft words or reasoned arguments. Any moment now, Charles would come downstairs for afternoon tea with William. He must not be upset, must not hear her wrangling with Werner. He must not even know that Werner had called her. At this stage of his convalescence, any shock or worry would be bad for him. She added briefly: 'William is not your son, he's my husband's.' That, at any rate, was true in the eyes of the law.

A protracted silence followed, then Werner said flatly: 'That is a lie. I did not think you would lie to me, Sarah.'

'Stop calling me Sarah in that stupid, formal way.' He was not to know that she found the repetition of it too full of poignant memories for comfort. To Werner, she merely sounded irritable and callous. 'And if you come to Washington,' she went on, 'it won't do you any good. I shan't be here. I'm going out of town.' There was no need to point out that William would not be with her.

'I shall come later, then, when you return to Washington.'

'No, you mustn't.' She could hear Charles's voice upstairs, speaking to William, and the child's shrill burst of answering laughter. She knew she mustn't give herself time to think or dream or hope. She had to be ruthless if she were to resist the temptation to tell Werner how much she still loved him; to tell him the truth. She continued rapidly: 'There is no point you coming here this month, next month or ever. William is mine. Mine and Charles's. I don't want to see you, Werner. What was

277

between us is over. Finished! Please leave me alone!'

She slammed down the receiver and sat rocking herself to and fro, drawing in gulps of air as if she were drowning. Charles was on the stairs. She made an enormous effort and pulled herself together. He must not suspect anything from her demeanour. She stood up slowly and pushed back her chair. William was shouting: 'Mom! Mom! Where are you, Mom?'

She propelled herself forward and out of the room. She managed to smile.

CHAPTER TWENTY-THREE

Somewhat to her surprise, Sally liked Dallas. After what Charles had told her, she had expected to be ill at ease; to feel, in some obscure fashion, threatened. Instead, she found the inhabitants outgoing and friendly, in a way foreign to the more conservative denizens of the capital. Everyone went out of his or her way to be helpful: nothing seemed too much trouble.

It was two weeks now since Werner had 'phoned. If she let herself recollect too clearly the things she had said to him, the tone of voice she had used, Sally felt she would lose her reason. To hear his voice again, after almost six years, and without warning, had torn her to pieces. It had brought back a vivid picture of him as she had last seen him, that cold winter's morning at Washington airport, as he boarded his 'plane, happy, excited, confident that she would soon be joining him in Hamburg. That was to have been their final parting; an end to that pattern of existence which had brought them together, their lives touching briefly, only to be forced apart by circumstances, old enmities and misunderstandings.

Sally tried not think about it. She busied herself with preparations for the trip to Dallas, realizing that it had now become vital that she and Charles get out of Washington, if only for a week. From anxiously trying to dissuade her husband from making the effort, she had proceeded to give Charles every encouragement to accompany her and the Kovaks.

'I'm sure it won't harm you, darling. You're so much better.'

Veronica, with no axe to grind, had added her mite.

'It'll be fun. You can rest during the day while Sally and I go shopping and Pete's at the convention centre; and in the evening, we can go out on the town as a foursome.'

Pete had been equally enthusiastic. Only Margery Graham had expressed reservations.

'Just remember, you're supposed to be convalescent,' she had told her son, adding bluntly: 'Remember, also, that you're not as young as the other three. You're sixty next year. A dangerous time of life for any man.'

Her words and attitude, however, had merely hardened Charles's resolve to go to Dallas. Sally was thirty-four and an extremely attractive woman: he had no wish to be reminded of his age.

'I shall be careful, naturally,' he had reassured his mother. 'Not simply for my sake. I have Sally to think of. And William.'

'William!' Margery had snorted. 'What sort of a fool do you think I am? The boy looks nothing like you.'

At the back of Sally's mind was the constant worry that Werner might telephone again. How had he found out about William? As far as she knew, her mother and Philip had had no contact with Werner. Yet he had discovered the truth somehow and had sounded angry. Surely he would not carry out his threat to come to Washington? But in case he did, it was essential that she and Charles get away. Perhaps she would persuade her husband to stay on in Texas for a while, letting Veronica and Pete come home alone. There were so many parts of the United States she had never seen. Maybe they could send for William. Time off from school at this early stage of his education surely could not hurt him. The three of them could stay away from Washington until after Christmas. She could think up some excuse for Charles. After that, he would be returning to de Courcy's and New York. She again suggested that she and William return there with him, to live.

But Charles, as Kay had predicted, vetoed the idea.

'I know you prefer Washington and I want, above all else,

for you to be happy. I like spending four nights a week with Kay and Mitch and the children. I get to see more of them that way.'

Sally had not argued. Dissension was bad for him at present. She would wait until he was stronger to press her point. At the moment, the most urgent problem was to get him away from Washington. The travelling would do him less harm than a confrontation with Werner.

She had her first sight of Dallas on the sixteenth of November as their aeroplane circled above the city waiting to land; the skyscrapers rising up like monoliths out of the surrounding prairies. The four of them were booked into the plush Adolphus Hotel, where, as Sally remembered, the Vice-President and his wife had been hissed at and spat upon three years earlier. And the Johnsons were themselves Texans.

Nothing, however, could have exceeded the affability of their welcome. Within a very few hours, Sally felt more at home than she had ever done in New York or Washington. It was only in the mornings, when she and Charles were sitting up in bed eating their breakfast and reading the *Dallas Morning News*, that she caught echoes of that other, untamed city, with its fervent hatreds and prejudices which had been described to her. There was a violence in the opinions expressed, an anti-Democrat and, above all, an anti-Kennedy bias, whose virulence shocked her. Its publisher was the man who had once told the President that what America needed was a knight on horseback, while all he was riding was his daughter Caroline's tricycle.

'I didn't know myself that I should be coming until the day before yesterday.' Werner stood once more on the doorstep of Grace Cottage, smiling at Dorothy. 'I flew into London yesterday and did the rest of the journey by train. My company has decided to open its first British factory in Bristol, and as all business was concluded by midday today, I thought I would drive out to see you. I took a chance that you would be in.' He did not add that he had deliberately

281

refrained from telephoning because he wished to arrive unannounced. He wanted to see the photograph of his son.

'How lovely. I'm so glad I'm at home.' Dorothy's pleasure was genuine. Since Werner's previous visit she had remembered him with something akin to affection, as the young man who had told her she would never look her age. 'Come in.' She held the door wide, and he stepped into the hall, where she took his hat and coat. She indicated the living room. 'My daughter Jennifer and two of her children are here, but you won't mind that, I'm sure. Philip's working in the studio, but I'll ring through and let him know you're here. We've had an extension 'phone put in. At my insistence. It saves me going into the garden in all weathers each time I need to get in touch with him.' Her voice was tart.

While she spoke, she ushered Werner into the living room, where a woman was sitting by the fire, reading to two small boys. Werner recalled her vaguely; one of the twins. The little boys, also twins, were like her, with soft brown hair and blue eyes; faces which he had seen recently in the photographs on top of the cabinet. His eyes, as though drawn by a magnet, switched to that cluster of ornate silver frames, and remained riveted on the largest of the group. There were two photographs of William, and Werner knew instantly that it was indeed his son. He had not really needed confirmation, but had he done so, this was it. The round, laughing face was not only his, at five years old, but was reminiscent also of his father at a similar age.

Jennifer, who had risen to shake hands with him after her mother's introduction – 'Darling, you remember! One of our German boys' – followed the direction of his gaze.

'That's Sally's little boy, William. I expect you recall Sally, my younger sister. She lives in America. Has done for years.'

Werner heard Dorothy's intake of breath. Then she looked at him, smiled and shrugged as if to say: 'Oh well! There's nothing I can do about it now. The damage is done.' He even had the impression that she was enjoying the situation, and thought that she was not a woman to whom

282

he would willingly entrust a secret. He remembered his earlier impression of her as a mischief-maker.

Philip arrived from the studio a few minutes later. Werner, struggling to maintain a polite flow of conversation with Jennifer, heard him and Dorothy whispering together in the hall. When they entered the room and greetings were over, Dorothy carried Jennifer and the children into the kitchen, on the pretext of needing their help. Philip warmed his cold hands at the fire, glancing sideways at Werner as he did so.

'Well, now you know,' he said.

Werner did not pretend to misunderstand him. 'I know William is my son. I don't know why Sally kept the information from me.'

'Because she decided to stay with her husband, presumably.'

'I have never understood that, either.'

Philip replied with asperity: 'I see nothing to understand about a wife staying with her husband. You had your chance years ago, Werner. You chose not to take it.'

Werner ignored him, pursuing his own line of thought.

'I telephoned her the week before last. She told me that William is not my child.'

'Then she lied,' Philip said quietly. 'But knowing Sally, she wouldn't have done so without good reason. Charles Graham has recently suffered a heart attack. Only a mild one, but for the time being, he needs rest. He must not be worried. How did you find out about William?'

'I went to see Mrs Younger after I left here that evening. Until then, as you are aware, I did not know of the child's existence. She mentioned him and was struck by his likeness to me. She just thought it an odd coincidence. She had no idea, of course, that I could possibly be his father.'

'So what do you intend to do?'

'I told Sally that I was going to America to claim my son.' He added bitterly: 'But naturally, I did not mean it. I just wanted to think it was possible, but I know now I could not do it without disrupting too many lives. Not least that of my son. Is he happy?' Werner asked wistfully.

283

'Yes,' Philip answered gently. 'He's a very happy child. He has a good life in America and Charles is very kind to him.'

'Mr Graham knows that William is not his son?'

'Yes. And there may come a time when the boy will have to know, too. But that will be up to Sally.'

'Do you see him often?'

'Not as often as we'd like. We were in Washington in the summer.' Moved by the look of sadness on Werner's face, Philip said: 'If you like, I'll write to you and let you know how the boy is. I'll send you some snapshots. But you must promise not to get in touch with Sally directly. She's chosen her life, and you must try to let her live it.'

For a moment, Werner made no reply, then he gave his head a quick shake, as though ridding himself of fantasies, and raised his eyes to Philip, who was regarding him anxiously.

'I give you my word,' he promised. 'I shall not bother Sarah again.' He added: 'There is a girl, a friend of Trudi Rossman's, who likes me, I think. A nice girl who would make a man a good wife. In time, who knows what may come of it?' He got up from the armchair where he had been sitting. 'Will you and Mrs Jackson forgive me if I leave now? I have to return to London this evening and I have to pack. I am booked on the early flight tomorrow.' He held out his hand. 'Goodbye, Mr Jackson. Write to me, please. But I don't suppose we shall see one another again.'

Philip laughed and shook hands. 'When you reach my age,' he said, 'you'll know that nothing is ever quite as final as that. Fate usually has some trick or other up her sleeve to confound us poor mortals.'

It had been a pleasant evening, passed by the four of them in the bar of the hotel. Charles was more relaxed than Sally had seen him for a long time. Pete's speech at the Convention that day had gone well and earned him a standing ovation. He was pleased with himself and all the world, and he and Veronica seemed, temporarily, to have overcome whatever differences there were between them: their marriage had lost its edge. Sally and her sister had been recalling old times.

Earlier in the evening they had watched television; the arrival that Thursday morning of the President, his wife and entourage in San Antonio. The Kennedys had received a warm welcome in a town which had recently returned a liberal Democrat to Congress. Later, the more conservative citizens of Houston had appeared equally friendly, and tonight, the Presidential party would fly to Fort Worth. Tomorrow, it would be in Dallas.

'Sally and I are going to watch the motorcade,' Veronica said. 'What about you, Charles? Pete, of course, is going to be mewed up listening to speeches even more boring than his own.' The old animosity sparked between them for a second, then was quenched by a spurt of mutual laughter.

'Yes, I'll come with you,' Charles agreed, sipping the weak whisky and soda which, nowadays, he made last all night. He beckoned to a passing waiter. 'Where would be a good place to watch the President's motorcade tomorrow?'

The man hunched his shoulders as though renouncing the Democrats and all their works. 'Almost anywhere,' he replied off-handedly. 'You can bet your life they're not turning out in force in this town to welcome that Commie-loving bastard.'

He moved on and there was silence at the table, the fellowship of the evening suddenly shattered into fragments. Pete looked apologetic. As a staunch Republican, he didn't much care for the Kennedy administration himself, but he would never have expressed his dislike in those words.

He got up and went over to the bar. When he returned, he said: 'The bartender thinks just off Main, on Elm, by the book depository, will be as good a place as any. Near the underpass. He reckons the crowds should be fairly thin thereabouts. You ought to get a pretty good view.'

'Good. I want to see what Jackie's wearing,' Veronica said. 'The clearer the view, the better.'

A bell-boy approached with a telephone trailing its lead.

'Mrs Kovaks?' Veronica glanced up. 'A long-distance call for you. From England.'

As soon as Veronica lifted the receiver, her twin's carrying voice sounded all round the table, as clearly as if Jennifer were in the next room.

'Ronnie? What on earth are you doing in Dallas? Look, I'm sorry I forgot our birthday, but . . .' The authoritative voice was muffled as Veronica cradled the ear-piece against her right ear.

Pete laughed. 'Isn't technology wonderful? If Jennifer was calling from Houston, you probably wouldn't be able to distinguish a word. Thousands of miles of sea and land, and everyone in the place can hear what she's saying.'

Charles smiled. He was holding Sally's hand, and they sat in contented silence while Veronica grew bored and impatient as her sister droned on.

After ten minutes, Pete mouthed: 'Give her the brush-off, for God's sake . . . What the hell is she finding to say all this time? It must be costing her a fortune.'

Veronica, a look of resignation on her face, held the receiver away from her ear, so that they could all hear. Jennifer might have been speaking through a megaphone from the bar.

'. . . called on Mother yesterday, while I was there? One of those German POWs, Werner Neumann. Do you remember . . .?'

Veronica pressed the receiver to her ear again quickly, and burbled: 'Darling, I'm awfully glad you found me . . . Yes . . . Yes . . . Well, I'm sorry you had an abortive call to Washington first . . . Yes . . . I know . . . Look, it's been lovely hearing from you, Jenny, and I wasn't the least put out because you forgot our birthday . . . Whooping cough . . . Of course, I understand. 'Bye. Love to Tony and the children . . . 'Bye, now.'

She slammed down the receiver and signalled to a waiter to take the instrument away.

'Heavens!' she exclaimed with false brightness. 'I thought

she'd never stop. Jenny's such a bore at times . . . Who's for another drink?'

'I'm fine as I am,' Charles said evenly. 'But I am a little tired. I think I'd like to go to bed.'

'I'll come with you.' Sally swallowed the last of her gin and vermouth. 'A decent night's rest will do us both good. Tomorrow could be a tiring day.'

During the night, Charles was restless again, turning and muttering in his sleep. No word had passed between them concerning the telephone call; but as Sally lay wakeful, watching the pattern of shadows on the bedroom ceiling, she cursed, in rotating order, Jennifer's piercing voice, the efficiency of the trans-Atlantic telephone system, and the sheer bad luck which had made them a party to the conversation at that particular moment. Veronica's flurried reaction had not improved matters. It had demonstrated an understanding of the situation which had only fuelled the general embarrassment. Worst of all, however, was the information that Werner had been visiting Grace Cottage. It was that, more than anything, which had obviously disturbed Charles. When he woke the following morning, he looked grey and ill.

The arrival of the *Dallas Morning News* with their breakfast of orange juice, toast and coffee, did nothing to console him, carrying as it did a full-page, anti-Kennedy advertisement. It accused the President of going soft on Communists, fellow travellers and ultra-leftists, while allowing his brother Bobby, the Attorney General, to persecute loyal American citizens. For Charles, John Fitzgerald Kennedy was not only a Democrat, but also a very fine man. He thought him simply the best hope that the United States had had since, for him, the squalor of McCarthyism; an intelligent, tolerant, liberal-thinking man. The bludgeoning criticism of the advertisement angered Charles.

'Ignore it,' Sally advised. 'Darling, take it easy. You know you're not supposed to get excited.'

Charles pushed the newspaper aside in disgust. His face

was now suffused with blood, a purplish-pinkish colour, as unhealthy as its former pallor.

'What in God's name did we fight the last war for?' he demanded passionately. 'Wasn't it to fight these fascist ideas?'

'I know. I know.' She tried to soothe him. 'But that kind of abuse can't hurt a man like the President. It won't make him change his policies or his mind. Now, eat your breakfast. We'll be going home tomorrow.'

'I thought you wanted to see more of Texas?'

She laughed. 'I've changed my mind. For the time being, at least. We'll fly home with Veronica and Pete as originally planned. We can always visit again when the climate's a little less emotional; not so charged with political undercurrents as it is at present.'

Charles sighed with relief. 'I'm glad,' he said. 'I admit, I shan't be sorry to get back to Washington.'

'Are you feeling all right?' Her concern was growing. 'I wish you wouldn't come with us this morning.'

'I shall be fine.' His tone was clipped, a sure sign that he was feeling unwell, and resented being reminded of the fact. He pushed back the bedclothes and went into the bathroom. A few minutes later, Sally heard his slightly off-key rendering of *Marching Thro' Georgia*.

She switched on the bedside television set. The President was addressing the residents of Fort Worth, in the rain, outside the Texas Hotel. Later, it showed pictures of him going off to a breakfast given by the Fort Worth Chamber of Commerce, where he would give a speech. Shortly, he would board Air Force One for the trip to Dallas.

Sally got up and set about getting bathed and dressed.

Veronica, her camera at the ready, hissed in her sister's ear: 'Charles doesn't look so good this morning. Is he OK?'

'He didn't sleep well, that's all.' Sally's tone was curt. She did not want to discuss the matter. If she ignored her worry, perhaps it would go away.

Veronica, however, refused to let the subject rest. 'I was

so upset about that 'phone call. If I'd guessed for a moment what Jenny was going to say, or that you'd all hear it so plainly . . .'

'You couldn't possibly have known. Forget it.'

Sally and her sister had spent the early part of the morning shopping at Neiman-Marcus, returning to the hotel to pick up Charles, who had been resting on his bed. He had looked, if anything, worse than when he had first got up, and Sally had once more urged him to let them go alone. He again refused, this time with a burst of irritation which confirmed his wife's worst fears. But she judged it best not to argue with him, and to let him have his own way. She suspected that some of his tetchiness was due to the prospect of playing the undignified role of tourist: it was not becoming in the son of the late Senator Graham, who could meet the President and his wife on equal terms any day of the week in Washington. But to back down now would be a sign of both physical and mental weakness which Charles was not prepared to tolerate, least of all in himself.

They were standing on the slope outside the Texas School Book Depository, a multi-storeyed building some yards to their rear. The barman at the hotel had been right in thinking that the crowds here would be thin. The lines of people on the grass verge were nowhere more than two or three deep. From the distance came the first, faint sounds of cheering, an indication that the motorcade was at last on its way. Sally and Veronica edged nearer to the road, which ran downhill to the triple underpass. Veronica steadied her camera between both hands. Charles was standing a few feet behind them, trying, Sally thought with amused affection, to look as unobtrusive as possible.

As the presidential car came into view, bearing not only John and Jacqueline Kennedy but Governor and Mrs Connally as well, all the women's eyes were riveted on the elegant figure of the President's wife, sitting upright and smiling beside him.

'Pink,' muttered Veronica, focusing her camera. 'I think I prefer the cream outfit she was wearing yesterday.'

The motorcade purred down Elm Street towards the underpass. Mrs Connally, who had obviously been making some remark to the President in the back, turned to face front once again.

There was a noise which, to Sally, sounded like the popping of a champagne cork. It meant nothing to her until someone screamed. The President had slumped forwards and sideways against his wife. Then all hell and pandemonium broke loose.

CHAPTER TWENTY-FOUR

Dorothy was in the kitchen, thoughtfully inspecting the contents of a chicken casserole which she had made for supper. She tasted a spoonful of the hot broth, added a pinch of herbs and a sprinkling of black pepper, and tasted again. Satisfied, she prodded one of the chicken joints with the tip of a knife blade and decided that another half-hour should do it. She called to her husband: 'Supper at half-past seven.' The television set was on in the living room: Philip was watching *Tonight*.

Things were much better between them. That trip to Washington, five years ago, had taught her something, if only to appreciate those who appreciated her. Philip loved her, and she realized that she had always taken love for granted, as her right. But she had learned that it was no one's prerogative: it had to be earned.

'God!' she thought in disgust, pulling on her oven gloves and putting the casserole dish back in the oven. 'I'm getting philosophical in my old age!'

Jennifer had told her recently that she had mellowed, and Dorothy supposed that she had, although the idea did not greatly appeal to her. But today was a good example. Philip had spent practically the entire day in the studio, trying to beat the deadline on an article he was writing for one of the Sunday newspapers. There had been a time when Dorothy would have resented being left to her own devices for almost eight hours. This evening, however, when he finally emerged from his seclusion, she had told him to sit down and put his feet up.

'You look worn out. I'll make the supper. Have a drink and relax.'

She had poured out two generous measures of vodka and tonic and carried hers into the kitchen. She looked round for what remained of it now.

Philip was standing in the kitchen doorway. 'Kennedy's been shot,' he said. 'They've just interrupted the programme.'

'Shot?' Dorothy paused in the act of sorting out the cutlery for their meal. 'Is it serious?'

'Don't know.' Philip was as yet unconcerned. 'I shouldn't think so. No one seems very perturbed. It was a news flash. They'll let us have more information as it comes in.'

A thought occurred to Dorothy. 'Isn't it today he's in Dallas? Sally and Veronica were going to watch the motorcade. Veronica told Jennifer when Jenny 'phoned her yesterday. Pete's there, attending some convention. Ronnie persuaded Charles and Sally to go along.'

'Very sensible,' her husband commented. 'It will do them both good to have a break. It's high time they paid us another visit. Now that I've finished this book, and while Charles is convalescent, we must see about it.' He turned away. 'I'll let you know as soon as there's any more news.'

Dorothy stacked a tray with cutlery and crockery and carried it into the dining room. She had just finished laying the table when Philip reappeared, a look of disbelief on his face.

'It's serious,' he said. 'Kennedy's been wounded in the head. Governor Connally's been injured, as well.'

'Oh my God, no!' Dorothy followed Philip into the living room and huddled with him round the television screen. The announcers and presenters seemed stupefied. Many looked ready to burst into tears. Gradually, piece by piece, the news trickled through: the President was in hospital; his injuries were not as bad as had at first been feared; they were worse; far worse; a priest had been sent for; a mere precaution, which would be taken for any Catholic in the circumstances; the President was in the operating theatre; everything was going to be all right . . .

John Fitzgerald Kennedy, thirty-fifth President of the United States, was dead.

Programmes, the announcer said, would continue more or less as scheduled, although there would be special tributes to the murdered statesman later that night. News and pictures would be transmitted as and when they were received.

Dorothy stayed where she was for a moment or two, unmoving on the edge of her seat. Then she said: 'The casserole! I've forgotten all about it. It'll be overdone.' The full horror of the news had as yet to sink in.

Philip nodded and switched off the set. He, too, felt as if he were trapped in a bubble of unreality, his mind temporarily numbed by shock. Later, when he and Dorothy had eaten, he would contact Jennifer and find out the name of the hotel where Sally and Veronica were staying. They might be able to give him some up to the minute news. Until then, he might as well enjoy his meal. He crossed the hall to the dining room.

It was halfway through the main course that Dorothy suddenly pushed aside her plate and burst into tears. Philip laid down his knife and fork, no longer hungry. He got up and went round the table to his wife, kneeling beside her and putting his arms around her.

'This is ridiculous!' Dorothy gasped, searching for a handkerchief and defiantly blowing her nose. 'I didn't know the man. I've never even seen him. And I've certainly never forgiven him for that Bay of Pigs affair. I really thought we were for it that time. It was the most scary few days of my life. If Kruschev hadn't climbed down . . .! And yet, here I am, howling my eyes out because Kennedy's dead. What in heaven's name is wrong with me, Philip?'

He kissed her cheek.

'I don't know, my darling, but I feel exactly the same. And I suspect we're not the only ones. All over the world, millions of people are trying to come to terms with the fact that a light has gone out, leaving the rest of us to flounder in the dark.'

Veronica came back with two plastic cups of coffee which she had obtained from the vending machine. She handed one to her sister, who sat crouched in a corner of the orange-upholstered couch. An outsize rubber plant, in an orange plastic tub, adorned one corner of the waiting area.

'Drink this,' she ordered, 'while it's hot. The doctor said you could see Charles as soon as possible. Just be patient. You can imagine the confusion this place is in. Kennedy died half an hour ago, did you know? Johnson's going to be sworn in immediately.'

Sally made no reply, but she took the proffered cup and set it down on the low table in front of her. It was no surprise to learn of the President's death: the back of his head had been shot away. She had seen it. Nor, at that moment, was she affected by the news. Her whole concern was for Charles.

Veronica sat beside her.

'Pete's on his way over,' she said. 'I telephoned the convention hall and someone managed to find him for me. Of course, the meeting had broken up as soon as they heard about the shooting. Pete says everywhere in Dallas is in total chaos. A policeman's been killed, presumably trying to intercept the assassin. Governor Connally is badly hurt and is undergoing surgery.'

Sally still made no comment, leaning back and closing her eyes, trying to sort out in her own mind the sequence of events. She remembered the noise of the shots, the sight of the President slipping sideways, the screams and commotion as she and the other people outside the book depository threw themselves to the ground, and the wail of the police sirens as the motorcade's stately progress suddenly accelerated and changed course for the hospital.

After a while, when it had become apparent that the assassin had no intention of firing indiscriminately into the crowd, people began to pick themselves up, stumbling towards one another in a dazed, blind way, seeking confirmation that what they had witnessed had indeed happened, and that they were not the victims of some terrible, mass hallucination. Sally had scrambled to her feet, looking round for Veronica and Charles.

Her sister was already standing, brushing the dust from her skirt, a reflex and mundane action which belied the shock and horror in her eyes.

'Where's Charles?' Sally had asked, before she saw him still lying prone on the ground. One arm was thrown forward, clawing at the earth. She knelt beside him. 'Charles! Charles, darling, it's all right now. You can get up. The shooting has stopped.' But somehow, she knew, long before she called to Veronica to help turn him over, that he had suffered another heart attack. And this one was serious. She could see that by the deathly colour of his face, hear it in the laboured breathing . . .

The next thing she could recall with any clarity was being in the ambulance as it rushed Charles to hospital. She presumed Veronica must have summoned it, but she had no recollection of when or how, nor even of its arrival; only of the young doctor bending over her husband, striking his chest with regular blows in an effort to make his heart keep beating.

At the entrance to the hospital, a crowd of people had gathered, many openly weeping, a few with the light of excitement in their eyes, a kind of eager anticipation. Kennedy was dead or dying: for good or ill, the world would never be the same place again.

Charles was taken straight into the intensive care unit, and Sally and Veronica had been told to wait. The hands of the clock on the waiting-area wall had slowly traced out an hour, minute after interminable minute.

'It must have happened when he threw himself to the ground,' Sally remarked suddenly, speaking for the first time since entering the hospital. 'He wasn't well this morning. I asked him not to come with us.'

'I know.' Veronica sipped her coffee. 'Charles was always stubborn.'

'What do you mean, "was"?' Sally rounded angrily on her sister. 'He isn't going to die!'

'Of course not. I'm sorry. It was just a turn of phrase, that's all.' Veronica added awkwardly, lowering her eyes:

'You are fond of Charles, then. I'm glad. He deserves it.'

'I have always been fond of him,' Sally snapped, in a tone of voice which precluded any further discussion of the subject. Her sister's remark had touched her on the raw. Did Veronica really think her incapable of appreciating Charles's true worth? Wherever were the doctors? What were they doing in that room, behind that firmly closed, all-excluding door?

A nurse appeared, and the brief, camera-shutter impression which Sally obtained between the opening and shutting of the door was of several medical staff gathered around a bed, and a bank of awesome looking machinery. She was overcome by a sudden faintness and leaned forward, putting her head between her knees. The shock of everything that had happened that morning was beginning to take its toll. She was vaguely conscious of Veronica's arm about her shoulders and the nurse's voice coming from a long way away.

'Mrs Graham.' The soft Texan drawl penetrated the yellow mists which clung about her. 'Are you feeling OK? Can you try to pull yourself together? The doctor thinks you ought to see your husband now.'

Werner was working late. He had returned to Hamburg from Bristol the previous evening, and had spent most of the day finalizing plans, in consultation with Kurt and the rest of the board, for the establishment of Gabler and Neumann (UK). Later, when all the meetings were over, he had been seized by a sudden doubt as to the validity of his choice of site. Was Bristol truly the best English city of all those he had visited? Did it really offer the necessary amenities and strike-free work force to which Gabler and Neumann were accustomed? Or had he, perhaps, allowed his personal preference to influence his judgement unduly? Was he pandering to the self-indulgence, the luxury, of returning as victor and benefactor to the city where he had once been one of the vanquished?

So, at four o'clock, he had returned to his office, called for the files and gone through them with merciless thoroughness once again. Three hours later, with nothing to be seen beyond the windows but the chill November darkness, he was satisfied that his decision was a sound one, uninfluenced by any personal considerations. He heaved a sigh of relief and closed the last file.

His office door opened and Kurt came in. He, too, had been working late with Josef Stirtz from the accounts department, going over the financial details of the British venture. Werner half-rose from his chair, about to suggest a drink, then paused, unable to fathom the expression of sadness on his partner's face.

'Is something wrong?' he asked. 'It's not . . . It's not Magda?'

'No, no! You haven't heard, then? It was Magda who telephoned me just now with the news. Kennedy's been assassinated.'

The moment seemed to stretch and dissolve, then re-assemble itself in broken fragments. Kurt, standing half-inside the doorway; the closed file on his desk, green against the white expanse of blotting-paper; the dark brown filing cabinets, ranged against one wall; the drinks cabinet in one corner; the reddish-brown patterned carpet; afterwards, Werner could recall all those things with an amazing clarity, but only as separate and disparate items. Everything in the room lacked cohesion and purpose. He felt as though he had suffered a deep and grievous personal loss.

'W-When?' he managed to stammer out at last. 'Where?'

'In the southern states of America, somewhere. Dallas, I think Magda said. Is that right?'

'How did it happen? Who killed him? Does anybody know?'

But what did it matter, the where and the when and the how? Or even the why! Kennedy, who had captured the hearts of the West Germans, as he had captured the love and imagination of a vast portion of the world, was dead. The answer to all those questions would not bring him back again. All the same, Werner felt a burning desire to know.

Kurt shook his head. 'Magda didn't say. Details are

coming in slowly. I'm going home, and I've told Stirtz to do the same. I can't work any longer.'

'No. I was leaving anyway.' Werner went over to the coat rack and took down his coat. 'The only place to be now is beside the radio or TV set. It's going to be a long, sad night.'

'It's going to be a long, sad winter,' Kurt answered, and went out. Werner heard his footsteps receding down the corridor.

As always, with any news concerning Britain or America, Werner's thoughts went instantly to Sally. In spite of the anger and resentment which burned inside him, his mind seized upon any opportunity to remember her and his son. His son!

He swung on his heel and slammed shut the door of his office with a violence which seemed to shake the whole building.

'Come to bed,' Philip said gently. 'It's nearly midnight.'

Dorothy looked up at her husband with puffy, tear-stained eyes. Her face was drawn and haggard. Then, suddenly, grief was replaced by anger.

'Why am I feeling like this?' she demanded, impotently banging her fist on the arm of her chair. 'Why are we both sitting here, feeling like death? Why do I feel as though I'd lost my dearest friend? It's ludicrous!'

'Everyone's the same,' Philip answered. 'You've seen the faces on TV. The Horobins, the Youngers, even Lady Quintrell have all been on the 'phone. We all need to be in touch; to seek reassurance in one another's company. We're all shocked and dazed and grief-stricken.'

'But why?' Dorothy's irritation increased. She disliked being prey to emotions which she could not understand. 'Kennedy was a foreign statesman. If someone told you de Gaulle was dead, had been assassinated, would you care? Eisenhower was one of the best loved Americans in this country. Do you remember, a few years ago, when he paid a visit to London, how thousands of people turned out to cheer him? But if he'd been shot and killed, would we have felt like this? We'd have been shocked, but not . . . not devastated! You saw all those people crowding into Grosvenor Square, just to stand outside the American Embassy all night! Explain it to me, Phil!'

He shook his head wearily. 'I can't. It's impossible. Obviously Kennedy had some special quality which made him universally beloved. He belonged to the whole world. At least, that's what people felt.' He held out his hand. 'Come along. Come to bed. We'll be up again at the crack of dawn to read the newspapers.'

'What's that quotation?' she asked. 'From *Richard II*?'

'*O, call back yesterday, bid time return.* Is that the one you mean?' She nodded. 'There will be millions of people wishing that tonight.' The telephone began to ring and Philip frowned. 'Whoever is that, at this time of night? I'll answer it. You go on up. You look all in.'

Dorothy's anger had subsided, to be replaced once more by the dull, unremitting ache of loss. She climbed the stairs, almost too weary to put one foot in front of the other, and went into the bedroom. She could hear Philip murmuring into the telephone and wondered idly who it could be, but was really too tired to care. She had kicked off her shoes and was unbuttoning her dress, when her husband came into the room.

'Who was it?' she inquired, but without much interest.

'Veronica.' Philip's voice sounded odd, and Dorothy glanced up questioningly. ''Phoning from Dallas.'

Sleep went flying. 'Did she tell you anything? Did she have any further news?'

'She and Sally and Charles were outside the book depository when it happened. They saw it all. What Veronica called "a grandstand view".'

'Dear God!' Dorothy was wide awake now, her weariness forgotten. 'Well, tell me! What did she actually say?'

Philip crossed to his wife's side and pulled her gently down on to the bed. He held her tightly against him.

'Charles is dead,' he said quietly. 'Another heart attack.

299

A fatal one, this time. Veronica thinks it was caused by the shock of witnessing the assassination. He died in the same hospital as the President.'

Charles Graham was buried the day following the state funeral of President Kennedy. After the service, Sally and her guests returned to the house. Margery Graham looked old and ill, and Sally had a sudden premonition that her mother-in-law would not outlive the winter. Her son's death and the assassination of John F. Kennedy had been a double blow from which an elderly and frail woman would not easily recover. Kay and Teddy and their families fussed around Margery as much as she would let them, but she had never pandered to weakness, her own in particular, and none of her old astringency had left her.

'I thought your mother might have flown out for the funeral,' she remarked to Sally in her well modulated, ice-cold tones. 'Old acquaintance and all that.'

Sally felt herself flushing, and Veronica, who had overheard, retorted hotly: 'What are you meaning to imply, Mrs Graham?'

The well-marked eyebrows rose. 'I was not meaning to imply anything. I merely thought Mrs Jackson would have wanted to be with Sally.'

Sally's colour had receded, leaving her very pale. 'Mother would have come if I'd asked her, but the time was so short. We only returned from Dallas ourselves on Sunday.'

'Ah.' Margery waved away a plate of cold meat, which one of her grandchildren was proffering. 'She'll join you later in the month, no doubt?'

'No,' Sally replied, keeping her voice even. 'There wouldn't be any point. As soon as I've settled my affairs here, I'm going home for good.'

Veronica, who had foreseen this move, and done her best to dissuade her sister from making it, exchanged a look with her husband and shrugged. Over the past few days, she had gradually come to accept that Sally would not stay in Washington.

Kay and Teddy had both regarded it as inevitable from the moment they heard of their father's death. They liked their step-mother, but had never been close to her, and the events of five years earlier had left their mark. William was so patently not their brother.

That evening, when everyone had gone, Sally went upstairs to her young son's bedroom. She had politely urged her step-children and their families to stay overnight, but they had as politely refused. Standing on the doorstep, waving goodbye as they were driven in their taxis to the airport, Sally had experienced an unexpected sadness. She knew that she was saying farewell to a part of her life; that a familiar door was closing. Veronica and Pete, too, already seemed to be distancing themselves from her. Veronica's parting kiss had been reproachful, but without tears or fuss. In the remaining weeks before Sally's departure she would not try to make her change her mind.

Margery Graham had said: 'Come to see me before you leave, and bring the boy.' But there had been no sadness or regret in the invitation.

William was lying on his side, propped on one elbow, ostensibly reading. But Sally could tell from his face illuminated by the amber glow from the bedside lamp, that he had been crying. She sat down beside him, on the bed, and gathered him into her arms.

'Isn't Pops ever coming back?' he asked after a moment.

Sally stroked his hair. 'No. He's dead, sweetheart. I told you.'

'Like President Kennedy? Did some bad man shoot him?'

She sighed. It was so difficult to explain death to children. At William's age, one seemed immortal.

After a long silence, she said: 'Bill, there's something I have to tell you. Charles — Pops — wasn't really your father.'

The little boy drew away from her in sudden alarm. 'But you're my mother, aren't you?'

Sally smiled reassuringly. 'Yes, of course.'

William relaxed against her with a huge sigh of relief.

'That's all right, then. Why wasn't Pops my father? Are you and my real father divorced, like Emmeline Groves's parents?'

'Who's Emmeline Groves?'

'Just a girl at school. Are you?'

'Not . . . Not exactly. It's . . . well . . . a bit difficult to explain. Your real father,' she added hastily, fudging the issue, 'lives in Germany.'

As she had cravenly hoped, this information was enough of a novelty to constitute an explanation in William's mind. He nestled closer.

'Shall we go to find him?' he asked sleepily.

Sally smiled mockingly at herself. She had been dreading telling William the truth, and only her conviction that, now that Charles was dead, it was better to reveal it sooner than later, had made her screw up her courage tonight. But, after all, she need not have worried. Young children were so adaptable to new ideas that they accepted with ease facts which their elders would find unbearably traumatic. Already, for William, Charles was fading to a pleasant memory.

Sally pillowed her cheek against her son's fair hair. 'I can't make any promises,' she told him.

CHAPTER TWENTY-FIVE

On Sunday, the twenty-second of December, Sally, holding William by the hand, was among the many thousands of people who gathered at the Lincoln Memorial in Washington. Each person carried a candle, and as dusk fell over the city, the first of these was lit with fire brought from the eternal flame at Arlington, burning on the murdered President's grave. Little by little the light spread, flaring and flickering into the night until, all around, there was a sea of brightness. It was bitterly cold, but no one seemed to notice, and after a little while the crowd gently and quietly dispersed, the glitter of candlelight melting away, drop by drop, flame by flame into the anonymous, all-embracing darkness.

The next day it snowed heavily, and Sally had to resign herself to spending Christmas in America after all. In the month since her husband's death, there had been too much to do, too many legal matters to attend to, for her and William to get away. She knew the terms of Charles's will, and had tried to overset them. He had left a third of his estate to her, and she had wished everything to go to his children. Kay and Teddy had firmly resisted.

'Papa wished you to have the money,' Kay wrote from New York, 'and neither Teddy nor I would want it otherwise.'

The Georgetown house was sold, but the final contract of sale was not yet completed. Sally fretted at the delay. Suddenly, she needed to be home; needed to be in her own bedroom at Grace Cottage; needed to feel the closeness of Philip's comforting, reassuring presence; needed to smell the scents and hear the sounds of the English countryside.

303

She wanted to see again those winter mornings of heavy frost and needle-sharp sunlight, all white and gold. Beyond that, she could not think at present. She tried not to think too much of Werner. It was too soon after Charles's death.

She missed Charles more than she had thought possible. He had been part of her life for nearly twenty years, and the sense of loss, of emptiness left by his sudden death, was often acute. She felt regret that she had been unable to give him the love he had wanted; but at least, during these last years, she had given him the affection and support which had helped him to live with his guilty secret.

She stood at her bedroom window, looking out at the snow, at the lengthening evening shadows staining it the colour of bilberry juice, and at the setting sun hanging low and red above the white landscape. All the important events of her life had taken place during the winter.

The door opened and William came in.

'You're crying,' he said accusingly, slipping one of his hot, sticky hands into hers. 'Don't be sad. I'm here.'

Sally turned and smiled. 'I'm not crying,' she lied, 'it's just a trick of the light. Did you have a good day at Aunt Veronica's?'

He grimaced. 'So-so! She's awfully fussy. I guess because she has no little boy of her own. Mom, when are we going to England? When are we going to find my real father?'

She sat down on the window-seat and drew him to her. 'We're leaving in there weeks' time. You won't be going back to your present school, after Christmas. You'll attend the village school in Coldharbour instead. Do you remember? I pointed it out to you once, when we were staying with Grandma and Uncle Philip. As for your real father . . . darling, I don't know. I can't promise anything. It will depend, you see, if he wants us.'

William shrugged and wriggled free of her embrace. Life was for living day by day. He couldn't concern himself for long about what was going to happen in the future.

For the moment, the only thing which mattered was his supper.

'Let's go eat,' he commanded peremptorily. 'I'm starving.'

'Darling, you've been home six weeks now. It's almost the end of February. Don't you think it's time you got in touch with Werner? He doesn't even know that Charles is dead.'

Sally, who was standing at the kitchen sink, peeling potatoes for Sunday dinner, could see, through the window, the fields beyond the garden. Philip and William were trying to fly a kite. The little boy was laughing, his cheeks pink with exertion and cold. At her mother's words, however, Sally turned her head.

'Don't worry, Mother. You won't have us here for ever, I promise. I fully intend finding a place of our own for William and me.'

Dorothy, who was arranging carrots and onions around the half-cooked joint of beef, felt justifiably annoyed. For once, her question had contained no hidden implications, and she resented her daughter's assumption that it did.

'That isn't what I meant,' she protested in an injured tone. 'I like having you both here. You're company for me when Philip locks himself away in the studio, and God knows you pay your way! Charles may not have left you a fortune, but you're very comfortably off. I just thought . . . Well, surely, darling, Werner ought to be told.'

'Why?'

'Why? Because William's his child, that's why. And don't let's keep up the fiction that he isn't. It's so terribly wearing.' Dorothy returned the meat and its accompanying vegetables to the oven. 'Besides, Werner's quite well-to-do now, I imagine.'

'For heaven's sake, Mother!' Sally threw down the potato peeler and stripped off her rubber gloves. 'What has that to do with it?'

'If you think money isn't important,' Dorothy retorted, 'you're a fool! However, it's up to you. But mark my words. Gabler and Neumann is going to be big. Big! I rather fancy having a son-in-law who's the partner of one of the biggest toy manufacturers in the world. Because it will come to that, so don't say I didn't warn you.'

'She hasn't changed a scrap,' Sally confided later to her sister, as she and Jennifer took a walk through the village, leaving Dorothy and the two men to cope with the influx of young Lathams, who, with their parents, had come to Sunday tea. 'I think "I", "me" and "mine" are the three most overworked words in Mother's vocabulary.'

'She's too old to change now,' Jennifer said with philosophical calm. 'She always sees every situation in relation to herself. I suppose, if we're honest, we all do.'

'Perhaps. But I couldn't live with her. Six weeks, and I'm more than ready to move on.' Sally grinned. 'Philip deserves a putty medal, as we used to say when we were children. I don't know how he puts up with her.'

'He adores her. He always has done. Warts and all! And when she gets too much, even for him, he shuts himself away, just as Father did, in that dilapidated summerhouse they call a studio.'

The two women walked in silence for a while, past the closed and shuttered village shop and silent school, through the twisting lane of Fairmile Street, emerging eventually on to the main Bristol road. As they crossed to The King's Head and entered Manor Walk, Jennifer asked: 'What do you intend to do?'

'Find a home for William and me,' Sally answered. 'A house with a room which would convert to a decent studio. But I must do it soon. William's getting too settled at the village school. It won't do him any good to keep changing. I should like to find a place in Clifton.' They passed the turning to the Youngers' farm and, a little further on, the Manor House, now restored to all its former glory behind its sheltering belt of trees. 'This is where it all started,' she thought. 'Charles and me, Veronica and Pete . . . and Werner.'

Jennifer said awkwardly, as though reading her sister's thoughts: 'What about William's father? It's all right. I

306

know all about it. Mother told me a few weeks ago. God knows how she'd managed to keep the secret so long. Don't you think, Sal, that you should tell him?'

'Don't you start, as well!' Sally exclaimed irritably. 'It's too soon after Charles's death. I feel I owe him the tribute of at least a few months' mourning.'

'Philip told me that the last time he spoke to Werner, he was talking about some girl, a friend of Trudi Rossman's. He said she'd make someone a very good wife.'

Sally slowed to a standstill, looking anxiously at her sister. 'Philip hasn't mentioned anything about it to me. Is it . . . serious, do you know? Why didn't Philip tell me?' She was engulfed by a wave of panic. Who was this unknown woman whom Werner fancied? On the other hand, if he really wanted her, had she any right to object? There were so many years of estrangement and misunderstanding between them, that Sally had no idea what could be expected either of herself or of him.

Jennifer shrugged. 'You know Philip. He wouldn't interfere. I expect Mother knows about it. Why don't you ask her?'

But that was the last thing Sally wanted to do. She knew her mother well enough to realize that Dorothy was bound to exploit the situation to her own advantage. She wanted Sally to marry Werner, and she could easily force her daughter's hand by exaggerating the danger.

Suppose, however, that there was nothing to exaggerate; that Werner was indeed on the brink of proposing marriage to another woman? Then she, Sally, had no right to present him with the dilemma of choosing between this woman and his son.

Dorothy noted her youngest daughter's preoccupation throughout the rest of the afternoon and evening, and when they were at last alone, Jennifer and her family having gone home and Philip withdrawn to the studio, she said bluntly: 'You're very quiet. What's the matter?'

Sally glanced up from the contemplation of her son's fair head. She had been reading to William, but he had fallen asleep, overcome by the heat of the living room fire, which Dorothy had banked halfway up the chimney.

'I've been thinking,' she answered. 'Making some decisions. And I've reached the conclusion that William and I must make a go of things alone. I don't know how Werner feels about me any more. There may be someone else in his life, and I can't use William as a bargaining counter. "Take me and you can have your son." That would be a kind of moral blackmail. If Werner wanted me for myself, not just as William's mother, that would be different. But I don't see how I can be sure unless the first move comes from him.'

'But he doesn't know that Charles is dead!' Dorothy cried in exasperation. 'So how can he possibly make the first move?' She raised her eyes to the ceiling as though seeking divine inspiration. 'And you've forbidden Philip and me to write to him, so how is he ever going to be informed? You are infuriating, Sally! Scruples are all very well in moderation, but you carry yours to excess. Besides, you're being most unfair to Werner, who not only wants, but has a right to see his son.'

The telephone rang and Sally jumped. Her mother had noted before how telephone bells seemed to upset her. Dorothy swore at the interruption and went into the hall to answer it. Sally remained where she was, too tired even to get up and put William to bed. The distant murmur of her mother's voice had a soporific effect. By the time Dorothy returned to her seat by the fire, Sally's eyes had closed. She roused herself sufficiently to inquire: 'Who was that?' but her lids were drooping again before Dorothy answered.

'Just Nick Horobin. He – er – had a proposition to put to me. He wants me to be on the committee for . . . for the parish summer fête. Isn't that nice of him?'

Sally did not reply. Her mouth fell open. She was fast asleep. Dorothy smiled with secret satisfaction.

It was late in the evening before Werner let himself into his apartment. He had worked late every night for a month, making sure that everything would run like clockwork when the Bristol project finally got under way, and he was dog-tired. There were three letters in his post-box, in the main entrance hall, but he was too exhausted even to look at the inscriptions. He tossed them on the dining-room table and went straight into the kitchen. Coffee and a meal, in that order, were his main priorities.

He had just turned on the hot plate beneath the coffee percolator, when the bell of his apartment rang. For a moment, he hesitated, tempted to pretend that he wasn't in, before he remembered that there would be a line of light visible beneath the door. With a muttered imprecation, he went to answer it.

It was Erich, who pushed his way inside in his usual ebullient fashion, without waiting to be asked.

'I came to find out if you've had your invitation,' he said. 'Are you going? I can get time off, and I thought it might be fun. Trudi doesn't object, as it's only for a couple of days.'

'What are you talking about?' Werner demanded. 'What invitation?'

Erich paused, his glance taking in Werner's overcoat, which he had not yet had time to remove.

'Working late again, eh? Being your own boss is never worth it.' He saw his friend's abandoned post, lying on the table. He picked up the letters and quickly sorted through them. 'Here! This is probably it.' He waved a pale blue envelope and slit it open.

'Would you mind explaining what this is about?' Werner asked in annoyance. 'And who gave you permission to open my mail? That's a criminal offence.'

Erich took no notice, but calmly read the letter.

'It's from Mrs Jackson. I've had one, too. Why don't you see what's in it?'

Werner took the letter and skimmed through its contents. Then he turned back to the beginning and read slowly through both pages again.

'Well?' Erich demanded impatiently, before he had

finished. 'What do you think? A prisoner-of-war reunion. For all of us who went to Coldharbour village. You see what she says. They've formed a committee and are trying to get in touch with as many of their "boys" as possible.' He chuckled richly. 'I'm afraid they'll find a lot of their "boys" have developed paunches and are losing their hair. How many of us were there going to Coldharbour, at the finish? Nine? Ten? Maybe more. As I recall, the padre had three of us, and there were quite a few other families in the village who entertained men from the camp. Mind you, we might find we're the only two idiots to accept, but what the hell! I'd like to see Frau Jackson again. She was a damned handsome woman!'

'She still is,' Werner answered, and Erich grimaced.

'I keep forgetting you've been there recently. I suppose, in that case, you're not keen on the idea. But I don't fancy going on my own. My English isn't good enough.'

Werner put the letter back on the table, and Erich noticed that he was looking rather dazed. Poor old Werner! He really was working too hard.

'Oh, I'm coming with you,' Werner said slowly. 'Nothing would stop me. And as it's Bristol, I can combine business with pleasure. At least, that's what I'm going to tell Kurt.' He turned the letter over. 'When is it, again? March the twenty-sixth to twenty-seventh. Another four weeks.' He didn't know if he could wait that long.

When a jubilant Erich had at last departed to inform Trudi that the trip was definitely on, Werner picked up the letter once more. Underneath the flamboyant signature were a few lines of postscript.

'If you decide to come, please send your reply to the Reverend Horobin at Coldharbour Vicarage. PPS I hope you and Erich won't mind sharing a room, but I have my widowed daughter and her son staying with me at present. William is five now, and likes his own room.'

Werner's hands were shaking and the words danced before his eyes. 'My widowed daughter . . .' 'William likes his own room . . .' Sally's husband was dead and she was free to remarry. Four weeks! Werner resisted the temptation to catch the first 'plane out of Hamburg. He got an impression of secrecy from Dorothy's letter. Just for once, he would play by her rules.

'So this is what all the secrecy of the past few weeks has been about!' Sally accused Dorothy grimly. 'Parish summer fête, indeed! I thought it odd that you'd allowed yourself to be co-opted on to the committee. You deliberately lied to me, Mother!'

'Yes,' Dorothy admitted happily, 'I did. I thought if you really knew what we were planning, that tender conscience of yours would force you to pack up and leave. Now, it's too late. Philip will be back with Erich and Werner in just under twenty minutes, providing, of course, that the train from London is running on time. Ten of our boys are coming altogether, including all three of the Horobins'. Quite a reunion for all concerned. There's a buffet supper and informal dance at The King's Head tonight. I know you'll enjoy it. Now, I must go and put the finishing touches to lunch. The boys'll be hungry.'

'Well, I shan't be here!' Sally exclaimed petulantly. 'I'm meeting William from school and we'll have our meal in the café behind the village shop. And don't expect to see me this afternoon, either. I will not be manipulated, Mother!'

'Hoity-toity,' Dorothy said, and went singing into the kitchen, putting her own words to the old music hall song, *Oh, I do love to be beside the seaside*. 'Oh, I do hope to be the mother-in-law of a very wealthy Ger-her-man tycoon . . .'

Sally slammed out of the house. She was halfway along Church Lane, when a car came round the corner and she stopped, her heart beating ridiculously fast. But it was only the Vicar's old Ford, with his 'boys' sprawled on the front and back seats. The three skinny, underfed young prisoners had become three large, jovial-looking men.

She had reached the corner, when the big green Peugeot, with Philip driving, came into view over the brow of the

311

hill. Sally pretended not to see it, cast a hunted glance to right and left, then plunged across the road, regardless of traffic, making for Fairmile Street and the school. Out of the corner of her eye, she glimpsed Erich's face at the wound-down window and heard him shout: 'Sall-ee! Sall-ee!' Then she heard Philip jam on his brakes, a car door open and shut and the sound of running feet. Her own pace quickened as she saw the children streaming out of school.

The next moment, William was greeting her with a casual: 'Hi, Mom!' as he slipped his hand into hers. His expensive American clothes made him stand out from the shabbier British children.

'Hullo, darling,' she answered breathlessly. 'I thought we wouldn't go home to lunch today. I thought we'd – '

Two hands gripped her shoulders and the well-remembered voice said: 'Hello, Sarah.' She had guessed Werner was behind her, but she jumped all the same. Releasing William's hand, she slowly turned to face him. Werner's grip transferred itself to her wrists. 'Why did you run away?' he asked her gravely.

'I . . . I wasn't sure . . . that you'd want to see me.' She added inadequately: 'It's been a long time.'

'Too long.' Werner's glance fell on William, an interested spectator. 'Hullo,' he said uncertainly.

William smiled sunnily. 'Hi! Are you my real father?'

Sally gasped. 'Now, why should he ask you that? He's never put that question to anyone else.'

Werner squatted on his haunches and drew his son between his knees, encircling him with both arms.

'Yes,' he answered simply, 'I am your father. Do you mind?'

William shook his head, suddenly overcome by shyness, and gave Werner a quick hug. Then he looked up at his mother as if for confirmation that he had done the right thing. At her encouraging nod, he leaned forward and planted a smacking kiss on his father's cheek. Werner stood up abruptly, blinking back the tears.

'Did you say we're not going home to lunch, Mom?'

William was indignant. 'Why not? Grandma's promised me chocolate steamed pudding with vanilla sauce. I'll miss it if we don't go back.'

'In that case,' Sally replied dryly, 'I have no option. Never let it be said that I came between you and your grandmother's culinary delights.'

William frowned suspiciously. 'What are cul . . . cul . . . thingy delights?'

'I'll explain later. Look, there's Uncle Philip come to fetch you. You run on with him, and your . . . your father and I will follow in a minute.'

Philip had appeared at the top of Fairmile Street, and William ran up the road towards him. Sally and Werner watched the two figures cross Hill Road and turn into Church Lane before walking slowly after them.

There was a moment's silence before Werner asked: 'Why didn't you let me know that your husband was dead? Mr Jackson tells me it was as long ago as last November.'

'I didn't return from America until after Christmas. And then . . . Well, then I heard that you might be thinking of getting married. Some friend of Trudi Rossman's.' It wasn't the whole truth, but near enough to suffice for the present.

'But how – ? Of course! I told Mr Jackson about her. I remember now.'

'I didn't feel I had any right to blackmail you with William. If you were really in love with this girl, I thought it would be unfair.'

They had reached the corner of the street and were standing in full view of the main road. Regardless of who could see them, Werner stopped and swung Sally round to face him.

'I've never loved anyone but you.' He took her face between his hands and kissed her. 'What happened, Sally? Why did you stay with your husband?'

She answered quietly: 'I had a very good reason. I can't tell you about it yet, but one day I will, I promise. When Charles has been dead a little longer. It was his secret, you see, not mine. Please trust me.'

313

'Do you still love me?'

'I have always loved you.'

'Would you ever have left Charles Graham and come to me?'

'No.' Her eyes did not waver from his face. 'Not as long as he needed me.' His arms went round her again, holding her tightly. She protested: 'Werner, Werner! People are looking at us!'

'Let them look,' he retorted, but he released her and they crossed the road. As they passed Saint Andrew's, he asked: 'Will you marry me, Sally?'

'Yes, if you're sure you want me.' But the look on his face gave her all the answer she needed.

She took a deep breath. Spring was coming; she could smell it in the air. There were crocuses and forsythia in the gardens; primroses and sweet violets in the woods. The winter world of silence and obscurity was yielding up its secrets. The leafless trees were bursting into life. All along the branches were the first pale, stickily gleaming buds.

Grace Cottage came into view, and they could see William swinging impatiently on the gate. He saw them and yelled: 'Hey! Hurry up, you two! Lunch is ready. I'm starving!'

Sally laughed and put her arm around Werner's waist.

THE END

THREE WOMEN
By Brenda Clarke

'Her work has that rare quality of being difficult to put down'
British Book News

When Joseph Gordon – owner of Gordon's Quality Chocolate factory – married a girl from the factory floor he made it quite plain that her two young nieces were no responsibility of his. Elizabeth and Mary, born to a humbler walk of life, could expect no handouts from their Uncle Joe and their lot was not to be compared with their beautiful pampered cousin, Joe's treasured only daughter, Helen.

But these three girls, Elizabeth and Mary, and the delicate Helen, were to form a bond that all Joe's venom could not break. The passage of two world wars and the years between were to see violent and dramatic changes in their lives and it was Elizabeth, strong, vibrant, working-class and beautiful, who was to be the saviour of the family.

0 552 13260 8

A SCATTERING OF DAISIES
THE DAFFODILS OF NEWENT
BLUEBELL WINDOWS
ROSEMARY FOR REMEMBRANCE
By Susan Sallis

Will Rising had dragged himself from humble beginnings to his own small tailoring business in Gloucester – and on the way he'd fallen violently in love with Florence, refined, delicate, and wanting something better for her children.

March was the eldest girl, the least loved, the plain, unattractive one who, as the family grew, became more and more the household drudge. But March, a strange, intelligent, unhappy child, had inherited some of her mother's dreams. March Rising was determined to break out of the round of poverty and hard work, to find wealth, and love, and happiness.

The story of the Rising girls continues in The Daffodils of Newent and Bluebell Windows, finally reaching it's conclusion in Rosemary for Remembrance.

A Scattering of Daisies   0 552 12375 7
The Daffodils of Newent   0 552 12579 2
Bluebell Windows   0 552 12880 5
Rosemary for Remembrance   0 552 13136 9

COPPER KINGDOM
By Iris Gower

The Llewelyns lived in Copperman's Row – a small back-street where the women fought a constant battle against the copper dust from the smelting works. When Mali's mam died there were just two of them left, Malia and her father, sacked from the works for taking time off to nurse his wife. Mali felt she would never hate anyone as much as she hated Sterling Richardson, the young master of the Welsh copper town.

But Sterling had his own problems – bad ones – and not least was the memory of the young green-eyed girl who had spat hatred at him on the day of her mother's death.

COPPER KINGDOM is the first in a sequence of novels set in the South Wales copper industry at the turn of the century.

0 552 12387 0

THE SUMMER OF THE BARSHINSKEYS
By Diane Pearson

'Although the story of the Barshinskeys, which became our story too, stretched over many summers and winters, that golden time of 1902 was when our strange involved relationship began, when our youthful longing for the exotic took a solid and restless hold upon us . . .'

It is at this enchanted moment that *The Summer of the Barshinskeys* begins. A beautifully told, compelling story that moves from a small Kentish village to London, and from war-torn St Petersburg to a Quaker relief unit in the Volgag provinces. It is the unforgettable story of two families, one English, the other Russian, who form a lifetime pattern of friendship, passion, hatred, and love.

'An engrossing saga . . . she evokes rural England at the turn of the century with her sure and skilful touch'
Barbara Taylor Bradford

'The Russian section is reminiscent of Pasternak's *Doctor Zhivago*, horrifying yet hauntingly beautiful'
New York Tribune

0 552 12641 1

RUTH APPLEBY
By Elvi Rhodes

At twelve she stood by her mother's grave on a bleak Yorkshire moor. Life, as the daughter of a Victorian millhand, had never been easy, but now she was mother and housekeeper both to the little family left behind.

As one tribulation after another beset her life, so a longing, a determination grew — to venture out into a new world of independence and adventure, and when the chance came she seized it. America, even on the brink of civil war, was to offer a challenge, that Ruth was ready to accept, and a love, not easy, but glorious and triumphant.

A giant of a book — about a woman who gave herself unstintingly — in love, in war, in the embracing of a new life in a vibrant land.

0 552 12803 1

A SELECTED LIST OF NOVELS AVAILABLE FROM CORGI BOOKS

THE PRICES SHOWN BELOW WERE CORRECT AT THE TIME OF GOING TO PRESS. HOWEVER TRANSWORLD PUBLISHERS RESERVE THE RIGHT TO SHOW NEW RETAIL PRICES ON COVERS WHICH MAY DIFFER FROM THOSE PREVIOUSLY ADVERTISED IN THE TEXT OR ELSEWHERE.

☐	12638 1	**SPINNERS WHARF**	*Iris Gower*	£2.95
☐	12637 3	**PROUD MARY**	*Iris Gower*	£2.95
☐	12387 0	**COPPER KINGDOM**	*Iris Gower*	£2.50
☐	12565 2	**LAST YEAR'S NIGHTINGALE**	*Claire Lorrimer*	£3.50
☐	10584 8	**MAVREEN**	*Claire Lorrimer*	£3.95
☐	11207 0	**TAMARISK**	*Claire Lorrimer*	£2.95
☐	11726 9	**CHANTAL**	*Claire Lorrimer*	£2.95
☐	12182 7	**THE WILDERLING**	*Claire Lorrimer*	£3.50
☐	11959 8	**THE CHATELAINE**	*Claire Lorrimer*	£3.50
☐	10249 0	**BRIDE OF TANCRED**	*Diane Pearson*	£1.95
☐	10375 6	**CSARDAS**	*Diane Pearson*	£3.95
☐	10271 7	**THE MARIGOLD FIELD**	*Diane Pearson*	£2.50
☐	09140 5	**SARAH WHITMAN**	*Diane Pearson*	£2.95
☐	12641 1	**THE SUMMER OF THE BARSHINSKEYS**	*Diane Pearson*	£2.95
☐	12803 1	**RUTH APPLEBY**	*Elvi Rhodes*	£3.95
☐	12367 6	**OPAL**	*Elvi Rhodes*	£2.50
☐	12607 1	**DOCTOR ROSE**	*Elvi Rhodes*	£1.95
☐	11596 7	**FEET IN CHAINS**	*Kate Roberts*	£1.95
☐	11685 8	**THE LIVING SLEEP**	*Kate Roberts*	£2.50
☐	12579 2	**THE DAFFODILS OF NEWENT**	*Susan Sallis*	£2.50
☐	12375 7	**A SCATTERING OF DAISIES**	*Susan Sallis*	£2.75
☐	12880 5	**BLUEBELL WINDOWS**	*Susan Sallis*	£2.50
☐	13136 9	**ROSEMARY FOR REMEMBRANCE**	*Susan Sallis*	£2.95

All Corgi/Bantam Books are available at your bookshop or newsagent, or can be ordered from the following address:
Corgi/Bantam Books,
Cash Sales Department,
P.O. Box 11, Falmouth, Cornwall TR10 9EN

Please send a cheque or postal order (no currency) and allow 60p for postage and packing for the first book plus 25p for the second book and 15p for each additional book ordered up to a maximum charge of £1.90 in UK.

B.F.P.O. customers please allow 60p for the first book, 25p for the second book plus 15p per copy for the next 7 books, thereafter 9p per book.

Overseas customers, including Eire, please allow £1.25 for postage and packing for the first book, 75p for the second book, and 28p for each subsequent title ordered.

NAME (Block Letters) ....

ADDRESS ....

....